HIGHLAND
SURRENDER

HIGHLAND SURRENDER

SONS OF SINCLAIR

HEATHER

USA TODAY BESTSELLING AUTHOR

McCOLLUM

Entangled Publishing, LLC
644 Shrewsbury Commons Ave., STE 181
Shrewsbury, PA 17361
Visit our website at www.entangledpublishing.com.

Amara is an imprint of Entangled Publishing, LLC.

Edited by Alethea Spiridon
Cover art and design LJ Anderson, Mayhem Cover
Creations and Bree Archer
Stock art by VJ Dunraven/Period Images and
kamchatka/Depositphotos
Interior design by Toni Kerr

Print ISBN 978-1-64937-494-3
ebook ISBN 978-1-64937-495-0

Manufactured in the United States of America

First Edition November 2023

AMARA

ALSO BY HEATHER McCOLLUM

To Kyrra and all her bravery.

You'd stand up to the Four Horsemen and never let anyone put you in a corner.

Love you to Pluto and back! Mom

At Entangled, we want our readers to be well-informed. If you would like to know if this book contains any elements that might be of concern for you, please check the back of the book for details.

FOREIGN WORDS
USED IN *HIGHLAND SURRENDER*

beò – alive, living (Scots Gaelic)

brann – fire (Norwegian)

daingead – dammit (Scots Gaelic)

faen i helvete – f*cking hell (Norwegian)

fy faen – damn or f*ck (Norwegian - pronounced fee fawn)

Helvete – Hell (Norwegian)

jævlig bra – damn good (Norwegian)

logn – calm (Norwegian) pronounced log-en

mo chreach – my rage (Scots Gaelic)

Seieren – Victory (Norwegian) Name of Erik's ship

sgian dubh – black-handled dagger (Scots Gaelic)

slå hjertet – strike the heart (Norwegian) Battle cry of the Wolf Warriors

tolla-thon – arsehole (Scots Gaelic)

uhyre – monster (Danish)

uilebheistean – monsters (Norwegian)

vær fri – be free (Norwegian)

vennen – term of endearment, sweetheart (Norwegian)

In the year 866 AD, King Herald Fairhair sought to unify Norway under his rule. So he set out on a quest of conquest to enforce the petty kings who ruled small territories along the Norwegian coast to yield to him. A unified country was a strong country. Herald conquered ten kingdoms along the coast of Norway, leaving behind slaughter and dead kings.

When Herald Fairhair journeyed to the farthest area of northern Norway to the district of Naumudal, he planned to make the two kings, Herlaug and Hrollaug, bow to him. King Herlaug, though, had refused to ever surrender.

He gathered eleven companions and some food and ale, and they all entered a burial mound. When he, his companions, and his finite store of food and drink were in the burial mound, Herlaug had the tomb sealed shut. Herlaug decided to die as a king rather than surrender to a foe he could not beat.

SNORRI STURLUSON, TWELFTH CENTURY ICELANDIC POET, HISTORIAN, POLITICIAN

CHAPTER ONE

"Sköll is the name of the wolf
Who follows the shining priest
Into the desolate forest,
And the other is Hati,
Hróðvitnir's son,
Who chases the bright bride of the sky."
GRÍMNISMÁL – ORAL MYTH WRITTEN DOWN
IN THE FOURTEENTH CENTURY.

Mythological poem about two celestial wolves
who chase the sun and moon. At Ragnarök, the
end of the cosmos, they catch their prey, and the
sun and moon are defeated.

COTTAGE OF BÀS SINCLAIR
FOREST OF CAITHNESS IN NORTHERN SCOTLAND
20 JUNE 1592

His senses alert, Erik Halverson stepped from a
mossy hillock to a smooth stone outcropping in the
thick forest of Caithness, Scotland. His laced leather
boots touched down without a whisper that might
alert whoever was up ahead past the bramble covered
in white blackberry flowers. The birds were still or had
flown off, and he'd spotted a thin rope that would signal an intruder if he'd been foolish enough to brush
against it. The only sound was the burble of the narrow river that emptied into the sea bordering

Girnigoe Castle.

He was alone, having left his horse and three friends back with the Sinclair wives discussing possible trade with Norway. All lies, of course. Erik drew his short sword from the belt that wrapped his hips, cinching his tunic, as he crept to the edge of the dense, fragrant bramble. The drone of a foraging bee vibrated close to his ear, but nothing could draw his attention away from the muffled sounds ahead. His hand clenched the familiar hilt, making the sharpened blade an extension of his arm.

He stepped past the buzzing bush, and his breath, and possibly his heart, lurched to a stop for a second. He blinked but the image continued. The forest opened into a clearing with a cabin and barn to the left and the river to the right. The summer-green trees cast moving shadows and golden light on the homestead before him. Right in the middle of the yard was the largest wolf he'd ever seen. However, what caught Erik's gaze wasn't the beast but the vision standing in the river behind it.

A woman, fair of hair and face, stood in a wide pool within the river. She stared at him and rose, stepping up the bank quickly with small bare feet, her damp hair swinging. She wore only a white smock that was completely soaked. It hugged her curves, showing everything as if she stood naked before him. Her nipples were hard and surrounded by a light rose hue. The sopping linen stuck to her gently rounded stomach and long legs, revealing her darker pelt at the crux.

She spoke, but her words were in foreign Gaelic, which Erik hadn't bothered to learn. They were musical and burbling, not unlike the mix of German, Norse, and Danish he knew. Even without translation, her tone was clear enough. And if her tone didn't communicate her desire for him to halt, the bow and arrow she grabbed off the ground did. With a fluid motion, she nocked an arrow and pulled the bowstring back to her chin.

Switching to French, she said, "If you come closer, I will shoot you through the neck and my wolf will dine upon your face." As if to add his support, the large gray beast growled low, showing sharp, white teeth. His thick tongue dropped out to lick his lips as if already savoring Erik's shin bone.

"Do you understand?" she asked in English.

"Aye," he said in English, which he preferred to French. The guttural sounds were more familiar to his Norse tongue. "Your wolf will eat my face after you shoot me if I come closer."

Standing there with the arrow trained on him, her white garment displaying her womanly form, and her long blond hair spread in waves over straight, brave shoulders, Erik recalled the stories of the old pagan gods that his great-grandfather would tell around the fire on winter nights. This ethereal, courageous creature would be Freyja if the goddess walked among mortals.

"Surrender your sword and any other weapons on your person," she said, her elbow tipped high as she held the arrow ready to spring forward.

"'Tis impossible," he answered, his grip tightening around his leather sword hilt, his gaze never moving from hers.

"Why?"

"I do not surrender." He allowed his thick accent to show in his English.

"You arc from Norway?"

He gave a nod.

"Why are you here? And how did you find this place?"

"I come here without malice."

"Either leave or answer my questions to avoid being shot and eaten, although Beò is rather hungry, and he might eat you either way."

"Are you good with a bow?" he asked, challenge in his voice.

Thwack. The arrow lodged into the tree directly behind him at a point above his head. In fact, he'd felt the breeze of a fletching feather as it grazed his hair. Before he could turn back to look her way, she'd nocked another arrow, this one centered on his chest.

"Answer or leave," she said. "On second thought… answer and still leave."

Smiling didn't come naturally to Erik, but his lips relaxed out of his severe frown. This woman had beauty, courage, and boldness. "I am Erik Halverson. My friends and I have come from Norway with permission from Sophie of Denmark-Norway to discuss trade with the great Sinclair Clan of Scotland. And I was following what I thought was a deer trail to bring down a stag to gift the Sinclair Clan for their harvest festival."

"Gift the Sinclairs with one of their own deer?"

He inclined his head. "'Tis my hunting abilities that I gift."

She didn't lower the bow but continued to stand there, the wind blowing against the wet smock. "You can wrap the blanket around yourself," he said.

"You can turn around and leave."

He indicated her white smock that showed her peaked nipples and curves, the flare of her hips that looked perfect for holding onto. "I can see right through that wet smock. Everything."

She didn't even flinch. "Have you seen a naked woman before?"

He wasn't sure what to say. "Uh…I have."

"They are the same breasts, stomach, hips, and legs that all women have," she said without wavering. If her arm was starting to burn from holding back the bowstring, she didn't show it.

He snorted softly but didn't answer her aloud. *You look nothing like the other women I've seen without clothes.* She was lithe, with smallish breasts and flared hips. She was taller than most women and had a grace that showed in her strong arms.

"Wrap the blanket around you, woman. I have questions to ask."

"I lower my bow, and you charge," she said, taking side steps toward the cottage, the angle of her body changing to keep the arrow pointed directly at his chest.

"I charge," he said, "and your wolf eats my face."

Her frown lessened, and slight humor lit her eyes. "Yes, he will, but I'd rather not have to clean up the mess." She backed up the steps onto the porch, obviously planning to barricade herself within the cottage.

Erik dropped his short sword and three dirks on the ground and held his hands out to the sides. As the leader of the Wolf Warriors of Norway, a royal warrior of Dowager-Queen Sophie, and as a man, this was the closest act of surrender he would ever permit. "I am unarmed."

She snorted, and he couldn't help but be impressed with the loud noise that came out of such a petite nose. "You are armed with what God gave you." She nodded toward his frame. Reaching behind her, she worked the latch, pushing the door open. Smoke puffed out from within.

"Fire," he said, pointing, but the woman's shriek overrode his warning.

Erik watched, fascinated, his mouth open, as a red squirrel dropped onto the woman's head, one paw clutching the woman's finely arched brow as it clung to her damp golden hair. The woman's cursing came in rapid Gaelic, and she turned, running into the smoke-filled cottage.

Erik looked at the wolf. The yellow eyes stared back. Erik had seen his share of wolves in Norway. His grandfather had taken him hunting for one when Erik had trained to become a Wolf Warrior, so he could wear the animal's hide during battle. But he had never seen one as large as the woman's protector. Perhaps the wolves in Scotland were larger or... His gaze lifted to the open door. "Freya lives in Caithness, Scotland, and you"—he looked into the wolf's eyes—"are Sköll, or Hati, who chases the sun and moon."

Erik crouched to gather his weapons. He kept his gaze on the wolf, preferring not to slay the magnificent beast.

The woman ran back out, the squirrel still flat over her head like a strange fur cap. She emptied a smoking bucket of charred paper into a trough of water that was fed from the roof by a gutter. Her smock was

smudged with black now, her face red, her bow forgotten inside.

"Is the fire out?" he asked, straightening to his full
height. "I can assist if—"

"'Tis out," she said. "And I thank you to leave."
She stood on the porch, her bare toes curled upon
each other. The squirrel leaped off to run up a beam
to the porch roof, chattering at him, its tail twitching
in reproach.

He backed to the edge of the clearing. The wolf
trotted up to the porch, sitting before the woman who
watched him leave. Her gaze was sharp and curious.

Goddess of a dead religion or not, Erik's interest
was snared.

• • •

"And you just stood there in your wet smock, keeping
your arrow trained on his heart?" Ella Sutherland,
Hannah Sinclair's sister by marriage, asked her.

They sat across from each other at a table set outside in the outer bailey of Girnigoe Castle. They'd
been stringing garlands of fall leaves and twiggy, purple heather for the annual Lunasdál Harvest Festival.
Cain's wife bit into a bannock as she bounced her
two-year-old daughter, Mary, on her knee.

Hannah swallowed the delicious hare stew they
were eating. "I wasn't about to lower my weapon."
The wind blew a strand of her hair, which tickled her
cheek, and she tucked it behind one ear.

"And he said he could see your nakedness?" Kára,
Hannah's second sister by marriage asked from behind. Hannah turned in her seat to see all four of her

brothers' wives staring at her. Kára was Joshua's wife from Orkney Isle who'd led her people to war herself. She was tall and blond, similar to Hannah except fuller in the breasts from already bearing four children.

Hannah nodded. "And I told him that they were merely breasts and legs and stomach and hips, which I'm sure he'd seen before." Hannah felt her face warm at the memory of the warrior's intense gaze. Even if she'd been properly clothed, Hannah would still have felt stripped naked under it. It had taken every bit of her training to keep the tremors out of her arms to hold the bow steady.

Kára laughed and raised her cup of honey ale as she leaned against the table. "You have the courage of your brothers. Wait until I tell Joshua."

"Oh, I wouldn't do that," Cait said, slowly shaking her head. She was a teacher and married to Gideon, Hannah's third and the most sensible brother. "Not unless you want this stranger dead in a bloody, painful way."

"You're right." Kára chuckled. "What did he say?"

"He said he was from Norway." The roll of his words had added to his masculine display, sending more tingles over her skin.

Kára studied Hannah, tilting her beautifully plaited head. "And from the red in your cheeks I'd say this stranger was attractive. Someone you might wish to protect from a grisly end."

Hannah touched her hot cheeks with cool palms. "I suppose he could be considered handsome, but he didn't smile. In fact, he looked incapable of smiling."

"I thought Bàs would never smile," Shana,

Hannah's fourth brother's wife, added. She played with the end of her plaited red hair. "But he did, he *does*." Her saucy grin added a passionate bend to her words. *Bloody hell*. Her brother and Shana tupping was not something Hannah wanted to think about. She'd raised him with her aunt after their mother died. Bàs was almost like a son to Hannah despite her being only four years his senior.

Ella held up an oatcake to her daughter, who took it, squirming to get down from her knee. Ella had strapped hard pieces of leather to the wee one's feet so the pebbles wouldn't hurt. "Don't give it to the dog," Ella warned as Mary trotted off toward the two huge wolfhounds. Bàs's dogs, Apollo and Artemis, had been staying at Girnigoe while the brothers were away to Orkney Isle doing the king's work.

"We've met his three friends," Ella said. "Traders of silver from Norway. I bought several pieces outright." She touched a delicate silver chain that dangled a small, hammered circle of silver. She held it up. "'Tis supposed to be a shield to protect my heart." She smiled, rubbing the shiny symbol.

Cait narrowed her eyes, one finger tapping her lip. "The Norwegians say they are trading silver for wool, but they were exceedingly brawny. Not what I would expect of mere traders. Two had pigment etched in the skin of their faces and necks."

Hannah remembered the chiseled muscles that strained against the confines of the stranger's sleeves. He'd worn breeches that were caught in his leather boots below the knee. "He definitely looked strong, and he had weapons that he dropped on the ground to show he wasn't going to hurt me."

All four ladies snorted.

"A man like that doesn't need weapons to be deadly," Cait said.

Hannah crossed her arms, catching the edge of her billowing shawl. "That's why I kept the arrow trained on him, and Beò stayed between us as I moved to Bàs's cottage." Hannah inhaled, her palms going to her cheeks once more. "But when I opened the door, smoke billowed out."

All the ladies paused, their eyes wide. "You set Bàs's cabin on fire?" Shana asked. Since Bàs had sailed to Orkney, Shana had stayed within the castle's safety rather than living alone out in the forest.

"I didn't," Hannah said. "Betty did." Betty was her brother's pet squirrel who had decided that the cabin in the woods was her home. "She knocked over a stack of brittle paper sitting on the mantel, and a piece or two touched the hot coals. The fire caught and followed the paper out into the room."

"Do we need to fix anything? Wash the walls down?" Shana asked.

Hannah shook her head. "It wasn't a big fire, but it complicated my survival if the warrior had been bent on violence. Thankfully, Beò was there."

"I don't like you caring for Bàs's animals by yourself," Ella said.

"We can all take a day to go with you until Bàs returns," Cait said. "Except for Shana, who doesn't need to be fighting any giant men while carrying a bairn." Shana and Bàs were expecting their first child that winter. There were bairns popping out everywhere in the Sinclair Clan. Hannah sighed softly.

Shana clasped her chin as if she were deciding on

a good price for a pound of milled flour. "Brawny, powerful, armed with weapons, didn't smile... Sounds like all four of your brothers." She grinned.

Hannah made a face. "Hopefully, he's left the area. I don't need to meet up with someone as stubborn as my brothers." And the man's gaze on her near-naked body had definitely not been brotherly.

Kára leaned over to check on the sleeping twins in the large cradle Joshua had built. They'd moved it outside with them, since the weather was so fair. "All men are stubborn, just some more than others."

All four wives looked at one another. "Like the Sinclair brothers," they said in unison and broke out in laughter. Several older men, carrying bushels of oat groats to be crushed, and the few guards left to keep Girnigoe fortified, looked their way.

The friendship of the women brought a smile to Hannah's lips. She breathed deeply the warm summer air. Girnigoe Castle was vastly different from her father's time, which ended merely three years ago. Since then, her brothers had all found wonderful women to love, and the nurseries at Girnigoe and Varrich Castles were beginning to fill with bairns. Right now, there were five children under the age of three, and Shana and Bàs's bairn would be a welcome sixth addition.

A familiar tug of melancholy weighed down Hannah's smile. With the absence of any suitors, being an aunt, like her Aunt Merida, might be the closest Hannah would get to having a child herself. She was already a score and nine years old without any prospects. She expected Ella was pregnant again, although she hadn't said anything yet. She was probably waiting for Cain to return home before letting people know. If he was gone much longer, whispers would start at her rounding middle.

Kára stood to gather their empty bowls. "The three men said they couldn't sign one of Gideon's contracts, but their leader could."

"The man you met must be he," Ella said and chased after Mary, scooping her up from trying to throw her leg over the back of one of the wolfhounds that trotted around the bailey. "It would be quite nice to complete a trading deal before the brothers return from Orkney." She set Mary on Apollo's back, holding her upright while the dog walked gently around as if she knew the precious age of the rider. Ella looked at Hannah. "Helping the clan grow and remain prosperous will make us stronger."

"Too strong and King James will convince himself once again that we are all traitors," Cait said.

Kára rolled her eyes. "The man is afraid of witches more than us, but you're right. We don't need to let him know we're getting silver from Denmark-Norway." She shrugged. "He should set up trade with the country, too, since his wife, Anne, is from Denmark, daughter of the dowager-queen, Sophie."

Thomas Sinclair, one of the guards who'd remained behind, clomped over the drawbridge. He strode directly to their table after signaling to the gatekeeper that all was well. He bowed his balding head to the ladies. Ella stood, her hand absently going to her stomach. She was certainly pregnant. Hannah's lips pursed. *I am happy for her. I am happy for Cain.* She repeated the reminder until the tightness lessened.

"What is it?" Ella asked.

"A Sinclair ship has docked."

"Have they returned?" Shana asked, rising along with the other two and Hannah.

"A small group only. Keenan brought this from Cain." He held out a folded parchment, sealed with wax, the press of the horse's head clear. When she took it, he hurried back to the gate.

Ella's thumb broke the seal, and she scanned the letter. "They will journey home soon."

Kára groaned. "They won't be home for the harvest celebration tomorrow."

"Looks not," Ella answered. "There's been some difficulty rounding up Lord Robert's children to go to Edinburgh for trial along with their father. They all seem to have abandoned him and refuse to be put on trial for treason with him."

"I didn't know one could refuse," Hannah said.

"They cannot," Cait answered, rolling her eyes.

The weight of disappointment soured the light atmosphere as if a cloud had passed overhead. "Cain says they should be home within a few days, a week at most," Ella continued. "But that he wishes us all a healthy and happy harvest celebration. That we should visit the clootie well with white, red, black, and pale green ribbons to tie there to bring the Four Horsemen luck."

Hannah's brothers had been raised to be the biblical Four Horsemen of the Apocalypse by their mad, warlike father. One by one, thanks to love being stronger than their upbringing, each brother had broken away from the dreadful expectations, focusing on growing the clan together. But there were still some strategies they continued, like having the four armies of white, bay, and black horses, and horses dyed a pale green. When they acted like the biblical Horsemen, they often frightened enemies into surrender, saving lives in the end.

Cait let out a huff. "They missed midsummer too." She picked up her fussing son, wee Gavin, from the basket where he'd been sleeping. "I'll be back. Someone is hungry," she said, heading toward the comfort of Girnigoe's great hall to nurse him.

As if the crying had reminded Kára's twins that they too were hungry, they woke. Kára lifted Astrid from her cradle while Shana lifted Alice. "We can chat before the fire inside while you nurse them," Shana said.

Kára patted Astrid's back. "Adam is probably giving Aunt Merida fits in the nursery," she said about her two-year-old son. "He hasn't been wanting to nap."

"This one either." Ella followed her sisters toward the keep.

"Ivy is planning to come up from the village today with Edward," Shana said about her sister and nephew. "The three can toddle around together and torment the dogs."

Hannah stood silent, watching them stride away, a lovely parade, glowing with motherhood. The ache she felt cast a hollowness to her chest, and she blinked against the tears welling in her eyes.

"Foolish," she whispered to herself. She was truly happy for her sisters by marriage, but she couldn't help envying them. She'd been four years old when their mother had died birthing Bàs. With their father's anguish, Hannah had jumped right in to love the infant, helping to mother him. She'd been too young to do everything, and now she was almost too old to mother her own. She wiped away an errant tear.

Kára ran back out, her arms empty. "I forgot Alice's rattle," she said, snatching the wooden toy from the cradle. Her gaze rose to Hannah's, and she froze. "What's wrong?"

Hannah shook her head, blinking, and tried to smile. "I but wish…well, that I was a mother too."

Kára's brows bent in sympathy, and she walked around the table to give Hannah a hug. Stepping back, she rested her hands on Hannah's shoulders, the wooden rattle clutched with her thumb. "You know, Hannah," she whispered, "you don't have to have a husband to have a bairn."

Hannah's eyes widened at the ruinous thought.

Kára laughed lightly, interpreting the look on Hannah's face. "Yes, you could get yourself pregnant, but the poor fellow might end up skewered by one or all four of your brothers. I was thinking of the orphanage that Viola and Rhona run over in Varrich Village. They're sure to have bairns coming in, unfortunately. Let them know you wish to take a child as your own."

Hannah's look of shock relaxed. She'd considered adoption. "Thank you," she said. "I will. 'Tis…to feel a life kicking within me…" She rested her hands over her flat belly. "Being able to nurse the bairn myself… There is still so much I would miss."

Kára met her gaze. "You'd also miss fiery heartburn, chapped nipples, sore breasts, months of nausea, being split in two… I could go on."

Hannah smiled genuinely. "That sounds horrid."

Kára nodded.

"But you do it again and again," Hannah said.

Kára sighed and gave her a sad smile. "Yes." She squeezed Hannah's hand, leaning in to her ear. "If you decide to go the other route and get pregnant, I'll support you, too, and try to get Joshua not to kill the man."

Hannah snorted a laugh, and Kára looped her arm through hers. "Right now, though, I would love your help in entertaining Adam while I feed the twins. He ran Aunt Merida around so much that she's gone to take a nap herself."

Hannah strode with Kára toward the keep, nodding to everything she said, but her thoughts were elsewhere. Who would be strong enough to survive her brothers if she were to get pregnant without a husband?

CHAPTER TWO

Tradition of the Clootie Well – "Pilgrims would come, perform a ceremony that involved circling the well [natural freshwater spring] sunwise three times before splashing some of its water on the ground and making a prayer. They would then tie a piece of cloth or 'cloot' that had been in contact with the ill person to a nearby tree. As the cloot rotted away, the illness would depart the sick person."

UNDISCOVERED SCOTLAND

Erik stood on the bluff overlooking Girnigoe Harbor where a Sinclair ship had docked, letting off a dozen men, leaving more to unload supplies. None of them congregated in a group of four. Dowager-Queen Sophie had said that the four Sinclair Horsemen would be back from fighting on Orkney Isle by now. He crossed his arms, his hands fisted, watching.

Erik's lifelong friend, Nial Kristiansen, traipsed up the hill, spotting him. Nial was bulkier in form with a long, light-brown beard and blond hair that he wore loose past his shoulders. Still a fearsome warrior, Nial had a false friendliness that earned him information. Whereas Frode and Sten, with their faces marked with lines and swirls of pigment etched into their flesh, often put strangers on guard.

"The Four Horsemen won't be back to these shores for a week," Nial said, wiping an arm over his sweaty forehead. "Damn, but 'tis hot here," he said in the Norwegian dialect of Bokmål.

"All four of them?" Erik asked, his gaze sliding back to the ship where several horses had been led off. A large man took the lead of one steed, mounting him to spur him into a run up the path from the sea.

Both Nial and Erik watched the fluid movement of the horse and warrior. 'Twas as if they were one. The man had a long sword sheathed across his back, and a special leather holder held an ax against the side of the horse. The man's hair flew out behind him, and as he rode up the hill, his gaze fastened onto Erik and Nial. A prickle of unease coursed up Erik's spine at the intense look.

"Is his horse…green?" Nial asked.

Even though the warrior continued to ride toward the castle, his face turned to follow their position until he had to turn forward or change the horse's direction to keep them in view. The effect was strangely eerie. Like the gaze of a devil marking you.

"'Tis gray but looks like greens have been washed over the coat," Erik said, turning to watch the man race across the moor. "He must be one of the Sinclair brothers."

"The fourth named as Death," Nial said. "Bàs in their language." Nial gave an exaggerated shiver. "Pis! I'd say the man was rightly named."

Erik turned on his heel and began to walk toward Girnigoe where he and his three friends had paid to stay in a vacant cottage at the edge of the village. Their story as silver traders had been accepted by the women and few remaining men in the village. At least so far. Bàs Sinclair's gaze, meant to convey that he saw them, had looked far from welcoming. If he hadn't been charging off somewhere, Erik was certain the man would have swung around to confront the strangers on his shore.

Nial kept up with Erik. "If the other three brothers are as big as that one, we should finish our quest before they return," he said.

"There's more to be assessed before we act," Erik said. "Sophie's orders are to find their weakness, a way to control the Horsemen."

"We could take one or all of their wives," Nial said, but before Erik could scoff, Nial raised his hands. "I know. Control them without causing each to become a crazed berserkr."

"I will not bring death to our shores," Erik said.

"Kronborg Castle is not on *our* shores," Nial grumbled. Kronborg Castle, north of Copenhagen, Denmark, was the current location of Sophie, the dowager-queen and queen mother of young King Christian IV of the united country of Denmark-Norway.

"We are loyal to our dowager-queen," Erik answered as they walked, his neck tense.

"We are loyal to her son and his regents." Nial was correct, of course, but he knew they would do anything Sophie wanted because she had control of Erik's sister, Iselin.

They walked on in silence, Erik contemplating the plan they needed to execute. He hoped that Sophie's information was correct and not inflated. He needed to get closer to the Sinclair family to make certain before acting. If he chose wrong, Iselin would be forfeited, something he refused to let enter his mind.

Erik spotted the Horseman of Death riding

through the village, across the first of Girnigoe's two drawbridges and under the raised portcullis to enter the impenetrable fortress on the sea. He was certainly in a hurry to reach the hall.

"They celebrate their harvest tomorrow," Nial said. "Perhaps the man will get drunk and be easily slain. Then we can leave his body and take his head to Sophie."

"How would that control the remaining Horsemen?" Erik asked. They spoke in Bokmål, so he wasn't concerned with them being overheard.

Nial shrugged his wide-set shoulders. "Maybe they will worry they'll also lose their heads."

"Did the man who rode by us look like he'd worry?"

Nial exhaled. "Nay."

"We must stick to the original plan," Erik said. "Killing one Sinclair brother won't bring the three others to heel." Erik broke into a jog, looking back at Nial. "If you were killed, Sten, Frode, and I would go after the bastard, not bow to his ruler."

Nial caught up to Erik even though it took him some effort as they dodged the large boulders jutting out of the purple heather that blossomed under the summer sun. The man didn't speak until they slowed, entering the village.

Nial wiped his forehead again. "And we aren't to kill them *all*, because Scotland still needs them for defense against other nations."

"I will confirm that our other target is much beloved, and then we can act," Erik said. So far, the villagers had held their tongues around them. "We haven't even met the sister yet. She might complain like a banshee and plot murder against their wives. If the Horsemen wish her gone, Sophie's plan won't work."

"She's their sister," Nial said as if that should be evidence enough that the Four Horsemen would do anything to keep her safe.

'Twas true enough for Erik, especially after sickness had taken his family, all but Iselin, his younger sister. As his warriors were witnessing, Erik would even set aside his honor to keep his sister well and happy. She was the only person left in the world whom he loved, would ever love. Because, as he'd seen quite clearly, love made one vulnerable. Death could take a loved one away even if he was there to protect them with his sword. Nay. He'd never love anyone other than his sister. His hand squeezed the pommel of his sheathed sword.

The two men walked along the path, their boots crunching on the fine pebbles and broken shells that ran between stone walls and thatched homes. Flowers decorated many lintels and were planted in boxes outside glass windows where shutters were cast open. Come winter, they would be shut tight like the windows in Norway to protect against the cold.

Two young girls stood together staring up at the thatched roof where a black and white cat crouched, watching them. One girl was blond and propped her hands on her hips in a gesture that didn't fit with her youth. The other had freckles cast across her face, reminding him of his sister when she was young. Their mother had called her one of the fae with her large eyes and full, mischievous smile. This girl had two braids that reached down behind her as she tilted back her head to see the cat. Both girls looked to be under ten years old.

"How could you let Boo climb up there?" the frowning one asked.

"How could *you* let Boo climb up there?" the freckled girl retorted.

"Ballocks, Trix," the blonde said, not seeing the men approaching. "Lady Ella is going to be so upset that *you* chased her cat up on—"

"Libby, you were holding Boo, not me." The one named Trix crossed her small arms.

Erik paused behind them, and it took Nial a couple strides to realize his commander wasn't walking next to him.

"The cat will come down on its own," Erik said, his Norwegian accent impossible to hide.

The girls spun around in unison, their eyes wide as they tilted their heads back to meet his gaze over the stone wall separating them.

"Good day," Trix said with a smile. "Boo is stubborn. We've been trying to coax her down for hours."

"Well, not hours," Libby said, frowning at the other. "But long enough that we think she's afraid to try, and we are supposed to be up at the castle helping to string garlands around, but we are stuck here, and Mistress Cait will be worried, and—"

"She's quite chatty," Nial said in Bokmål.

Both girls looked at him. "What did he say?" Libby asked.

"That you talk a lot," Erik answered.

Libby frowned, narrowing her eyes at Nial, who actually blushed under the girl's unspoken fury. It was sometimes hard for Erik to believe that his friend was one of the deadliest, most coldly calculating warriors he knew. With his slight paunch, long beard, and kind eyes, Nial Kristiansen looked more like someone's harmless uncle who told bedtime stories to children about sprites and unicorns.

Trix giggled. "Where are you from, good sirs?"

The lasses didn't seem intimidated by their size like many adults were. Erik's mouth relaxed. "We are from Norway, little girl."

"Why have you come here?" Libby asked.

"To trade silver for wool," Erik said, digging out a thin silver chain to dangle in the air.

The girls inspected it like they were shrewd traders, their small chins jutted out.

Meow. The cat above attempted to move down the slope but stopped, crouching, its stomach flat on the roof.

Erik walked over, and the cat shimmied back. He turned to the girls. "May I lift one of you to retrieve the cat?"

Two arms shot up as each girl lifted onto their toes to be picked. Their eagerness tugged at his heart as he contemplated Sophie's worry. If civil war came to Girnigoe, would that enthusiasm turn to fear and hiding? Erik's mission, though dishonorable, might save these two girls, or at least their carefree smiles.

Libby frowned at Trix. "I was the one holding Boo, so I should be the one to retrieve her."

"She likes me better," Trix said, stamping one booted foot.

"She likes both of us," Libby argued and raised her arms before Erik in a silent order to be lifted.

Erik crouched, wrapping his arms around her legs,

and lifted. The little blonde girl weighed little more than a loaf of brown bread. He could have thrown her up and over the roof if she'd desired.

"Here Boo," Libby crooned.

Meow.

"Just hold her up there for a few minutes," Trix whispered to Erik. "And try not to look so threatening."

Erik looked past Libby's skirt at the other girl. "I look threatening?" The girls certainly didn't act threatened.

Trix tilted her head and then shrugged. "To a cat."

Nial coughed into his hand, but Erik didn't miss the smile on his face. His friend would surely spout about how the leader of the fierce Wolf Warriors was frightening to cats but not little girls.

"With the Four Horsemen about, they must be used to terribly ferocious warriors," Nial said in their language, which made Trix frown at him.

"'Tis rude to speak in another language before someone," she said, taking the hands-on-hips stance to which Libby seemed inclined.

Erik kept his face stern. "He said you two are brave. And you shouldn't trust warriors you don't know."

Trix narrowed her eyes at Erik. "Do you have villainous intent, traders from Norway?"

Aye, they did. Erik shook his head and swallowed the lie. 'Twas one thing to deceive adults who could be dangerous but to lie to children seemed wrong. *Like this mission.*

Trix smiled. "Well, then, welcome to Girnigoe, kind sirs. Libby and I actually live in Varrich Village to the west." She pointed north with great confidence. "We are practically the daughters of The Horseman of Justice, Gideon Sinclair." She nodded, watching him as if to see if he was impressed.

Daughters of a Horseman? Erik glanced at Nial who raised his eyebrows in an unspoken question. Should they steal the girls? Erik gave a slight shake of his head and looked back at the roof where the little girl he held inched her fingers closer to the cat. Were the Sinclairs so confident in their power that they didn't guard their children?

"I've got her," Libby yelled, and Erik lowered the child and cat from the edge of the thatched roof, setting Libby's feet on the ground.

"Hold tight to her now," Erik said.

The girls nodded in unison. "Thank you for your assistance." Libby bowed with great seriousness but then smiled.

Trix grabbed his hand, shaking it briskly. "Yes, thank you." Then she pulled her partner's elbow, and they ran around the rock wall and headed toward the lane that led to the castle.

"This mission will be easy," Nial said.

"They have no idea why we're truly here," Erik answered. "And they're so strong that they leave their women, children, and livestock unguarded. Perhaps the dowager-queen is right to worry about her daughter's kingdom."

Sophie of Mecklenburg-Güstrow was the mother of young Christian VI, the king of Denmark-Norway and Anne of Denmark, wife of the Scottish King James. Sophie loved her children dearly, raising them without sending them away like many royals did. With regents controlling her son now that he sat on the throne, Sophie's mind slipped often to her daughter in Scotland. Sophie worried over her, especially when she'd received word about how the Sinclair Horsemen might try to take the Scottish throne from James and Anne. Not being one to sit back and let her daughter become embroiled in a civil war, Sophie and her chancellor had sent the head of her elite Wolf Warriors to find a way to control the Sinclair Horsemen.

As Erik watched the two girls near the corner, a woman strode out, and the girls stopped before her. "Where have you two been?" she asked.

Erik stood completely still inside the stone wall. Even his inhale halted as he took in the woman with golden waves of hair that trailed past her shoulders. Her smock sleeves were short, showing the slim arms he remembered holding an arrow trained on him. She looked as magnificent dressed in the pale blue costume as she had in a wet, completely see-through smock. Her hair looked even more golden, and the smile she cast on the girls with the cat transformed her already beautiful features into something angelic.

"If we act before the Horsemen return from Orkney…" Nial's words trailed off as he followed Erik's unwavering gaze. "Jævlig bra," Nial murmured. "Who is she?"

"The woman I found in the woods," Erik said. Yet she'd come from the castle.

"The one with the squirrel on her head?"

The woman had felt Erik's gaze, and her eyes raised to his and then widened. She straightened, saying something to the girls. Trix pointed back at Erik and Nial while Libby hugged the cat. Trix waved. Nial lifted his large paw in a friendly gesture.

The woman gave a small nod and turned, taking Trix's hand and waving Libby to follow.

"I bet her hair feels like silk," Nial said. The woman's waves reached all the way to her arse. A loose blue ribbon held her tresses partly together, but errant curls escaped.

Nial adjusted his jack under the front of his tunic. Erik noticed, and his voice came out low and edged with ice. "You'll not look at her that way."

"Because you saw her first?" Nial asked, challenge in his voice, a grin on his face.

"Because she's probably one of the Horsemen's wives."

Nial shook his head, and they both turned back to watch the woman walk the two girls across the first drawbridge into Girnigoe Castle. "I met the four wives. She wasn't present."

Hair at Erik's nape prickled. Could she be Hannah Sinclair, the Horsemen's sister and the key to harnessing the powerful Horsemen of Scotland?

• • •

In the folds of her skirt, Hannah carried the small doll she'd made from heather and wheat, braiding them together into little arms and legs. Hannah wore a wreath of heather, like she'd made for the doll, and climbed the root-tangled path toward the sacred clootie well.

Laughing children ran past her on both sides with mothers calling for them to take care climbing over the rocks. She smiled at Trix and Libby as they dodged the many trees along the path, at times holding hands and at times squabbling. They hurried to be sprinkled with water from the freshwater spring that burbled up from the earth.

The clootie well was at the top of a rather steep hill to the south on Sutherland land and fed the stream that ran by Bàs's cabin. For hundreds of years, local people had journeyed to the well to leave trinkets and tie ribbons on the clootie tree beside it. If someone ill tied a ribbon to the clootie tree, as the ribbon faded away, so did their illness. The clootie well was also said to help women conceive and bless those who left offerings or were sprinkled with its waters. Hannah carried ribbons of white, red, black, and green for each of her brothers, and the hidden doll made of heather to nurture blessings for a healthy bairn if she ever had the opportunity to become with child.

Hannah glanced around, but not many men had returned yet from Orkney. Over the last two years, she had considered man after man as a possible husband. Keenan had finally wed Millie, who'd had his child. Osk, Kára's brother, was younger than Hannah by eight years and acted more like Kára's twelve-year-old son than a potential mate. If Hannah wed someone, the man would have to be clever and kind at heart, and she hoped he would be handsome and tall, but she certainly wasn't picky at nearly thirty years old.

She caught sight of one of the Orkney settlers named Aiden, who was helping Kára's grandmother step over some thick roots. He was fairly handsome, certainly not ugly, and he trained with the warriors.

But when she looked at him, imagining herself naked and touching him, her stomach felt queasy, and not in a nervous fluttery way but in a stop-imagining-or-I-might-vomit way.

The path before her was well-worn by centuries of people traversing it, stomping down the soil so that the tree roots presented many opportunities to trip and fall on one's face. Hannah certainly didn't want to do that in front of the villagers climbing with her, so she held her skirts up to spot the arching hazards. Her mind flitted from warrior to pastor to widowed craftsman to the horse trainers that Cain had employed. But no particular man stood out as someone she'd allow to see her naked.

The Norwegian trader, who'd seen her in the wet smock, didn't make her feel queasy. Although, that might have been because she'd been defending herself, steeling herself to kill him if he attacked. However, thinking of his brawny form and obvious power now brought on a flutter that spurred heat in her abdomen. He was large, maybe even better formed than her brothers. He was brave to lower his weapons before a growling wolf and hadn't tried to attack either of them.

Even though she'd been practically naked, he hadn't leered, although his glance had held appreciation for her form. Just the thought of his eyes sliding down her exposed body made a tingle slide over her skin, pearling her nipples under her laced bodice. She rubbed her free hand over her stays as if to quell the sensitivity.

He'd been outside Girnigoe yesterday when she'd gone out to collect Trix and Libby for Cait. The girls thought he was honorable and spoke highly of the silver chain he'd displayed. Some of her brothers' wives had bought silver rings from them.

Hannah turned her etched gold ring on her finger with her thumb, the one Gideon had given her proclaiming her their sister. She wore it on the middle finger of her right hand, since it wasn't a wedding band. So, the brawny man shouldn't think she was wed.

"He'll return home soon," Hannah whispered, thinking of the man's intense stare. If she became pregnant by him, and he returned to Norway, her brothers couldn't kill him. She could have a strong bairn to love all on her own. "Perfect," she whispered, but the fluttering in her stomach made her snort.

How could she entice a stranger to her bed? And did she have that type of courage? On the other hand, he hadn't met her brothers, who had scared off too many men to count. Did the stranger already know who she was? The protected sister of the Four Horsemen? Bloody hell, he'd never touch her if he knew.

Up ahead, Bàs walked with Shana, refusing to relinquish her arm, to prevent her from tripping on the roots. He was even more protective now that she was pregnant, which was why he'd returned to Girnigoe as soon as Cain didn't need him to finish their mission on Orkney.

Bàs glanced behind him, easily finding Hannah. "So ye almost burned down my cabin?" he asked. Shana gave him a playful punch to his arm.

"Pish," Hannah exclaimed, catching up and sliding her arm through his free one. "*Betty* almost burned down your cabin. I saved it."

Bàs's teasing smile faded. "And one of the Norwegian traders found ye there, alone?"

She squeezed his arm as if comforting him. "Beò was with me and made certain the man didn't get close, even when I was distracted at putting out the fire *your squirrel* started." She would not take the blame even though it wouldn't have happened if she'd just fed the animals and left without starting a fire in the hearth. After mucking out the cow paddock, she'd desperately wanted to bathe in the cold creek and dry her hair before the heat of the flames.

His gaze drifted over the line of people on the short pilgrimage to the clootie well. "I will speak with these traders. I don't want any of them near ye."

"I think your sister found him quite handsome," Shana said.

Bàs narrowed his gaze at Hannah as if she'd said she wanted to run away and become English. "We know nothing about these men. Just because he didn't attack ye with a wolf blocking his way—"

"And my arrow trained on him," she added, cocking her head in irritation. All her brothers thought of her as a wee lass, weak and unable to avoid trouble. They forgot how she and their wives had coaxed King James away from arresting them during the mess with the Oliphant Clan. They forgot Hannah trained with Ella and Kára in knife throwing and combat, and that Shana was helping Hannah hone her archery skills.

"Is the man here?" Bàs asked, straining to look down the hill.

"No," Hannah said. She dropped his arm but didn't bother to look behind her again. She already had, and the man, who would surely have stood out, hadn't been there.

They reached the spring where children were tying their ribbons onto the low tree branches and setting out their offerings: pretty stones, flowers, and handmade dolls. Aunt Merida, with a full wreath of purple heather and yellow toadflax on her silvery hair, stood on the bank where the water gurgled out of the earth. She dipped willow branches, tied into a broom with a red ribbon, into the gentle water. The children squealed and laughed as she sprinkled water over them.

"A blessing on these children," Aunt Merida called. "To keep them healthy and growing in peace to bring on more and more Sinclairs."

Hannah hurried past Bàs and Shana to catch some of the sprinkles on her upturned face. She laughed with the children, dancing in Merida's rain. For the rest of the summer morning, Hannah greeted children, women, and the few men who made the journey up the hill. She'd already tied the ribbons for her brothers onto the tree, but she wanted a moment of privacy to set out the longed-for bairn in offering to the sacred spring.

"Are ye going to stay up here all day?" Aunt Merida asked as she began to descend with several new brides who had set their own little dolls at the well's edge.

"Go on," Hannah said. "I'll be along soon. I wish to pray a bit."

Aunt Merida snorted slightly, but who could deny a lass asking for a moment alone with God. "Say hello to our heavenly king for me."

Hannah watched her aunt walk down the path while the brides from last Beltane followed her, chatting about their hopes for children and plans for the harvest festival that afternoon and night. Finally, their voices faded until all Hannah could hear was the gurgle of the spring and one bird tweeting high in the canopy of the summer trees. A breeze wove through the leaves, sounding like the whispers of her ancestors.

Crouching along the bank where the spring water collected in a shallow pool, Hannah pulled the woven doll from her skirts. "Pish," she murmured, pressing the doll into the mud, close enough to the water without washing away. "I don't need a husband." A husband might treat her like her father had, ignoring her except when he wanted her to do something for him. In the case of her father, it was acting like the lady of Girnigoe Castle since her mother had died. For a husband it might be doing whatever sexually deviant thing he forced upon her.

Not that she was opposed to the passionate fun she heard her sisters by marriage whispering about, but the thought of having a silk scarf tied around her eyes or being tupped from behind after she was run down in the forest was not something she wanted to do with Aiden or Thomas or any of the men in the village.

The stranger came to mind. His powerful body looked so strong and chiseled. Even the knicks of scars she'd seen on his cheek and jaw added to his mightiness, like he'd been formed from the frozen mountains of his rugged country.

As if conjuring him from the forest, Hannah, still

crouched by the spring, saw that very man lower from the thick branches of an oak tree several yards away. She gasped softly, her eyes wide and watching. Thick arms bulged as they extended over his head, his laced boots stretching toward the ground, showing his narrowed waist and hips. The man dropped from the tree into a crouch.

Hannah's heart pounded as she leaned over the pool. Suddenly, the mud on the bank shifted under her feet, and she lost her balance. She yelped as the cold spring water embraced her like a mantle of ice.

CHAPTER THREE

"Naiad, (from Greek naiein, "to flow"), in Greek
mythology, one of the nymphs of flowing
water—springs, rivers, fountains, lakes. The Naiads,
appropriately in their relation to freshwater, were
represented as beautiful, lighthearted,
and beneficent."
BRITANNICA.COM

In three strides, Erik dropped from the bank into the
pool, catching the woman who was spluttering.
Thankfully, the spring that the local people had been
visiting all morning was shallow and not fast flowing.

Erik steadied her by the shoulders so she could get
her feet under her. The wobbling rocks on the
stream's bottom added a challenge. "Are you hurt?"
he asked in English, helping her slosh back to the
bank where she'd crouched, holding what looked like
a fertility doll.

Was she one of the brides who'd brought the other
dolls? Her husband still with the warriors in Orkney?
He'd thought she might be the Sinclair sister after
seeing her walk with Bàs Sinclair and his wife on the
path.

"I am sodden," the woman said, her syllables snapping like little bolts of lightning.

Erik stood to his full height and lifted her onto the
bank, following her out of the refreshing pool. She
gazed down at her bodice and skirts that dripped

spring water and *tsk*ed.

He squeezed the water from the edge of his tunic. There was no helping his dripping trousers, which would need to dry on his legs. "When I saw you in the forest the first time," he said, "I'd thought you were from the race of wood fae, a dryad perhaps or the goddess Freya, but two of the three times I've seen you, you're covered with water." He stared into her large blue eyes where a couple droplets clung to her long lashes. "Perhaps you are actually a naiad, a water sprite."

Her gently arched brows narrowed even though her lush lips seemed close to smiling. "I am neither, sir. Today you surprised me. I blame you for making me wet."

I made her wet? Erik kept the lines of his face neutral.

Her cheeks flushed immediately upon her words. So…she realized how improper that sounded. Perhaps she was married then, to a man who made her wet with passion? The thought tightened his gut and his loins.

She threw out a hand toward his perch. "You were hiding in a tree." Her tone was sharp with accusation.

"I was *observing* in a tree your…customs here in Scotia. Leaving bits and dolls by this sacred spring." He leaned over the water, fishing out the wreath of purple and yellow flowers that had fallen from her head. Shaking off the water droplets, he handed it back to her.

When she took it, he saw a gold ring on one of her slender fingers, another indication she might be married. The Sinclair sister was unwed. "Where is your husband that he would leave you alone when you are obviously prone to drowning?"

"I am not prone to drowning." She sniffed, placing the wreath back on her head, weaving a few curls around it to hold it in place.

"And your husband? Where is he?" He caught her hand, sliding his thumb over the gold band.

Snatching her hand back, she looked at him. "I…" She looked away and sniffed, blinking as if tears threatened, and her face pinched with sadness. "I have no husband. Now anyway."

So, she was a widow, still mourning her dead husband. She hadn't seemed sad, only thoughtful at the well. He studied her youthful beauty, the expressive movements of her smooth face. "You still wear a ring."

She kissed the ring but answered him only with a terse tone. "I do not like being surprised by a stranger who's been *observing* me." Despite her slender appearance, she was a warrior, this woman, not some meek girl who swooned easily.

Erik had seen her beauty when she'd smiled with unguarded friendliness while greeting her neighbors. But the indignant flash of fire he saw in her gaze drew him even more. The woman had courage to stand up to him when others cringed under his gaze. He was scarred and battle-honed, obviously deadly. Usually, he didn't mind frightening people, letting them assume he killed without much consideration. But he didn't want this courageous woman to fear him.

He tried to smile. "I am Erik, Erik Halverson from Norway, here with my three friends to trade silver for your thick wool that repels water."

His gaze slid down her wet front. The wool didn't cling like her linen smock, but the woman's sleek curves were still obvious. "I believe you're dry under your costume since 'tis made from the soft wool we seek." Unless she was wet between her legs from a carnal heat. Just the thought made his jack twitch, and he hoped it would behave. It was particularly unruly with his forced abstinence on mission.

Her head tilted to the side as she studied his face. "You don't do that often, do you?"

For a moment, his gut tightened. Bed women? Was she asking him if he bed women often? "Do…what exactly?"

"Smile," she said, showing her own teeth, and pointed at his mouth. "'Twas more like a snarling wolf maw."

He relaxed his lips, clearing his throat. "I suppose I don't have reason to smile often."

She pulled her skirts out from her and then her bodice, as if seeing if her skin was wet, and tutted. "There is always a reason to smile." She tipped her face to the sky. "Perhaps not the sky today, but the flowers and the fresh breezes, the birds." She shrugged. "Happiness is a choice and finding things to smile over as well."

"You are wise, Lady…?" he said.

"Hannah."

The name caught his breath, his pulse giving a jolt. "Hannah Sinclair?" Hannah was a common name, and she lived with the Sinclairs. "Sister of the infamous Four Sinclair Horsemen?" Maybe the information from the Danish court was incorrect, and the sister had married, even if briefly. He waited, his entire body tight, including his fists that had curled at his sides.

"We are almost all Sinclairs here," she replied with a shrug that ended with a shake of her head. "Cousins are thick in the streets of Girnigoe."

"Hannah," he said. "'Tis a...lovely name." Had he ever said someone had a lovely name before?

"Hannah is a common name in Scotland."

They began to walk down the heavily rooted path while Erik weighed his evidence for thinking she lied. The fact that he'd seen her walking with the girls into Girnigoe Castle, and her name was Hannah, both flagged her refusal as a lie. But Dowager-Queen Sophie had assured him the sister was a maiden, unmarried.

"Have you been attacked by pirates?" she asked suddenly. "Do they attack your ship for the silver you carry?"

"Nay."

She touched a fingertip along her own cheek as if tracing his face. "Your scars. They mark you as a warrior, not a trader." She didn't tremble or glance around furtively. Only curiosity bent her brow.

"I've been called to defend the border between Sweden and Norway on occasion."

"By Dowager-Queen Sophie or her son?"

Erik's brows rose. The woman kept up with world politics. "Her son's advisors and regents."

Hannah looked off into the woods. "That's right, the poor woman had all her power taken from her when her husband died."

Oh, Sophie of Denmark still held a huge amount of power, which she wielded expertly, even over Erik.

"Do not mourn for her," he said, his familiar scowl back. "She is not hurting in any way."

Hannah squeezed her skirts. "I must change before the festival," she said, hurrying down the path.

Erik easily kept up, stepping behind Hannah when the path was too narrow. "I saw you leave a fertility doll at the well," he said. "Do you wish for a child?"

She tripped on a high-reaching exposed root, and he caught her arm to keep her from tumbling down the steep trail. She adjusted her balance, letting him assist her. "That is not something I talk about with strangers."

"I'm not a stranger," he said, stepping downhill. If she fell again, he'd be in a better position to stop her. "I saved you from the spring. In some kingdoms, you would owe me your life for that."

She snorted. Even that noise enticed him, or perhaps it was the relaxed courage she showed around him. Women usually scurried out from under his gaze unless they were brazen and came to his bed. Hannah, on the other hand, didn't seem afraid of him.

"You want a child."

"I have no husband," she said. "I don't have a way to become with child. Not honorably anyway."

"Perhaps that's why you hid the doll until everyone left."

She stared hard at him. "You *were* spying on me," she said with a look very much like the scalding one she'd given him when she'd leveled an arrow at his chest. "Not just observing our customs."

"I thought that was clear."

She blinked, anger reddening her cheeks. She glanced back up the slope. "You waited in the tree until I was alone." She backed up.

He exhaled, showing his palms, although he had half a dozen weapons on him. "I mean you no harm, Hannah. I followed the procession up here to see the sacred spring and stayed when I saw you coming up the path, hiding in the tree so as not to disturb you, and I waited."

"Why?"

What could he say that wouldn't make him sound like a poacher of women? Why had he waited until she was alone to lower from the tree? "To apologize," he said, although his friends would laugh. Erik Halverson never apologized and never surrendered.

She tipped her head to one side. "Go ahead."

He frowned. "I apologize for frightening you the other day at your cabin. 'Twas not my intent."

"You were intent on taking down a stag for the Harvest Festival," she said, repeating the explanation he'd given. She tried to step around him to continue down the path, but he blocked her way.

"Aye, like I said."

She tipped her head, studying him. "You were hunting a stag with your sword." She indicated the long double-edged sword sheathed at his side. "And without a horse." She shook her head. "Do you just run down a stag, leaping upon its back to slice him with your sword?" She drew a line with her finger across her throat.

Even with all the chaos of being soaked and nearly naked, with a squirrel clutching her head and the cabin on fire, the woman had realized his explanation was flimsy at best. He met her challenging eyes. "I was exploring."

They stared at each other for a long moment, Erik directly in her path. Erik was known for keeping his secrets, not letting people in, and yet he felt like she was sliding under his layers of armor, nimbly seeking truth.

"I accept your apology," she said brusquely, and he stepped to the side. She gave a wry grin and continued her quick march down the path.

They walked in silence for several minutes. The sun broke through the clouds and canopy of leaves to land on her hair like sundrops. Despite falling into the spring, she moved with grace, holding her wet skirts out from her legs so they wouldn't drag in the dirt. Gathering them, she squeezed the wool and shook it.

"So," he said, "you aren't the sister of the Four Sinclair Horsemen?"

She didn't answer.

"And you want a child but don't have a husband and want to retain your honor. Perhaps, you wish to become with child through the Holy Spirit."

Hannah stopped and turned to him again, her mouth open, aghast at his sacrilege. Erik found that he liked saying things that made her stop and stare at him, especially if her mouth opened. "I…" she stammered, "I wish no such thing. 'Twould be inappropriate, devilish even."

"Would it be better to wish to get with child with a man out of marriage?"

She put her hands on her slim hips, almost like the wee girl yesterday named Libby. "You are practically a stranger, Erik Halverson, and yet you ask me the most personal, outrageous things. When you attack people with wildly inappropriate questions—"

"I have insulted you," he said and tried to look sorry for it.

"Me, God…" She threw an arm out to the woods. "Anyone listening. We are all insulted."

"There is no one listening," he said and then realized how threatening that could sound. But Hannah seemed without care that she was alone in the woods with a strange man who could easily abscond with her.

She poked his chest with one finger, the nail clean and nicely filed. "That doesn't make your words any less rude." She crossed her arms again, scowling at him. "God and I are insulted and angry."

"You speak for God?" His brow rose.

"Are you trying to anger me?"

He almost smiled at her wide eyes that looked innocent when he suspected she carried a blade on her and was tempted to stab him.

"I apologize again," he said, wondering what Nial would say if he could hear him. Two apologies in one day from the man who never gave in. "For insulting you and God."

"Hmph," she said. "Very well." She flapped her hand at him and started walking again. "People will dislike you regardless of the quality of your silver, Master Halverson, if you ask outrageous things. A better tactic is to ask mild questions first and then move forward with your quest for information if you must. When you push hard, people become obstinate, but if you acquiesce, they listen. Like I did back there on the trail."

He glanced the way they'd walked. "You acquiesced?"

"Yes," she said. "You wouldn't step out of my path until I accepted your apology. 'Tis basic human strategy."

"Another word for acquiesce is surrender," he said. "Which I do not."

She looked sideways at him as she shook her damp skirts again, letting the wind catch the soggy wool. "Call it what you want, but taking a step back instead of stubbornly forcing people and happenings around you works better in many situations." She stopped again. "Do you know the tale about the wind making a wager with the sun?"

The woman was intriguing, clever, and brave. Even if he'd heard the tale, he'd have said he hadn't just to hear her retell it. "Nay."

She spoke as she began to walk again. "The wind made a wager with the sun one day that he was stronger, because he was blustery and forceful while the sun merely sat in the sky. The sun looked down at a man walking on a road while wearing a jacket. The sun said, "I wager that I can get that jacket off the man while you cannot. The wind laughed."

She flipped her hand, smiling at him. "As wind can do in my tale as much as a sun can talk and wager."

"Of course," Erik said, enthralled by the musical quality of her voice and the expressive way her hands moved while she told the tale. The glint of her old wedding ring made him wonder how much she mourned her lost husband.

"The wind said," she continued, "I will have his jacket off in no time. And he huffed and blew huge gusts at the man, trying with all his might to tug the jacket off. But the man held tighter, never letting go, as he bent his head into the wind and continued his journey. Finally, the wind gave up. He said, you, Sun, will not be able to get his jacket off, either. But the sun smiled—"

"As a sun can do in a tale," he added.

"Of course." She smiled, although she looked ahead as they continued to walk, holding out her skirts that dragged through the tall grass.

"So, the sun began to shine brightly on the man, its rays heating him. And…the man took off his jacket."

She turned a bright smile on Erik, and he nearly tripped over a hummock at the beauty in her features. Hannah was lovely, but when she smiled, really smiled, she rivaled a goddess with her wide blue eyes filled with laughter.

"The sun won the wager," she said, "because he didn't force the man to take off his jacket. He warmed him, and the man did what the sun wanted him to do."

The day had brightened overhead, and he steadied her arm as she stepped over a narrow creek that cut through the grass and wildflowers. She didn't pull away. "So you see," she said, "victory is not always won with force."

"An interesting notion." He inclined his head to her.

"When you are a sometimes-warrior," she said, casting a glance at him although her face remained straight ahead, "you should remember that. And as a trader of goods, you must be more subtle in your confrontations."

"Acquiesce?"

"When 'tis called for."

They'd reached the moor that led down to the

village that sprawled before Girnigoe Castle on the sea. Erik had the overwhelming desire to see Hannah again, listen to her tales, and maybe catch one of her bright smiles.

He cleared his throat. "There is a festival outside the village today?"

"Yes," she said. "Lunastain, our harvest festival." A gust of wind blew, and she reached up to hold her flower wreath on her head. "There will be competitions of strength and agility and then we will have fires and feasting when the sun goes down."

Erik had already planned to go, trying to learn everything he could about the target of his mission. "I will attend." Maybe Bàs Sinclair would drink heavily and foolishly recount how he'd do anything for his sister, who Erik still must locate if this woman wasn't she.

• • •

Erik Halverson is the one.

Hannah paced across the floor of her bedchamber. The man was ruggedly handsome with just the right number of scars to show he battled but often won. Although, she hadn't yet seen him without his tunic. Perhaps, he would take it off while competing that afternoon. Either way, Hannah had seen the man's muscles straining within his sleeves, and he'd lifted her out of the water like she weighed nothing. And the way he'd looked at her, his deep blue eyes meeting her gaze without glancing away, it caught her breath.

"Hannah...'tis a lovely name," she repeated his

words from their walk. And he'd waited in a tree to catch her alone. He said it was to apologize, but he could have waited to see her in the village or at the festival.

She pressed a hand against her lower than usual neckline and felt her heart thumping with giddy excitement. *I'll seduce him. Tonight, at the festival.* She would have a chance of getting with child. There would be no evidence for months after Erik was safely back in Norway without a way for her vengeful brothers to find and kill him.

"He's the one," she whispered, lifting her breasts in the bodice so that they swelled a bit over the edge. She didn't have an overly full bosom, but there was enough to rise above a tightened set of stays.

Just the thought of Erik touching her breasts made them feel fuller, and the sensation of warmth spread in her abdomen and lower until she shifted against the heat blooming in the crux of her legs. She pressed there through her skirts for a moment, trying to rid herself of the ache.

Hannah examined the blue, laced bodice in the polished glass. She'd embroidered it with flowers and birds with white thread. The motif ran along the curved bottom of the bodice too, accentuating the rise of each hip and the deep *V* in front that pointed down into the layers of blue skirts. She'd spent extra time on her hair, replacing the soggy wreath with a new one that Libby and Trix had made for her. The two girls seemed to want Hannah to find a suitor, making Hannah wonder if their adopted mother, Cait, had said something to them about pitying their aunt.

"I'm done being pitied," Hannah said to her

reflection. All her life she'd been expected to stay quiet and out of the way, like a mouse that no one was to notice. But her father was no more, and her brothers were married. It was her time to shine and be noticed. Starting today. And if she became with child and people whispered about her, so be it. At least they wouldn't think she was a meek mouse anymore. It was now or never at nearly twenty-nine years old.

Hannah dabbed a bit of red-hued beeswax on her lips but didn't bother to add it to her already blushing cheeks. She grabbed up her bow and quiver of arrows from the bed. She'd been practicing with Ella and Shana and planned to compete in the contest. It gave her a perfect reason for being out in the fields where the warriors were competing. She'd be sure to happen upon Erik there.

Hurrying down the steps, she strode through the archway into the great hall of Girnigoe Castle. Kára stood wearing the trousers she used to wear on Orkney Isle when she was the leader of her people. "Thank you, Osk," Kára said to her tall, thin brother who was holding Kára's two-year-old son, Adam. "He'll have more fun with you today, especially with me taking care of the girls." She smiled down at the two infants in the large basket at her feet.

"We'll have fun, won't we?" Osk said, tossing the boy slightly in his arms. The child laughed.

Osk turned to see Hannah and stopped, his eyes widening along with his grin. "Good day, Lady Hannah," he said. "You look…quite fetching." He glanced around as if he thought Bàs might be near, but the rest of the hall was empty. He met Hannah's gaze, his brow rising. "Very fetching."

Kára smiled at her. "What a lovely gown on you. I haven't seen it before."

That was because Hannah hadn't had a reason before to wear something that might attract a man. She smiled back. "It was my mother's. I adjusted it to my taller height." She pointed to the wide darker blue ribbon sewn around the bottom of the skirt.

"And the embroidery?" Kára asked, rocking the basket a bit with one foot as the bairns began to make soft waking noises.

"I've been working on it a little at a time," Hannah said, smoothing her fingers over the stitches along her low neckline.

She noticed Osk followed her fingers. With Adam on his hip, he offered Hannah his open arm. "May I escort you out to the target field?" He nodded to her bow.

Hannah looked at the bairns in the basket. "I should help Kára with Alice and Astrid."

"Oh, go ahead," Kára said, using muscle to lift the basket, carrying it to the hearth where a cheery fire flickered. "These two need to nurse before we go out."

Hannah lifted the front of her skirt and took Osk's free arm. "Well then, thank you, Master Osk." With wee Adam in one arm and her on the other, they looked like a young couple stepping out to enjoy the festival. She could almost imagine Erik there on her arm, their first bairn in his other.

Her smile faltered. *I merely need his seed.* She blushed thinking it and pushed the happy family image from her mind. She didn't have time for courting and wedding.

The August air was warm, and the sun beamed

down, casting cloud shadows that raced across the
moor above the village. The men who'd returned from
Orkney and those of Clans Sutherland, Gunn, and
Oliphant gathered in small groups near the various
competitions. There was archery, sparring with weapons, caber toss, dagger throwing, and stone tossing.
Hannah scanned the groups, seeing Bàs among the
warriors. His large arm gestures, along with the shaking heads and occasional laughter, showed he was
telling tales of the battles on Orkney to take Robert
Stewart into custody for King James of Scotland. She
didn't see Erik Halverson nor his Norwegian friends.

"Lady Hannah," Kenneth Sutherland, Ella's father, greeted her. His gaze shifted to Osk. "And
Masters Adam and Osk."

Osk's gaze was on Bàs. "I think Adam and I will go
listen to some tales of my homeland."

Osk carried the unbreeched lad away on his arm,
and Hannah turned back to Kenneth. "Are you helping organize the games today?" she asked.

"Aye. With so many Sinclair men still on Orkney, I
volunteered to help."

"So kind of you." She smiled broadly at the older
man in spectacles. After Ella left the Sutherlands to
marry Cain, Ella's younger brother became the chief,
with Kenneth advising him every step of the way.

"Could I ask ye, milady, if ye could help with the
awards?" Kenneth said. "The winner of each competition receives a silver penny and a blue ribbon they
can tie around their upper arm. Instead of me fasten-
ing the ribbon on…" He waved one of the bright blue
ribbons. "'Twould be more festive if a bonny lass did
the honors."

She smiled and gave a little nod. "I can tie."

His brows rose high over his spectacles. "And a kiss for the winner will make it extra special."

Hannah laughed. "Will they want a kiss from you, Master Kenneth?"

His kind face crinkled with humor. "Not likely, but from ye…I'm sure to get more men signing up to compete."

She smiled broadly at his flattery and gave a small nod. "Very well," she said, wondering if Aunt Merida had implied to Kenneth that Hannah needed some male attention. The two spent a suspiciously large amount of time together.

Kenneth clapped his hands together. "Thank ye, Lady Hannah." The loud crack made several people turn his way, and he looked out toward them.

"Lady Hannah Sinclair will give the winner of each competition a silver penny, a blue ribbon, and a kiss!"

A small volley of cheers rose, and Hannah felt the heat wash up her neck to her cheeks. *Bloody hell. What have I done?* Erik would find out very quickly that she'd lied earlier, that she wasn't a widow from town. She glanced out at the field, back toward the village below, and her breath caught.

A murmur replaced the cheers as people turned to watch four men striding up the hill, four broad, tall men with blond hair. Men who did not look anything like simple silver traders. Not with muscles to rival her brothers' and intentional pigment marks on two of their faces, swords at their sides. These weren't traders.

They were warriors, and Erik Halverson led their advance.

CHAPTER FOUR

"Lughnasa (pronounced LOO-na-sa; Scottish
Gaelic: Lùnastal) is a Gaelic festival marking the
beginning of the harvest season that was historically
observed throughout Ireland, Scotland, and the Isle
of Man. Traditionally it was held on July 31 – August
1… The festival is named after the god Lugh, and
involved great gatherings that included religious
ceremonies, ritual athletic contests, feasting,
matchmaking, and trading. There were
also visits to holy wells."
New World Encyclopedia

Let the people look.

Erik was done hiding the fact that he and his
friends were formidable men. Nial had negotiated
with the Horsemen wives, because he looked the
mildest of their pack. But to confirm Hannah
Sinclair's identity and the love her clan had for her,
more importantly the love her brothers had for her,
Erik needed to interact. The quicker he could identify
the sister, the quicker they could complete their mission and regain his own sister's freedom from Sophie.
Love was the Horsemen's weakness.

Whispers and gazes followed him and his Wolf
Warriors as they made their way across the grassy
field. Most people gave them a wide berth. Their obvious strength and fine weaponry brought on cautious
looks, but the designs on Sten's and Frode's faces,

along with scars on all of them, made an obvious statement that they were not men to bother.

"I see we aren't going with the docile trader masquerade anymore?" Nial asked in Bokmål.

"Pokker," Sten swore. "I'm glad we can stop hiding."

"We need to return to Denmark soon," Frode said.

"We must be sure before we strike," Nial replied. He glanced at Frode. "Iselin will be well kept at court."

"As a prisoner," Frode said, his words gritted out.

"A well-fed, well-clothed, pampered prisoner," Nial added.

Erik said nothing. Nial was right. His sister, Iselin, was in a good place, protected while they performed their duty for Sophie. The reminder of her imprisonment, no matter how comfortable it was, made Erik's jaw ache, and he rubbed it over his short beard.

"One step at a time," Erik said. His words were low even though no one would understand their Norwegian dialect.

"We should act before the other three brothers return from Orkney," Sten said, "if they look as brutal as the youngest brother."

Nial's gaze swept the small groups of people talking, laughing, and imbibing. "The sister should be part of the celebration." He didn't say her name, which couldn't be hidden in their language.

Erik's gaze stopped on a cluster near a registration table, and he spotted the woman from the clootie well. A pale blue gown hugged Hannah's slim curves. Her golden waves fell like a mantle over straight shoulders. As they drew closer, he saw she wore a new flower crown that made her look like a forest queen, with late summer flowers of gold, white, and violet.

The younger warriors seemed to be playing court as they buzzed about her like bees around their queen. The young widow would remarry before winter set in, he concluded.

Erik walked in her direction. "We will sign up for the contests to show these Highlanders that they should not war against us."

Frode grunted acceptance, and Sten thumped his shoulder. "All will be well. Iselin is in no jeopardy." Frode was betrothed to Erik's sister, so he wished to rush through this mission so Iselin wouldn't be forced to wed anyone at the Danish court, a threat if they were unsuccessful.

"Let's get things done here and get back to Kronborg," Frode said.

"One step at a time," Erik repeated, his tone brooking no disobedience. A glance Frode's way showed the man nod in silent acceptance. "Sophie is trying to prevent a war in her daughter's country, not start one. 'Tis a tangle that requires planning."

"You hear that, Frode?" Nial asked, turning to walk backward to look at the scowling man. "Planning, not charging in and lopping off heads."

"I'm better at lopping off heads," Frode said with a snort.

"Which is why Erik is in charge," Sten said.

"Erik's good at lopping off heads, too," Nial said, turning to face front again. "Just that he plans to do it ahead of time."

Hannah looked more beautiful the closer Erik walked. The blue of her dress brought out the pale blue in her eyes. They were large like before. *A man could fall into them*, he thought poetically. Maybe she was a siren instead of a naiad, one who didn't even have to sing to draw his gaze. Her gown was simple wool yet thin, moving about her gracefully. There was embroidery around the lines accenting her trim waist and generous hips, hips he'd like to hold onto. If she was a widow, perhaps…

Her hair was blond with brown and gold shot through. The sun shone on the crest of each curl like the glisten off ocean waves. The pale skin above her bodice was smooth, and he predicted it would be as soft as the wool shifting around her legs as she turned to address the older man behind the table. The man said something to make her smile broaden, and Erik could see the white edge of her teeth between her rose-colored lips. By God, what those lips could probably do if given the chance.

Erik was glad for the longer tunic to hide the stiffness he felt in his groin. It wasn't like him to let a woman control his body or anything at all about him. His ire with his lack of discipline helped him get ahold of his carnal thoughts.

As Erik approached the table, his men with him, Hannah nodded to him but turned away, walking toward the archery field. His teeth clenched behind his frown. Did she think he would follow her as if she were a mare in season, as if he were a stallion trailing after her, hoping to mount her? Erik groaned at the thoughts battering him.

"You have a blister?" Nial asked, glancing down at his boot.

"What?" Erik asked, dragging his gaze from

Hannah's long, straight back and the way her tresses slid along it as she walked. Several young men sniffed after her.

"You look like you're in pain, and you made a noise." Nial followed his gaze. "'Tis the woman from before, the one herding the two girls with the cat."

The bespectacled man behind the table frowned at them. "That is Lady Hannah Sinclair," he said.

"You understand our words?" asked Sten in English.

"A few," the man said, his gaze taking their measure. "But your leader here is staring after milady, and you asked a question."

Erik's face turned to the man. "Lady? Lady Hannah Sinclair? Not Mistress Hannah, a widow from town?"

The man shook his head, his one brow rising. "*Lady* Hannah Sinclair is the sister of The Four Horsemen here at Girnigoe. Ye would do well to stay far away from her unless ye want to ask her brothers for her hand in marriage. They won't let any randy arse even look at her." He crossed his arms over his chest. "'Tis fortunate for ye that Bàs Sinclair isn't over here watching ye watch her or ye might find your head rolling down the hill."

Faen. His initial suspicion had been correct. The beautiful warrior sprite had lied to him.

"Her brothers care that much for her then?" Nial asked when Erik didn't speak. At least he was thinking of the mission instead of fuming over the fact he wouldn't be able to entice her into bed.

"Aye," the old man said. "We all do." He stood straight and met their eyes as he spoke. "Ye best remember that before ye do anything foolish."

Erik stood still, watching the man nod grimly, his arms crossed. And then he pivoted to see where Hannah stood surrounded by applauding men, some pointing to the arrow that had lodged quite close to the center. Lady Hannah Sinclair, with the golden waves and smooth skin, was not a young widow from town, but the sister of Dowager-Queen Sophie's enemy. His sovereign wanted to use her as a pawn to wage a silent war. And all Erik could think of was how he wanted to touch her.

• • •

"Very nice," Ella said to Hannah. "The wind changed the arrow's course right at the end of its flight. A little more power behind the release and it would have hit in the middle."

Cait, who stood next to them, squinted toward the five targets nailed to hay bales. "Still… 'Twould have killed the man."

"Definitely," Ella concurred. Her gaze slid from Hannah to somewhere behind her. "Good Lord," she murmured, making Cait turn.

Hannah's heart thumped wildly with the keen sense that someone was staring at her with intensity. She wet her lips and turned slowly. Even though she'd guessed that Erik Halverson was the one watching her, seeing his confident stride toward her made her heart lurch.

The Norwegian was dressed in a dry set of narrow gray breeches that tucked into his tall, laced boots, which were also dry and different from the ones he'd worn that morning. His white tunic was cinched with

a thick leather belt, studded with silver eyelets, and
his blue jerkin moved casually unlaced over it. His
light golden hair nearly grazed his shoulders, but part
was pulled back, which accentuated his square jawline, sporting a trimmed beard.

Hannah had never been mesmerized by the physical appearance of a man before meeting Erik
Halverson, but the piercing blue eyes that held her
gaze would not allow her to turn. His steps were firm
and sure as he blazed through the grass and wildflowers, stopping before her.

He inhaled through his nose, making his nostrils
widen the slightest amount, and Hannah watched his
perfect lips part. "Good day, *Lady* Hannah Sinclair,"
he said. "Sister of the Four Sinclair Horsemen of
Scotland." He tilted his head as if daring her to lie
again.

She tilted her head to mimic his movement and
gave a sly smile even though her heart pounded.
"Good day, Erik Halverson, trader and sometimes
warrior from Norway."

"Good day," Ella said, her voice cutting through
the tether that had wrapped around Hannah. "Have
you and your men come to compete today at our
Harvest Festival?"

Only then did Hannah notice that three men stood
behind Erik. Two of them had pigmented designs on
their faces, one with a full blond beard that didn't
cover the scowl he wore. The third of Erik's companions nodded to her, allowing a casual smile. He was
larger in girth with long hair and looked the friendli-
est of the group. Perhaps he was like Gideon. The one
who could talk without frightening normal people,

which was why he did most of the negotiations with King James.

"Aye," the friendlier-looking man answered Ella. "Since we await the return of the chief and Horseman of Justice, with his contracts, we thought we would partake on this fine day." The man held out a hand to the sky. "The Lord has blessed us with sun and cheerful breezes." His English was accented but seemed to hold authentic gratitude. He looked between Cait and Ella. "This is the fourth man of our silver trading group, Erik Halverson."

Erik nodded quickly to the ladies. It was almost rude how he turned immediately back to Hannah. "You lied to me," he said, his words hard but even. "About who you are."

Bloody hell, the man was slightly bigger than her mountain-like brothers with delicious-looking scars that showed how fierce he could be. A child he would father would be strong, living past all the risks of infancy. Just the thought of how he'd get her with child sent a sizzle twisting in her middle. Hannah held his gaze and kept her breathing even.

"You lied," he repeated.

Ella and Cait looked between them but didn't say anything. Hannah wet her lips. "Think hard on my words, Master Halverson." She turned to look out at the vast moor, the wind blowing her hair around her shoulders. "No lies passed my lips. I merely led you to believe something through my actions." She kissed her gold ring and sniffed as if she fought back tears. "You interpreted those actions incorrectly."

Erik snorted softly.

"Do you shoot?" Ella asked as if trying to pull his

gaze. She indicated the targets at the end of the field.

He glanced at Ella and shrugged. "I'm a simple silver trader."

Hannah highly doubted that. "You can try," she said, indicating the bows heaped at the top of the field for participants. "Even though the judging is nearly complete, there is still time to enter the contest."

"Good day," came a small, joyful voice, and Hannah saw Trix and Libby standing before the friendlier Norseman, heads tipped back to look up at him.

"Good day," he returned. "We were not properly introduced yesterday. I am Nial Kristiansen."

"I am Beatrix Sinclair and this is Libby Sinclair. But I go by Trix."

"We aren't sisters by blood, but we are sisters by heart," Libby said.

"Lady Cait and Chief Gideon have adopted us," Trix said, her missing front tooth adding to her charm.

"Girls, why don't you run over to see how the bonfires are being built?" Cait said, obviously worried about them being in the middle of such large strangers.

"Why would we need to learn how to build bonfires?" Libby asked.

Trix pointed at Erik. "He's the one who saved Boo from the roof, Lady Ella. He's quite valiant." Her voice sounded a bit dreamy.

"Who are the frowning ones?" Libby asked, nodding to the two pigmented strangers.

"They are Sten and Frode," Nial said.

Frode looked over to the girls. "And we eat kittens to break our fast."

The girls' eyes widened, but then big smiles broke across their faces. They giggled. They were used to big, scary uncles, and, unfortunately, saw no threat when they should be running off to safety.

"Kittens are scrawny," Libby said.

"You should eat cats," Trix added. "They are meatier."

Hannah noticed the smallest quiver to Sten's frowning mouth.

Erik stepped away and picked up a sturdy bow from the pile. He set the arrow in place but allowed it to wobble while he raised it. Hannah watched him struggle for a moment and walked over. "You aren't holding it right."

Erik tried again, but the tip of the arrow kept rising off its perch.

"No," Hannah said. "The tip must rest on the little shelf to keep it even so it will shoot straight."

Erik rested the tip, but his elbow sagged. He released the arrow, and it flew downward, sticking in the ground halfway to the target. Hannah covered her mouth with a hand so he wouldn't see her stifle a laugh. Maybe he trained only with a sword.

"Why did you put paint on your faces?" Trix asked from behind where Sten and Frode must be watching.

"That's not just paint, Trix," Libby corrected. "It was done with a needle and pigment."

"I know."

Libby stood right below Frode, staring up at him. "Didn't that hurt?"

Hannah turned back to Erik who had picked out another arrow from the quiver. He nocked it oddly.

Hannah huffed, coming beside him. "Rest the

arrow, keep your elbow back, and try to release smoothly." He stood in a strange way that would probably foul up his aim. "Here," she said, and stepped behind him. She wrapped her arms around him so she could steady his aim. She tapped his right boot with her foot to get him to slide it outward a bit. "Arm straight. Close one eye to help you aim."

Good Lord, he was large. Tall and broad, it was like hugging a thick tree or one of her brothers. But then, it was nothing like hugging one of her brothers, because her body was warming, and Hannah was almost painfully aware of her breasts pressing against Erik's back. He smelled clean, like an herb and leather, and his body radiated heat like a sunbaked brick.

He didn't move as she stood wrapped around him. She shifted so she could reach his hand holding the bowstring. Her hand rested over it gently. Slowly, she pulled the string back. "Keep your elbow up, higher than level," she instructed, her words soft. "You'll have to aim, because I can't see over your shoulder." The man really was massive. "Aim and release the arrow when you're ready."

The rise and fall of their breathing adjusted so that they inhaled and exhaled together. She would swear she felt his heart beating through his jacket, tunic, and flesh, but more likely 'twas her own. *I should step away*. She lowered her arm but didn't move back.

Twang! He released the arrow, and it shot straight and far, hitting the target in the middle.

A cheer went up behind them, and Hannah jumped back, realizing how she'd probably looked instructing the huge man. Instead of turning to thank her, Erik plucked a second arrow from the quiver. Without the smallest bit of hesitation, he drew back the bowstring, aimed, and fired.

Thwack! The arrow hit once again in the center. As everyone gasped, Erik plucked a third, fired, and hit the center. By the time he'd repeated the obvious skill with the fifth arrow, Hannah could feel the flush rising up her neck into her face. The man was a bloody expert.

The entire group of spectators watched with wide eyes and open mouths. *Thwack! Thwack! Thwack!* Erik emptied the quiver, hitting the very center every time, even slicing through some he'd first fired, and tossed the bow onto the grass beside the pile of contest bows.

He turned to Hannah, and she glared up into his brutally handsome face. "You lied to me," she said, her teeth gritted in humiliated anger, and lowered her voice. "To get me to…hold on to you like that." She waved a hand toward where they'd stood with her basically clinging to him before everyone. Her cheeks flamed.

He leaned in slightly, and she could see the edge of white teeth as he spoke. "I merely led you to believe something through my actions, and you interpreted it incorrectly," he said, using every single one of her earlier words.

She didn't have time to retort because Kenneth Sutherland hurried up to them. "What skill!" he said to Erik. Down at the end of the field, several lads signaled to Kenneth. "They say ye hit every time after… Lady Hannah gave ye instruction."

One of the boys ran up with the arrows in his arms.

"Two arrows are split clean through!"

"Very good," Kenneth said and turned to the on-lookers. "The winner of the shooting contest is Erik Halverson of Denmark-Norway." A smattering of applause sounded, mostly from the women and girls watching.

Kenneth held up a silver coin, handing it to Erik. "Ye can spend it here if 'tis no good at home," he said. "For more wool or whatever." He held out the blue ribbon to Hannah.

She stared at it for a few seconds before remembering she'd told Kenneth she would award the prizes. *Oh Lord.* And give the winner a kiss.

Kenneth waved the ribbon in the air, and she took it, going to Erik's arm. It was thick with muscle.

"'Twill be tight," she murmured.

He shrugged out of his jacket, leaving him in breeches and the white tunic that was cinched around his narrow waist. Hannah wrapped the blue ribbon around his arm. The muscle popped out quite high as he held his arm even. Her tongue teased her bottom lip as she fastened a knot, since there wasn't enough slack for a bow to hold the ribbon in place.

"And all winners have the extra prize of a kiss from the fair Lady Hannah," Kenneth called out. More applause.

Hannah swallowed hard and looked up into Erik's face, but his gaze was behind her at the hill leading to the village. *I'll only kiss his cheek.* She stepped forward. He stepped back but leaned into her ear. "I will claim my prize later when your brother isn't clamoring up the slope with his sword ready to spill blood."

Hannah whirled toward the hill where Bàs strode,

his gaze latched onto her, his sword in hand. Shana, who had come up to stand with Ella and Cait, saw him and hurried to intercept. Whatever she was saying had no effect on her husband as he tore his way through the crowd.

"Step away from my sister," Bàs said, making Hannah's stomach clench. *Daingead!* He was demonstrating to everyone what became of men who approached her, even at an innocent, well mostly innocent, contest.

Erik's three friends had come to his side, their own swords drawn, and Hannah found herself between them and Bàs. Several returned Girnigoe warriors joined Bàs opposite them, and Kenneth Sutherland grabbed Hannah's arm to pull her out of the fray. But Hannah tore away from Kenneth and stepped between her brother and the Norwegians. She shoved her palm into Bàs's chest as if he were a bull charging. Fortunately, her brother didn't run her over. "He won the archery contest, Bàs. I was but giving him his prize."

"See," Shana said, breathing heavily, one hand sliding down her gently curved middle. "No one's harming Hannah."

Kára came up behind them, one bairn tied to her front and the other to her back, huffing at the effort of striding with the heavy weight. So now all four sisters were there, too, witnessing her embarrassment.

"Keenan said they'd followed ye up onto the hill." Bàs pointed the tip of his sword at Erik. "That this one especially has been watching ye."

Erik's watching me? Bloody hell, Bàs! That would probably end now that her brother, The Horseman of

Death, was close to violence. Hannah huffed. "No one is watching me, brother, not with you charging up to anyone who might find me…worth watching." She waved her hand at Bàs. "Now put that sword away and greet these traders from Norway in a welcoming manner. I'm sure Shana has told you they bring silver with them."

"I did," Shana called from behind.

Bàs stared over Hannah's head at Erik, sizing him up the same way the traders were doing to Bàs and those who stood with him. Even though there weren't too many Sinclairs yet returned from Orkney, there were a fair number of Mackays, Sutherlands, and a few Oliphants. And all of them were on Bàs's side.

Libby and Trix wiggled through the gathered people to stand beside Hannah. The two little lasses were always climbing into trouble. They'd even risked their young lives to ride a huge horse to warn King James about an assassination attempt last winter.

"He saved Lady Ella's cat," Trix called to Bàs.

"Master Erik there," Libby said, pointing. "He lifted me up so Boo would come to me off a roof. So clever, because Boo would not come to a stranger, but she came to me."

"And Lady Hannah looks so lovely today, everyone is watching her," Trix said, making Hannah's cheeks heat again.

Crouched low, Cait moved quickly right amongst them and took each girl by a hand, leading them out of the fray.

Hannah turned her face to Erik so he could see her mouth move in a silent plea. "Back up to move forward," she whispered.

Erik's gaze was centered on her mouth, sending a little thrill through her. When had a man ever looked at her mouth or into her eyes or even at her bosom? Never, even without Bàs snarling behind her.

Erik took a step backward, sheathing his sword. "We mean no dishonor to the lady."

Slowly, Bàs lowered his sword, and those warriors on either side did the same. Erik's three friends sheathed their swords, too.

Nial stepped forward, addressing Bàs. "We but wait to greet your chief, Cain Sinclair, before we depart with the bartered wool the ladies of Girnigoe have traded. We brought silver from Norway." The man smiled. "We understand you were the first to return from war."

"Aye," Bàs said. "Cain and my brothers will follow within the week. They're transporting Robert Stewart to mainland Scotland for King James to take into custody for treason."

Nial shook his head. "We have heard of the Stewart earl's overstep at the Danish court. King James is fortunate to have such strong warriors behind him."

Even though Nial spoke, Bàs continued to glance at Erik as if he realized he was the leader and the biggest threat.

Bàs inhaled. "Welcome to Girnigoe. My brothers will be happy to speak with you upon their return."

Nial held out a hand, and Bàs grasped it. "Good," Nial said. "Let us enjoy this fine festival together then."

Bàs released Nial's hand and looked at Erik. "Now that ye've won the archery contest, let us see how ye fare in strength."

CHAPTER FIVE

How to judge a caber toss – "A perfect throw ends
with the 'top' end nearest to the thrower and the
'bottom' end pointing exactly away. If the throw is
not perfect, it is scored by viewing the caber as
though it were a hand on the clock. The ideal
position is 12:00. A caber pointing to 11:00 would get
a better score than one pointing to 10:30. If the caber
lands on its end and falls back toward the thrower,
the score is lower than for any throw that
falls away from the thrower."

SCOTLAND'S ENCHANTING KINGDOM

Erik and his men followed Bàs Sinclair and the growing crowd over to an area flanked with cut and
cleaned trees.

The ground there was free of boulders that
seemed to erupt from the landscape like the bones of
mythological giants, the Jötnar perhaps. Hannah
walked with the wives of the horsemen while the two
little girls continued to follow Frode and Sten, asking
questions as they skipped along.

"How many days does it take to sail here from
Denmark-Norway?" Libby asked as she gazed up at
Sten.

"Four days from Norway and about a week from
Denmark," Nial answered when Sten didn't.

"But they are the same country, right?" Trix said.

"Yes," Libby answered before anyone else did.

"Cait taught us that."

Trix nodded and then tugged on Frode's sleeve. "Do you get ill on the water?" Frode turned his frightening face down to the child, but she smiled up at him. One of her front milk teeth was missing. She didn't know how many people Frode had killed in war, although none of them were children. She continued when he didn't answer. "I think I would vomit if I had to ride up and down on waves for a week," Trix said and moved her hand as if it were riding a wave.

"I do not get ill," Frode said and turned his face back to the field ahead.

Libby grabbed up a handful of flowers without stopping. "'Tis fortunate for you as traders."

Two wolfhounds loped along beside the girls and gently maneuvered between them and Erik's men as if they sensed danger. The crowd spread around the felled trees, talking about their weights.

The man, Kenneth, hopped over one. He was spry for an old man. "If ye've signed up for the contest, pick your caber," he called out. "Otherwise, step back." Kenneth waved his arms together as if pushing back the crowd.

"Nay," said Cait Sinclair, shaking her head at a young warrior who had hair that wouldn't stay out of his eyes. "You haven't been trained in technique, Jack," she said, making the lad flush with a look of mutiny.

"The Norwegians probably haven't, either," the lad called.

"Have you heard of tossing logs?" Nial asked Erik in Bokmål.

Erik stood with his arms crossed. "They throw trees across rivers to ford them."

"How?" Frode asked, his apathetic mask slipping to real interest. They had many trees and water to ford in Norway.

"I suppose we will see," Erik said.

Cait Sinclair walked closer to the young man, speaking low so as not to embarrass him further. She frowned like Erik's mormor when she'd been determined to keep Erik alive as a boy. The memory of the elderly woman with the wrinkled apple cheeks tightened the spot in his chest. It sat high on the left where his heart had died with most of his family.

"Ye heard your mother," called an elderly woman with braided white hair. "Ye need proper training so ye don't drop a tree on yourself."

"She's not my mother," the boy grumbled, crossing his arms.

"She's the closest we have, Jack," Trix said, frowning at him.

Libby planted her hands on her hips. "And Erik Halverson and our friend, Frode, are obviously strong enough to lift the trees, so they won't drop them on themselves."

"Sten is just as strong," Trix said.

The look of annoyance on Nial's face, probably because the girls hadn't said he was strong, almost made Erik chuckle.

"Competitors should remove their weapons before competing," Kenneth said. It seemed that ten other men had signed up to throw these trees or cabers.

"Are ye brave enough to throw a caber?" Bàs

asked Erik, his question laced with challenge.

"Brave enough to battle a tree? I suppose I am," Erik said.

"They are about one hundred seventy-five pounds and nineteen feet long. There's a technique for tumbling them." Bàs's mouth relaxed a bit. It wasn't a smile but close enough to make Erik feel odd. He didn't need to befriend one of the Sinclair Horsemen.

"Ye aren't actually battling them but trying to toss one end over end to land in a straight line." The man moved his arm, his fingers pointing straight out from his body. "Perpendicular to the line." He indicated a rope that stretched out before them. "The one who throws it to land the straightest wins."

Trix and Libby hopped among the tall warriors, their heads tipped back to meet their gazes. "Warriors can throw them across rivers to make a bridge for crossing if needed," Libby said.

"You carry trees with you into battle?" Sten asked.

Another young man laughed. "I wondered the same thing when I came from Orkney." He nodded to them. "I'm Osk, Kára's brother. We didn't have trees on Orkney, so it seemed bloody odd. But they leave these trees near rivers so they can toss them over if needed."

"Girls, come away."

Erik turned at Hannah's voice.

"Pardon me," she said and slid against his arm to lean into the semicircle of men, her hands reaching for Libby and Trix. The ring on her finger reflected the muted sun, and a delicate flower fragrance came from her hair. Erik couldn't help but inhale fully, and his arm warmed at the spot of their contact.

Hannah backed up, tugging the girls. She looked over her shoulder at Erik, meeting his gaze. "Don't drop a tree on yourself."

His mouth relaxed, curving slightly at the corners, and he gave a small nod.

Frode grabbed Erik's shoulder, giving it a little shake. "Keep that up, and her brother will skewer you before we fulfill our mission."

Erik caught Bàs's watchful gaze. The man frowned fiercely at him, coming over. "The less that weighs ye down, the better," Bàs said, pulling a dagger from his sleeve, first one and then the other. Erik did the same. For every dagger Bàs Sinclair pulled, he waited for Erik to pull one, and they would drop them in unison on the ground at their feet. Four daggers, a short sword, and a long sword each. It was a competition in itself as the villagers watched, some of them counting.

"For a trader, ye carry a lot of blades," Bàs said, tilting his head.

"We have come to apparently hostile territory," Erik said, standing with his legs braced. He was finished with his weapons. "We'd be fools to come unarmed even if your queen's mother sent us."

Bàs's brows drew together. "Queen Anne's mother? Sophie of Denmark sent ye?"

"Aye," Nial said, giving Erik a glance that told him to hold his tongue. "Indirectly. We heard from her court that the Sinclairs had rich wool indeed." They'd also heard how the Sinclair brothers were strong enough to take Scotland away from King James and Sophie's daughter, but of course Nial didn't say that.

Bàs drew out one extra weapon, his ax strapped

to his back. It thumped on the ground, and his people cheered. He'd won the unofficial most-weapons contest.

Out of the corner of his eye, Erik saw Hannah watching them as they walked along the tree trunks that had been stripped of limbs and tapered at the ends. Bàs pointed to one. The caber was carried out by four warriors who held the tree upright, balanced on the ground. Bàs yanked his tunic off, leaving him in the wool wrap around his hips and tall boots. The man had scars from battle and an ax etched with pigment on his upper back, along with another in the shape of a horse's head on his upper arm. His muscles backed up the legend that he was a formidable opponent.

Bàs showed no hesitation as he gripped the bottom of the caber in hands where his fingers were interwoven. Once he got his hands under the cut bottom, he began to run with it, the upright length balanced against one shoulder. He stopped, throwing his gripped hands upward, making the top of the tree fall with speed toward the ground. As that end caught on the grass, the end Bàs had been holding flew through the air in an arc and the whole caber thudded onto the ground in a perfect perpendicular line.

The crowd roared with approval, and Bàs walked back, grabbing his tunic to throw over one shoulder. His wife hurried forward to plant a kiss of victory on his lips. He lifted her easily, turning her around in a hug. She laughed, kissing him again. The man was apparently quite loyal and openly loving to his wife.

Another two Highlanders went, one of them unable to get the tree end to fly upward high enough, and the tree shot across the grass without flipping. The third Sinclair warrior, Keenan, managed to get the tree to tumble but it didn't land exactly perpendicular.

"Ye going to try?" Bàs asked Erik and his men.

Frode shook his head. "'Tis more about a technique we haven't practiced."

"Nay," Sten said, and Nial shook his head.

"Halverson?" Bàs asked.

Erik stretched his arms overhead and rolled his shoulders. He nodded and walked over to the trees, picking out the one Bàs had used. He would never back down from a challenge, even if he wasn't sure of the outcome. Like the others, Erik pulled off his tunic, leaving only his breeches tied about his waist and his laced boots.

A murmur went through the watching crowd, probably from the markings Erik wore across his back. Symbols of old power gave him and his men strength and focus. A wolf's snarling face sat in the middle of his back. And there were eleven etched valknut symbols on his chest over his heart, one for each of his family members who'd succumbed during the great illness. The interlocking triangles of each valknut stood for the phases of life and afterlife where he would be with them again.

"Traders my arse," Bàs said and walked to the tree to help carry it with three others onto the field. 'Twas true that Erik was built for war with muscles honed from daily training. Strength and agility kept him alive as he led his group to guard the eastern border of Norway against the Swedes.

"Drop the tree on the horseman," Sten suggested

in Bokmål. "Bring his body back to court too."

Sten knew that wasn't the plan. "Nay," Erik said, continuing in their language. "If I kill him, we will be up against at least a hundred angry warriors with weapons and a weeping, pregnant wife."

"No killing before the children," Frode said. He glanced at Libby and Trix who were each lying across a wolfhound's back.

Erik walked up to the tree that Bàs continued to balance on one end for him. "Get under its weight," Bàs said. "And throw the end upward with all your strength. Then the tree will do its job."

Erik grunted at the tree that seemed to soar into the clouds. With the end of the caber on the grass, Bàs held it with one hand. His other clamped down in a friendly manner on Erik's shoulder. "There's no shame in failing the first time ye've ever tried."

The man wasn't the cruel, killing-without-provocation executioner described to Erik at the Danish court. Nay. Hannah's brother was rather…likeable.

Erik crouched, wrapping his woven fingers around the base of the caber, working his grip underneath; he had to tilt it somewhat so as not to squash his fingers. His muscles bulged easily as he lifted.

"Balance on your shoulder," Bàs yelled, backing up. "But keep it mostly upright and run forward."

Erik took two steps back as the weight moved, and everyone behind him gasped. But then he pressed his shoulder harder into the smooth trunk and the weight shifted forward. He took several running steps and snapped his arms upward with a fierce growl, the force nearly making him lose his balance. He caught himself from tumbling as he watched the caber flip bottom over top and landed, not perfectly perpendicular but not completely skewed, either. The crowd cheered. Erik turned, and Bàs strode forward to clasp his hand, a broad smile on his face.

"Not bad at all, Norseman," Bàs said, and they walked off the field together.

Norseman? So, the Sinclair Horseman suspected Erik's old Norse ancestry. It made him much more likely to be a warrior than a trader, but he didn't correct him.

Frode and Sten stood with their arms crossed but nodded at Erik. Erik accepted a tankard of cold mead from Bàs, but his gaze rested on Hannah, who stood with the Sinclair wives. Her eyes held a lightness that was more than the color. The slight curve of her lips added to her playful look, reminding Erik once more of a wood sprite.

Bàs glanced between them, his smile slipping. "Hannah is special to me, to all of us. I am most protective of her." His voice was even as if he merely informed, but Erik heard the undertone of a lethal threat.

Erik met the horseman's gaze. "Is that why she's not wed? No one would dare irritate the Sinclair Horsemen?" The woman had shown how much she wished for her own family with the fertility doll at their sacred spring. Despite caring for her, were her brothers ignorant of their sister's wants?

Bàs's jaw moved back and forth. "Perhaps. Or perhaps she has not met one she fancies."

Erik turned back to watch Hannah smile at the antics of the girls, her lips parting in laughter. It seemed so natural on her and made everyone around her smile and join in, increasing joy and banishing frowns like a wave of magic over the small crowd.

Feeling his gaze perhaps, she glanced at him. She nodded, keeping her bright expression. And just like that, Erik felt the wave of sunlight wash over him, too.

• • •

"Are you certain?" Kára asked, looking to Hannah. Even though Kára had seemed quite supportive the other day, she now glanced between Hannah and her other sisters by marriage.

"I'm certain I will never find a husband among our people," Hannah said, her face firm. "I have tried these past years since my father died, but no one looks at me once one of my brothers comes around and honestly, I think of them all as my kin anyway."

"Most of them are," Cait said where she sat nursing her son, Gavin. The Sinclair wives and Shana's sister, Ivy, sat in the candlelit solar in Girnigoe Castle. Four bairns nursed or slept nearby.

Hannah indicated wee Gavin. "I want a bairn, one that comes from my body with Sinclair blood running through him or her." She looked up at Ella. "Will you help me?"

"Bàs won't let you out of his sight tonight at the bonfires," Shana said, cradling one of Kára's twin daughters. Their newest sister wasn't due for another five or six months, but she was already showing outward signs of carrying a child.

Ivy sat beside her with her arms outstretched to keep her son, Edward, away from Apollo's swinging tail. The little boy tried to catch the wolfhound with chubby hands. "What do you know of this Norwegian?" Ivy asked. The poor woman had been tricked by a man and held them all suspect since then.

"I know he saved Ella's cat and is kind to Trix and Libby despite their constant chatter," Hannah said. "I know he didn't attack me the two times we were alone, once when he could see through my wet smock—"

"Beò stood between you two," Shana reminded her.

"Yes, but not when he had me all alone at the clootie well," Hannah said. "Then he could have attacked me, and he didn't."

"You know how…things work?" Ella asked. "Between a man and a woman?"

Hannah rolled her eyes. "The four of you whisper about it all the time."

"Do we?" Cait asked, looking at the others.

"I do," Kára answered with a little grin. Joshua's wife was especially happy to give details of their rigorous loving when asked and even when she wasn't asked.

"And I've seen horses," Hannah said. "I've also walked into the pantry a time or two to find Cain and Ella—"

"We need to make certain he's a gentle lover," Ella interrupted. "You're a virgin."

"The first time, he shouldn't take you from behind," Kára said. "Unless that's what you'd like."

"I don't know what I'd like," Hannah said, frowning. "How many different ways are there to choose from?"

A look passed between Cait and Ella before Cait

gently popped the sleeping bairn off her breast and closed her robe. "There's a book about different ways in the library. I sent it over to Girnigoe when the library at Varrich Castle began to be used by the children for our school. I'll get it." She set her bairn over one shoulder and walked briskly from the room.

"I can take care of Bàs tonight if you'd like," Shana said, glancing at Hannah. "I know how to distract him." She smiled broadly, obviously implying some erotic trickery.

Hannah tipped her hand toward her. "Like that. I want to know what you all know and insinuate."

Kára looked seriously at Hannah over the head of one of her daughters. "There's no going back once you lose your maidenhead. Are you sure you wish to do that? Not being a virgin might change a future suitor's mind about wedding."

Hannah wet her dry lips, trying to suppress the fluttering in her stomach. "I am nearly thirty years old. If I don't carry a child soon, I never will. I don't have time to find a man who doesn't turn my stomach, convince him to wed me despite my brothers, and then become pregnant."

"So, you don't want to *wed* Erik Halverson?" Ivy asked.

Hannah shook her head. "I will never leave Girnigoe and Scotland, and I doubt Erik would leave Denmark-Norway to live here."

"Raising a child alone is not easy," Ivy said, snatching up wee Edward as he tried to grab Apollo's ear. She would know after the betrayal she'd endured the previous summer.

Ella walked over to fix the flower wreath on

Hannah's head. She answered Ivy but held Hannah's gaze. "We would help her like Shana helps you, Ivy."

Ivy smiled at her sister and then looked to Hannah. "I get all the help with Edward that I need thanks to the Sinclairs and Mackays, but I'm talking about"—she laid a hand over her heart—"the hurt and loneliness when the man you love is gone for good, his child always there to remind you of the loss."

Ivy was sad, and it would take much more than a year to numb the pain with which she was living. Her sadness lay over them like a filmy veil, and silence filled the dim solar.

Hannah cleared her throat softly. "I am so sorry, Ivy, and I know you love Edward so very much and would never wish him gone."

Ivy cuddled her little boy in her lap. "Of course not."

"I'm fortunate I don't love Erik Halverson," Hannah said. Just his name caused excitement to bloom in her middle. "I want him to go away, because if he stayed here, and I was with child, my brothers would slaughter him in various appalling ways."

Kára chuckled, her brows raised. "Joshua can be horrifically creative to those he sees as enemies to his family."

Ella crouched before Hannah. "I will support you, but you must be sure."

"You did see that man's arms today, didn't you?" Kára said. "And his back and chest? Hannah would have to be a cold, stone statue not to want to make a babe with him."

Ella kept Hannah's gaze. "You could bed him, lose

your maidenhead, and not get pregnant."

Hannah drew in a full breath, which pushed her breasts to swell slightly over the edge of her blue gown. "I know, but there's a chance. Maybe a couple chances if he stays here until Cain arrives home."

Ella ran a hand down her face in worry. "You two will have to be careful not to be caught or Erik Halverson will…"

Kára drew a line across her throat and made a noise like her throat was being cut.

Cait whisked back into the room with Gavin over her shoulder. "Here it is." She laid a book with an ancient-looking papyrus cover down on a small table, and the sisters gathered around it. "'Tis one of several volumes, all of them written in an ancient language from the far east. But this one has pictures." She opened it, and Ivy gasped softly behind Hannah as they looked down on a woman kneeling before a man, his erection buried in her mouth.

"That's not for a first time," Ella said, quickly turning the pages to the front.

Hannah looked at her with wider eyes. "Is that pleasurable for the woman?"

"Oh, it can be," Kára said with a saucy grin. "But only if he's clean."

"Absolutely," Ella said. "Cleanliness is very enticing."

"But it won't get me with child," Hannah said.

"Not everything you do with a man is because you want to get with child," Cait said.

Hannah knew that, or at least…well, it made sense. Things that felt good were important too. Like when she touched herself. There was no outcome except pleasure.

In silence, they flipped through the images of a woman and man copulating in various positions, some twisted and bizarre.

"Are there instructions in the other books?" Ivy asked.

"I'm not certain. Gideon and I have had great success just focusing on the pictures," Cait said.

"There's the mounting from behind," Kára said, pointing to the detailed drawing. "Kneeling on the edge of a bench or bed works better than standing if he's tall."

"Again," Ella said, "not for a first time." She cast a frown at Kára.

"Unless she wants," Kára added with wide eyes.

Ella huffed. "We need to find out if Erik Halverson is gentle before…" Her fingers fluttered toward the book. "I don't want Hannah being scared of something that is wonderful when done correctly." She spoke as if Hannah wasn't sitting right there.

Kára nodded. "He needs to prepare her body beforehand. We will talk with him."

"What?" Hannah asked, her eyes widening. "You can't go up to a man and ask him if he…"

"He knows how to bring a woman to hot, wet bliss before entering her?" Kára asked.

"Exactly," Hannah said. "You can't ask him that or even how he…" She moved her hand in the air.

"Beds a lass?" Cait said.

"Tups?" Shana said.

"Aunt Merida calls it riding below the crupper," Ella said.

Ivy laughed softly, seemingly cheered.

"Tups, beds, threads the needle, does the deed of darkness…" Kára rattled off.

"Really?" Ella said. "Deed of darkness?"

Kára nodded. "Although I find doing the deed under a warm sunray much more fun."

Everyone laughed softly through their noses. "As long as he gets his seed in me," Hannah said. "To make a child."

"Oh 'tis so much more fun if he knows how to give you pleasure," Ella said. "'Tis a must." All the ladies nodded.

Hannah picked up the book again, flipping to a page that showed a man's face buried between a woman's parted thighs. "Not a way to get with child."

Kára looked over her shoulder. "It did for me."

Hannah's gaze snapped to hers. "How?"

Kára grinned devilishly. "Because after that," she tapped a curved fingernail on the page, "I was ready for everything and anything Joshua wanted to do with me, which then got me with these two sweet girls."

Hannah stared at Kára, feeling her face warm while Kára nodded, kissed her daughter's head while holding her against her chest, and twirled away with her as if she were blissfully happy. Lord, how Hannah wanted to be blissfully happy. She looked back at the pages, turning them slowly. One image showed the woman sitting upon the man's jack like she was riding a horse, and another showed both the woman's legs held up in the air while he entered her. Hannah couldn't imagine doing most of these positions, but the pictures alone were filling her with a hot, languid achiness.

Ella stood beside Hannah. "But no going off alone

without us talking to Erik Halverson first. And you be quite loud about saying no if you decide to stop or slow down or…well anything. Even if you've started something."

Kára nodded, a frown on her face. "You say no forcibly and walk away if you decide not to follow through."

Hannah looked at them both and nodded solemnly.

Ella glanced at the ceiling as if seeking heavenly guidance. "For I will never forgive myself if you come to harm and we allowed it."

"None of us would," Shana added, and all the ladies nodded.

"There ye all are." Bàs's voice came from the doorway of the solar, making Hannah jump, the book still open before her.

Cait slapped the book shut, but Bàs's gaze had already landed there.

He frowned. "Is that Gideon's—?"

Shana hurried toward her husband. "I had a question about…" She leaned up to his ear and whispered in it.

Bàs's brows rose, but then he frowned. "'Tis not something for ye, Hannah," he said. "Nothing in that book is for an unmarried maid to see."

Daingead. She frowned at him. "I'm nearly an *old* maid, brother. 'Tis about time I learn about these things. Knowledge is power." 'Twas an old saying that Gideon used often.

"Not *that* kind of knowledge," Bàs called back as Shana dragged him away.

Ella looped her arm through Hannah's while Cait took up the book. Ella leaned in to her ear. "Let

Shana take care of him."

As they headed out the door, Hannah mentally checked off her seduction preparation list. *Bathed, clean teeth, oil on the elbows and knees, rag tucked into my belt.* The last item was recommended by Kára who said she'd need it afterward. Hannah doubted she would have gotten such vivid instructions from her mother on her wedding day.

Hannah inhaled, her mind going to Erik's brawn and intense gaze out on the practice field earlier. Just the memory, mixed with the pictures in the book, made heat bloom inside her, sluicing down her body until it settled like warm honey between her legs. Yes, she wanted to be part of her sisters' camaraderie and not merely the sad, virgin auntie. And she wanted a child to love who was all hers. But she also wanted to grow this fire kindled within her, the one that roared a bit hotter every time she imagined being with Erik, running her fingers along the lines etched into his hot skin. The thought of putting her mouth on his erection like she'd seen in the book only made her ache turn more molten, especially at the thought of him doing something similar to her.

Everyone gathered their capes, Hannah's being the embroidered blue wool cape that her sisters had gifted her last Hogmanay. Bàs strode down the steps to rejoin the men already outdoors. The ladies would stop off at the nursery before heading to the bonfires outside. Several lasses from the village had been hired to care for the children so the sisters could dance and enjoy themselves even if their husbands hadn't yet returned. Shana was the luckiest of them. She was pregnant and Bàs was home with her.

Ivy's sad words came back to Hannah. *The hurt and loneliness when the man you love is gone for good…* "I don't love him," she murmured. "I want only to tup him."

She was a Sinclair, born to a family of warriors who fought for what they wanted. And she wanted a bairn, one who would have a chance to grow up into someone as strong as her brothers. Erik Halverson seemed like the perfect man to fulfill her plan. If she ignored the emotion behind being intimate with someone and focused on just wanting his seed, the whole situation was easier.

Hannah waited for nearly a quarter hour for the other sisters to come down from the nursery, and they walked out together into the night breeze. Over the first and second drawbridges and under the vicious-looking raised portcullis, the ladies talked and laughed. Hannah kept quiet. Kára looped her arm through hers. *Support.* What had Hannah done before without it? *I hid in a corner.*

All through her childhood, when her brothers were being taught how to conquer and war, judge and kill, Hannah had listened and learned. She knew things that other women didn't know, like where to cut someone's neck to pierce their carotid artery and how many troops were needed to take over Scotland. She knew the absence of birds over a battlefield meant men were probably hiding in ambush and that the gazes of liars flicked away quickly. Hannah had learned languages, sums, writing, and archery. And now she'd learn the art of passion, if Erik Halverson was good at it.

"There he is," Kára whispered in her ear, and Hannah's heart thumped with hot anticipation.

CHAPTER SIX

"An ingenious person should multiply the kinds of
congress after the fashion of the different kinds of
beasts and of birds. For these different kinds of
congress, performed according to the usage of each
country, and the liking of each individual, generate
love, friendship, and respect in the hearts of women."
ADVICE ON PHYSICAL LOVE (CONGRESS), KAMASUTRA
BY VATSYAYANA SECOND CENTURY AD

Erik stood on the far side of the bonfire with his men,
Bàs Sinclair, and some of the other Sinclair warriors
who'd come back from Orkney already. Many of the
Sutherlands and Mackays had also remained for the
drinking and camaraderie.

"Join us," Bàs said, indicating the logs set on the
other side.

Ladies danced around a bonfire farther off while a
set of talented musicians kept the beat going. The
women wore crowns of wilted flowers and laughed.
Erik sat down on a stump, searching the group, but
there was no sign of Hannah Sinclair. Did she hide
away in Girnigoe Castle behind ten-foot-thick walls
and two drawbridges?

"The children have found their beds?" Frode
asked in English as his gaze settled on a man and
woman sneaking away together into one of the sheds
beside the vast stables built near the castle. It seemed
the festival was taking a more carnal turn now that

the sun was fully down.

"Aye," said the soldier, Keenan, who seemed to be a high-ranking warrior in Bàs's army. "The night of Lunastain is for mature folk." He raised a small glass bottle of smooth whisky, took a swig, and passed it to Sten.

Conversations moved from Scotia's history, to great battles, and anticipation for a bountiful harvest. There was no mention of rebellion against their king and queen. But would they let plots slip with strangers present? Erik wouldn't.

Frode journeyed off into the night, likely to piss. Sten went with Keenan when he mentioned a new breed of horse the Sinclairs had imported from Spain by way of pirates sailing the coast. Bàs sat on Erik's other side and sipped the whisky, passing it to Erik.

An uncomfortable silence pervaded the space, broken by the crackle of the fire as Bàs placed more wood upon it. Nial cleared his throat. "I'm going to sample another of those tarts," he said, standing and walking toward a table where the treats were laid, even though Erik knew he was more interested in the two women talking beside it.

"Don't your wife and sisters partake in the festival after the sun disappears?" Erik asked.

"They will come out shortly," Bàs said, staring into the fire. He frowned at it. "Are ye interested in my sister?"

"The ladies of Girnigoe are married," Erik said, keeping his voice as amiable as he could make it. As if Hannah didn't coalesce in his head, her smile and bright features that could play the part of a warrior, grieving widow, and sprite.

"Ye know I speak of Hannah." Bàs turned his face to Erik. "What are ye about, Erik Halverson? Are ye sniffing after her?"

Erik rubbed his jaw. "If I admit I think her beautiful and a fine lady, will I find myself skewered by a Horseman of God?"

Bàs's lips turned into the faintest of grins. "Ye do not fear me. In fact, I think ye don't fear anyone. That might see ye skewered."

Erik let his grin fade. He feared *for* people but didn't fear them. "There are more dangerous things than swords and arrows."

Bàs's brows drew together. "Disease?"

Erik nodded. "Of my vast family, descended from ancient raiders and kings, only my sister and I remain." Erik looked out at the laughing ladies and Nial, who chewed with relish while the two bakers smiled up at him. "Girnigoe is fortunate that illness hasn't attacked."

"Plague?" Bàs asked.

"Three years ago," Erik said. "It ravished our village on the northern coast of Norway, Naumudal." He'd returned to find livestock unattended and surviving on fields that had been left to rot without people to harvest the food. His parents had made his sister flee the moment they realized what was befalling the village. He'd found her ten miles inland, living with a reverend and his wife. The pain of burning the bodies of so many loved ones sat as a dull ache in his chest, a reminder never to love anyone else who would make him vulnerable.

Bàs looked at him, weighing him and his words. Erik didn't care if he believed him or not, but sharing sometimes led to adversaries lowering their suspicions a bit. Hannah would probably approve, since giving information was rather like acquiescing.

"Even without the plague here," Bàs said, "we've had illness wash through our clans before. 'Tis bloody awful when a foe is not one we can battle."

Erik nodded grimly and took another big drink of the whisky. "You are lucky, like me, to still have your sister."

Bàs watched the fire and nodded in a slight rocking fashion. "Hannah protected me when I was a bairn and a lad, acting like a mother to me when I'd… lost mine." He turned his face to Erik, and Erik saw not a threat but resolve. "I will gladly lay down my life for her. I will do anything to see her happy and healthy. All four of us would."

Erik's whole body froze. This was what he needed to hear, the truth that the Sinclair Horsemen would do anything to keep their sister safe. It was the confirmation that meant they could enact the rest of their plan.

Bàs turned to face the fire and continued. "Several years ago, Hannah was tricked into helping a scoundrel. He abducted her, almost killed her. Since then, she hasn't seemed interested in any man." He shook his head and exhaled. "I would rather have her home anyway, safe and without a husband than in danger and discomfort with an ornery bastard who I would have to kill."

Erik's brow lowered, his chest constricting at imagining the smiling woman frightened at being taken. *Damn.* And yet she didn't cower or run when he approached her alone on the hill.

"Is the man who took her dead?" Erik asked, his gaze sliding among the men around them. Did the bastard still lurk nearby?

"Shot and burned," Bàs said as Keenan and Sten walked back to the fire.

Erik nodded, taking the tankard that Sten handed him. He swallowed some of the cold, honeyed drink. *Fy faen.* Hannah had been abducted and threatened. An added weight landed next to the boulder that had formed in his gut a month ago when he'd heard news of his own sister's abduction. The original boulder was made of fury and worry. This new weight was one of remorse.

From the shadows opposite the bright flames of the fire, a group of women emerged. In the middle, her arm looped through another woman's, was Hannah. Her hair reflected the bright flickers of the flames, and the light illuminated her lush form that peeked from her parted cape. Aye, she was lovely. No matter what must happen, he could still admit he found her beautiful. And alluring, clever, brave, and talented. *Faen i helvete.* He should take a bottle of whisky and find his bed.

"Slainte, lasses," Keenan called out to Hannah and her sisters. They nodded and smiled, but Erik stilled, feeling the perusal all six cast his way. Cait glanced at him surreptitiously, but Kára and Ella studied him blatantly. He'd met them all during the games, and they'd seemed pleasant enough. Now they reminded him of his grandmother and her friends assessing the young lads and lasses in their village, discussing which ones would make successful pairs. Ridiculously, Erik found himself sitting up straighter on the log.

Bàs stood, going to his wife and kissing her fully while his friends around the fire both cheered and groaned. Keenan leaned over to Erik, but took in Nial, Sten, and Frode, too. "They've been wed a year now but still kiss like they're newly married. And I've caught them tupping in the barn several times."

A warrior named Hamish shook his head and looked heavenward. "Actually, when all four brothers are back, ye can't walk into any shadowed place without announcing yourself or ye're bound to get an eyeful of flesh. Sights that will keep ye tossing yerself off unless ye have your own willing woman." He made a motion toward his cod and then rubbed the back of his neck as if it pained him.

Sten chuckled, and Nial nodded. "No wonder there are so many children in the village."

"'Tis too cold to fok outdoors in Norway," Frode said, sipping from the whisky.

"Not in the summer," Nial said and raised his ale in salute. The men raised their own cups and laughed.

"But not Hannah, the sister?" Erik asked Hamish. "She's a maid?"

"The fact that no poor bastard has been gelded or sliced open by one of her brothers makes me think she is," Hamish said. "But 'tis not something I ask. In fact, every man in Northern Scotland knows she's not to be touched. Hell, despite her…" He lowered his voice as if worried that Bàs would hear over the crackle of the fire, the wind, and the distant music. "Despite her obvious beauty, kindness, and lush form, we don't even look her way."

"Does she long for the church?" Nial asked.

"Not that I've heard," Keenan said. "And the nunneries are closed now anyway."

Hamish knocked Keenan's arm. "Now that ye're married, ye can at least speak with her."

Erik frowned. Did they all ignore the woman? Perhaps these men were cowards. If Hannah Sinclair had been a widow or simply no longer a maiden, she'd be less valuable to Dowager-Queen Sophie. But Hannah's clan had protected her, and that protection might see her married to a foreign chancellor against her will. *Dritt.* He took a gulp of his ale.

"My wife says ye might be interested in viewing our stables," Bàs called over the fire, looking to the four of them. "That ye have cavalry in Denmark-Norway."

The four stood, but as Nial, Sten, and Frode followed Bàs, Ella and Kára came up on either side of Erik. The ladies put their arms through his. He was startled enough to let them turn him around.

"Let us talk a bit," Lady Ella said, indicating a stump with a pointed finger.

He lowered to sit and tipped his head toward the line of his men fading away into the darkness that was broken by a few torches along the village path. "I am to view the—"

"You can catch up later," Cait said, sitting a few stumps over so she could stare directly at Erik. Hannah sat with the other woman in the group opposite Cait so that they created a semicircle around him with the fire throwing out heat and light right in his face.

"Good eve, ladies," Erik said cautiously, the feeling of his grandmother's judging eye intensifying until he felt like he sat before God on Judgment Day, the bright fire blinding to him. *Helvete!*

Ella started. "I would ask to see your hands, but 'tis obvious from the display at the games today that you're a warrior."

"I am a trader who is a warrior when called upon by my soveri—"

"We know," Kára said, cutting him off. "You've told everyone that, but you train." She squeezed his upper arm. "And have strength to rival the Sinclair Horsemen."

"You flatter me," he murmured, remaining still even though he'd have rubbed at his arm. The woman had a pinching grip.

"But what we need to know," Cait said, her words even like he'd heard men speak when leading a trial in court, "is how you treat a woman."

His mouth opened with his inhale. "A woman?"

"Yes," Ella said. "How do you treat the women you've been with? Kindly? Or like chattel to be used?"

"Been with?" he asked. Were they really asking him—?

"Are you a gentle lover?" Kára asked, making Erik's face snap toward her. She stared into his face without glancing away. When he didn't answer, she leaned toward him, pinning him with hard eyes. "We know you cannot be a virgin." She flapped her hand at his form. "So, we must know how you treat a woman you are…tupping."

Erik blinked, glancing over at Hannah who watched the proceedings with interest.

"Are you kind and considerate?" Cait asked.

Kára spoke again before he could even have time

to make sense of the interrogation. "Do you know how to bring a lass to pleasure?"

"Before you take your own?" Ella added.

"Yes," Cait said, nodding. "Do you make sure she feels pleasure too before you fall asleep?"

Five sets of eyes studied him. Would they ask him to strip down for inspection next? Erik's gaze slid across to Hannah who stared back. "Do you have a question too?" She had propped her hands on the stump, which made her breasts seem to swell even more over the lace edge of her smock.

"Do you know how to read ancient languages from the far east?"

A small bubble of laughter came from Cait, and Kára snorted softly.

"Nooooo," Erik said, drawing it out.

Ella frowned at him. "No to what exactly?"

"And do you bathe frequently?" Hannah asked on top of Ella's question.

All five women nodded as if the question was of utmost importance.

"Aye," he said slowly. "Whenever there is a clean body of water or bath available."

Hannah gave him a small nod, her gaze dropping for the slightest moment to his breeches. Kára Sinclair tapped his leg with one finger. "You haven't answered our other questions. Are you a gentle lover?" she repeated. "Do you treat women well, and do you make sure a woman is finding her pleasure when tupping?"

Erik turned his face to Ella. "Are these the types of questions you ask traders?"

She offered him a smile, but her gaze was piercing. "Sometimes. We need to get to know what type of man you are before we agree to do business with you. And how a man loves a woman, someone who is physically weaker than himself, says a lot about a man's morality and heart."

"How many women have you tupped?" asked the other woman who sat next to Hannah. She narrowed her eyes accusingly. "Are you diseased from it?"

"This is Ivy," Hannah said, introducing her as if he should know the names of his women inquisitors. "She's Shana's sister by blood."

Erik felt shot through by arrows rooting him to a tree trunk. He could stand up and walk away, act insulted, or give them false information. But to walk away might make Hannah believe terrible things about him. And that possibility didn't sit well with him.

He exhaled in a long sigh, deciding that even though he never surrendered, he would give them some answers. "I have a sister whom I love and respect, so I view women as important as men. They are not chattel, and I do not count the ones I have… tupped, as if they were sheep in a herd," he said. "I am not diseased," he said, looking at Ivy. His gaze slid across to Hannah. "And if a woman chooses to trust me with her body, I reward that trust by giving her… immense pleasure." He turned to shoot Kára with a hard gaze. "And I would never hurt her."

Kára glared back but eventually gave one nod. "That is good to know."

"And my friends"—he tipped his head toward the stables—"they would not harm a woman either. Frode wishes to marry back in Norway. Sten has a warrior mother who would slice his cod right off if he harmed a woman who wasn't trying to kill him in battle. And Nial is kind and even-tempered when not in battle."

Erik watched the glances slide among the ladies like pebbles rolled in a game, their frowns relaxing. "Very well, then," Ella said and stood. "I hope you enjoy your time here in Scotland."

All the others stood with her as if a council meeting had concluded. Kára stepped over to take Hannah's arm. "Let's go to the bonfire up there." She pointed to one where musicians played a quick-paced tune. "I think dancing will relax us."

Hannah walked away with them, and Erik watched her long hair sway, the ends touching the waistband of her skirt. The few glances that had flitted between the ladies during his questioning made him think it had to do with Hannah. It certainly shouldn't matter to the four women married to the Horsemen. He didn't know Ivy, but the ladies had glanced at Hannah, not her. Did Hannah want to know if he was a good lover? The thought jarred through him, making his cod stiffen. He adjusted it quickly. Did Hannah want him to bring her pleasure? "Fy faen," he cursed under his breath. If he kept thinking that she did, he'd be the one tossing off all night.

· · ·

Kára kept hold of Hannah's hand, with Ella taking the other one. Cait, Ivy, and other ladies from the village helped them complete the circle around the large, hot fire that reached up into the inky darkness above.

"I can't believe we asked him all that," Hannah

said over the music toward Kára.

Kára grinned. "He did well. You should have seen how Joshua paled when my amma asked him the same questions."

Hannah's mouth dropped open, and she laughed as Kára nodded deeply.

"That was after you'd already been together, though," Ella said, obviously having heard the story.

"Yes," Kára said, "but Joshua would have gotten detailed instructions from the women of our village if he hadn't answered correctly." She laughed at the shocked faces of Cait and Ivy and leaned toward them, yelling over the music. "Through their words, not their bodies." She shook her head as if dismayed by their perverse minds.

Despite the rough tactics, Erik had responded with patience and all the right answers. He was intelligent and able to survive the volley of personal questions. He was perfectly formed without disease, stayed as clean as possible, and he was honorable. *And he knows how to give a lass pleasure.*

The thought stirred the hot ache pooling inside Hannah. With the pictures in Cait's book fresh in her mind, seeing Erik in all his masculine beauty, and listening to him talk about giving pleasure, Hannah's body had been teased to the point that she wanted to break away from the fire circle and seek him out now. She didn't want to play any more games of enticement where she walked away with hopes he'd follow.

Has he bathed tonight? Hannah held her fingertips to her lips as a bubble of laughter popped out as she remembered the picture of the woman taking the man in her mouth. Lord, she'd had only a sip of whisky, but mixed with the heat in her, she was ready to risk everything to be with the brawny stranger.

Ella continued to tug her arm as they danced in a circle, but Hannah kept glancing about. Kára had been certain he would follow them, but so far, Hannah hadn't seen Erik walk over. Could he have sought his bed for the night? Alone? Gone back to the cottage that he shared with his three men? She almost groaned in frustration.

"I need a drink," she called over the music and stepped back. Kára grabbed Ella's hand, and they continued while Hannah hurried over to one of the tables set up with refreshments. There were pitchers of honey-sweetened ale, beer, and whisky. Hannah usually stuck with the least intoxicating.

She picked the honey ale and drank, her foot tapping to the strong beat of the drum. Shana was still gone, somewhere distracting Bàs no doubt, but Ivy danced with Cait, Kára, and Ella.

"Are you tired already?"

Erik's voice shot like a finely fletched arrow through Hannah, and she spun on the heel of her slipper. Some of her ale flew out of the cup, and she looked down at it, hoping it hadn't ruined her bodice.

"I didn't mean to startle you." Erik handed her a rag from his belt.

Hannah hesitated, staring at it. Did he carry a rag for a woman to use after tupping, too? Did all men? "Thank you," she murmured and used it to dab at the one spot on her skirt where the ale had landed.

"I was getting something to quench my thirst."

He raised his own cup. "Aye. I have a strong thirst, too."

Good Lord, she hoped he did. She swallowed and smiled at him. "Do you dance?"

"Not usually, but we practice footwork at home to help coordination. Sometimes to the beat of a drum."

Hannah narrowed her eyes at him. "You *are* a warrior, Erik Halverson. Maybe you also happen to trade silver, but in your heart, you're a warrior."

He went to shake his head, but she held a hand up to stop him. "I grew up among warriors, men who either thirsted for battle or built themselves into the strongest to withstand battle." She touched her finger to his hard chest through the white tunic. "And you, Erik Halverson from Norway, are a warrior."

She took another big drink of ale, her brows raised, and she nodded.

"And you, Hannah Sinclair, are clever." Although he didn't smile, there was a lightness in his eyes, and his mouth relaxed. It was probably the closest he ever got to showing merriment. That didn't bother her. She'd been raised with warriors who rarely smiled.

Feeling the heat that only grew in his presence, she stepped closer but didn't touch him. "I would show you some of our stables down near the docks. 'Tis where the gray horses are kept, and my sweet mare, Loinneil, is there."

Erik kept his gaze directly on hers. "I missed the tour earlier, so that would be…most welcome."

Hannah tipped the rest of the ale into her mouth and set the empty cup on the table. "I need to let my sisters know I'll be gone for a bit, else they'll worry." He nodded, and she ran over to Ella, grabbing her arm and talking into her ear.

"I'm taking him to see my horse. I put the blankets

and supplies there in a back stall."

Ella stepped back from the dance, glancing over to where Erik waited. "You are sure, Hannah?"

"Yes," she answered without hesitation. "I've made a bit of a nest in the stall next to Loinneil, so we may be there for hours, maybe overnight." Just the thought of exploring Erik's huge body sent a hot thrill through Hannah. "Don't come looking for me."

Kára overheard the last of her words and laughed. "You sound ready, Hannah." She leaned into her ear. "And may you be blessed with a babe."

Hannah smiled at them, nodding, and hurried back over to Erik. She slid her arm through his and turned him toward the darkness, leading him away. "They worry," she said.

"You are fortunate to have such loyalty here. Your brothers and their wives."

"Yes." Hannah's heart thumped like there were giant wings in her chest. *Am I really doing this? Yes. Yes, I am.* She just needed to get Erik to go along with it. No other man would be brave enough even with only one of her brothers nearby. There was no time to waste. With her other brothers returning within days, Hannah needed to bed Erik as many times as she could before sending him away to safety.

Their steps were slow but steady as she led him through the darkness toward the sound of the water slapping against the docks. Erik's ship sat tied to the deep-water frontage at the end of a long wooden walkway that extended into the protected bay. Hannah managed to keep putting one foot before the next as if this wasn't the most daring thing she'd ever done in her life.

"How many men do you have on your ship?"

"About six others. We don't need too many to sail," he said, and she could see lanterns lit on the deck, two flags flapping in the wind. Both were red, but one had a white cross for Denmark and the other a dark blue cross for Norway.

"How many ships do the Sinclairs have?" Erik asked over the crunch of the pebbles on the path under their feet.

"Three." Hannah pointed to the one tied opposite his. "That one, and two more still on Orkney, plus a few smaller ones to ferry us if needed. The Sutherlands also have two, and Gideon is having one built at Varrich, since they are also on the sea."

"They're large enough to hold horses," Erik said.

"Oh yes. We travel with our horses. My brothers wouldn't know how to win without them." She laughed lightly and clamped her lips tight when it came out like a childish giggle.

They reached the stables, and she tugged him to the door. "Good eve, Mathias," she said to the guard there. "I've come to give a tour of the stables."

"Good eve," said the man who'd once been a soldier for their Orkney enemies, Robert and Patrick Stewart.

"You must hate missing the festival," she said, knowing how the man liked the lasses.

"Aye."

"Go on then for a bit," Hannah said. "I will be here with Erik Halverson. No one will bother the horses with us here."

Mathias looked the large man up and down. "Are you certain, Lady Hannah?"

"Yes," she said, shooing him with her hand.

"I'll be back within the hour," he said, frowning at Erik, but Hannah smiled and took up his lantern to lead Erik inside. Ella would make sure he didn't return too soon.

"Loinneil is back here," she said, guiding him toward the empty stall next to her mare where she'd left blankets, along with some honey ale and cups.

"'Tis a Gaelic name?" Erik asked. His deep voice tumbled with his northern accent like a stroke over her skin.

"Yes," she said, realizing her voice sounded breathless. She inhaled fully. "It means nimble. She was so dainty when she was a filly. Now she's large and strong but still nimble."

"You train with her?"

"Any woman here, who wishes to train, may. Ella was a warrior of the Sutherland Clan before marrying Cain, and Kára fought on Orkney for her people."

"I can certainly see that."

Hannah felt warmth flood her cheeks. "They are rather direct. Cait too."

Hannah waited, but he didn't question her about the interrogation. They stopped in a circle of warm light from the lantern in the aisle that ran between the stalls.

Erik was close, and his fingers reached out to touch her bodice. "Intricate work." He ran a finger down the stitching she'd added. "Did you make this?"

"Yes. I ride and embroider."

"And shoot with skill and wrangle squirrels."

She sniffed a laugh. "Betty is Bàs's squirrel."

"The Horseman of Death has a squirrel for a pet?" Erik asked.

"Bàs has many animals. I don't know if he considers them pets, though. More like kin."

Erik's finger still stroked the embroidery that ran down to her waist. Just watching his finger, imagining it stroking her bare skin, made Hannah tingle. "I won the shooting contest earlier," he said and pointed to the blue band tied around his upper arm.

"Yes." She looked up into his handsome face with his short beard and little white scars.

"I was to be rewarded with a kiss from Lady Hannah, and yet I haven't received it." His words were a murmur that strummed inside her, making her shift.

She stepped forward. "I…I can remedy that." She rested her hands on his chest. The muscles were hard there, and she stroked upward over his chiseled form.

Tipping her head back, her breath caught as his mouth touched hers. Unlike the rest of him, so hard and unbending, his lips were soft, capturing her in the kiss. The heat that had started building inside her flared. His hands came around to her back, pulling her body into his without hesitation. She could feel his hard jack press against her, and it didn't frighten her at all.

As if answering his arousal, her own body responded, the skin under her smock prickling with awareness. She wrapped her hands around his neck, molding herself against his hard frame. The kiss turned wild, and the ache between her legs intensified, making her shift against his hard jack. He must understand by now that she wanted more than a kiss.

Erik brushed her hair back from her face, cupping her cheek to guide her against his lips as if she were his captive. He backed her up against the stable wall, and he released her mouth to kiss a hot path down her neck. The hard wood against her back and the massive man before her made Hannah throb with want. She tipped her head back, her lips parted to take in air, and he inhaled against the skin of her neck as if she were a sweet flower.

His hand slid up to cup her breast through her bodice, and she moaned softly, pressing the crux of her legs against his erection. "I prepared the stall for us," she whispered.

He pulled back to stare at her in the darkness. "Prepared?"

She couldn't see his face in the shadows, but maybe that was better. Hopefully, he couldn't see the blush staining her cheeks. Hannah was determined, but she was a novice at seducing a man. Tugging his hand, she led him into the vacant stall next to Loinneil's. "There are blankets and ale," she said. "And we have some time alone."

Without him kissing her, she felt foolish. The heat that had been all consuming started to cool, and she desperately wanted it back. Time to jump in with her whole self. She came forward, tilting her face up to his to reach his gaze in the shadows. She'd imagined saying things like "make me moan" or describing something she'd seen in Cait's wicked book, but the words failed her now. Instead, she brought his mouth back to hers, kissing him. It took only a few seconds for him to respond, pulling her closer again.

Erik stroked down her back, and she tentatively

slid her hand to his erect jack. Through the breeches it felt thick and long, perfect for pleasure and creating bairns. He groaned against her mouth, and she shivered at the thought of him touching deep inside her. Another moan escaped her as he palmed her breast, and she moved her shoulders to work the bodice down.

"Touch me," she whispered.

The words seemed to spark heat within Erik, because he picked her up, taking her to the spot where she'd laid out the blankets. Cool air brushed her bare legs as he rucked up her petticoat. "Oh yes," she breathed as his finger slid down her arse, and she spread her legs. Let him feel her desire for him. "Please, Erik," she murmured as he touched her there.

He said something in his rough foreign words that sounded like he was on the brink of losing control. It thrilled Hannah that she could do that to him. She plucked the ties of his trousers to loose his jack. Ella had said that putting one's mouth on it was not for a first time, but Hannah was sure Erik would groan with the feel of it. And she wanted to make this massive, strong man lose control.

But then he started to stroke across her sensitive nub, and she moaned low at the pressure he built with the rubbing. Swallowing, she raised her arms to his shoulders, clasping him as he nudged her closer to a release she'd only ever given herself. He slid his fingers inside her, and she moaned again, moving against his hand. Inside and out, he worked until she cried out on a gasp as she found her release. "Oh God, yes, Erik. Take all of me."

His fingers stilled, and he groaned, a painful groan. He withdrew his hand, letting her skirts drop down her legs, and pulled her closer. She pressed into him, feeling the ebbing waves of her climax. Erik rested his chin on the top of her head, so she breathed against the hollow of his throat. The masculine scent of him was a mix of some sort of musky soap, honey-ale, and fresh ocean breeze.

She reached down to find the rigid line of his jack. He was so hard. "I would make you feel as good as me," she whispered.

"Hannah…" He gently pulled her hand from his jack, bringing it up between them. "I cannot take your maidenhood."

She stiffened. "But you…we…?" she whispered. "Erik Halverson, I want you. Don't you…want to bed me?"

A deep chuckle rumbled in his chest. "You felt what's in my breeches, how badly I want you." His words made her shiver with hunger. "You trust me, and I am honored, but I cannot dishonor you by laying with you."

"My brothers—"

"And not because of your brothers." He backed up slightly, and the glow of the lantern cut across his face. A severe frown tightened his lips. "I don't fear your brothers."

She shook her head. "Everyone fears my brothers."

"I don't." He stepped farther from her, tying the laces of his breeches. "But I can't…"

She let her gaze move to the shadows. She wouldn't tell him how badly she wanted a bairn. That would make her sound like she was using him, even though that's exactly what she was trying to do.

At the front of the stables, the door creaked. "Erik," a hushed voice called. It wasn't Mathias, who would have called her name. It must be one of his men.

Hannah glanced down, relieved her breasts weren't exposed. She tugged the bodice back into place and ran a hand down her skirt to press against the ache between her legs. *Daingead*. She would ache all night.

Erik's eyes closed for a moment before he answered the intruder, and he did so in his Norwegian language. He stepped out into the aisle, and more discussion volleyed back and forth for a full minute, the words growing in speed until his friend ran off. A prickle of unease crawled up Hannah's spine.

"Is something wrong?" She looked between him and the stall door. *God's teeth.* Her plan of seduction had failed.

Erik clasped her hand, and she curled her fingers around his. "The tide is high," he said, picking up the blankets, shoving them under his arm. He managed to grab the lantern, too, and it swung from his fingers as he led her quickly down the stable hall, yelling something to Sten. The man had entered the barn, holding another lantern high to light the place.

Movement in the corner of an open stall caught Hannah's eye. She had only a second to see two little girls staring out with wide eyes, silent as the shadows where they hid. Trix and Libby? Hannah's cheeks flamed. What had they heard? *Good Lord!* She'd have to tell Cait they may have heard moaning.

Erik hadn't seen them. He was too busy tugging her along and yelling out more orders that made Frode stride down the stable aisle. The only words Hannah recognized were her own and Loinneil.

"What's going on?" Hannah demanded as she hurried to keep up with his strides. The passionate heat that had been all consuming before had begun to cool.

"'Tis time to go."

"Go? Back to the fire?"

Erik stopped. He set the lantern and blankets down and pulled Hannah's blue cape from her shoulders and handed it to Sten, who ran off.

"What…?" Hannah's confusion halted as the lantern light cast a glow over a lump on the ground. "Mathias?" she whispered. He was tied and gagged inside the barn door, his eyes open and narrowed on Erik.

"Bloody foking hell," Hannah said, using Joshua's favorite curse. She stared up at Erik, ice replacing the heat within her. "What the bloody foking hell are you doing?"

He let out a huff of restrained anger, his gaze focused slightly over her head while he spoke. "By the orders of Dowager-Queen Sophie of Denmark-Norway, we are taking you to her court."

"That is ridiculous!" she yelled, anger licking up inside her. Hannah grabbed Erik's tunic. Her fingers curled into it, and she jerked it around as if trying to shake him. She'd have had better luck shaking a two-foot-thick oak tree. "For what reason could she possibly want me? Me! I am nothing!"

Erik shook his head. "You, Hannah Sinclair, are

everything." He finally looked down to meet her gaze. "And she will use you to control the Four Sinclair Horsemen of Scotia."

CHAPTER SEVEN

"Sophie was only 14 years old when she was married to Frederik II, who was 23 years older than her. Nevertheless, they had a harmonious marriage. She had no political power while Frederik II was alive but after his death in 1588, she played a more prominent role, for example as Guardian of the young Christian IV in Schleswig and Holstein. As such, she came into conflict with the government, which expelled her to the palace of Nykøbing Slot on the island of Falster."

KONGERNES SAMLING-ROSENBORG

Take all of me.

The words picked at the wound inside Erik, the wound which Hannah's huge, unbelieving eyes delivered. *Erik Halverson, I want you.*

But Hannah Sinclair was figuring out now she didn't want him at all. He'd watched the softness of her features harden before him. Her gentle fingers curled into rocks in his palm as he tugged her toward his ship. In the shadows, he could see his crew rushing about in silence, uncoiling ropes, readying the sails. The few watchmen on the one other Sinclair ship were tied and gagged, watching helplessly as he forced Hannah aboard. *Fy Faen!* Why hadn't he told his crew to leave the men below deck?

"Let go of me!" Hannah yelled, and he drew her in to him, lifting her easily from the grass that had begun to grow damp with the night air.

He pulled her against his chest, one arm under her knees. She kicked, thrashing about, and aimed her nails toward his eyes. She was a kitten turned wildcat. Her nails caught his ear, and he swore she meant to tear it off his head.

He grunted, dropping her feet to the ground, working her fingers off his ear. She screamed, a piercing banshee scream, and his open hand covered her mouth. He realized his mistake when her teeth sank into his palm. "Dritt," he cursed and yanked the rag he'd seen dangling from her bodice.

"She's a banshee," Aksel, one of the Wolf Warriors watching the ship, said as he strode past them with their full provision bags.

"No," Erik muttered and pushed the cloth into Hannah's mouth. "She's a Sinclair Horsewoman, a Valkyrie."

She stopped struggling long enough to glare straight into his face. She couldn't scream with her lush mouth that he would always remember as soft under his. But she could curse him with her eyes. They spit accusations and hatred. In all his years of warring, he'd never deserved hatred more.

He had to look away, tugging her along toward his two-masted ship, both of her wrists caught in his one large hand, the one that didn't throb with her venom. His crew had waited for days, ready to sail with each high tide, waiting for the perfect moment when half the returned Sinclairs and their allies were drunk on harvest wine and whisky. Erik had tried to anticipate when Hannah could be lured away from the safety of Girnigoe, but tonight had been too good to pass when she asked to show him the stables near the ship. And Bàs had confirmed that they all loved Hannah and would do anything to keep her safe and happy.

Frode walked past him, a broad smile on his face. "I knew when I didn't see you nor the woman that you were somewhere near the ship. 'Twas high tide, too." He nodded with approval. "Now the Wolf Warriors will finish this mission in under a fortnight."

"Sten and Nial are executing the plan at the castle?" Erik asked.

"Aye," Frode said. "Sten made friends with a lass about Hannah's size and has persuaded her to wear the cape and meet him in the castle. He will dally only shortly and make his excuses, leaving the cape in Hannah's room and bundling her clothes under the bedding to make it seem she sleeps there."

"And Nial?" Erik asked, watching his men setting the poles out to push off the dock.

"He's making sure he's seen in good humor and drinking with Keenan and some of the warriors, but he'll soon beg off, heading to our rented cottage before circling around."

Hannah couldn't know what their words meant, but she saw the smile on Frode's face and twisted her wrists, yanking. She managed to jerk her wrist through the pinch of his fingers, but he caught her again quickly. "Hannah," he said, a bit of pleading in his voice that she ignored. Erik huffed and lifted her, setting her as carefully as he could over one of his shoulders. Her hair flung about her head as she struggled, pounding his back.

He caught her legs with one hand and held her arching back down with the other. The woman was strong and as slippery as the legendary mermaiden, her hair slapping at his legs as she tried to wiggle free. He'd have bruises under his tunic from her sharp knuckles.

"No harm will come to you," Erik said, trying to reason with Hannah, but she didn't pause until she saw Frode leading her horse.

Lifting her head, she watched as Frode walked past them, the dappled gray horse following on a lead. "We have stalls below deck," Erik said. "She will be safe, and you will have her in Denmark." He'd made that decision when he saw how much she cared for the horse. She was a Sinclair, after all. If the squirrel had been hers as well, Erik would have tried to capture it, but luckily it turned out to be her brother's. And the wolf belonged to Bàs as well, although one could argue that a wolf couldn't belong to anyone. Either way, there would have been no way to get a wolf on the ship. But a horse was easily carried across the sea with the proper preparation.

Purposely keeping the lanterns low so no one would happen to see their preparations or departure, Erik carried Hannah carefully up the wooden walkway onto his ship, the *Seieren*. Without stopping, he strode directly to his cabin, pushing into the small, private room. She'd stopped flailing once she saw her horse taken, and he lowered her to the bed.

Immediately, her hand went to her gag, yanking it from her teeth. He wiped the blood welling on his palm with his own rag. "I am sorry for that," he said, nodding to the gag. "You can scream in here without everyone hearing."

"You are sorry," she said, panting, "for the gag?

How about for tricking me, abducting me, using me to control my brothers and clan?" Her voice had grown loud, and Erik quietly shut the door behind him. He stood before her gaze that cut into him like a flail on the end of a whip. The pain was deserved.

"I know you hate me, Hannah," he said, his words even. "'Twas a mission to obtain you."

"I knew you lied about being a trader," she said, her teeth all but bared.

"I am the leader of the Wolf Warriors of Norway. We are an elite army under orders of Dowager-Queen Sophie of Denmark-Norway."

"You're Norwegian. Even if the countries are united, even if you do this thing for Denmark, it will be *you*." She spat the last word. "You and your damn Wolf Warriors who will suffer under the blades of my brothers. Whatever you're up to, you tolla-thon, my brothers will slaughter you for it."

He closed his eyes for a moment and shook his head. "No explanation will be enough." He turned, not wanting to see the snapping hatred in her beautiful eyes. "You are headed to Kronborg Castle on the coast of Denmark where you will be treated like lesser royalty. You will not be molested in any way, nor starved, shackled, or hurt, neither here nor at Kronborg." Surely, Sophie wouldn't torture the woman. "Food will be brought in the morning and there is ale by my bed."

"Your bed?" She glanced down as if only then noticing she sat on a bed.

"I will sleep elsewhere." He gave a nod. Fists clenched as hard as his chest, Erik pivoted on his boot heel and strode out of the cabin, closing the door. He

lowered a bar across it from the outside, which he'd
fastened upon their landing in Scotia. Something hit it
hard. Likely her dagger that he hadn't had the heart
to take away.

Sten stopped before him. "We are ready to push
off."

"To Kronborg then," Erik said.

Sten reached out to clap a hand on his shoulder.
"You will get Iselin back."

"Aye," he said and glanced at the door, hard and
barred. He could feel the condemnation slashing
through it, every lash deserved.

* * *

"She hasn't come down to break her fast?" Bàs asked,
setting his tankard with a *clank* on the long table in
Girnigoe's great hall. He frowned.

Anything past dawn was late for Hannah, and she
wouldn't miss a meal. Despite her slender frame, he
knew she ate heartily. Always had since the age of
nine when she confided to him that she wanted to
grow as big as her brothers.

Kára and Ella glanced at each other. "We were
letting her sleep after the dancing at the festival," Ella
said. "I checked in on her late last night and saw her
bundled up, sound asleep."

Bàs had asked the guard at the gate if he'd seen his
sister come inside Girnigoe. Thomas said she'd hurried in alone wrapped up in her blue cloak, raising
one hand to wave. Bàs had then spent a pleasure-
filled night with Shana, starting in the kitchens where
they'd found some rolls filled with cream. The last

time he'd seen his sister was when she danced with his brothers' wives around the fire. He hadn't thought of her again until now. When he'd crept from the room he was sharing with Shana, careful not to wake her, he'd expected to see Hannah finding her morning meal.

"Hmmm?" he murmured and took one of the butter crocks to slather the fresh cream on his scone. It was still early. Perhaps his sister needed her rest.

"I hope she's not ill." Cait glanced at the steps as she held wee Gavin against her shoulder. A healthy burp came from the bairn. "Perhaps we should check on her."

Kára and Ella were already striding past her to the stairs and disappeared through the archway, their slippers slapping the stone steps as they climbed.

Bàs stood, the force toppling his stool behind him. "Ye're worried? Why?"

The front doors of the keep opened, and several sets of boots thumped into the room. Keenan led the way, his face ashen.

"What's happened?" Cait asked, and everyone in the great hall stood. It felt as if they collectively held their breaths.

Keenan looked from her to Bàs. "The Norwegian traders," he said, panting from an obvious sprint to the castle. "They attacked the men on our ship last night, and Mathias in the stables."

"Dead?" Bàs asked.

Keenan shook his head. "Tied up but unhurt. And the traders left."

"Erik Halverson has left?" Cait asked. "Overnight?"

Keenan nodded, looking paler by the second.

"And he took…" He wet his lips as if his mouth was too dry to talk.

"Took?" Bàs asked, his warrior's blood pounding through him.

"Lady Hannah."

Bàs turned, running toward the stairs. "She's asleep in her bedchamber. People saw her." He bounded up the steps two at a time, meeting a breathless Ella at the top. She held Hannah's blue cape in her hands.

"There were bunched up clothes under her blankets," Kára said.

Keenan had followed Bàs up the steps. "The Norwegian silver traders took her, sailing east."

"Nay!" Kára yelled, but Keenan nodded vigorously.

"Took her horse as well," Keenan said. "Saddle and tack."

They stood in the spiral stairway at various levels, Cait below Keenan and Ella and Kára above. "Bloody devil," Ella said, turning to Kára, and the two women clutched each other's shoulders, the blue cape dropping in a heap at their feet.

"We must set sail at once," Bàs said, turning on the steps. The whole group tapped and stomped their way back down the staircase, emerging into the great hall. Everyone stood, their faces slack with horror and surprise. Bàs pointed toward the doors. "Gather supplies and men." Two of Keenan's men hurried back out.

"How much of a head start do they have?" Cait asked, looking around as if wanting to hand Gavin off to her friend, Rhona, but she wasn't there.

"One tide," Keenan said. "Two really, since we must wait for the next high tide to push off. That's tonight after dusk."

"A full day then," Cait said. "We have a day to prepare."

"I must get word to Cain," Ella said. "And then we will pack food, supplies. Enough for those bairns still nursing."

"Bloody hell, what?" Bàs asked, his voice booming in the room.

"Bàs?" Shana had just stepped out of the archway from the stairs. "Why are you yelling?"

Bàs didn't look at his wife but at the three wives of his brothers. "Ye are not coming with me."

"Where are we going?" Shana asked.

"Nowhere!" Bàs yelled.

But Ella and Kára spoke to Shana. "Erik Halverson abducted Hannah last night, taking her away from Scotland on his ship. He set her room to look like she'd returned there last night."

"Heaven help us," Shana said, lowering to sit on a stool as if the news was too heavy to bear standing.

"My men and I will go after them," Bàs said. "And then Cain, Joshua, and Gideon when they return."

But all four ladies were shaking their heads. "We are going with you," Kára said, her words forceful.

"With bairns?" Bàs yelled again and looked to Keenan for support. The man also frowned at the ladies.

"Alice and Astrid will come," Kára said.

"And Gavin," Cait said.

"The others are old enough to do well here with Aunt Merida," Ella said.

"And Rhona," Cait said. "Viola will help, too, and Willa and the girls."

Bàs ran his hands through his hair. "This can't be. Ye can't come."

"Oh, but we are," Kára said, her voice even with a force Bàs had never heard before. 'Twas as if she were turning into a Norse warrior right before his eyes.

Shana rubbed her forehead. "Bàs, we must go."

"Why?" Bàs asked.

The ladies looked at one another. Shana stood, walking over to take Cait's hand. The four of them clasped hands now in a row: Ella, Kára, Cait, and Shana.

"Because," Ella said, "we practically gave Hannah to them."

Before Bàs could utter a word in question, Rhona came running down from the steps yelling. "Cait! Lady Cait!"

Aunt Merida followed on her heels. "I'm sure those troublesome lasses rose early and headed out to chase butterflies or play with Boo." But the elderly woman's face was pinched, too, with worry.

Rhona stopped, her arms half lifted out to her sides. "Trix and Libby aren't in their cots. And they aren't playing in the solar or any of the hiding places that I can find."

"How about the secret staircase in my bedchamber?" Ella asked.

"I looked in your room," Aunt Merida said, "but the bookcases were all closed up tight."

"I sent Willa looking through the kitchens," Rhona said, "and she's going to send Jack hunting through Girnigoe village." The woman wrung her hands.

Cait looked to the other three ladies. "They were sweet on the fierce-looking ones."

"Which ones? They were all fierce-looking," Shana said.

"Frode and Sten," Kára said. "With the pigment markings down their faces and necks."

"They must be here somewhere," Shana said. "Two little girls wouldn't just run off, and there is no reason for the Norwegians to take them."

Bàs remembered the winter before last when the girls had borrowed a horse to gallop off together to warn King James of treachery. Even though Shana knew the story, she hadn't lived the fear that had gripped them all at the girls' jeopardy. The king had rewarded them, which had only increased their desire to interfere and save creatures big and small. They worked together to get into never-ending bouts of trouble.

Keenan motioned to one of the men with him, who handed him a yellow ribbon. "We found this in the stables. Thought it might belong to Lady Hannah."

Cait blinked rapidly as if tamping down tears and took the ribbon from him. "'Tis Libby's. See," she said, pointing to the tiny *L* embroidered on the bottom edge. "She didn't want anyone else to take it, thinking it was theirs."

Cait raised her gaze to Bàs. "Rhona," she said while looking at him. "We need to pack up Gavin with everything I need to care for him on a journey."

"Where are you going?" Rhona asked.

Cait kept Bàs's stare, and the other three ladies, including his Shana, came up around Cait. She clutched the yellow ribbon. "We're going to rescue Trix, Libby, and Hannah."

• • •

"Beat to windward," Erik called above the growing storm.

"Heard," his helmsman called back. The man steered with the ship's whipstaff below the half deck.

Damn this whole mission. Erik stared up into the gathering storm clouds that had taken on the hues of a bruise, swollen with festering across the sky. It looked like the bruise on his palm around Hannah's bite print. God was surely against the abduction of the beauty who'd been smoldering with rage in his cabin for a day now. They'd departed Scotia during the night, sailing quickly with a strong wind, but now as day surrendered again, a storm had frothed up with rage.

He wanted to yell at the heavens that he'd had no choice, but, somehow, he imagined the heavens yelling back that he had. *I have to save my sister.*

Erik looked out at the slip of land northward, knowing that it was the Shetland Isles of Scotland, more Norwegian than Scottish despite King James's claim on it. Erik hadn't counted on having to stop during their seven-day journey homeward, but God had a different timeline and had pushed them north off their course.

Waves pushed the ship upward only to vanish underneath, letting the ship drop in the gully. Much more of this, and his beloved *Seieren* would start breaking apart, and they'd all be lost. Nay, they must make it to the shelter of West Voe of Sumburgh, Shetland's southernmost bay.

The rain beat down sideways with the lashing wind. They'd lowered most of the sails so they wouldn't be shredded, but they must tack into the wind to make it to the isle.

"God's not happy," Sten said next to Erik.

"God and I have something in common," Erik responded, wiping the cold rain off his face. He thought only of the silence emanating from his cabin. Hannah hadn't yelled or cursed or even spoken since he left her. She looked out the window only when one of his men had brought her food and ale. But she sat straight, undefeated. For that, he was thankful. It was one thing to force Hannah to leave her home; it was another thing to break her spirit. He wasn't sure if he could live knowing he'd done that.

Of course you could live, he told himself. He was a Wolf Warrior on a mission, fulfilling his duty. "Fy faen," he cursed low, glancing at the barred door. Not that Hannah would ever understand that.

"Frode's happy we are getting closer to Iselin," Sten said. Frode was wrapping rope around one of the sails they'd lowered. He worked hard but didn't frown. The man was in love with Erik's sister and would do anything to rescue her from Sophie's court, same as Erik.

Erik exhaled. "We must shelter while the storm rages."

"Agreed," Sten said. He glanced around. "Where's Nial?"

"Probably puking over the rail," Erik said. The big man sickened when the waves bounced them about. "There he is." He pointed through the rain at the large form of Nial striding toward Frode. Nial's face was serious, and he hugged something into his body, trying to block it from the wind. Behind Nial, clutching his woolen long coat, was a little form.

"Hva i helvete?" Sten cursed and lurched forward.

"What the devil?" Erik repeated and ran with Sten toward Nial and the drenched little body holding onto his coat.

"Look what I found hidden under a barrel," Nial yelled over the wind and rain. He opened up his coat to show the little blond lass, Libby.

Erik grabbed up Trix from behind Nial. She shivered so hard she was almost convulsing, her eyes wide. "What are you two doing on our ship?"

Nial ran to the rail, vomiting. Erik felt his own stomach drop with the deck. As the ship plunged again, Frode grabbed Libby, who looked almost like her feet had left the deck, her little weight unable to hold her earthbound.

Libby's hair was out of its ribbon, streaking with rainwater over her pale face. "Little girl?" Frode said, staring back at her with wide eyes of his own. "What are you two doing here?"

Libby opened her mouth, but instead of words, vomit shot out, hitting Frode's chest in a yellow, lumpy mess.

"We're here to save Lady Hannah," Trix yelled from Erik's hold and turned to glare at him, her freckles more prominent in the paleness of her face. "And I'm sure you're all going to Hell for this."

Erik stared back. He agreed.

• • •

Hannah's queasy stomach hardened the moment she saw what Erik was holding in the open doorway. She ran toward him, her fury momentarily forgotten in the face of two frightened, drenched-through girls.

"Trix? Libby?" She yelled their names, trying to pull them from Erik's arms. But he walked past her, setting them on the bed that she'd managed to fall asleep on sometime during the day before the waves began to swell.

Her face snapped to his. Even drenched and blown with wind and rain, the blasted man looked like a hero from the ancient past. *Not hero. Villain.* "You stole them away? For what purpose?"

"They snuck onto the ship when we were preparing to sail," Erik said, yanking out some blankets from a chest and a few men's tunics.

"We came to save you," Trix said, her teeth chattering. "But then…they sailed away, and then the storm started. We found a barrel to hide in."

Oh good bloody Lord. The two reckless, albeit noble and brave, girls had risked their lives to hide onboard, not realizing that the ship would sail before they could free her. Despite wanting to yell at them, Hannah dropped to her knees and hugged them tightly.

"I threw up," Libby murmured against her as if ashamed.

"So did Nial," Trix pointed out. "And he's a warrior."

Hannah stroked their cold backs. "We will get you dry and warm. You're probably starving."

As if waiting for his cue to enter a stage, Frode walked in through the door where dusk had been eaten away by the storm behind him, bringing on night to hide them in the pitching sea. He set a tray down with rolls and cheese, but the rolls instantly tumbled onto the floor. He was bare chested and soaked through. "In case they feel up to eating," he said, chasing after the rolls. He set the recaptured rolls on the bed, gazed briefly at Libby and Trix, and strode back out.

"We will land at West Voe of Sumburgh," Erik said. "On Shetland Isle, to wait out the storm."

The winds must have blown them north. Hannah hugged the frightened, freezing girls to her. "The southernmost bay," she said, kissing their wet heads. "It will protect us from the wind and waves." And likely save the ship and their lives.

The two girls nodded, wide eyes looking up at her. "We will be well then," Trix said and patted Libby's shoulder. The blond girl turned to her friend, burying her face against her. The sight of such fear curdled Hannah's stomach, and she turned her glare to Erik as if he was responsible. *He* is *responsible*.

His face was tight, his frown hard as he watched them. She saw him swallow, the muscles of his throat working. "Once we are in the bay, I will come to take the three of you across to shore."

Hannah said nothing but felt everything. Simmering anger at Erik and even more so at her own foolishness. How could she have missed the signs of his deceit? Even if he'd been gentle with her as he stole her away from her home, he was still a depraved devil for doing so.

"They won't come for me!" she yelled the lie with as much conviction as she could. "My brothers. They aren't even back from Orkney. Your government cannot control them. No one can, especially not through a lowly sister."

Erik's gaze rose to hers. "You are anything but lowly, Hannah Sinclair. And sure as this storm is raging with fury, your brothers will come for you."

CHAPTER EIGHT

"Shetland [made up of approximately one hundred
islands] belonged to Denmark until 1469, when
Princess Margaret of Denmark married James III of
Scotland - the Islands were part of her dowry."
SCOTLAND.ORG

"There's a homestead over that ridge," Nial called
through the wind as he and Erik dragged the dinghy
high onto the pebble-strewn shoreline. Cold rain
pelted them so hard, Erik wondered if it was sleet.
"We visited it several years ago during another
storm," Nial said, his mouth facing Hannah in the
second boat in an attempt for her to hear.

Sten and Frode dragged their boat up. Hannah
was seated in the middle, surrounded by the other
men from the ship. Two had stayed aboard to keep it
secure but would head for shore if it began to sink.
They would release Hannah's mare if it came to that.

Hannah held fiercely to the two girls under layers
of wool blankets to protect them from the cold and
wet. Only her face was visible, staring toward the
shore with pale determination. Perhaps it was a blessing the girls stowed away. Hannah wouldn't think of
drowning herself with the need to protect them.

He thrust the horrid thought away. Life as a chancellor's wife at the Danish court must be preferable to
death. Although his sister certainly didn't think so. *I'll
kill myself if you leave me here.* Dowager-Queen

Sophie might not be her son's regent, but she controlled her powerful court, the authority of which stretched like strong, grasping fingers up into Norway. And she'd made certain her order was taken seriously by stealing Iselin away. *Just like I stole Hannah.*

Erik had told Nial to take care of Hannah, knowing the woman felt only spitting rage toward him now, but Erik found himself striding over to the tossed dinghy to help her stand. She opened the blanket she'd been using as a cape. "Take them," she called. Erik lifted first Libby to Frode and then Trix to Sten and turned back to Hannah.

For a moment, it looked like she wouldn't take his hand, mutiny on her face that reminded him of how his sister had looked when she delivered her threat of suicide. But then Hannah took his arm, steadying herself as she climbed off and onto the rocky beach. She dropped it as soon as her footing was sound. As it was, the slippers she'd worn to the harvest festival were soaked through and ruined.

"There's shelter this way," he said, beckoning with a wide sweep of his arm. Frode and Sten carried the children, and Erik led the way with Nial, their crewmen bringing up the rear behind Hannah. Erik motioned for his four other crewmen to take shelter in the barn across the yard. There was no need for all of them to stampede into the single-story, stone roundhouse before them.

Rap! Rap! Nial knocked on the door of the roundhouse so prevalent on the treeless isles whipped by wind. *Rap! Rap!* "We are friends caught in the storm," Nial called through the door in Bokmål, following it in English. The scrape of a bar on the other side heralded the door cracking open, the tip of an arrow pointed out.

"We mean you no harm," Erik said, choosing the language that most spoke on the Shetland Isles, Norm, despite them being under King James's Scottish rule. The isles were actually closer to Norway than mainland Scotland. "We are journeying home to Norway and were set upon by the storm."

The door cracked a little wider and a man stared out, his eyes wide, taking them in. Suddenly Frode pushed past them, Libby still in his arms. "We have children who are wet and cold," Frode said, his one hand rising to push the arrow away so he could carry her inside the squat little house.

Erik rushed in, hoping no one inside would shoot at the warrior and hit the girl. Frode didn't think things through. Erik dodged around them, showing his hands empty of weapons to the middle-aged man holding the bow. An older woman hugged a younger woman in the corner by the hearth, blatant fear pinching their faces.

"We'll do you no harm," Nial repeated. "You're Leif Pedersen, aren't you? I visited some five years ago when your daughter there was not much bigger than the two little ones with us." Nial pointed at Libby and Trix, who'd been lowered and were holding hands before the fire in the middle of the room, the smoke rising out of a hole in the roof that was partly covered to stop the rain from coming in.

Trix smiled timidly, waving her open hand. The women just stared, but Leif relaxed the trembling hold on his bow. "I remember," he said, nodding to Nial even though his wary gaze remained on Erik,

Sten, and Frode.

"They won't harm you." Trix waved toward the men.

"Unless you're a sister to the Sinclair Horsemen," Libby said with a glance at Hannah who remained mute while she studied the women in the corner. They huddled there as if they were abused hounds.

Trix left Libby to go over to Frode to tug him closer. The man frowned but bent closer as she whispered, although Erik could hear her. "You're scaring them. Don't look so ferocious." She glanced over at Erik. "You, too, and Sten."

"Not Nial?" Erik whispered back.

Trix smiled. "They remember him, and he looks soft enough."

Frode snorted, his mouth bending in a grin that Erik hadn't seen for over a month.

Nial frowned, crossing his arms. "I do not look soft." He walked closer to Leif to tell him about the storm and ship anchored in the bay off his beach.

Trix turned her attention back to Erik, whispering, "Bend your shoulders some so you don't look so… menacing and tall."

With another glance at the two women in the corner, Libby went to stand before Frode, inspecting him. "Perhaps walk with a limp so you don't look like you could catch them if they must run."

Trix tilted her face to study Sten. "Stop staring directly in people's eyes. 'Tis disturbing."

Libby nodded. "You do that, too." She frowned at Frode.

In answer Frode stared directly at Libby, so she did the same and made a pinched ugly face before whirling around. "Just trying to help you be more likeable."

"We don't want to be more likeable," Sten said as she trounced away. "I might end up looking soft. Like Nial."

Nial made a rude gesture behind his back at Sten as he negotiated with Leif for them to sleep in his barn. Nial spoke evenly, gesturing at the girls and Hannah. Eventually, he turned back to Erik. "Leif says the children and Hannah may stay in the house, and we can have the barn."

Erik didn't like the idea of leaving Hannah alone, but where would she go? She didn't have a horse, 'twas storming, and she couldn't steal a boat to sail over a day back to Scotia. He nodded at the older man. "Thank you."

Hannah had walked closer to the two women, her smile reassuring. "We truly mean no harm." She had a gentle strength about her, courage to do what must be done to forge ahead.

The older lady nodded back and released her daughter. "I am Elizabeth, and this is our daughter, Eydis," she said in accented English.

"I am Hannah Sinclair, sister to the Four Sinclair Horsemen of Caithness in Scotland." Hannah seemed to wait. "Have you heard of them? They are great warriors who lead armies of horses. White, bay, black, and pale green."

"Like in the Bible?" Eydis asked, her brows furrowed. "Do they come from the heavens?"

Hannah smiled. "No. They are men, but great warriors. Do you not know them?"

Both women shook their heads, and Elizabeth

slowly raised her finger to point at Erik. "We know of him," she said, glancing at Nial and then nodding at Erik. "The Wolf Warrior and his pack. Protector of Norway."

Hannah's lips quirked to the side. "Hmph. I thought they were merely silver traders." She crossed her arms with simmering fury. Did it irk her that the woman and her daughter didn't recognize her brothers on this remote isle, that she'd known Erik instead, or because she'd been tricked by someone obviously known? Any option merely added to the hate she now exuded toward him. Any hope of another kiss, even to bury his nose in her glorious mane, was slashed apart forever.

Fy faen, he shouldn't care. But Erik did. A lot.

• • •

"Did they"—Hannah lowered her voice to the slightest whisper—"rape her?"

Elizabeth's eyes welled with tears, but she shook her head. "Leif came upon a man holding her…inappropriately in the barn, but stopped it before he could…" She shook her head. "He still beat Leif, and Eydis is terrified that they will return. We all are."

Hannah glanced at the sleeping young woman who had shared her room with her. "I am deeply sorry." She shook her head. "The man should pay for what he did and the fear he sows."

"He and his men still threaten us," Elizabeth added, "if Leif does not continue to let them steal half his crop of bere barley and several sheep each year."

Hannah's stomach, which had alternated between

the hardness of fury and the queasiness of the waves, ached in a new way with this terrible information. These kind people lived in fear without any type of protection. The small group of villains were working on Patrick Stewart's stone tower in the small village of Scalloway just north of the coast. Patrick, of course, had turned a blind eye to the plights of the native people who were being extorted and abused. He was like his father, Robert Stewart on Orkney Isle, whom her brothers had captured for trial in Edinburgh.

"If my brothers were here, Elizabeth," Hannah said, "they would strike down those criminals or cart them off to Edinburgh to hang for their abuse." But her brothers weren't there. What could she do to help?

"How about the Wolf Warriors?" Elizabeth asked, glancing at the curtained-off archway that separated the sleeping room from the main house. "Can they help us?"

Wolf Warriors? Hannah snorted softly. *What a ridiculous name.* Although, the idea that her brothers were the Four Horsemen of the Apocalypse could be seen as ridiculous, too. But her brothers would never steal away an innocent woman. Well, Cain had captured Ella, but they'd been at war with her clan. And as far as Hannah knew, they were not at war with Denmark-Norway.

"Will you ask them?" Elizabeth asked, bringing Hannah's mind back to the terrible fear that hung over the small family.

Hannah nodded. "I'm not sure how long we will be here on Shetland, but I'll ask them to do what they can. I'm their prisoner, so they probably won't listen to me."

Elizabeth shook her head. "Why would they take you prisoner if they are honorable men?"

Hannah had been too angry to ask. She shook her head. "I don't actually know. I think it has to do with my brothers and their king's mother wanting to control them."

"Controlling God's Horsemen? Impossible," Elizabeth said.

Controlling them with me. She'd told Erik that her brothers wouldn't come for her. A lie. One he'd seen through immediately.

When she thought of Bàs, growing up under her constant care and mothering, healing his wounds and calming his spirit when those around him hurt his feelings, she knew he would come for her. When she remembered the last time she'd seen Gideon, how she'd made him laugh despite his pinched brow, his look of brotherly love cast upon her, she knew he would come. And Joshua would tear the world apart for those he loved, which definitely included his younger sister. And Cain...the leader of their clan. Sober with dignity, he would use every means available to him to bring her home. Even starting a war against Denmark-Norway.

Hannah closed her eyes, willing the tears to stay inside. *Bloody hell.* They would all come for her, falling into whatever trap Sophie of Denmark had set, that royal bitch. Her eyes flew open. She must find out as much as she could about her enemy. The dowager-queen was the mother of King James's wife, Anne of Denmark, who was now queen of Scotland. Surely, the mother didn't want to force her brothers to war against her daughter. For what purpose was

Hannah's abduction?

"I need to talk to Erik," she murmured, rising from the fur-draped bed she'd shared with the two girls, Eydis and Elizabeth, while Leif slept out by the fire.

"He brought this sack for you," Elizabeth said, standing and motioning to the corner where a woolen bag sat. "This morning. Leif brought it in while you slept."

"What's in it?" asked Eydis from the bed. She yawned, pushing up to sit.

Sensing movement, Libby rolled over, blinking, and Trix sat up in a cross-legged position even though her eyes were still closed.

It was past dawn, the dark clouds finally giving way and letting light down to brighten the morning. Hannah unlaced the binding on the satchel, which was actually a large woolen blanket. Undone, the blanket fell apart to reveal clothing.

Eydis hurried over with a hushed gasp, her fingers touching the soft fur around the collar of a short cape. "'Tis all the pieces of a costume from Norway. So rich." The soft woolen gown was the blue color of summer cornflowers, and the stitching in an intricate woven design along the cuffs, collar, and hem of the overdress was a sunny yellow. White daisies were sewn among the yellow design. Eydis helped Hannah pull each piece of the ensemble out, shaking the wrinkles free as best they could, while Libby and Trix hopped out of the large bed wearing clean tunics donated by Erik's crew.

A smock of white linen was edged with lace. White stockings of warm, thin wool had embroidered flowers around the edge that hid ribbons to tie them just above Hannah's knees. The underskirt was white, as were the stays, which were made of fine silk. The bodice was a work of art with wide, embroidered ribbons stitched to hide the clasps that closed the front over the stays.

"Let's put it on you," Trix said, rising on her toes.

"Is there one in my size?" Libby asked, rubbing sleep from her eyes.

"I don't think those who sent the Wolf Warriors to find Lady Hannah knew there would be two liten jenter with her," Elizabeth said.

"Liten jenter?" Libby asked.

"Little girls," Eydis translated. "Mama, perhaps we could see if Mistress Rachel has some dresses her girls outgrew."

Elizabeth nodded. "For the Wolf Warriors, I am sure she will find something."

"How have you heard of the…" Hannah turned from inspecting the fine garments. "Wolf Warriors?"

"Oh, they are legendary," Elizabeth said, her eyes growing wide. "The strongest and most clever warriors in Norway and Denmark. They guard the border against Sweden, keeping them from stepping a foot in their great country without permission."

"And they work for King Christian and his mother, Sophie of Denmark?" Hannah asked, holding the soft fur edging the short cape under her chin.

"I do not know," Elizabeth said. She looked at her daughter. "I thought the Wolf Warriors stayed up in Norway along the northern coast, protecting the border there. 'Tis far to reach the court in Denmark."

Eydis nodded agreement but turned her attention

back to the beautiful costume. "This will be lovely on you and comfortable. And look," she said, lifting a pair of boots off the wooden floor. "There are boots for you, too."

"Erik Halverson sent Leif to the trading post to buy them for you," Elizabeth said. She looked at Hannah. "To replace your ruined slippers."

"How thoughtful," Eydis said, and it was obvious from her tone that she thought Erik was a legendary hero and not the abductor of women and children.

To be fair, he hadn't expected Trix and Libby to come along. Poor Cait and Rhona must be frantic with worry over the missing girls. And, soon enough, Gideon would be, too. No matter what, Hannah would get them back to Girnigoe.

An hour later, Hannah was dressed in the joyful ensemble, and Elizabeth had found two smaller gowns for Libby and Trix from their close neighbor, Rachel Nilsen. They weren't as fine as the one provided to Hannah, but the girls twirled around in the soft wool frocks, Libby in a pale rose color that seemed a shade lighter than the heather across the moors and Trix in a green costume that reminded Hannah of the bright moss in the woods around Girnigoe. The girls loved them, and Hannah assured Elizabeth that Erik would pay Rachel for the garments.

"They are not your daughters?" Elizabeth asked as Trix and Libby ran out of the house to scatter some beans and barley for the chickens.

"No," Hannah said, helping chop some root vegetables to be served later with fresh trout. "Their birth mothers have died, and my sister by marriage has adopted them. They snuck onboard the ship we came on." She shook her head. "Cait must be so worried."

Elizabeth *tsk*ed sympathetically and then looked at Hannah. "You do well with them. Do you have no children yourself?"

Hannah shook her head, feeling her cheeks warm. "Not yet. I hope to one day." The woman didn't look too much older than Hannah and had a daughter nearly grown.

"Erik Halverson is a Wolf Warrior and would make a strong child, I'm sure," Eydis whispered to Hannah when she walked past. Hannah smothered a snort and blinked against the embarrassed tears in her eyes.

"Why do you have no husband?" Elizabeth asked.

Hannah felt battered by both whispered comment and question. "I... I..." She stood straighter, fluffing the white, pleated apron that Eydis said was part of the traditional ensemble. "My brothers are protective and big. They scare off any man who would dare court me."

"They are not here," Eydis said. "And the Wolf Warriors are." Elizabeth frowned at her daughter. "Not for me," Eydis said quickly. She shook her head and glanced down. "I don't want to get near any man." Fear and sadness twisted her words, squeezing Hannah's heart for the girl.

Hannah went to her. Without a word, she hugged her, wishing she could pull some of the nightmare she'd experienced away from her. "We must teach you to feel strong," she said over her shoulder. Elizabeth nodded her agreement. Hannah pulled back, keeping hold of Eydis's shoulders. "I'll teach you how to shoot with your father's bow and arrows. 'Tis a skill of mine."

They ate around the central fire in the outer room. In all this time, no man had stepped inside. "Is Leif helping with our ship?" Hannah asked.

"He's nearby," Elizabeth said. "'Tis all I know." She glanced at Eydis and back at Hannah. "Since Lord Patrick's men came, Leif doesn't go far from our home."

The poor man carried the lives of his wife and daughter on his shoulders, and it seemed all he had was a crude sword and a bow with a few arrows. Where the overseer of Shetland should have been the protector of his people, instead Patrick Stewart let his brutish men steal and abuse his people. Hannah would get word to King James about this issue. Hopefully it wouldn't be too late. If she could find ink and paper, she'd write a letter to him on the Pedersens' behalf and another to Queen Anne about her capture.

"You need a dog," Trix said, nodding.

"A big wolfhound," Libby added. "We have several around Girnigoe. They could protect you."

Elizabeth smiled, looking dubious. "An extra stomach to fill."

The two women looked thin, and yet they'd given so much to their visitors. Hannah suddenly didn't feel as hungry, finishing just the one oat cake before standing. The short cape fell only over her shoulders, but it gave enough warmth on the summer morning to stave off the chill as she stepped outside.

Leif waved from the barn, and she returned his gesture, adding a smile so he wouldn't think anything was amiss inside. Although, she wondered if she'd ever have a genuine smile again with all this bitter anger inside. It felt like poison creeping through her veins.

She looked across the pebbled yard where chickens scratched, and a milk cow munched on summer grasses. But she didn't see Erik or his men. The storm had moved off, leaving a breezy morning, and she stepped down toward the beach. They were probably working on the ship, checking it for damage. "Poor Loinneil," she murmured. The mare had been stuck on the ship through the tossing storm overnight.

As she climbed over the rise that protected the farmstead from the sea, Hannah gasped, pausing on the top ridge. She blinked, gazing out at the protective inlet from the bay. The water was flat with small waves washing up on the pebbled beach. A large waterbird swooped down to land on the dark greenish surface right where the ship should be. But it was nowhere in sight.

Erik's ship, the *Seieren*, was gone.

CHAPTER NINE

"Once it arrived in Norway [in the fourteenth century],
the plague tore through the country. Estimates
are between one third and two thirds of the population
being killed. While exact numbers of deaths aren't
known, the country didn't fully recover to its
pre-pandemic population level until the 17th century."
LIFE IN NORWAY.NET

"Vær fri," Erik yelled from the back of the mare, letting her run. His smile widened, his unbandaged hand holding loosely to Loinneil's reins, his bitten palm protected in a fist.

The horse stretched her legs, galloping across the hardpacked ridge he'd surveyed before helping his men with the *Seieren*. Covered with wild grass and summer flowers tossing like waves with the wind, it was the perfect spot to peer down into the sheltered bowl that held Leif Pedersen's homestead.

Erik's gaze stopped on the figures beyond the barn. Two women stood across from a filled sack. He recognized Hannah immediately. She wore the Norwegian costume that he'd bought with the dowager-queen's coin before leaving on Sophie's mission. The blue, white, and yellow looked fresh hugging the Highland woman's soft curves. *Hannah*. To think of her caught his breath yet pinched tightly in his chest. His smile dropped away from the mixture of pleasure and pain.

Gathering the reins tighter, Erik guided Loinneil down the hill toward her. Hannah was helping Eydis hold the bow, her arms around the girl, guiding her like she'd guided him during the festival competition back on Scotia. He remembered the warmth of Hannah against his back, hugging him.

As Loinneil's hoof thuds caught their attention, both girls turned. Eydis looked on with a smile while Hannah's frown was ferocious. "Get off my horse," she said sharply as he neared.

"She's beautiful," Eydis said, setting the bow down to hurry over to where he stopped the horse. Eydis slid her hand down the mare's neck, over the unique gray dappling of the coat.

"She needs exercise after being stuck on the ship," Erik said to Hannah, who looked like a Norwegian princess full of snapping wrath. As if she could summon lightning bolts to throw like javelins through his chest.

"And where exactly is your ship?" she asked but then didn't let him answer. Her finger poked hard into his lower leg, punctuating her words. She threw one arm out to the homestead. "I thought you'd left. Stolen Loinneil and left me here to defend these good people. Luckily, Leif was here and told me you would return. From a port somewhere?" She gave him no time to answer her question. "It would have been considerate to let me know or take me with you to see to my horse." Hannah stepped close to Loinneil's face, rubbing her palm down the horse's gray nose.

Eydis's eyes grew round as she glanced between them. "I will…check on your…nieces." With one more pat on Loinneil's side, she strode down the path toward the homestead, glancing back over her shoulder more than once.

Erik let the girl retreat from hearing range before turning back to Hannah, who stood at the horse's head. Hannah's cheeks were rose-hued, either with exercise or anger. By God, she had a bursting spring of passion within her. Right now, 'twas all fury.

"Why would I leave you here when I was tasked to bring you to Denmark?" He continued to sit on her horse.

"Don't smile at me," she snapped. "There's nothing funny about abandonment." Even though he was much higher than she, Hannah Sinclair had a way of bringing herself level in every confrontation. He liked that about her.

Erik's fingers rose to his mouth. Was he smiling? Or did this woman, raised with the Four Sinclair Horsemen, view a relaxed mouth as a smile or the closest she'd ever seen on a warrior? His fingers grazed the still sore scratch marks along his cheek where her claws had sought his eyes. Elizabeth had given him ointment and a poultice for his hand.

Erik took a deep breath, easily letting his mouth fall into his familiar frown. "The horse needed to disembark and there are a few repairs that must be made to the *Seieren* before we can continue our journey." He pointed over his shoulder. "Just north along the west coast is a deep-water dock where I could maneuver the ship into a berth. 'Tis tied up there and being worked on. I was able to lead your mare off."

He saw Nial and Sten walk over the rise. Erik had overtaken them before he'd let Loinneil have her head across the flat meadow. The two men carried the one splintered top of the main mast between them. They'd sand it and lash it as securely as they could to take them to Denmark-Norway where they'd find a replacement mast. On an isle with no trees, there were no masts to be found.

"You could have left a message," Hannah said. She crossed her arms. "Libby and Trix were worried you'd left them."

"I apologize for worrying all of you," he said, letting his gaze drop to the splendid ensemble. It tapered around her waist to flare out over her hips. "The costume fits you well," he said. "And the colors suit you."

Hannah's hands slid along the short cape around her shoulders. "Yes," she said. She·glanced down. "And the boots are appreciated."

"They fit then?"

"Yes." Hannah looked up at him. "I appreciate them like a prisoner appreciates the scraps from the kitchen thrown into his cell."

She was still furious, but he didn't blame her. "Hannah, I am…"

He was what? Sorry? He'd already said that. Was he sorry he was trapped in his role of savior to his people and elder brother to Iselin? Sorry he wasn't still kissing her, touching her, letting her seduce him? Sorry he'd ruined anything that had started between them?

None of that was useful. "I am…glad the clothes and boots fit you. My wish is for you to be comfortable."

"Then take me home. That is the only place I will feel comfort."

He swallowed, looking away. "Would you like to

ride with me?"

"I will ride alone."

Normally, he'd worry about a horse taking the combined weight of two adults, but Loinneil was large, a breed with muscle and huge hooves. He shook his head. "I would not have you riding off through Shetland, trying to convince the people to sail you back to Scotia."

She snorted. "There are apparently too many villains on this small isle to make that a wise plan."

"Aye," he said, nodding. "I spoke to the workers at the dock. Patrick Stewart has employed immoral and cruel men to work for him on his tower house. And then he left them here to do as they will."

"One attacked Eydis," she said, her mouth tight.

Erik inhaled abruptly, his nostrils flaring as his gaze followed where the girl went. "Drittsekk," he murmured, looking down into the vale where she held Trix's and Libby's hands. "I will ride to Scalloway and let it be known that the Pedersens are under the protection of the Wolf Warriors."

"Ride?" she asked, narrowing her eyes at him. "*My* horse of course." She huffed. "For Eydis, you may. But right now, climb down."

Instead, he reached a hand to her. "Ride with me for a short bit before I must help with the mast." Erik held his breath and realized he was a fool to think she'd take it.

But then she placed her hand in his. She rose with his lift, and he slid back to set her before him, her legs opening to sit astride. The edge of her skirts rose nearly to her knees, showing the white of her stockings. He could point out that they might get dirty sliding along the horse's bare back, but he wouldn't do anything to make her retreat from this closeness.

He let her take the reins, thankful she sat in the safety of his legs. Bareback was dangerous enough. She leaned forward, and the backward shift in her hips against his groin caught him off guard. Only the strength in his thighs kept him seated as the mare leaped forward, ready to fly once more. She glanced over her shoulder at him as if to see if he was still there.

Hannah guided the mare back up the path to the ridge. Her hair, loose down her back, flew up around him like whipping silk. It still held the flowery fragrance from the night they'd kissed in the stables on the shores of Scotia. It reminded him of the crown of flowers she'd worn at the holy well when he'd watched her before knowing she was the sister of his sovereign's enemy. If she'd have kissed him then, had wanted him then, before he knew… His cod hardened with the carnal thoughts and the rub of her arse against him. He leaned forward, almost over her, to keep his seat. Perhaps she was trying to knock him off.

He heard her laugh and realized he, too, was smiling into the wind, smiling with the false sense of freedom. She was an excellent horsewoman. He'd expect nothing less from the sister of the Four Sinclair Horsemen.

Hannah guided the horse down the next hill and pulled to a stop before a nearly ripe field of Shetland barley, called bere. Wind blew across the pale gold stalks in the field, making waves, but the rise blocked the constant whoosh of wind over the isle. They stared out at the field in silence. Erik would sit there as long as she allowed, soaking in the feel of her against his chest. He blocked his thoughts, allowing himself only to feel her warmth.

"Why does Sophie of Denmark want to control my brothers?" Hannah asked, still looking out at the waving field.

The thought of his mission soured the moment. He wasn't privy to the dowager-queen's thoughts, but fear was easy to spot, especially by a warrior. "She's afraid of them taking over Scotia, taking it from her daughter."

Hannah shifted in the seat, turning halfway around to face him, her brows pinched. She'd rested the reins on Loinneil's neck and leaned the slightest amount closer to him. "Anne? *Queen* Anne?" He nodded. "I've spent some time with her," she said. "She was so pleasant. Loves children and animals. Loves her husband, King James."

Hannah stared up into his eyes, and he took a moment to remember every part of her pale blue irises, the little flecks of gray bathed in blue. Long, dark lashes framed her eyes, eyes that flashed with fury or sparkled with humor. 'Twas as if every emotion Hannah felt could be discovered in those eyes.

"Why would the queen's mother attack her daughter's warriors?"

Erik inhaled. "The dowager-queen must have heard about the Sinclair Horsemen from her daughter and has decided that there is a danger of civil war in Scotland. Sophie of Denmark is protective of her children. Where children born to royalty are usually sent away to be raised by others, Sophie refused to be separated from her children."

He shook his head and reached forward to catch a golden piece of hair that had been caught in Hannah's lips. Her gaze followed his fingers. Would she bite him again? Gingerly, slowly, as if she might attack, he tucked it behind her ear. "When Sophie was queen," he said, "she kept her children close, formed strong bonds with them. She will not tolerate her daughter living in jeopardy."

Hannah sat silently staring up into his eyes as if drawn to him. Could she feel this pull between them? This pleasure-pain caused by the tug?

He'd felt the attraction since walking with her down the hillside from the sacred well. The feeling was forbidden and traitorous. And now she hated him, would hate him more before this mission was over, and yet he couldn't pull away from her.

Hannah Sinclair was a clever, mischievous siren from her golden tresses down to her toes that had left his thighs bruised as she kicked him while being carried over his shoulder. And she'd wanted him enough that she'd taken him to the stables to seduce him, something that had never happened to him in all his years, because women were frightened of his scars and fierceness. Only the experienced, thrill-seeking widows followed him to his bed. Innocents were too frightened, but not Hannah. Not the brave woman raised with battle-sliced warriors. Despite her innocent look, she was a warrior, too.

Hannah ignored the bit of hair that fell immediately from behind her ear. She threw an arm out toward the field with a graceful arch as if to take in the whole isle.

"But my brothers protect King James and Queen

Anne. Right now, they're risking their lives to bring in James's traitorous uncle who has declared himself king of Orkney and Shetland."

He glimpsed the soft skin of her wrist at the edge of her sleeve before she dropped her arm.

"If I could write a letter to Queen Anne and her mother," she said, "this could be solved without force."

Erik almost forgot what they were talking about. He shook his head. "I don't know why I was sent on this mission, only that I must…" He swallowed hard, tearing his eyes away from the face that had haunted his dreams last night. "I must complete it. I'm sorry."

"Why? Why must you go along with such a horrid, dishonorable mission?"

"There are circumstances…"

"Erik!" a voice called down from the ridge. 'Twas Sten. He waved a hand, beckoning him.

Without further words, Erik took up the reins and turned Loinneil toward the homestead. His one arm wrapped firmly around Hannah's middle, and she didn't protest. The softening was real, but he wouldn't wish for it to mean anything. He would leave her with the dowager-queen, and Hannah would hate him forever.

• • •

Hannah didn't understand the Norse words exchanged between Nial, Sten, and Erik, but the inflections and postures showed they were angry, maybe disgusted. Hannah walked over to them after leading Loinneil to a water trough. Frode and Sten worked on sanding the splintered mast while Nial continued to talk. He even spat on the wind-swept dirt.

Erik looked at Hannah. "We will do something about the men harassing this homestead," he said. "And the devil who attacked Eydis."

"Only Leif is here to protect his family."

The door was open to the stone hut, and Hannah could see Trix helping Elizabeth cut root vegetables while Libby braided Eydis's long hair into plaits.

"I will make a plan." Erik strode off toward Leif at the barn.

Nial walked past Hannah with a sanding block in hand. "Don't worry," he said. "Erik is not someone who can walk away from an injustice."

She snorted, following him over to the splintered mast that had been laid upon two boulders. "But he can abduct an innocent woman, carry her away from her family across the sea to control her brothers." Hannah watched Erik wave Sten and Frode over to Leif, and they all listened to the man, frowns on every face.

Nial didn't say anything for several strokes of the sanding block. "Has Girnigoe ever suffered sickness?" he asked suddenly.

"Yes. No village is immune to illness creeping in," Hannah said, turning to watch the man that Trix had called soft. Nial Kristiansen might be broader around the middle than the others, but there was nothing soft about his muscles.

"You're fortunate then to still have so large a family," he said, glancing at her.

"A family who is worried sick over the disappearance of two little girls."

He kept sliding the ridged stone over the wood. "Imagine that a serious illness rolled through Girnigoe, all of Caithness," he said, not looking up. "Imagine those four sisters you have by marriage died, that their children died." He hooked a thumb toward Trix and Libby in the doorway. "Imagine those two closing their eyes, their sweet faces turning gray with death."

Hannah's stomach clenched, but she didn't say anything as Nial continued to paint the horror. "And then your Aunt Merida and Kára's grandmother and aunt, them all dying. And your brothers." He met her gaze, his hand stilling on the mast. "Erik has suffered."

Hannah blinked as tears stung behind her eyelids, but she kept her lips firmly pinched. Nial could be lying to gain her sympathy, so she'd cooperate.

"Erik has little left," Nial said and turned back to the mast, stretching to reach higher. "You can't swing a sword at illness…disease. So…" He paused as if thinking, but then continued. "Erik battles for his country, saving people, doing his duty for his sovereign. Don't your own brothers do the same for King James of Scotland?"

"King James doesn't order the abduction of women. Why would King Christian and his regents order something like that?" And why would Erik agree? Duty? Hannah wished she had Cain and Gideon here to think things through with her. She'd listened to their discussions over proclamations and political moves, as if Scotland were one big chessboard. But Gideon had the mind to understand secret maneuvers and clandestine reasons.

"Perhaps one abducted woman can prevent war

and the deaths of many," Nial said.

Hannah looked toward the barn where Sten and Erik stood with their arms crossed, listening to a widely gesturing Leif while Frode paced. "What war?"

There are circumstances…

The scrape of the plane continued against the wood as Nial spoke. "A war that our sovereign feels is on the horizon."

•••

"When will the ship be ready to sail?" Erik asked Nial as they walked the few miles back to the homestead, having left the *Seieren* behind at the dock, guarded by all six of the crewmen.

"A day at most," Nial said. "I left Kyle in charge of re-rigging all the sails this eve. The others will help. They're as anxious as we to reach Denmark."

Erik nodded, his gaze sliding across the barley field. "We must do more for Leif before we go. To give half his harvest to Patrick Stewart's men without recompense is blatant thievery."

"And they deserve to lose their balls or their life for attacking that girl," Nial said darkly. Behind them, Frode grunted his agreement.

They'd gone to the tower grounds in Scalloway before continuing on to the dock, but only a few servants scurried about. None of Patrick's hired men were there or in the village beyond. One wide-eyed, hunched man said he thought they'd journeyed north collecting taxes on the land.

"We could stay—" Nial started.

"Nay," Frode said with force. "We must get Iselin

without further delay."

"The dowager-queen did not give us a time frame," Nial said. "She knows the Horsemen were on Orkney, so we'd have to wait to confirm Hannah's importance to them. We were lucky Bàs came back early."

Erik rubbed his jaw. "When those Horsemen come, and they will, they will be as ferocious as a pack of wolves rescuing their pup. And I doubt Sophie has considered that they might have little care about insulting or threatening her." He shook his head. "'Twill be a battle to the bloody death either way, and Sophie will call us to wage it."

"As long as we get Iselin away from the vipers at court before she's forced to marry that walrus of a man," Frode said. "I'll steal her away if I must."

"Peter Kaas." Nial murmured the name of the Chancellor of Denmark. If Nial was considered soft, Peter was a melted pile of pudding with a large belly, swollen fingers, and pasty skin.

"We will rescue her, but she won't marry a dead man," Erik said, glancing at Frode, his friend and future brother by marriage. Frode cursed under his breath, knowing he must be patient.

Erik stared out at the field, his mind drifting back to that morning when he held Hannah before him on the horse. "We will stay to speak with the tax collectors. Make a lasting impression on them."

Frode raked fingers through his hair. "You are delaying our mission. 'Tis for Hannah Sinclair, isn't it?"

Erik turned to Frode who stood in the middle of the path. His friend's face was red with anger, and Erik fought to tamp down his own. If Frode could read Erik's mind, he'd probably see some truth in his words. But the man couldn't read Erik's mind nor any weak part of his body, like his traitorous cod or his tight chest.

Erik stepped close to look directly in Frode's face. "I've loved my sister since she came out as a newborn from my parents' bedchamber, swaddled and held in my father's arms. You've loved her only for the past year. So, you can hold your thoughtless, damnable tongue before I yank it from your crusty, sneering lips." Neither Sten nor Nial said anything or tried to step between them.

Frode inhaled but didn't respond. Erik turned away, trudging forward along the ridge. "We will remain on Shetland until we've tried to help the situation for Pedersen and his family, but no more than a couple days." He listened for a snort of derision or curse behind him but all three of his men remained wisely silent.

They continued toward the homestead. Erik inhaled the breeze, which had shifted to come in off the bay where they'd initially landed. *Smoke?* The tang registered in his mind, and he broke into a run before he could say the word.

"Brann!" Sten called behind him.

Erik charged forward and crested the ridge to see down into the little valley.

Fire! The homestead was on fire.

CHAPTER TEN

Health manuals encouraged bathing during the medieval and Tudor periods. "The bath cleans the external body parts of dirt left behind from exercise on the outside of the body. ...if any of the waste products of third digestion are left under the skin that were not resolved by exercise and massage, these will be resolved by the bath."

REGIMEN SANITATES, ITALIAN PHYSICIAN, MAINO DE MAINERI, FOURTEENTH CENTURY

Fire crackled along the thatching and dry peat on the roof of the barn, spreading under the summer sun. And with it, war had been declared on this poor farmer and his small family. *So war it will be.* Hannah's brother, Joshua, Horseman of War, would surely agree.

"Give me your bow!" Hannah yelled at Leif. The man's hands were shaking so violently that he wouldn't be able to hit the barn, let alone one of the fiends who'd set it ablaze.

"She trains every day at home," Trix called, jumping up and down.

"Just give her the bloody bow," Libby yelled.

Leif practically threw over the weapon and quiver sparsely filled with arrows. "Get your family to safety," Hannah said to him. "And you two, get in that room and hide." The two little girls clasped their hands together and ran back into the bedroom.

Leif shook his head. "I fight for my home."

Elizabeth nodded, and so did Eydis, even though her eyes were large saucers in a pale face. Elizabeth stood before her like she'd scratch someone's heart out of their chest if they came near her daughter again.

"Then give everyone some type of weapon. Even rocks if nothing else." Hannah had been on the fringe of battles several times, big and small, but she'd never been in the smoky middle of one. At least she wasn't shaking as much as the Pedersens.

I'm a Sinclair, a Sinclair horseman, a horsewoman. "A Valkyrie," she whispered Erik's description of her, a mythological warrior woman on horseback. The words licked up inside her like the fire beyond. "I condemn these men for destruction and attempting to kill us," Hannah said. *Kill us or worse.* Torture and rape were worse than a quick death, and she would use everything she'd learned to prevent that from happening to Eydis, Elizabeth, the girls, and herself.

Tears had bled down Eydis's cheeks with her fear when the six men arrived that day to demand payment, twice as much as the agreed-upon taxes. When Leif said he didn't have the amount they'd threatened to take Leif's livestock. The leader of the group, a brute with greasy blond hair, had suggested that Eydis come with them in exchange for the sheep. He'd leered, and one glance at Eydis's gray pallor and the blood that marked her lip from her biting down on it told Hannah that this was her attacker.

He wouldn't survive for long if Hannah had anything to do with it. "Guilty," she whispered, as Gideon, Horseman of Justice, surely would. In a land without law, someone must help these good people survive against devils. She suddenly understood why Joshua had remained with the Orkney people led by his yet to-be wife Kára. Not helping or turning a blind eye was a crime in itself. A crime of dishonor.

Hannah stepped out of the house, raising the bow. Loinneil screeched inside the barn. *Mo chreach! Loinneil!* The torch-waving men stood between her and the burning barn.

"There's a horse inside the barn," she yelled to them. "Get her out!"

The blond leader motioned to one of his men who threw the doors open to the building. It took Hannah all her control not to run toward it, desperate to save her sweet mare. But the men would grab her if she ran close, and she must stand apart to use the bow. Hannah's stomach released its knot with an audible sob when she saw Loinneil led out from the smoke, shaking her mane and tossing her head, her nostrils flaring, searching for clean air.

"We'll take the horse," the blond called, a Scottish lilt to his words, reminding Hannah that he was employed by Patrick Stewart. If the son was as bad as the father, Robert Stewart, his goal was to subjugate and break the people in his realm. Hiring like-minded workers would continue Patrick's efforts while he was off the isle.

"She is *my* horse," Hannah yelled back.

The blond grinned savagely. "Then we will take ye, too."

Without another thought, Hannah raised the bow, nocked her arrow, aimed, and shot in one fluid motion. *Thwack!* The arrow pierced the man right between the eyes, slicing through his brain.

Gasps behind her didn't slow her down. She'd learned war from Joshua, quiet and swift action from Bàs, and how to shoot from her sisters. She drew another arrow and aimed toward the man holding Loinneil. He yelled, dropping the halter, and charged toward Hannah, his red face twisted with vengeance. She fired, noticing as it left her bow that the cock feather was missing. *Daingead!*

The arrow shot askew, hitting short and skidding across the hard ground pocked with puddles. Despite the storm the day before, the winds had dried the thatching enough that the fire was spreading.

She grabbed another arrow, trying to nock it, but the man reached her, barreling into her. The impact was like hitting the ground from off the back of a horse, and for a moment the world went black, her breath knocked out of her as her teeth clacked together. Hannah struggled to inhale and was yanked off the ground to be thrown over the man's broad shoulder, his hand roaming over her arse. She couldn't breathe and concentrated on trying to inhale despite the man's shoulder pressed into her stomach.

"Bloody foking hell!" he yelled as they spun around, adding to her dizziness. She couldn't see what was making him curse.

Hannah began to kick ferociously, and the bastard almost dropped her. She felt her sgian dubh press hard against her hip where it lay in her pocket tied under her skirt.

The sound of swords hitting swords made her arch up in desperation to see what was happening. Hopefully, Trix and Libby weren't charging into the fray with kitchen knives but had remained hiding under the pile of furs in the corner of the backroom. But what met her gaze flooded her with relief. Erik Halverson, shirtless and full of vengeful power, sliced through one of the bandits with his long, two-handed sword. Without watching the head roll across the ground, he swung back around, his gaze stopping directly on Hannah. He strode toward her as Sten, Nial, and Frode fought against the other three men.

"Release her." Erik's voice carved the air as sharply as his sword.

"Ye can't strike me without striking the lass," the man said. There was no fear in his voice, only deadly determination.

Hannah's fingers sought the folds of her skirt as she shifted on the man's shoulder. "Hold still, ye little harpy." But she didn't obey and slid the sgian dubh from her skirt.

Taking the dagger in both hands, she aimed toward the man's meaty calf above the edge of his boot and stabbed. The man screamed, falling. Once again, Hannah landed on the hard-packed ground. Before Erik could strike, a large rock came down on the man's head. He went still, his eyes wide with surprise. Hannah saw Eydis standing there, her teeth bared.

Leif grabbed his daughter as she crumpled. Hannah watched from the ground, the sounds of battle muted by the ringing in her ears. She blinked several times, trying to clear her head of the lethargy that had fallen over her upon impact.

"Can I lift you?"

Hannah turned her face to the deep, comforting voice that promised safety. The irony that Erik was also her captor wasn't lost on her, but right now he was all she wanted. "Yes," Hannah said, trying to identify where she hurt. Her back, hip, and shoulder screamed the loudest as Erik lifted her from the ground as if she were broken. His arms didn't falter, his strength evident in the smooth glide to right her, holding her steady as she fought the weakness of her limbs. "They came for taxes that were beyond what was agreed."

Erik studied her face with desperate eyes, brushing her hair back from the side of her head that stung with a scrape. "Nay. They came to steal and abuse the innocents in this house."

She nodded, feeling heaviness in her chest. Still meeting his gaze, she whispered, "I killed a man."

He nodded, pride wiping away some of the worry lines around his eyes. "I saw. 'Twas a most perfect shot."

"The fletching was broken on the second arrow."

"And yet you still felled the brute."

Hannah realized she was trembling. She'd never actually killed anyone before. Her brothers did in every conflict. Had they shook after their first? She'd have to ask Bàs.

Hannah swallowed past the smoke on her tongue. "Is Loinneil well?" She looked around him and saw Trix and Libby scratching her horse's face. They hadn't stayed hidden for long, the two urchins who continuously sought to help and always fell into danger.

Erik glanced over. "If you are well enough, you should go see. I must help put out the fire and dispose of the bodies."

The barn roof was still ablaze, and Sten, Frode, and Nial were helping the Pedersens, who were trying to throw water from the cistern on it.

Hannah nodded, and Erik waited until she pulled away from him, watching to see if she was steady.

"You should put their heads on stakes on the back edge of the fields. Far enough they won't stink down here, but they will stand as a warning." Erik's brows rose. Did he wonder if she was sound in the head? "'Tis called a ghost fence," she said, sliding a hand through the air as if showing a fence. "To warn others from doing harm on this family." She shrugged. "You should leave some indication that the killings were done by the Wolf Warriors, so the family isn't blamed."

"I will consider it."

"My brother, Gideon, says it intimidates those who bluster or want to start trouble." Joshua liked the not-so-subtle message, too, and teased Gideon that Cait wouldn't let him set one up any longer.

"I will ask Leif if he would like the…ghost fence."

With the briefest of smiles, she turned, walking toward the girls and her mare. But she looked back at the large man running to help save what they could of the barn. The muscles moved under the tanned skin of his back as he dodged the bodies of their attackers. His shoulders were large and toned, and his longish golden-brown hair brushed below his nape, giving him a primitive look. Strength was evident in his smooth stride and through the cut of his breeches, showing the taut lines of his arse, an arse she still wanted to see naked.

He stole me away. Hannah let out a long exhale

that contained her bitterness. It slid out across her tongue as if exorcising a demon. "He has no family left, nothing but his pride," she whispered. What would she do if she'd lost everyone, and her king and queen asked her to act? She had no answer.

• • •

"We will patch the roof, and I'll take responsibility for killing Patrick Stewart's men," Erik told Leif.

The older man wiped a cloth over his face. "We would all be dead without your help today. I am truly grateful for the Wolf Warriors." He glanced toward Loinneil where Hannah worked to make sure the horse was well. "And Lady Hannah Sinclair." Leif shook his head. "I've never seen a woman so brave."

She'd washed the mare, scrubbing the smoke from her dappled gray coat, and was now drying her flanks with a rag, massaging the muscles around the horse's eyes and the sharp planes of her face. "She was raised with warriors in Scotia and trains with them," Erik said.

"Given arrows with proper fletching, a bow, and a lofty perch, and she could have taken them all out," Leif said. "I swear my Eydis started making new arrows before the bodies were cold, and Hannah gave her some lessons after the midday meal. We will all be practicing."

Hannah turned, saw them staring at her, and nodded their way before walking across the yard to the roundhouse. She grabbed a towel from inside the door to throw over her shoulder and a small leather satchel. Without glancing his way, she strode away from the homestead up the ridge. Where was she going now? If she planned an escape, she'd have taken her horse.

"Elizabeth probably told her where we bathe when 'tis warm," Leif said, following his gaze. "There's a pond east of the bere field." He pointed.

And Hannah was walking there alone? They had just disposed of the initial threat to the homestead and its people, but that didn't mean she was safe.

Erik made certain Loinneil was breathing easily. She'd sneezed a couple times, spewing forth soot-stained mucus, but she seemed healthy enough and smelled free of smoke after Hannah had washed her down. Luckily, the bastards' greed for the horse had won out over their bloodlust.

As he made his way up the path, he glanced down toward the sea where Nial, Sten, and Frode were weighing down the six bodies. Only one of them was without a head, which stared outward on a pole at the back of the Pedersens' territory. Erik continued to follow the path toward the pond. Hannah seemed rather accident prone near water. Could she swim? The question hastened his step until he spied the water.

Hannah's wet head broke the surface. Then a slender arm slid out, and she used some soap to wash it. The next followed, and then she scrubbed her long hair, probably trying to rid it of the acrid smoke.

A bird darted out from the low scrub that hid him over the ridge. *Fy fean*. He was looking while she bathed, and she was completely naked this time. His mother, had she been alive, would be appalled. Was he a common peeper now? Erik stood straight and walked down the slope. "You shouldn't be alone out here."

She turned toward him in the water up to her neck but didn't look frantic or even startled. "Apparently, I'm not alone," she called back, her musical voice skimming over the surface where a little bee touched down only to soar high above her. She raised an arm, pointing at Erik.

"Before I got here," he said, walking to the edge of the pond where the rays of the lowering sun caught on the water, glittering. Once again, he was reminded of the mythical naiads or water fairies. "'Tis dangerous to swim alone too. You could drown from a leg cramp."

"I smelled like a burnt caldron. Elizabeth is helping me release the smoke from the costume you brought that I was wearing." She tipped her head to the side, staring at him. "If you're here to bathe, you can do so over there." She pointed across the pond.

Erik would bathe, but if he were to disrobe before her, she'd see his weakness for her. His cod was an unruly sort and didn't seem to care that Hannah hated him.

"I will sit by that outcropping." He pointed to three boulders that rose from the sod a few feet back from the pond's edge. "My back to you. Yell if there is any trouble."

He turned, striding through the taller grasses fed by the damp edges of the pond. His ears picked up the gentle splashes of the water as Hannah moved around. It almost sounded like she was following him with her strokes, but he didn't look. She'd only accuse him of spying on her.

Erik lowered to the ground, adjusting his foolishly

hopeful cod. He heard her splash a bit as if going under for a moment and popping back up. He saw a pile of white clothes near him on the bank, her smock and petticoat, and some drying sheets. She must be naked in the water.

"Don't come out here alone again." He realized his heart was pounding as he scanned the fields to the east. "Anyone could be lurking, and you don't have a bow."

"They'd have to be willing to swim into the middle of the pond to get me," she said, her voice closer than he'd thought. "I'm an excellent swimmer."

He remembered that she'd been bathing alone at the cabin in the woods that he'd discovered was Bàs's home. "'Tis best we travel in groups or pairs here now that we've retaliated against Patrick Stewart's men."

"If we'd made a ghost fence around the pond, there'd be less chance of retaliation."

The slight pout in her voice made Erik grin. "I put one head at the edge of the field." He motioned to the barley undulating in the wind.

"Six would have been better."

"And would have smelled worse."

"I suppose," she said, water moving around her. "I'm coming out."

"I won't look."

In his mind, Erik followed her through the water and up the bank incline. She sounded surefooted. No scurrying for cover as if she thought he'd look. He knew she didn't trust him. Did she not care if he looked? He kept his back straight and his eyes focused on the field, the tiny spot that was the fiend's head at the far end.

The flap of the drying blanket paused, and he

could hear the slight brush of linen on skin while she dried herself with it. The fabric whispered as she wrapped the towel around herself, and he held his breath at the sound of her footsteps. She stopped before him. Hannah was a water goddess who'd taken human form, her mermaiden's tail splitting into two solid legs draped in linen, her feet poking out of the bottom. Hannah's hair lay long and dripping down her back, darkened by the water. Droplets of water still sat on her naked shoulders and face.

She studied him. Her face was a mix of subdued anger and something else. Regret? "Just so you know, when you decided to abduct me that night in the barn, this is what you gave up."

With that, her fingers opened where they clutched the drying sheet, and the whole thing fell away, pooling around her feet. Hannah stood there in the golden light of the lowering sun, glistening from the moisture left on her skin. Her breasts were perfect, small moons, pale with dark nipples peaked with a rose hue around them. She was tall and slender with hips that flared out, tapering along her sleekly muscled legs. The landscape of smooth skin ran down her middle to the dark patch that hid the crux of her legs that had been so hot and wet for him previously.

With dignity, she turned, pulling her hair to lay across one shoulder. Her spine was long and straight, leading to a generously rounded arse and the backs of strong legs. Finishing her rotation to face him again, she held her chin even, her large eyes like moons gazing down at him. Erik drank in the sight of her, speechless.

His mouth had gone so dry that his tongue caught

on its roof. Blood and heat pulsed through him as all his senses came to life. He realized he was standing. She watched him for several long seconds as if to see what he'd do. What could he do?

I could pull her to me and kiss her, touch her, love her. The traitorous thoughts sent enough ice through him to give him control.

He wet his lips, and her gaze dropped to them. "I..." he started. His hand dropped to his obvious erection, and her gaze followed it. He adjusted himself, watching her closely, but she gave no sign of apprehension. He started again. "Even if we had not been interrupted, I would have abandoned my own desires, Hannah." He shook his head. "Knowing what I must do as part of my mission. Knowing I would hurt you when you learned the truth." He wanted to look away, but Erik never surrendered, even in something as simple as staring. He swallowed against the tightness of regret in his voice. "And I will forever regret the loss of such a gift."

Hannah stared back into his eyes, and he felt her judging him. She dipped to the ground to clutch the drying sheet, sliding it back up around her body, hiding away the beauty.

Without a word, she walked around him. He didn't turn, even though his cod yelled a bloody war cry for him to follow her. He listened as fabric fell over her and looked only when she walked up the bank toward the homestead on the other side. She'd slid on a clean smock and wrapped in a second drying sheet to traipse uphill in unlaced boots. She never looked back.

Erik rubbed absently at his tortured cod as his chest squeezed with pain.

CHAPTER ELEVEN

"Sirens are a type of creature found in ancient Greek mythology. Commonly described as beautiful but dangerous creatures, the sirens are remembered for seducing sailors with their sweet voices, and, by doing so, luring them to their deaths."

ANCIENT-ORIGINS.COM

Hannah's heart thudded, her cheeks growing so warm that she imagined them bursting on fire. But she'd done it, and the look on Erik's face, a mixture of pain, remorse, and barely concealed passion, brought a smile to her lips as she marched away.

She'd known he would find her after she walked away from the homestead. And some part of her knew that he might still want to tup her. After all, his jack had been very erect back in the barn before her abduction, and he couldn't hide it just now at the pond, either. The sight of him adjusting it brought back a picture from that book Cait had brought to the solar, one of the man holding his hard jack to slide it into the waiting woman's body. A hot ache pulsed between her legs. Bloody hell, her foolish body still wanted him, too, even after he lied to her. Well, his body couldn't lie and neither could hers, apparently.

Hannah stepped to the side of the roundhouse and paused at the sound of conversation. "I don't understand." It was Elizabeth. "Is she a prisoner of theirs then, taken from her home?"

"There are reasons," Leif said. "Their queen is try-ing to prevent a civil war from erupting in Scotland."

"By stealing her away, they will start a war between Hannah's clan and Denmark-Norway," Elizabeth said.

Hannah nodded in agreement but kept to the curve of the house, leaning against it. The stones had absorbed the sun and radiated some warmth.

Leif replied so softly that Hannah couldn't hear him.

"But ten men? The woman could be in danger!" Elizabeth said. The anger in her raised tone warmed Hannah.

"Shhh," Leif warned. "She's not to be touched by any of them, Lizzie," he said. "Their queen wants her to come as a virgin."

"What if she is not? Will the dowager-queen re-turn her home?"

Hannah held her breath, clutching the cloth around herself.

"I don't know the whole of it, but the two with the paint on their faces assured me they couldn't touch Hannah even if they wanted to. None of them can."

"I see how their leader watches her," Elizabeth continued.

Erik watched her? Hannah's heart sped faster, and she glanced back toward the pond. So far, Erik hadn't followed. Was he bathing too? She remembered the talk about having a man bathe before attempting the picture in the book with the man's jack in the wom-an's mouth. Her foolish body responded with a clenching below.

"No matter what he does with his eyes," Leif said, "he cannot touch her."

"She might not be a virgin," Elizabeth continued. "She's older." She huffed. "If she were with child, surely the dowager-queen wouldn't keep her."

Hannah's frame straightened at her words, and she stood away from the curved wall. *If she were with child... Their queen wants her to come as a virgin...*

Hannah's breathing quickened, her mind playing over Elizabeth's and Leif's words. When she heard the crunch of boots on pebbles, she pulled back, hurrying toward the front of the roundhouse. Leif paused when he stepped around, and Hannah began to walk forward as if she'd just gotten back from the pond.

"Good eve, Master Pedersen," Hannah said. "Is Elizabeth still working on my costume?"

His face flushed at seeing her, whether from nearly being caught talking about her or because she was wearing only a smock and under petticoat beneath her drying shect. "Aye. She is behind the house." He gave a brief bow and hurried toward the half-burnt barn where Trix and Libby fed a turnip, cut in half, to Loinneil.

Hannah breathed deeply, her hand on the stones of the house. *I want a bairn, and I want to go home.* The flutter in her stomach moved lower again. And Erik's lust for her could give her both.

• • •

Hannah Sinclair was a siren.

Every time he turned around, there she was, bending over so that an image of him loving her from behind popped into his head. Then she would snap upright, her golden tresses flying about in wild disarray as if she were in the throes of passion. Several times over the past two days since she'd dropped her bathing sheet before him, she'd spilled water over her front and had to take her bodice off to dry. She'd been left in a damp smock that she covered with a shawl. And then the shawl would slip from her shoulders whenever Erik walked around the corner.

His cod was in constant agony, and his mood was becoming more vicious by the hour. He didn't even have to close his eyes to see the smooth, pale skin Hannah had shown him. Her peaked breasts and full hips appeared in his dreams every night, too, as if to taunt him further about what he'd given up in the Girnigoe barn the night he'd stolen her away from her home.

They were finishing repairs on the ship and, since killing the worst of Patrick's men, they would sail the next day for Denmark. The sails had been sewn. The mast had been rubbed smooth and just needed to be fitted against the broken base. Eric had poured his restless energy into repairing the Pedersens' barn and instructing the two small Sinclair girls on making a flag with a wolf's head on it. They would hang it from the barn facing outward to let Patrick Stewart's men know that they'd be back if they continued to harass the homestead.

Erik stretched his back in the doorway of the barn, his gaze going to Hannah standing next to the roundhouse. She wore the blue dress he'd commissioned with Sophie's money. It was in the Norwegian style instead of the Danish, a small triumph against the dowager-queen's orders in this mission.

Hannah poured creamy milk into the tall bucket of a butter churn. Eric's breath swelled in his chest as she gripped the smooth wooden plunger, her long fingers wrapped around it. And she began to stroke the wood. Was she even moving the plunger or merely sliding her hands up and down the length? He didn't care. His breath came out in a loud rush, and he watched, her arms going up and down, her fingers sliding faster along the wooden cod, for that's what it looked like. Hannah giving pleasure to an erect cod.

When her lips parted slightly as if to catch more air or moan, Erik heard a strangled noise next to him. Glancing beside him, he saw Nial and Sten standing there, mouths open, eyes wide. "What is she doing?" Sten whispered.

"Churning butter," Nial said, but his voice was low, husky.

Sten rubbed a hand down his front. "But her lips—"

"Get back to work," Erik said, stepping in front of them. He shoved at their shoulders to get them to retreat into the barn.

"I've never seen a woman churn butter like that," Sten said, shaking his head as if to rid himself of the image or break a spell cast upon him. "My mother surely doesn't."

Nial groaned. "Ugh, Sten! Now I have a picture in my head of your mother stroking a butter churn."

Sten's face pinched into a horrified grimace.

"Go down to the dock and find a farmer willing

to sell us some provisions," Erik said, his words a definite order. "We will be on the ship four or five nights, since we were blown so far north."

Sten frowned and looked out toward the shore. "The bloody Sinclair Horsemen will get there before us."

"I left my generals prepared to detain them if they do," Erik said.

Nial crossed his arms. "You might lose a hundred men doing so."

"They are mortal," Erik said. "Now go. Leif doesn't have provisions that we can buy, so we need to find some. Let Nial talk," he said to Sten. "You frighten people."

"And Nial is soft," Sten said and ducked when Nial threw a punch. Sten laughed while Nial cursed, and they both strode off toward the ship.

Erik watched them leave out the back of the barn and then went to the door facing the roundhouse, but Hannah was gone. The churn sat abandoned until Eydis came out and began working the plunger, the correct way. He turned, his gaze scanning the homestead for Hannah. The woman was graceful and lithe, strong and clever, not to mention the beauty of her features and form. No wonder he was taut with lust for her. He glanced down at the bulge in his trousers. If the children came out now, he'd scar them against men.

"Faen i helvete," he cursed, grabbing a drying sheet from a small stack Elizabeth had brought out for them to use with a bit of soap that smelled of thyme and lemon balm. He'd go take another plunge in the cool water of the pond and bring himself to release there if his erection wouldn't abate. He'd already had to take care of himself the last two days with his increasingly erotic thoughts about the Sinclair siren.

Without looking anywhere that Hannah might be bending over, stretching her long neck, drenching her fine breasts with water, or beating a butter churn, Erik strode toward the pond with brisk steps. The sun was going down, and he welcomed the shadows that would hide his embarrassing state.

He exhaled through his nose, listening to the evening birds calling to one another as they swooped over the barley field that Leif had begun to harvest. He pulled his tunic off, letting his sweat dry with the breeze, and his mind turned to the final phase of his mission. *Fy faen*. He didn't want to give Hannah to Sophie. The dowager-queen could very well be wrong about the Sinclairs wanting to depose her daughter and her husband, James of Scotland. There'd been no hint of it at the festival at Girnigoe. Bloody hell. The Sinclair Horsemen were working to bring traitors to heel for James.

Erik dropped the drying sheets and his tunic by the boulders where he'd witnessed the beauty of Hannah's naked form. His hands fell to his leather belt, and he unbuckled it, letting his loose trousers fall to his feet. He looked at his cod. Even with the cool breeze, it stood hot and ready still. "Calm down, you hopeful fool," he murmured and plucked the ties lacing his boots, shucking them.

He ran his hands over the scruff on his jaw, turning to face the breeze. The mission hadn't been one he wanted to take on, but he'd had no choice. It was simple. Confirm that the Sinclair brothers loved their sister and bring her untouched to Sophie in order to trade her for Iselin. Hannah would wed the chancellor, Peter Kaas, and remain at the Danish court. Then if her brothers sought to overthrow Sophie's daughter in Scotland, she'd threaten to imprison Hannah or worse.

As if to escape his duty, Erik stepped to the bank and, throwing his arms overhead, dove into the fresh, rain-fed water. *I could marry Hannah.* The thought shot through him with the cold embrace of the water. Sophie could keep her in Denmark-Norway, but Erik would keep Hannah with him, even if they were on the march. She was strong and brave, and he'd make sure she was protected. He surfaced, gulping the air. As if the inhale had refocused his mind, disappointment tightened inside him. Hannah hated him. Forgiveness was unlikely.

He touched down in the soft mud that made up the bottom of the pond, and straightened, pressing pebbles farther into the muck under his feet. It was shallow enough for his chest to surface, and he froze. "Hannah," he murmured. She sat on one of the three boulders, watching him.

• • •

Hannah had remained completely still as she watched Erik undress and dive. His jack rivaled the ones Hannah had seen in Cait's tupping book. It had been thick and stood straight and long when he'd turned to look left before diving in. His muscular arse and legs had propelled him forward, his broad shoulders and straight arms breaking through the surface. Every bit of him had commanded attention.

Before he'd come up for air and turned around, she'd hurried to perch on the boulders as if she'd been there all along. From that distance, he wouldn't be able to tell that her breath came in shallow pants from her jog to keep up with him nor that her heart thudded at the audacious seduction she'd been trying to execute over the last two days.

She'd used every technique she could think of to lure him to lust, using ploys she'd seen her sisters use, especially Kára when she teased Joshua. Time was slipping away, and the ship was nearly fixed. Once they were sailing with ten men and two little girls, it would be nearly impossible to get Erik alone long enough to make him forget his mission and take her maidenhead. With luck and clootie-well blessings, she'd also get with child from the encounter.

Hannah held his gaze as he waded through the water toward her. "I didn't know you were here," Erik said. Tentativeness edged his tone. 'Twas probably the closest Erik had ever sounded to afraid. The idea that she made him nervous bolstered her, and she raised a brow.

"I came to bathe." She stood to shrug off the short cape from her shoulders and untied the pleated apron that marked the costume as traditionally Norwegian. Her hair was already free of any pins or ties, since she'd been letting it blow free around her the last days. Ella said men loved free-flowing hair.

"I can swim to the other side," he said but didn't move.

She kept Erik's gaze and unlaced the bodice,

sliding it off the sleeves of her white smock. A sharp tug of the ties, and her two petticoats fell from her hips in a heap from which she stepped out.

"This area is deep and big enough for both of us, And swimming alone is dangerous. You could get a leg cramp," she said. Before he could respond or she could lose her nerve, Hannah caught the bottom edge of her smock and lifted it over her head. It floated down next to her to land on her pile of petticoats. She stood straight before him in only her stockings that were tied above her knees.

Erik's mouth dropped open. "Hannah," he murmured but didn't add anything else. He glanced left and then right, but she knew no one was there. She'd asked Eydis to watch the girls, and Hannah had seen Leif walk toward the docks where Sten and Nial had hurried off. And the longer she took, the deeper the shadows were becoming. Night was moving in like a rising tide.

She bent forward, which presented her breasts at their fullest, and plucked the ribbons of her stockings. Sliding them down and off, she stood again, her hair sliding around her shoulders and down her back. The tresses tickled her sensitive skin like the whisper of silk. The calm breeze in the valley and Erik's intense gaze made her nipples pearl sharply.

A throb began between her thighs, just from him touching her with his gaze. Hannah walked to the bank, letting her fingers slide down between her breasts, over the planes of her stomach, to reach the ache increasing at the crux of her legs. His gaze followed her fingers, and she thought she saw him swallow as she rubbed herself. Erik murmured something in his language, his voice rough as if he endured torture.

Before he could move away, Hannah lifted her arms and leaped off the bank, diving toward him. Cold slammed into her, but she'd dived many times into Lake Hempriggs at home, and it was the end of summer. Her fingers bumped into his stomach, and Erik lifted her upright with his hands grasping her upper arms. She blinked the water off her lashes and stared up into his face.

"What are you doing?" he asked, his gaze hard.

She pinched her nose quickly to rid it of water and raised her arms to pull her hair behind her. Her neck bent, her chin tipping up at the weight of the wet mass. "Making certain you don't drown."

Hannah settled her feet on the tops of his, which lifted her enough that the top swell of her breasts rested on the water. She glanced at his one hand where a sliver of soap nestled in his fingers. "And washing, of course." She plucked it from him and inhaled the herby lemon scent. She preferred flowers, but this would do. "I can help you and you can help me."

"Help you? Help me?"

He seemed incapable of forming a coherent thought, and she smiled slightly. Stepping back off his feet, she ignored the squish of the mud under her toes and rubbed the soap on his chest. Bloody hell, he was well made. Her hands slid along the muscles and sinew of his forearms, biceps, and shoulders while he stared into her face. He didn't move. 'Twas as if he were a statue, a statue with warm, smooth skin over evident strength. Hannah moved to his back, sliding her hands up and down over the pigment picture of a wolf. Her hands slipped below the surface, and her heart thumped hard as she ran them over his taut backside.

Erik groaned, turning in the water to face her. "I cannot...touch you," he said, his voice choked.

"But you want to," she said, trying to keep confidence in her voice. She was putting herself in a position to be crushed by his rejection, something she never thought she could do.

"Fy faen," he cursed low. "Hannah..." He exhaled. "I want you with every inch of my being."

Hannah exhaled too, and stepped closer until her nipples nearly touched his chest where hair curled in a light fur across scars that looked white in the waning light. "Do you know how old I am?" She tore her gaze from his body to look up into his face.

"Nay."

"I will be thirty years old next year," Hannah said. She blinked at the confession she rarely made. "I am a mature, adult woman with mature, adult needs."

She raised her hand out of the water to touch the smooth skin over her collarbone. She let water drip down into the valley between her breasts and then slowly followed it with her fingers before sliding the pad of a thumb over one tight bud at the center of her breast. "I can satisfy my own needs." Her hand slipped down below the water to the throbbing between her legs. The look on his face told her he was imagining the touch even if he couldn't see through the now dark water. "But I prefer..." With every bit of brashness she could muster, Hannah reached across the short distance for Erik's jack. "Thisssss."

She let the word hiss softly out between her teeth. Could she convince him she was already devoid of her maidenhood, so his honor didn't stand in her way?

He groaned, his eyes shutting, as she wrapped her fingers around the rigid length. She'd seen the picture in the tupping book, a woman pleasuring a man by sliding up and down, which was what she'd mimicked with the butter churn.

Erik's jack was as hard as the granite that made up this isle, standing tall, reaching for the surface. "Hannah," he said, his voice tortured as she moved. His hand found hers, stopping her.

"Nay," he said. "You cannot."

"Cannot?" The seduction evaporated from her voice, and she breathed evenly to bring it back. It was hard to think straight with her own body responding to his groans. "I can't pleasure myself or I can't convince you to help me find the pleasure that we can create together?"

He pulled her hand away from his jack, holding her fist in his large palm. "I can't touch you."

She slid her hands under her breasts, lifting them, pinching the nipples. "So, you can watch me touch myself, but you won't let yourself touch me?" Her breasts felt swollen as she plumped them, lifting onto tiptoe so that they fell above the waterline. "Why will you not help me find pleasure?" She stepped up to him so that he could easily grab her.

He stepped backward as if she were a wolf stalking her prey. Maybe she was.

"Am I not enough for you?" She raised the finger she'd touched herself with to gently touch his bottom lip.

Erik swallowed. "'Tis my mission to bring you to the dowager-queen untouched."

"Untouched?" she said, lifting her breasts in an obvious touching manner. "I am nearly thirty years old. Why would the dowager-queen think I'm untouched?" Hannah wouldn't lie outright about her virginity, but questions, said in the right tone, could lie for her. "Why would I place a fertility doll by the clootie well if I never…was never touched?"

They stood before each other in the calm water. The wind that tore across the treeless isle remained muted in the valley where the pond collected rainwater like a large cistern. Hannah fought off a shiver of cold born of the stillness as they stared at each other.

"I want you, Erik," she whispered. "Before I go to Kronborg court. I ask for pleasure before I must go there and feel pain."

He grabbed her shoulders, his large hands engulfing them, and looked hard into her face, his lips pulled back as if he snarled. "You will not know pain. I won't allow it." The words rolled out of him with the ferocity of a blood oath. They caught her breath, making her heart thump like a war drum.

What type of oath was he making? Her fingers caught the back of his neck, pulling his face closer.

CHAPTER TWELVE

"A girl who is much sought after should marry the man that she likes, and whom she thinks would be obedient to her, and capable of giving her pleasure."
KAMASUTRA, VATSYAYANA SECOND CENTURY AD

Hannah's lips fell open as Erik's met hers. The coolness of the water and air was forgotten with the heat unleashed within her. The throbbing below bubbled up like a pot boiling over.

Using the buoyancy of the water to her advantage, Hannah lifted her legs and clamped them around Erik's waist, bringing the crux against his abdomen as she kissed him back. The heat of her core rubbed against him underwater. Arms wrapped around his neck, she opened her mouth, her tongue tasting him, and she hoisted as if climbing him while their kiss continued unchecked and wild. She was desperate to hold on to him, desperate to save herself.

The rasping mews she made against his mouth seemed to urge him on, and he trailed his mouth down to her neck. Tingles shot along Hannah, under her skin, and she threw her head back, exposing her throat as if she didn't mind if he bit into her. He supported her back as she arched, and he lowered his mouth over one taut nipple. The heat and the pressure of his swirling tongue made her moan and rub her open crux against him. He was all man, hot, thick, almost violent in his need, and it brought the Valkyrie out in her, her nails scoring down his back.

Darkness draped them in shadows as they moved together in the pond. Naked skin rubbed against naked skin, the sensations bringing out a wild side of Hannah she didn't know existed. It should shock her, but it matched Erik's own wild response. The water lapped around them as they made waves on the calm surface.

Her hand dropped down into the water, reaching under her arse to find him. He groaned, and she lowered her legs so she slid gently down between him and his straining erection. It slid hot along the cleft between her legs as if searching for her heat. Using the water, she rose to his ear.

"You are thick and long," she whispered. "And I ache." She ground her pelvis against him.

He growled, gathering her to him so that his jack once more lay against his taut abdomen. He ravished her wicked mouth and carried her step by step through the water to the shore. She'd brought a blanket but wouldn't stop kissing him to tell him. He could find it by chance or take her in the wildflowers and grass for all she cared.

Arms wrapped completely around each other, Erik walked as if they were one being toward the shadow of the boulders. The blanket sunk into the grasses as he lowered Hannah to its softness. Erik grabbed one of his drying sheets, kneeled beside her, and wiped her limbs as she lay spread there in the darkness. Hannah raised her arms overhead, raking her fingers through her wet hair to make it disperse out around her like some shadowed sun. Her legs shifted and rubbed on the blanket, her legs spread, and her breasts sat perched, the nipples hard. One hand stroked her sensitive nub while the other cupped her breast. "Can you see me in the dark?"

"Aye. Utsøkt skjønnhet," he said with reverence. She didn't need to understand the words to know it was praise.

"I need your heat," she said.

Erik scooped up the second, folded blanket and snapped it open. He threw it over his shoulders like a long cape and slowly lowered over her. Their body heat was caught between them, the cloth hiding them from everything but the feel of each other.

"Bloody hell, I want ye," she said, her Scottish accent growing thicker. "Inside me."

He growled low, holding himself half over her, his forearms flanking her shoulders. Dipping his face, he inhaled along the skin between her breasts and moved his face up her collarbone and throat, kissing and nibbling as he went. Hannah's fingers shot through his hair as he reached her lips, holding his face to hers. She moved restlessly against him, her legs tangling with his.

For long moments, they explored with abandon, kissing and stroking each other. He cupped her breast, and she gasped when he teased her nipple, dipping his mouth to its hard peak. Sensation prickled like lightning, and she felt a deep, aching need as he stroked along her flared hip, grasping the bone for a moment as if he claimed it as his. And right then, it was.

His large hand slid down her loin inward to the mound between her parted legs. She groaned loudly as he touched her sensitive nub outside, rubbing it briskly until she panted, bending her knees. He dipped his finger between her legs like he had in the barn. Could he feel that she was intact? He'd already touched her there, so if he'd felt her maidenhead, there was no hiding she was a virgin.

He was a shadow above her. Even his outline was hidden by the blanket, but she could feel him staring down at her.

She reached for his jack, bringing the tip to her. "I want you inside me."

"I will bring you pleasure first," he said. His strong fingers dipped into her, and she moaned, riding against his hand.

She could feel her own wet heat. "But I ache."

He covered her mouth with his, swallowing her moans and words with kisses as he rubbed her most sensitive spot outside as he moved fingers inside.

Leaving her mouth, he kissed a trail to her ear. "I want to do something to you, but I'm afraid you'll wake the homestead with your cries." His voice sounded hoarse as if he strained against his need to fill her.

She reached down his body to stroke his hard jack. "I'll pretend I'm gagged."

His lips moved back to her ear. "I want to taste you."

She shivered at the wild promise in his tone. When he began to kiss a trail down her stomach, sliding under the blanket, the picture in the tupping book rolled through Hannah's mind. She stifled a moan at the thought and squirmed, the sound of her breath shallow and fast.

Hannah's knees fell wide. He looked up her naked

body as he moved downward, the blanket dragging back with him. The moon had risen somewhat, casting a cool glow. She watched him with hooded eyes, her lips parted, and he lowered his mouth between her parted thighs.

"Bloody hell," she murmured as he loved her there with his mouth and tongue. "Oh God." His hair brushed her inner thighs. She curled her fists in the blanket under her at the building tension inside. Her breaths increased with the rhythm his talented mouth created, until she gave a small cry against the hand she'd thrown over her lips. Jerking against him, she reached her pleasure, and he continued as she rode the waves.

"Erik, please," she whispered. She held her arms out to him as he stared down at her pale body, so open, so ready. Sliding his rock-hard, hot body along hers, he kissed her mouth as he propped himself over her. Her hands held his face, her thumb rubbing his damp lips. "One day I will do the same for you."

"Aye. But now…" he murmured, moving the head of his jack against the flooded heat below.

She smiled in the darkness, spreading her legs in an angle that welcomed him. She pulled her face to his. "Yes, bloody hell, yes." She wrapped her legs around his hips, thrusting herself higher to him.

Hannah had never been so wound with lust, even when she'd brought herself to pleasure.

He kissed her and moved to her ear. "Hold on, Hannah love," he murmured. With a nudge against her heat, he thrust inside. She gasped, and he stilled, fully embedded inside her body. Could he tell she'd been a virgin? She'd felt no pain, perhaps the tiniest of stings.

She thrust upward against him. "Please, Erik," she whispered, and he started moving. The feel of being completely impaled thrilled her. As he leaned in to kiss her, thrusting below, all her worry turned to ash. Now she could just enjoy.

Hannah clung to his shoulders, her body throbbing still with her first release, and words bubbled out of her, sliding wickedly from her tongue. "Oh yes," came from her lips on narrow exhales. "So full of you. Oh God. Yes."

Thrusting inside her, his body surrounded Hannah on all sides too. Muscular biceps propped from his elbows and forearms on both sides of her head, his undulating torso sliding in concert with hers. His hot breath tickled along her ear, his words rumbling from her ear straight to her core.

"Through the tightest of sheathes, I plunge through. Tell me, sweet Hannah, how you like my cod ramming deep inside you."

His words struck like lightning straight through her. Sliding back out, he thrust in fully, and she gasped, meeting him.

"Tell me," he whispered in her ear, grazing the skin along the rim with his strong teeth.

"Erik," she breathed. "Such wild pleasure. Yes, oh yes. Plunge deep." She struggled to keep the words to a whisper in the silent night air.

He groaned low with animalistic resonance, sending a chill teasing her fevered skin. This man was like a beast marking her as his, and she loved it. Reveled in the taking, in the full ravishing of her body and maybe her soul.

Her breathing matched their rhythm, increasing with her frantic moans. He reached between them to rub her outer nub as he continued to plunge into her hot core. She teetered on the brink of release. "Oh yes, Hannah, squeeze me tight with your pleasure."

Hannah's whole body felt like it was exploding and clenching at the same time, coming apart as the taut sensations shot through her. Back arching, she was about to call out when Erik's palm landed over her mouth. Her deep moan was muffled, but still the waves flooded through her. She squeezed her eyes shut, letting it carry her away.

"Leif's wife said Hannah was headed to the pond to bathe." The voice cut through the darkness above them on the ridge.

"Erik!" a second voice called, cracking through the night like a hammer.

Hannah's eyes flew open. In the light of the cloud-muted moon, she watched Erik's tight features harden, his mouth open with a silent yell. Her pelvis remained braced high, and he thrust in once more as he lost himself, spilling within her open body. She felt the swell and heat of it, their movements still fast but shallow.

"Erik? Hannah Sinclair? Are you out here?"

Erik stilled into a statue of granite over her and in her, but inside she felt his throbbing heat. *Filling me. Gifting me with a bairn?* She smiled in the darkness despite the danger of being discovered. What did she care if others knew she was no virgin?

Footsteps came down the hill toward the pond. They clung together, joined and throbbing while their bodies wrung the last bits of pleasure from their mating.

"If she drowned—"

The other man cut him off with brisk words said in their Norwegian language. The first man was surely Nial, who seemed to prefer English much of the time. The second sounded like Sten.

Erik didn't move off her but lifted slightly to allow her to breathe easier. There was no running away. Their only escape was to remain unnoticed in the deep shadows under the dark blanket she'd taken from the cottage. The two men continued to talk and call for them periodically as they tramped through the tall grass.

"Faen i helvete," Erik murmured the curse he favored as if to himself.

Hannah held her breath, the sound of her heart thumping in her ears. She could only see Erik's face before her as he hovered.

Stomp. Oomph! "Fy faen!" Sten yelled.

Hannah squeezed her eyes shut as Erik covered her completely with his body, protecting her from the flailing legs and arms as Sten tripped over them. The yelling warrior tumbled beside them in the tall grass.

Nial yelled too. "A body? By God! Where?"

"Here on the ground," Sten answered. "I fell over it."

Erik's curt retort overrode both their continued questions. "Hva pokker! Get off us!"

"Erik?" Sten asked.

"Us?" Nial yelled, and Erik cursed again. He remained covering Hannah. Thank God, it was dark. "Is Hannah with you?"

Sten found his feet again. "What the hell are you two doing here hiding in the…?" His words trailed off. "Fy faen!" he yelled, easily putting together the obvious conclusion. "Fy faen!" He rattled off a string of punctuated Norwegian.

"Get off her," Nial said, yanking back the top blanket. "By God, you're naked."

"Naked?" Sten said with a fair amount of despair. "Are you well, Lady Hannah?"

"What have you done?" Nial asked, dropping the cover. She wasn't sure which one of them he was asking.

Hannah felt Erik tense, but he wouldn't move away from her, covering her. She peeked out past Erik's shoulder to see the dark form of Nial's large head, the moon behind him. "I am quite well. I am wonderful, in fact."

Sten choked, coughing into a fist. The two men stood on either side of her and Erik, staring down at them lumped together under a woolen blanket, the edge hovering under Hannah's chin now since Erik kept lifting it higher on her.

"I can't bloody believe this," Nial said, anger punctuating his words. "Untouched, Erik. She's to be untouched."

"And you're bloody well touching all of her right now," Sten said, his voice rising. "Like...*all* of her!"

Hannah crossed her arms under the blanket at their rebuke. "I seduced him. He hadn't a chance of escape."

Sten choked, the noise somewhere between an angry grunt and laughter.

Erik slowly extricated himself, leaving her wrapped up. The sight of his taut arse and long, muscular legs in the moonlight sent tingles through her body. Lord, he made her wanton. Despite his naked-ness, he stood proud before his men. "Go on back to the homestead. I'll bring Hannah along in a bit."

"I will stay," Nial said, his arms crossed. Standing there in the moonlight fully dressed, he should look more imposing than a naked Erik. But the size and obvious sturdiness of Erik's muscular form and strong stance made him still the leader.

"I said go," Erik replied as if he were swathed in armor and fully armed.

Sten slapped Nial's arm. "'Tis not like he could make her less untouched." He pulled Nial's arm to get him following him uphill, and they trudged away in silence that felt heavy like an incoming storm.

Hannah sighed and let her gaze roam over the beautiful figure of her lover. Broad back straight, his spine leading up to shoulders thick with muscle from wielding his sword. His hair reached just past his nape and moved about his face as he turned back toward her, walking briskly to crouch beside her.

"Do you have a rag?" she asked, and he stood again, retrieving one from the lump that was his dis-carded clothing.

"Thank you," she said when he handed it to her. "I was warned about…the mess."

He exhaled and sat beside her on the blanket. "Hannah…" He searched her face. "You said you were not a virgin, but I'm now certain you were." His brows furrowed. "You lied."

Hannah's chest constricted, and she swallowed past the tightness in her throat. Was that guilt? Shame? Remorse for tricking him? "Think over the words I said. I never lied."

"Not with words, but with…everything else." He shook his head. "And I…released in you."

Despite what they'd shared, she felt suddenly shy and…villainous. She had used him for more than simple pleasure. She sat straight, feeling the slight discomfort of her nether regions pressed to the hard ground. "I want a child, and I want to go home. Seducing you might answer both my prayers."

"You tricked me," he said, the warmth in his voice icing over so much that she shivered.

Hannah pulled the blanket around her form, suddenly feeling more exposed than when she'd spread herself out on the blanket before him. "I…" *He abducted me. Took me from my clan and homeland.* She tilted her chin up as she wrapped her arms around her knees. "I am a Valkyrie, a warrior woman who must do whatever she can to battle for her own life and happiness. Surely, you of all people understand."

Erik stared at her mute. "Faen i helvete!" he yelled suddenly, making her jump. From her time with the Norwegians, she knew it was a terrible curse.

Hannah struggled to stand and wrapped the blanket around herself as she stared into his murderous features. "I am not the villain here, Erik Halverson. I am the victim, the one stolen away. I must do what I can to make myself less desired by your dowager-queen. If she wants a virgin, I am no use to her now. You might as well sail me home."

"You used my own lust against me." With a grunt, he turned away, striding to his clothes.

She followed after him. "I must use the weapons I have, Erik. Your attraction to me was the only one available." And it wasn't all about tricking him. The pleasure they'd shared had been completely real, but saying as much now... He wouldn't believe her.

Blanket wrapped around her tightly, Hannah hobbled on her tiptoes to catch up. "Why does Sophie want me untouched? Does she have someone there who wants to marry me if I'm a virgin?"

He didn't answer, throwing his tunic on instead.

"Erik?"

His head emerged through the hole. "A lady of pure reputation will be of better use to her," he said.

"Better use? For what?" Hannah pushed out of the blankets and strode through the cool night to grab up her own clothes next to him. "To marry a Danish aristocrat perhaps?" He didn't answer. "I don't want a husband from Sophie," she said, her words tart with anger. She let it well up inside her chest, filling the hollow that her guilt and embarrassment had chiseled away. "I want to return home, Erik, not be forced into marrying some stranger in a foreign land."

He turned to look straight at her. "So you... spread..." He stopped as if catching his wickedly damning tongue. Hannah was glad for the darkness because her cheeks flamed red. "And now your maidenhead is broken."

"I thought you'd been able to tell I was intact from our time in the barn at Girnigoe."

He ran a hand over his face. "This was a trick. You are a bloody siren."

She inhaled fully through her nose, walked up to him, and shoved her pointed finger into his chest with each word. "I remind you, Erik Halverson, that I had planned to...lie with you back at Girnigoe before I knew you to be a dishonorable abductor. I want a child. I wanted to experience the fiery pleasure between a man and a woman. And I wanted you. That is all." She dropped her hand. "However, I also want to be free."

After a moment of staring at each other, he looked down and yanked on his trousers. Hannah walked back to the boulders, stepping into her petticoats. She yanked them up with as much force and tied them over her smock, forgoing the stays, which she'd carry. Her hair was still damp and heavy, bringing a chill to her scalp.

"I cannot return you to your home," he said, shoving one foot into a boot. "I must complete my mission." His anger had dulled.

She found it easier to inhale and shoved her bare feet into her boots. "Your mission is no longer possible, since I am no longer the virgin bride."

"Fy faen." His hands raised to shoot his fingers through his tousled hair. He looked at her. "Even so, you must act the part of a virgin, Hannah. To Sophie at Kronborg."

"I will not," she snapped, hands propped on her hips.

"You must."

She stepped up to him, ignoring the pull of his large, warm body, and stared hard up into his shadowed face. "Then you, Erik Halverson, are the bloody villain, not me."

Erik looked heavenward. Was he praying for God to give Hannah back her virginity? Without lowering his gaze back to her, he drew in a large breath and spoke. "I have a sister named Iselin."

"Liar."

He dropped his gaze to her, his brows bent. "I do."

She raised one hand toward the ridge where the men had traipsed. "Nial said all your kin died from a great illness that swept your village. That you fight now for your sovereign, doing your duty. 'Tis the most important thing to you now." It was apparently more important than her.

The clouds moved, and the moon beat down on them like a cold sun. The silver glow made him look like a marble statue, strong yet sad. "'Tis true the illness wiped out my family, all of them, save one." He leveled a look at her. "Iselin is twenty years old now, old enough to marry." He swallowed, glancing away. "Two months ago, I was called home from the camps near the Sweden-Norway border where my Wolf Warriors patrol against those who continuously press into our territory. When I arrived at our cottage, I was told I must hasten to Denmark, to the court, that Iselin had been taken there."

He inhaled, turning toward the pond. His tunic hung untucked, and he stood there with the moon reflected across the water and the stillness of the breeze in the small valley. Erik emanated sadness.

It squelched Hannah's fury as thoroughly as water dumped over a candle. "Sophie has Iselin?" she asked, her words even, without emotion.

"Aye."

She walked over to stand next to Erik, both of them looking out at the water that had enveloped them a mere hour ago. "Why? And was she taken against her will?" Hannah asked.

"Aye. Sophie's soldiers abducted her. Took her to Denmark." He turned his face to her. "Unless I accomplish my mission, she will be married off to Peter Kaas, the chancellor, something Iselin says will push her to…take her own life."

Hannah's heart sank, and she pressed her palm over it. "You are trading me for Iselin." It wasn't a question, but she waited to see if he'd deny it.

He crossed his arms over his chest. "I was to confirm that you are indeed beloved by your brothers, so much so that they would heed the word of the dowager-queen of Denmark if she possessed you."

"Why does Sophie want to control a Scottish clan? Her daughter is the Scottish queen."

He looked at her again as if it were easier to talk about politics than his mission. "Sophie has heard from her daughter, Queen Anne, that the Four Horsemen are so strong they are likely to take over Scotia from her husband, King James. That she fears for her life, that of the king, and their kingdom. Sophie is convinced from her daughter's information that the Sinclair Clan and their mass of allies will start a civil war in Scotia. Although the council that acts for our young King Christian does not care so much, the dowager-queen loves her daughter beyond reason and has ordered that the Horsemen be brought to heel."

"She controls you through Iselin and plans to control my brothers through keeping me hostage in Denmark." Although Hannah's legs felt wobbly, she shook her head. "My brothers will not allow it."

"If they try to take you from Denmark, they will be killed," he said. "Either way, Sophie succeeds in bringing the Four Horsemen to heel."

"Who can kill my four fierce brothers?" But she

already knew the answer. Sophie meant for her Wolf Warriors to kill them. "You…" she whispered. "You're supposed to kill my brothers if they refuse to abandon me."

Erik tipped his face to the few stars that sparked brightly between the clouds. "Frode is betrothed to Iselin. He'll do anything to get her back."

As will you.

Hannah ran a hand down her cheek. *Daingead.* An innocent girl was imprisoned in Denmark. She was probably frantic with loneliness and fear, and prepared to take her own life, leaving Erik completely alone in the world.

Erik walked back to their blankets, gathering them while Hannah shrugged into her bodice. He waited until she tied her boots, and they climbed the hill to reach the ridge, both of them silent as if their fury had ebbed like a dissipated hurricane.

The ache between her legs reminded her of the delicious adventure they'd shared, but Nial's and Sten's anger had tainted her first experience with ultimate carnal pleasure. For the last three years, Hannah had been shaking off the shackles that had dragged her into a sad, lonely corner of life. And now she'd been forced into another type of prison. This time, however, she was determined to take her life and her deepest desires into her own hands.

CHAPTER THIRTEEN

"In Norse mythology Loki is the son of Laufey and the Jötunn Fárbauti and is Odin's blood brother. He is known as the God of Trickery and Mischief and The Father of Monsters.

He sired the vicious wolf Fenrir and the serpent Jörmungandr as well as Odin's eight-legged horse Sleipnir. He's also the father of the Goddess Hel who reigns over the realm of the dead."

LIFE IN NORWAY.NET

Crack! Erik yanked his fist back from Frode's face as the man flew backward onto his arse on the floor of the barn. "You think I don't love Iselin?" Erik said, his words low like a growl. "That I would turn my back on saving her?"

The early morning sun from the cracked door shone down on Frode lying flat on his back, legs spread, one hand to his eye. "You foked Hannah Sinclair."

Erik was going to rip the man's tongue from his mouth. "Shut your foking mouth, Frode Hansen, or I'll slice off that offensive tongue and feed it to swine."

Nial stepped before Erik as if to hold him back. "The accusation is true. He loves your sister, which makes his tongue unwise."

Erik rubbed his bruised knuckles. It added to the

still sore bite wound. He stepped around Nial, close enough that his shoulder knocked him with enough force to make him stagger back. "Hannah and I last night… What happened between us will not stop Iselin's release," Erik said, standing over Frode who pushed up to sitting.

"It has everything to do with it," Frode said, bending his knees. "Perhaps as the leader of the Wolf Warriors, your father was in truth Loki, since you're full of lies, and mischief taints your heart." Frode glared up at him.

"You did name your horse Loki," Sten said to Erik.

Frode continued. "You've failed our mission to bring an untouched Sinclair Horsemen sister to trade for Iselin. Untouched, Erik."

The man was a fool. Loki? Frode talked like a pagan of old.

"She lied to him and said she was already ruined," Sten said from somewhere behind.

Ruined was a horrid word. Hannah was certainly not ruined. In fact, she would probably have been jubilant if they hadn't fought. And she hadn't actually lied.

Erik met Frode's healthy eye, since the other one was swelling closed quickly. "We will say naught of… what went on between me and Hannah. Sophie will not know, and I will still trade her for Iselin."

"She will tell Sophie," Nial said, his face red and pinched. "'Twas Hannah's plan to destroy our mission in an attempt to go home. She will yell her ruination from the bloody rooftops."

"Maybe she's a mythical seductress or witch, and

you fell right into her trap," Sten said, shaking his head, and then leaped backward when Erik spun around toward him, his fist ready.

"Fighting among us will only weaken us," Nial said, rubbing the back of his neck.

"Then you three need to hold fast to your wild tongues and have trust in your leader," Erik said, his words like thunder cracking through the Jotunheimen mountain range. "I have never failed in a mission. I have led us through battle after battle without a single surrender or retreat."

"You certainly surrendered your clothes quickly enough," Frode mumbled, still on his arse.

Erik considered kicking him in the face but turned away. "I will talk with Hannah. We will save Iselin, and then perhaps there will be a way I can talk Sophie into letting me wed Hannah myself. She will stay in Denmark-Norway then." But he could still ensure her safety and comfort.

All three of them stared at Erik with mouths open like hooked trout. Nial recovered first. "You…will wed Hannah Sinclair?"

Erik caught the back of his neck and rubbed at the tension there. "If it will save her too." Lord, what was he thinking? He'd sworn off all future attachments that could be used against him like Iselin. Caring for someone made him vulnerable, and the pain of losing someone like he lost his family was too great a risk. Even before the plague had decimated his village, he'd never considered marrying anyone. And he surely hadn't considered that Hannah would forgive him enough to kiss him again. He was wrong about a number of things, it seemed.

Frode finally gave a series of small nods. Erik
threw his left, uninjured hand down for the man to
grasp, hauling Frode to his feet. "Offer that to her,"
Frode said. "Sophie won't exile us for not guarding
Hannah's virtue if she never learns what happened."

Nial shook his head. "I've never known you to de-
viate from a plan, Erik. And marriage…? Are you
certain you have no spell upon you?"

Erik snorted. "Even a mighty river deviates when
an obstacle falls in its middle. But…" He met the
gazes of his three loyal men, his three best friends. "I
will not sacrifice Iselin, and to think I would, insults
me."

Sten had enough shame to glance away.

"Whatever deviation you decide," Frode said, "it
better stop that old walrus Peter Kaas from wedding
Iselin."

"Neither Iselin nor Hannah will wed Kaas," Erik
said as if his words, cast into the world, made them
true. His three friends looked dubious. Erik crossed
his arms. "Hannah would assassinate him within a
fortnight of their wedding, and as much as the man is
a slovenly walrus, Denmark-Norway needs him as
chancellor."

"He might not take a woman who isn't a maid to
wife anyway," Nial said.

Erik didn't change his expression as his friends
stared at him. Had he considered that when he'd broken the shackles of restraint on himself last night?
The action would be considered treason to act against
Sophie's plan.

Erik was a man of control, full of intent, strong
and clever enough to stop an army of Swedes coming

across the border, but he'd lost all control last night. And what was worse, he wasn't furious over it. In fact, he'd woken with a lightness inside, a feeling he hadn't had since the sickness had spread through his family.

Nial sighed long. "What's done is done." He sniffed, resigned.

"Goddess or not, I bet it was bloody amazing," Sten said, his voice soft even though he spoke in Bokmål. There was a smile in his voice, but Erik turned hard eyes on him.

"I won't talk of such things," Erik said.

"She said it was…" Nial glanced up as if recalling the exact words. He spoke in a higher pitch. "'I am wonderful, in fact.' That's what she said."

"Wonderful?" Sten said, his face breaking into a teasing grin. "'Tis a fairly strong word." He moved his head side to side as if judging it.

Erik rolled his eyes and strode away. He knew the truth, and he wouldn't be goaded into sharing the experience with his men. Traipsing across the yard, the quiet made him frown. He'd defended himself after the sixth underhanded comment from Frode, and despite them being inside, the doors had been open. He'd at first worried that Hannah or the young girls would hear the small, personal battle and come running, but no one seemed about.

Erik rapped on the door to the cottage. Leif left early, walking Loinneil out of her stall to be watered at the trough outside. Perhaps he'd taken the horse with him to check the fields. Did Hannah like to sleep late? Surely, Elizabeth and Eydis would be up.

Slowly, the door opened, and Elizabeth met his gaze. At her wide eyes he said, "There's no trouble. I but wonder where Hannah...why the ladies and children are not about this morn. 'Tis so quiet."

"They departed two hours ago."

"Departed?"

She waved toward the barn. "Leif took the horse out for them."

Erik followed her gaze as if that might give him clues, but all he saw was the water trough. "He let them ride off? All three of them?"

"Four. Eydis went along." She smiled. "Lady Hannah's horse is strong, but it took some creative seating to get Trix and Libby sitting on top of Eydis and Hannah on the horse. And all of it quietly so they wouldn't wake you."

Unease sent gooseflesh up his arms, the short hairs at his nape standing on end. He looked back and forth between the barn where his friends were emerging and Elizabeth in the doorway. "Where did they go?"

"The docks."

• • •

Hannah climbed higher in the rigging. The boots Erik had provided did a fabulous job of keeping her feet on each rung. She grunted as she pushed into the topcastle attached around the mast that had survived the storm. From there, she could see the men working on the broken mast that Nial had been smoothing with the plane.

"Slightly right," she called across, holding her hands up to show that she meant for them to tip the heavy wooden arm to make it straight. Only one of

Erik's crew who'd remained with the ship spoke English and none spoke Gaelic, so using her hands was the easiest way to guide them.

"I want to climb up," Trix said from below.

"There's no room," Hannah answered. It was also dangerous being that high up and disconcerting with the slight swaying.

"You don't like heights," Libby said to Trix.

"I might like them if I'm ever given the chance to climb high, but you're always jumping before me."

The two girls squabbled for a full minute before dashing off to the rail when Erik's yelling in his native tongue filled the air. Hannah, holding onto the thin rim of the curved wall that surrounded her, looked over the edge.

Eydis glanced up. "He sounds angry but the type of angry my papa gets when he's worried."

"Hannah!" His voice preceded him onto the deck of his ship. He was dressed in his usual white tunic, trousers, and laced boots. He strode with purpose and strength, a warrior with just the right number of scars upon him to give his handsomeness a robust ruggedness. He was like a Norse god ready to throw thunderbolts. Delicious fire flared within her, but she hid it behind an apathetic glance down the mast.

Tipping his head back, he frowned at her. "What the pokker are you doing up there?"

"I will take your anger as a sign you were frightened I had turned your crew against you and absconded with your ship."

"I am never frightened," he said, "and you could never turn my crew against me nor sail this ship."

"Then why are you yelling?" she asked with wide

eyes and a slight shake of her head like she was some
simple lass who had no idea how to move her pieces
about on a chessboard. For her mission to counter
Erik's mission was most certainly a game of strategy.

He looked about, his hand sliding without thought
over the pommel of his sheathed sword.

"I worried Stewart's men could have taken you
four." He glanced back up. "What are you doing in
the topcastle?"

"Helping your men tie the mast on straight," she
called back and threw her arm out toward the soaring
main mast where the crewmen worked with silent ferocity. Hannah had lit a fire under them when she'd
woken them at dawn, demanding through gestures
and a few English phrases that they should get working. She had a mission now and wouldn't rest until she
saw it through.

"What are you doing out here at the docks?" Erik
asked.

"Ridiculous," she murmured. She wasn't going to
keep yelling back and forth for everyone to hear. So,
she moved her arms and mouth as if speaking but
didn't make a sound. It was something that Joshua did
to annoy her, especially while their father was still
alive, and she spoke very softly to remain unnoticed.
The gesture had the same irritating effect on Erik, his
face darkening with more ire.

"Come down from there."

She glanced back at the main mast, which was
straight. Her work was done up there anyway, and his
bluster certainly didn't worry her. She'd been raised
with yelling and raging around her. Anger was closer
to love than people thought. It was apathy, the numb

uncaring, that stood opposite of love and passion.

Hannah tucked her skirts against her legs to climb down through the hole in the forecastle and set her boot on the first rung.

"Slowly," Erik called up. "One foot at a time."

His order, barked with obvious annoyance, certainly wasn't uncaring. Hannah grinned as she curled her fingers around each rung on her way down. When her arse came level with Erik, he reached up to grasp her hips, pulling her from the narrow rope ladder.

Hannah was fairly tall for a woman, but she still had to stare upward to meet his eyes when he set her down. She kept a pleasant, neutral expression.

"What the bloody hell were you doing up there?" he asked.

"I already answered that." Her lips pinched in annoyance at his continued loud voice. "And I will say no more if you keep yelling."

He ran a hand up his forehead. "I'm not yelling," he said in a quieter voice. But then he threw his hand out toward the ladder and his voice rose again. "You could have fallen. 'Tis the smallest of rope ladders. Climbing it in skirts is foolish. Dangerous."

"I have excellent balance and grip, and the men were needed to hold the heavy mast in place. And if I hadn't gone up," she lowered her voice, "Libby or Trix would have."

"'Tis dangerous to walk the miles from Leif's home by your—"

"We rode Loinneil."

"Patrick Stewart's men could—"

"We killed the worst offenders, and the horrid man is off the isle."

She knew cutting into his statements was pricking his ire even more, and she wondered how far she'd have to go to make him curse, throw up his hands, and stomp away. If he was like Gideon or Cain, it would take a long time. Joshua would explode with a few more nudges, and Bàs would have already exited the confrontation without a word.

Brows furrowed, Erik seemed to be trying to loom over her. Tall people, like her brothers, utilized their height like a weapon. But a successful looming required the shorter person to fear, which she did not.

After a moment of silence, Erik began again. "There's no reason to come out here this earl—"

"We were up, and I wanted to get started. There's no time to lose."

He took hold of her shoulders as if he wanted to hold back her words. "Hannah…" He searched her face. "You want to sail from Shetland soon."

"At the next high tide if possible."

He shook his head and lowered his voice. "Do you think…? I can't take you back to Scotia, Hannah."

"I don't want to go back to mainland Scotland."

Erik stared at her, and Hannah studied his beautiful blue eyes. *If I have a child, I want him to have your eyes.*

"You don't…want to go back to Scotia?" he finally said.

"Not yet." She flattened her hand on his chest between them. "We have a mission to complete," she said, thumping him with each word.

"We?" he asked, his brows lowered.

She tilted her head slightly to one side as if he weren't keeping up. "Your sister, Iselin."

"Iselin?"

Hannah's fingers curled into his tunic, and she raised onto her toes to close the distance. She tried to ignore the heat radiating off his chest and the now familiar scent of him. She had a mission, and that required focus, which meant not giving in to this pull between them. At least not when there was work to do.

"Yes," she said. Her brows narrowed and her face hardened with determination. "'Tis time we go get her."

• • •

"And then she walked away?" Nial asked as Erik recounted the reason why Hannah was helping them fix the *Seieren* while it sat docked.

"Aye," Erik said. He watched Hannah smile and touch the arm of the elderly islander with whom she was negotiating the best price for their foodstuff. The gruff man seemed to melt a bit, nodding his gray head as they walked toward his cottage along the wharf.

"She will get the ogre to sell us his entire garden with that smile," Nial said. He turned back to Erik. "So now she *wants* to go to the Danish court?"

Erik nodded, watching the way the thin wool swayed with her steps. The woman was graceful with confidence, and shined in the face of conflict, especially with stubborn, irritated men. It must be from her upbringing with her brothers.

"I told her about Iselin, and she wants to help free her." Erik's gaze followed her through the gate in the stone wall around the man's garden. The blue

Norwegian costume hugged her waist and flared gently over her hips. The color made her blond hair look even more golden After her bath in the pond, it lay in wild curls all the way down her straight back.

"Does she realize she will be trading herself for your sister at the court?" Nial asked, also watching Hannah take the arm of the old man as he pointed to things in his garden. "And that her brothers will be killed if they try to retrieve her?"

Erik huffed through his nose. "I believe she has formed a different plan, one that will free Iselin without sacrificing her own freedom and her brothers' lives."

"Has she shared the details on how this miraculous plan will happen without us being killed or exiled?" Nial asked.

Frode crossed his arms with silent questioning.

"Aye," Sten said, standing with them. "Is that part of her plan? Because us not dying is an important detail that cannot be forgotten."

Hannah thanked the old man and pointed at the *Seieren*. He nodded back. His ruddy cheek reddened when she leaned in to place a kiss there among the bristles before turning to stride away, waving to him as she left. From the triumphant look on her lovely features, she'd accomplished her goal of obtaining food for the rest of the trip.

"I don't think she cares about our outcome," Frode murmured.

Nial snorted. "Maybe if Erik keeps bedding her—"

"And do it even better than merely wonderful," Sten added, his foolhardy grin showing he was poking the wolf to see if he still wanted to bite.

Nial nodded. "Then she will want to keep you, and thus us, alive and out of Kronborg's dungeons."

Hannah walked over to them. "With the mast fixed, we can launch at high tide now that we will have fresh vegetables to go with the smoked fish, bread, barrels of stream water, and ale."

Nial and Sten stared at her with blank expressions. Frode openly frowned. Erik's mouth relaxed with pride at all she'd accomplished once she'd set her mind to it. Perhaps he should have explained things from the start.

Nial cleared his throat. "Erik says you have a plan for getting Iselin out of the Danish court," Nial said. "Care to enlighten us?"

She glanced between them. "No."

Erik almost snorted. Hannah was not prone to positive responses. "Why not?" Nial asked.

"'Tis still coming together," she said, raising her hands overhead as if pulling ideas from the sky. "But we will have at least four days to reach Denmark to discuss onboard. If Dowager-Queen Sophie thinks you're waiting for my brothers to return from Orkney before luring them to her country, then we will arrive early. Joshua would agree the surprise will benefit us."

"Joshua?" Sten asked.

"The Horseman of War, my second brother," Hannah said, shaking her head. "Don't you even know who is hunting you now, to kill you? Kill you viciously?"

"I do," Sten said, defensiveness in his tone. "I don't think of them as having given names."

Hannah gave him a pitying look. "Even that villain whose head is rotting on a stake by Leif's barley field had a given name."

Sten mumbled something about it not being worth knowing their names. Hannah turned back to Erik. Her eyes were bright, and her cheeks flushed with exuberance. He could easily imagine her organizing a battalion.

"Denmark has a lengthy shoreline," she said. "Where were you planning to land, and how will my brothers know where to find me when they come to my rescue?"

"I left them a message," Erik said.

She stared at him a moment. "A message? Like… We have your sister. Come get her in the town of so-and-so?"

"Kronborg Castle," Nial said.

"It was pinned to your horse's stall," Erik said. "They are to land north of Copenhagen in Denmark. Iselin is being kept at Kronborg Castle in Helsingør with the dowager-queen and her chancellor."

Hannah frowned. "With our delay here on Shetland Isle, we might be late to my rescue."

"Then you will have to add rescuing your brothers to your mission," Sten said. He quirked an eyebrow at her.

Hannah frowned at Sten. "You remind me of Joshua, and not in a good way."

She looked back to Erik. "I need a map of where we will land with hills and valleys indicated. And other bodies of water besides the sea. And a layout of Kronborg."

Erik crossed his arms. "Is there anything else, Captain Sinclair?"

She smirked at him. "You're the captain." She

patted his crossed forearms. "I'm merely using the knowledge I've learned from all the schooling afforded my brothers in order to make this terrible mission into one that is successful to more than just Dowager-Queen Sophie."

"We were successful until last night," Nial murmured under his breath.

Erik cut him a severe look, but before he could see how Hannah took Nial's words, she turned in the direction of the ship when one of Erik's men yelled. "An army is coming."

His words were in Bokmål, but his pointing to the ridge could be understood by anyone. Hannah followed it. Riders were galloping toward them, riders bearing the Scottish flag and a nobleman's heraldic banner. Two of its quadrants showed the gold lion of Scotland on a field of red with a black slash through them. The black slash showed that, though related to the royal Stewart house, they were illegitimate. The other two quadrants showed a ship on a field of blue. 'Twas the symbol of Orkney Isle.

"Bloody hell," Hannah murmured. "'Tis Patrick Stewart."

CHAPTER FOURTEEN

"Patrick Stewart, 2nd Earl of Orkney lived from 1569 to 6 February 1615. The son of Robert Stewart, 1st Earl of Orkney, Patrick adopted his father›s tyrannical approach to governing the islands: though unlike his father he took his political maneuvering a step too far, losing his head in the process, and bringing to an end the short and brutal Stewart dynasty on Orkney and Shetland."
UNDISCOVERED SCOTLAND.ORG

Hannah's heart was already pounding from being so close to Erik, moving around him as if they hadn't shared the most exquisitely delicious experience of her life the night before. And that she hadn't tricked him into thinking her already devoid of her maidenhood, revealing she was nearly an old maid.

Now she'd confidently asserted she had some strategy that would win the day for them while not sacrificing Erik's sister, herself, or her brothers. What that strategy was, she didn't know. She was acting without having any clear path. If only Cain were there. His brain had been trained to calculate odds and devise unbeatable plans since he could move a chess piece on their father's board. Gideon, too, would know what to do to maneuver royal minds, since he did so with King James and the chiefs of their allied clans. But neither were there, and now she had Patrick Stewart riding toward them with twenty men.

"Don't tell Patrick Stewart who I am," Hannah whispered. "He might take me to control my brothers." She hmphed. "I hear that men employ the dishonorable tactic often."

Erik ignored her jab. "Take Eydis and the girls onto the ship."

Hannah glanced around for Trix and Libby but saw that Frode had already shooed them up the plank leading to the *Seieren's* deck, and Eydis was already aboard.

Hannah turned back to Erik. "Don't get killed," she said and walked away.

Erik called something Norwegian, which brought his additional six crewman off the ship. They were all armed with multiple daggers and swords. Their number would make it ten on the ground against twenty on horseback. Terrible odds for normal warriors. Her brothers would still be favored, but Hannah didn't know how well Erik's warriors could fight. "They are Wolf Warriors," she whispered to herself, hoping that meant something.

After the sixth Norwegian soldier trotted off the plank, Hannah strode quickly up it, wondering if she should struggle to pull the board away. But they wouldn't be able to sail the ship if the Norwegians were killed, and Patrick Stewart would easily find another board for his men to swarm up like ants drawn to honey. Hannah's stomach churned, and she scooped up Leif's bow and the quiver of repaired arrows.

"They're Scots," Libby said, pointing to the plaid wrap that half the soldiers wore. "But I don't trust them."

"Good instincts," Hannah said, and Libby's chin

lifted with the praise. "That's Patrick Stewart out front."

"The one with the floppy hat and pointy beard?" Trix asked.

"Yes." Hannah watched the man in his mid-thirties dressed in velvets and silk, sitting on a sleek bay horse. He was of medium height and build, and had dark, shifting eyes.

"They call him Black Patie," Eydis whispered. "Because his heart is black as wet coal."

Hannah would order the girls to hide, but they'd already been seen. "If Patrick's men make it past Erik, get away from them as best you can," Hannah said.

"We will climb up high into the topcastles," Trix said.

Hannah didn't tell her that Patrick would send his men up the poles to carry them down. "Go find as many weapons onboard ship as you can," she said instead. "Eydis can shoot, too, if you find another bow."

Trix and Libby ran off with their important mission. Eydis stood next to Hannah, trembling slightly, but the girl didn't run off to hide. Hannah nocked an arrow, one she quickly inspected to make sure the feathers were attached. She kept it down by her side, partially hidden by the gunwale.

"Who are ye, causing mischief on my isle?" Patrick called.

"I am Erik Halverson on a mission from King Christian of Denmark. Our ship was blown off course in the storm four nights ago. We will depart after I am certain the Pedersen family, who sheltered us, is treated well here on this isle." He indicated the heraldic crest. "Earl Patrick Stewart."

"Six of my men went missing after visiting that homestead," Patrick said.

"They attacked a farmer, setting his barn ablaze. One had attacked the daughter, a mere child, with carnal intent," Erik said. Hannah squeezed Eydis's hand where it curled around the rail.

"The farmer didn't pay his taxes, and the daughter is a whore." Patrick's face took on a red complexion that showed his well-known bad temper. The men beside him held the same frown. Hannah's heart sped as their gazes shifted beyond Erik and his men to land on her and Eydis on the ship.

"I'll drown myself before I let them take me," Eydis whispered next to her.

Hannah wasn't sure what her choice would be. She'd been taught that where there was life there was hope, but she hadn't been assaulted like this young woman. "Kill as many as you can first," Hannah whispered back.

Her words seemed to make Eydis stand straighter. "From your lips to God's ears to my hands," she whispered.

Breathing heavily, Libby and Trix came running back on the deck. They carried three bows and more arrows, dropping them at Hannah's feet. "There are swords too," Trix said.

Libby plopped down on a crate, her hand to her heart in a dramatic gesture of exhaustion. "But they were heavy, and we thought you could do more damage with arrows."

Eydis quickly picked a bow up and nocked an arrow. "We can pluck them off one by one if they come up the plank."

"Or even along the waterfront," Trix said.

Erik slowly drew his sword, apparently deciding there was no negotiating with a liar. The heat of anger on behalf of Eydis and her family, on behalf of many Shetland natives up through the string of northern isles, grew inside Hannah. If Patrick Stewart wanted war today, she would add her skill to Erik's Wolf Warriors. She lifted her arrow, pointing at the man next to Patrick who leered their way.

"Your men attacked innocent people for their own gains. So their bodies are being feasted on by sharks and eels now."

"Except for one head," Hannah yelled out. "Which stands guard against other cruel, lying uilebheistean."

"Monsters for certain," Trix said, picking up a bow that was as big as her.

Patrick's gaze shifted to Hannah, and he narrowed his eyes. "She's Scots, a Highlander. We'll take her too."

"And I will shoot this arrow straight through your eye, Black Patie, traitor to King James along with your bastard father, Robert Stewart," Hannah said with words so forceful she imagined them as arrows. Words, and the way they were spoken, could weaken an enemy before the first sword strike. If they survived the day, she'd order the Wolf Warriors to come up with something to say like her brothers reciting the Horsemen part of Revelations from the bible.

Patrick chuckled. "Feisty wench. I'll bring ye to heel."

"And I'll cut your floppy cod off and shove it down your screaming throat," Hannah called back with cold, calm words that seemed to spread across the group of men like a wave of wide eyes and some grins. Joshua would be proud, although when he threw out grotesque threats, no one grinned. Gideon would shake his head, but no one found his threats humorous. Bloody hell, she missed her brothers. And if she died out here, they'd never know what had become of her.

Libby came up alongside her. "Look how worried they are."

"You're definitely a sister of The Horsemen," Trix added with a sharp nod. "Tell them you'll…shred their hearts with your sgian dubh."

"No," Libby said, "your fingernails."

But Hannah was listening to Erik's cold words. "I understand that you, Earl Patrick Stewart, are a wanted man in Scotia. That you and your father are ordered to Edinburgh to stand trial for treason against your king."

Patrick narrowed his eyes. "Keep to your own politics, Dane."

"We're Norwegian," Nial said. "Wolf Warriors for our king and dowager-queen in Denmark."

At the name Wolf Warriors, faces of several of Patrick's men snapped to Erik and the three other men on either side of him. They apparently had heard of them, and their sudden mutinous uncertainty showed clearly in their faces.

"The Wolf Warriors will shred your hearts," Hannah said slowly, her voice strong but even. Her hard stare without moving made it look like a fact rather than some fantastical exaggeration.

"With their fingernails," Libby whispered, but Hannah didn't add it.

"I don't answer to Wolf Warriors," Patrick said,

ignoring her. The man next to Patrick said something that sounded more guttural, like he spoke in Gaelic, but Hannah couldn't hear the words.

Patrick's face was sharp with hatred, and he met Erik's gaze directly. "You and your women are fortunate I feel lenient today. Be gone at the high tide, and I won't persecute you for the slaughter of six of my good men, though I will be charging you with the crime and reporting it to my king."

Eydis released a breath of relief next to Hannah.

"Would that be King James or your father?" Erik asked. His tone showed plainly he didn't appreciate Patrick's leniency.

"It's like he wants to fight," Libby murmured.

"Cain Sinclair wouldn't back down," Trix pointed out. "Even if he were outnumbered."

"Frode won't let them get to us anyway," Libby said, shrugging.

"Neither will Sten," Trix added with every confidence.

Eydis glanced at Hannah, and she wished her eyes reflected the assurance that the girls had.

"Maybe we should pull the plank in." Libby looked to Hannah.

She nodded, and the little girls ran to the board. They grunted as they struggled to slide it from the dock. Trix was nearly launched into the air as the weight of the board, freed from the dock, pulled it down toward the water. Eydis ran over, catching the end and the three pulled it onto the deck.

It was comical, but not a single chuckle came from the tense group behind Patrick. And Hannah certainly didn't find it humorous knowing people were destined to die today. But she would do anything to make certain it wasn't the three girls on deck with her.

"Sail away now, Norwegian," Patrick said, "or die. 'Tis your choice."

Erik said something to his men in their language. He didn't keep his voice down, but Hannah didn't understand it. Eydis gasped, and two of Patrick's men quietly turned their horses around and walked away as if back to Scalloway, causing the men around them to murmur. One called after them, but they continued, picking up speed as they fled.

"What's that?" Patrick demanded. "Speak in English, barbarian."

"To show support for our dowager-queen's daughter, Queen Anne, now of Scotland, I arrest you, Patrick Stewart, for your crimes against your people and your treason against your sovereign." Erik took two steps closer to the man on horseback. "You are coming with us."

Erik stared up at the finely dressed aristocrat. Dowager-Queen Sophie would like the Scot's horse, too, but he hadn't brought food for more than Hannah's horse.

Patrick's lip curled back like a dog about to attack. "Ye are a foking idiot, Halverson," the rotten Earl said. "I rule this isle and will control Orkney soon enough. Ye're outnumbered, and I've run out of patience." He drew his sword as if to strike Erik from his seat. It was all Erik and his men needed to signal the start of a battle.

Erik knew that a man wielding a long sword on horseback was unbalanced. Unless he practiced and honed his skill, he was easily toppled. With one yank

and lift of the man's boot out of his stirrup, Patrick
Stewart flew over the far side of his horse, knocking
against the seated man next to him before thudding
to the ground in a tangled heap with the horses' legs.
His horse sidestepped away as his master's sword clattered on the worn flagstones built into the edge of the
meadow.

Without waiting, Erik's men flew into action.
Using their steel-plated shields, his six crew ran
among the men on horseback.

"Slå hjertet!" Erik's men yelled their battle cry as
they used their shields to protect their heads while
slashing the legs of Patrick's men. They snarled and
showed their teeth. Erik hadn't brought his wolf's
hood off the ship, but Wolf Warriors didn't need the
skin of their spirit animal to attack with the vicious
strength and cunning of the magnificent animal.

Many of Patrick's men wore the Highland wraps,
leaving their legs devoid of any protection, not that a
pair of breeches would sufficiently defend against the
slash of a honed sword. Some of Stewart's men
screamed, wheeling their horses around.

Nial rotated his sword in the air in the figure eight
pattern they practiced, but he wouldn't run into the
fray like that. There would be no loss of equine life if
they could help it. Noble beasts who had no control
over who feeds and houses them were to be protected
if possible.

Frode and Sten ran in low, yanking men off horses.
Those who chose to fight them lost quickly while a
few retreated. The numbers were changing in Erik's
favor quicker than he'd anticipated.

Patrick yelled something in Gaelic to two large

men, and they dodged toward the cottage housing the old man with the vegetable garden. Erik must keep his focus on the leader, though. Capturing a man was trickier than killing him. Erik sheathed his sword and stepped toward Patrick. The man struck, and Erik easily deflected it with his shield. The foolish Scot didn't seem to carry any defensive weapons. Erik shoved his steel shield into Patrick, throwing the man off-balance with the force. He fell to the ground where he cursed wildly, trying to avoid the hooves of the confused, prancing horses.

As if flying, Frode ran past Erik toward the ship, his arms pumping. "Go to Hell!" Frode yelled in Norse as he swung at one of the two men who were trying to board their ship. The other one crouched to grab the underside of a mast beside the cottage wall, the one the old man had tried to sell them. Even though it was too short for the *Seieren*, it was long enough to replace the plank the wee girls had yanked onboard.

Patrick rolled, leaping up to raise his sword again, making Erik draw his own. The old grumpy fellow with the garden ran out of his cottage, yelling at Patrick's man to drop the mast. But the soldier picked it up as if it were a caber at the Sinclair's Harvest Festival to drop it across the space between dock and ship.

Erik deflected several two-handed strikes from Patrick, unable to aid Frode in stopping the Scotsman. The wooden mast fell across. *Crack!* It hit perfectly.

"Ye're going to break it, ye oaf!" the old man yelled and threw a turnip at the man.

Two more of Patrick's men ran past to reach the ship, shoving the old man out of the way.

Thwack! Erik glanced up to see the one who'd

dropped the mast fall from it into the water. He couldn't see the bastard, but from the look on Hannah's face, Erik guessed he had an arrow sticking out of his chest. Hannah quickly nocked another arrow beside Eydis, her gaze following the two who now attacked Frode. The girls were trying to dislodge the mast while the old man yelled at them not to drop it in the water.

Erik parried another clumsy thrust of Patrick's. "I'd have thought you were a better fighter, Stewart," Erik called as he shoved the man back. "Having survived the Horseman of War's wish to see you dead." He'd heard the legendary tale from the Sinclair men at Girnigoe.

At the name of the Sinclair, Patrick's red, angry face drained of color, leaving him ashen. He tried to strike again, but it seemed he barely had the strength to lift his sword. Had merely the name of the Horseman frightened the man?

Patrick backed off, sucking in large draughts of air. His chest rose and fell as if he wished to collapse into a seat and order a bracing cup of whisky. "Did he send ye then? Sinclair? Joshua Sinclair? Send ye here to Shetland for me?"

The thought seemed to scare the piss out of him. More so than the fact he was face-to-face with and fighting the leader of Norway's Wolf Warriors. Erik frowned.

"He was dead, ye know," Patrick said. "I watched him be buried in the foking ground." The genuine fear in Patrick's face surprised Erik.

"Did you run away to Shetland when you saw him return to Orkney, Stewart?" Erik asked. "Did you abandon your father to The Horseman of War come back to life and sail away to hide here in your tower, abusing the populace?"

Patrick didn't answer. Behind him, Frode sliced through one attacker and Hannah shot the other. The girls cheered at the rail while the old man tried to drag his mast back. Before he could dump it in the sea himself, Frode lifted it to carry back to his cottage, the old man following behind.

Sten, Nial, and the *Seieren's* crew had killed or routed the rest of Patrick's little army. Erik sheathed his sword and used his shield to knock Patrick's aside, leaving the man open to a deadly strike. Erik grabbed the man by the neck, squeezing enough to make it impossible for him to talk.

"You are my prisoner now, and your people are set free," Erik said and grabbed the man's arm, dragging him toward the ship.

Nial mopped his sweaty face. "What do we have here?" He took hold of Patrick so Erik could find a rope along the dock.

Erik wrenched Patrick's hands behind his back, tying them together. "We have a gift for Dowager-Queen Sophie to give to her daughter, Anne, Queen of Scotland."

He glanced toward his ship, his gaze meeting Hannah's. Relief was in her eyes as she hugged Trix and Libby to her, but there was unease there, too, because she knew what Erik must admit to himself.

A gift of Patrick Stewart wouldn't replace the sister of the Sinclair Horsemen.

CHAPTER FIFTEEN

"When a man and a woman support themselves on each other's bodies, or on a wall, or pillar, and thus while standing engage in congress, it is called the 'supported congress.'

In the same way can be carried on the congress of a dog, the congress of a goat, the congress of a deer, the forcible mounting of an ass, the congress of a cat, the jump of a tiger, the pressing of an elephant, the rubbing of a boar, and the mounting of a horse. And in all these cases the characteristics of these different animals should be manifested by acting like them."

KAMASUTRA, VATSYAYANA, SECOND CENTURY

Hannah stroked along Loinneil's long neck. "'Tis not my favorite way to travel either," she said to the horse who'd had to be lured onto the ship with half the turnips she'd bought from the elderly man, Sven.

He'd let them borrow his wagon to carry the five dead out of his yard to Scalloway Tower, or rather he'd ordered them to carry the dead away, not wanting them in his side yard.

"We should be across in three days," she said to the horse as if Loinneil understood time. She nickered and lowered her muzzle to drink from the freshwater trough.

"She's well?" Erik's voice made Hannah's heart jump, and she turned to the low stall door to see him standing there.

"With all those turnips and the swaying ship, I expect it will smell pretty rank down here before too long, but yes, she seems well enough."

He nodded, his longish hair falling forward to brush one broad shoulder. How could such a simple movement cause her to warm? She remembered the feel of that soft, full mane skimming her stomach and inner thighs as he'd dove lower. The memory would stay with her always. She felt a flush infuse her cheeks.

He stared at her and raised one arm to brace himself easily on the low ceiling against the ship's movement. His biceps swelled with the easy effort, straining against the white sleeve of his tunic. "Patrick Stewart is confined to a closet with a small open window high above to allow light and air, but closed off enough that we don't have to hear his constant tirade."

"What will you do with him?"

"At the very least give him to Peter Kaas to hand over to King James. But your brothers would probably like to take him to King James themselves."

"You won't try to persuade Sophie with him then?"

Erik shook his head. "Unfortunately, he's not a big enough prize that Sophie would trade him for Iselin. Sophie wants your brothers under her control."

Silence stretched as the ship creaked around them. Hannah's heart layered a thudded rhythm over it at his continued stare, pinning her in the dark hull. They hadn't been alone since the meadow, and there was little privacy on a ship, especially when all females were sleeping together in the captain's room. "Do you…" She hesitated. "Do you want me for something? Come to fetch me for the girls?"

After his accusations about her lies and trickery in the meadow, accusations that were sadly true, she'd wondered if he'd talk alone with her again.

His lips moved, sliding against each other as if they were dry, and he dropped his arm, keeping himself steady with braced legs. "Frode and Sten are making valiant nursemaids, answering their thousands of questions about sea travel, and Nial and Libby have bonded somewhat over their queasy stomachs."

Hannah tilted her head. "So, I am not needed above?"

He shook his head. Good lord, he was brawny with his sculpted form and roguish look. She'd accused him of being a villain in this epic story. Since her temper had cooled, she'd seen how he could think the same about her. "We will free Iselin," she said at last.

"Have you devised your plan yet? One where everyone wins?" He crossed his arms, his hands tucking into his armpits. "My men…Nial especially, doesn't believe 'tis possible."

Hannah crossed her arms, too. "Earlier this summer before Gideon left to Orkney, he spent some time educating us about the powers that might affect Scotland. At the time, he said that King Christian's mother had little to no power in the Denmark-Norway government, that the regents for her son had forced her out of control."

His brows lowered. "Sophie has much pull, behind the scenes."

"Her daughter, Anne, confirmed that she did not when we asked."

"You've spoken with her daughter?"

"Yes. She came to visit us at Girnigoe and Varrich Castle. She's the patroness of our orphanage and contributes to our school." Hannah washed her hands with a bit of the fresh water and sliver of soap left in the corner of the hull where the single horse stall was situated among supplies.

"The dowager-queen may not understand the extent of her daughter's friendship with the Sinclairs," he said, and she could feel his gaze following her.

Drying her hands on the apron that was part of the Norwegian costume, Hannah turned to him. "I plan to enlighten her."

"It may be too late for words," Erik said. "She has recalled my army from the Swedish border to await your arrival and guard our shores from the Four Horsemen who will follow."

"We will get there first," she said with false confidence.

Hannah walked over to stand directly in front of Erik. He looked down into her eyes and seemed to look deep within her, something no one ever did. She was the Horsemen's sister, untouchable. To look so closely at her would show interest, an interest that was hardly allowed. But Erik Halverson was not someone her brothers could scare off.

His eyes looked dark in the low light of a single lantern and the bit of muted daylight through the portholes. "Your men would listen to the leader of the Wolf Warriors if he told them to stand down long enough to listen to reason. They would pause if you ordered them to."

"'Twould be best for your brothers to surrender

when they reach our shore," Erik said.

She shook her head. "The Four Horsemen do not surrender. Perhaps you should tell my brothers you surrender to stop them from running off their ships to cut a swath through your men to reach me."

Erik sniffed a little laugh, his sensuous mouth relaxing in a half grin. "I don't surrender either. 'Twould go against everything I believe in."

"What do you believe in?"

"Saving my family," he said, his voice serious. "And Iselin is the only family I have left."

"But you won't concede to save her?"

"How would yielding to your brothers save her? Surrendering when they have but a hundred men and I have two thousand waiting, armed and ready?"

She rolled her eyes, breaking the intense stare between them. "'Twould just be a farce to get them to pause to see reason." She sighed long. "Remember what I said back at the festival? Sometimes, pulling back is the only way to move forward." Why were warriors so pigheaded?

"If I show weakness, your brothers will gnash at my throat."

She shook her head. "Gideon and Cain will listen. Bàs is probably quietly livid over you stealing me out from under his watch." She could imagine her youngest brother swinging his ax about while wearing his hideous skull mask. "And Joshua is deadly and barely controllable most of the time." Especially if Kára wasn't with him to remind him to be more than a dangerous pain in the arse.

Hannah let out a long, hefty sigh. "But if we can talk with the other two without you ending up having a sword or ax through the skull, we can make this work. Horsemen and Wolf Warriors working together to fix this...misunderstanding between mother and daughter. For that's what this is, a misunderstanding that might lead to war between Scotland and Denmark, something I'm certain Sophie does not want."

Erik rubbed a hand behind his neck. "Her chancellor, Peter Kaas, has had confirmation from his envoys to Edinburgh that King James worries about the strength of the Sinclairs. He supports Sophie." Erik looked up at the low ceiling. "'Tis who...Iselin is supposed to marry if I fail to bring you to court."

"Peter Kaas," she murmured. "Is he horrible?"

Erik face tightened. "Nay. He is mild, at least in public. Soft and round in build, balding, and has an easy smile. He works hard to help our country, but he's easily swayed by Sophie. Iselin would never consider him."

"And she's betrothed to Frode."

Erik nodded slowly. "Aye."

"And she wants to wed Frode."

"Aye."

"Well then," Hannah said, "marrying Peter Kaas won't do. We will rescue Iselin and stop this ridiculous war, and once everyone talks and understands that we aren't planning to take over Scotland, you and your men won't be exiled or executed or anything you fear."

"I don't fear anything."

She laughed, letting some mocking into the sound. "You sound very much like my brothers. But even though they don't like to talk about it, each of them has realized fear." She touched his sleeve, rubbing it lightly between her thumb and finger. "It means there's something precious to lose, someone."

He looked down at her fingers. "I have already lost everyone except my sister, and I will do anything to save her from being forced to wed Kaas. I will not lose her too."

Hannah dropped her hand and stepped back. "Of course, you will do anything to save her." The man was a sculpture of cold marble.

Her voice was even. "Since you have no attachments except for her, once you give her into the safekeeping of Frode, you will never know fear. How fortunate for you."

Her teeth clenched, and it took a moment for them to relax. "But you won't win against my brothers." She thought of them with their wives and children and shook her head. "You love but one, your sister. They love many, and the accompanying fear has been honed with bravery, determination, and practiced skill to protect. 'Tis made them unstoppable. Without that passion, you, Erik Halverson, are at a disadvantage."

Wishing to leave with the last word, Hannah traipsed across the short distance toward the ladder that would lead her aloft. As she slid by Erik in the cramped quarters, his arm shot out to brace against her chest so she couldn't continue. "Hannah." The block was solid, not threatening. If she'd tried to duck or dodge, she knew he'd let her, but she didn't.

He gently pulled her around toward him with his arm. The look on his face was tortured, and she wanted nothing more than to lay her palm against it.

But she kept her clasped fists lowered and her face a mask of indifference.

"I am not a heartless monster," he said, his flinty voice quiet. "I promised Iselin I would do what must be done to rescue her. And that meant finding the weakness in the Horsemen of Scotia."

"And that weakness is me."

"We heard from the villagers and your brothers' wives how important you are to your family. When Bàs returned and confirmed it, and the opportunity presented itself, we had to act."

"Your dowager-queen plays with fire," she said. "If I die at the hands of Denmark, the Four Horsemen will rage war on Sophie and your government no matter what our king orders," Hannah said, drawing closer so Erik could see the conviction in her shadowed features. "Sophie will bring war to her daughter's country as well as her own."

Erik's hands landed on her shoulders. "Your plan will prevent war when you convince Sophie of your friendship with her daughter. She must see reason when you explain the civil war that your abduction will incite."

Hannah met his dark eyes. "And if I am with child…" She kept a strong gaze. "My brothers will assume the worst and rampage against you." She shook her head. "My initial plan back on Girnigoe included you being gone when it became known I was with child. So my brothers couldn't kill you."

He reached up to tuck a strand of her hair behind an ear. "You truly want a babe, even on your own."

She clutched his tunic in her fist, her fingers curling tightly. "I did not lie about my age, Erik. The older

I get, the more dangerous it will be for me to carry a child. I want one now, and you were my chance. You still are." Her voice was low, a mere vibration that matched the thrumming through her body.

Was it the graze of his thumb on her cheek or his nearness that sent warm honey through her veins? Maybe he drew her because he talked and listened to her. As much as she loved her brothers, they still treated her like a newborn kitten who couldn't handle the pressure of life. But not Erik. He'd realized quickly she wasn't easily broken, that she wouldn't cower.

She stepped closer until she was right up against him. Her body called to his, her very womb tightening with desire. "You are my chance to conceive a child, something I yearn for. And not only to save me from wedding some Danish aristocrat. I want a child with your bright blue eyes and strength." Her brows pinched with feeling and absolute sincerity. "I want my son or daughter to be strong, brave, and…" She swallowed. "Honorable, like their father." Had she said too much of what was in her heart?

She had no time to consider it, because Erik pulled her in to him, his mouth coming down on hers, and, as if the invisible ropes he'd tied around himself since their night together had been severed, he enveloped her.

His familiar scent filled her nose, and she slid her mouth against his, tasting and feeling the wildness of his need for her. She let her own desires answer and clung to Erik in near desperation. Her fingers curled into his tunic and then rose to cup his bristled face. His hands found her face, too, their bodies pressed against each other, and they gave and took and loved each other with their kiss.

Hannah could feel the hardness of his jack through her petticoats, and it broke through the dam on her own heat. Lord, how she wanted him, needed him, if only for this short time they had. Because once they reached Denmark, everything might end.

Her hands slid down his body to his jack, rubbing against it. He spoke in his native tongue, the deep tenor vibrating against her exposed throat where he kissed. The deep desire in his words coursed from her flesh directly down between her weakened legs.

Beside them, her mare thumped the floor of her stall, her bucket rattling. Hannah stiffened. "I can't beside Loinneil," she whispered.

Erik raised his head and kissed her parted lips. Growling low, he lifted her under her arse and walked them to the back of the hull into the deep shadows where crates of wool and barrels of fresh water were stacked.

Without words, only breathing and the sound of their mouths moving over lips and skin, their hands explored and teased. Wet heat spread throughout Hannah, and when Erik's fingers found her under her rucked-up petticoats, he muttered words at the evidence of her desire. The reverence in them sent tingles through Hannah.

She turned in Erik's arms to face the wall, keeping her skirts bunched up around her waist. Perhaps he'd seen the book before or this warrior was well versed in tupping, but he knew exactly what she wanted. Breasts now bared above her stays, his hand cupped one, teasing her nipple with his fingers. The other hand guided his hard length down the cleft of her arse, and she arched back. His mouth found her neck, kissing it as his granite jack found her parted legs where the ache was quickly becoming unbearable.

"Erik, yes."

As if waiting for her words, he thrust into her, and her breath caught. Head thrown back, she could barely support her weight as he began a rhythm that she knew beyond a doubt would send her into erotic oblivion.

CHAPTER SIXTEEN

"The Viking war cry was an essential part of the Viking warrior's arsenal. It was a battle cry that was designed to strike fear into the hearts of their enemies, and it was often accompanied by the beating of drums, blowing of horns, and other loud and intimidating sounds. The war cry was used to rally the Vikings and boost their morale, as well as to intimidate and demoralize their enemies."

MODERNMAN.COM

Erik had lost his mind. Again.

His arm wrapped around Hannah's middle while she faced the hull's wall, her skirts bunched up and his breeches undone to give his cod its randy freedom. Her sweet breast rested in his free hand. He cupped and teased her nipple until she quivered. Their passion had taken them like a storm, and there had been nothing to do but hold on and ride it out until they both peaked and their passion ebbed like a retreating tide.

Erik liked to think of himself as restrained, careful with strategy, and disciplined. But nothing about his passion for Hannah Sinclair followed any of his better characteristics. With her, a need to touch her, to bury his face in her hair and his cod in her slick heat, took over everything.

She leaned forward, her hands flat against the wooden hull, and he slid one hand past the layers of petticoat to the place of their joining. She gasped as he brushed against her hidden nub, so sensitive and waiting for some attention. He rubbed across it rapidly, listening to her breathing grow raspy and shallow. Caught between wanting to arch backward into him and forward against the friction of his fingers, Hannah stood helpless while he took his pleasure and teased out her own.

Erik's mouth fell onto the bared skin at the base of her neck, kissing and sucking upon it. She moaned and thrust toward his fingers in front and then back against his pelvis, and he found the rhythm to match the movement. Faster and harder, they plunged together, the heat and friction raising the intensity until her gasp fell over into a moan. The clenching around him pulled him over the edge into his own release, and he buried his face in the back of her hair, inhaling like a bull in a rose patch.

His arm wrapped around her middle to hold her against him as he curved over her back. Their rhythm slowed into long, languid ins and outs, and he kissed the delicate skin on the side of her slender neck, marveling in its softness. "Smoother than the costliest silk," he murmured.

He pulled a rag from his belt, pressing it into her hand.

"Thank you," she whispered, and he stepped back, allowing her to drop her petticoats. Her breasts were still perched on top, looking luscious, and he had the need to suck on them.

He moved forward, kissing her lips. "We should put those away before I ravish you again." Her smile made his chest open, and he felt lighter in the glow of it.

"Another ravishment?" Her brows rose with her teasing voice. "Perhaps there is time for that now." She plumped her hands under her breasts, and Erik felt his cod twitch.

Nial might opine that she was merely using him for his seed to get out of wedding a man at the Danish court. *But she wants her child to have my eyes.* The thought made him step up to her, bending to kiss her lips gently.

A noise in the corner made him pivot, but then he remembered her horse tethered in the one stall that he'd had built for his own horse, which he'd left this time in Norway. Hannah's mare tossed its head and nickered.

Someone cleared their throat. "All done down here?" came a voice speaking Bokmål.

Erik spun around to see Nial's head poked through the hatch as if he bent double to peer down before climbing.

"By the devil, Nial," Erik swore and turned back to Hannah. She'd already tugged her bodice back into place. Her hair was askew, but everyone's hair was misshapen when sailing. The wind tangled knots and sucked out pins.

Nial held a lantern and jumped down the last two rungs, landing with a thump. He turned, a wry grin on his mouth. "There are no secrets on a ship, Erik. You know that."

"We were talking," Erik said, which was only a half lie, since they *had* exchanged words. Wicked words.

Erik glanced at Hannah, who now held a horse's brush. "And grooming my horse," she said, holding it up. Her face was innocent enough, but her petticoats held deep wrinkles from being rucked up around her waist, pressed between them with vigor and heat. *Faen.* Just the thought made him long for her nipples.

"Well, you can thank me for keeping the innocent children at the other end of the ship while you two *talked.*"

"I will finish with Loinneil and come above soon," Hannah said, stepping into the stall.

"I will see you above," Erik said, and Nial stood aside while he climbed the ladder into the evening calm, the gentle wind barely filling the sails.

Nial followed him up, lowering his voice. "You might want to tie your trousers."

"Faen," Erik cursed and yanked the ties closed.

"We are two days out from the strait before Kronborg," Nial said. "Our army of two hundred will be stationed at the docks. Another two thousand over the ridge beyond with platoons riding between Kronborg and the docks to ensure the dowager-queen's safety. They will be waiting for your orders once we land." Nial cocked his head to the side. "Do you know yet what those orders will be?"

Trix and Libby sat with Frode and Sten at the stern of the ship. Trix and Libby gestured as they spoke over each other, but their smiles showed no fear or agitation.

"I will soon," Erik said.

Nial exhaled. "If you don't have a new plan," Nial said, walking next to him, "we will continue with the plan we started with. Deliver Hannah in exchange for Iselin, and if the Sinclair Horsemen land and attack, we kill them."

They dodged thick coiled ropes and the other

crewmen as they kept the ship on course. "We will come up with a better plan," Erik grumbled as they approached the children.

"Really?" Trix asked Frode. "You say nothing?"

"How does your enemy even know you're the Wolf Warriors?" Libby asked, hands landing on her hips in her favorite chastising pose.

"We have a banner," Sten said, his face snapping around until he saw their flag flapping high on a mast. "'Tis a wolf's head."

"We don't need a banner," Libby said. Her hands shot out before her as if depicting a wedge. "We have four armies with the horses divided by color. White, bay, black, and pale green. Like in the Bible."

Frode took a drink from a flask and wiped his mouth on his sleeve. "There are no such thing as green horses." It was likely nothing stronger than watered-down ale.

Erik turned at Hannah's step behind him. "They are gray and white horses," she said, stopping next to the girls. Her hair had been tidied, but her skirts were still quite wrinkled. "Bàs's men use a mixture made from green plants to paint on their horses before battle," she explained, looking at Frode. "When they appear greenish gray, riding together, the effect is—"

"Terrifying," Trix said with a big grin and wide eyes, "with Bàs Sinclair, The Horseman of Death, riding in front of them, his skull mask over his face and his sword and ax strapped across his bare, tattooed back."

"And Joshua, The Horseman of War." Libby threw her arms up as if Hannah's second brother was a giant. "He rides a bay horse the color of fire, and he spouts off curses and throws his sword about so that everyone in his path quakes."

"Gideon rides a shiny black horse and Cain rides Seraph, a beautiful white horse," Trix added. "Although Seraph is as deadly as the other horses." She looked at Hannah. "Keenan once told me he saw Seraph bash a man's skull in during battle."

"How is that possible?" Libby asked, hands back on her little hips.

"The bastard had fallen off his horse, and Seraph trampled him."

"I doubt Cait would want you cursing, Trix," Hannah said, and the little girl covered her mouth as if to suck the word "bastard" back in, but she smiled behind her hand.

Sten leaned against the gunwale with his arms crossed. "And they ride in separate armies by horse color?"

"Yes," Hannah said. "'Tis intimidating and sometimes stops a battle before it begins. The other army hears my brothers roar the words from Revelations in the bible, and they surrender before blood can be spilled."

Frode snorted. "Cowards."

Hannah's gaze slid to him, hardening. "When you hear them recite the words of Revelations about God sending the Horsemen of Conquest, War, Justice, and Death down to conquer the world, let me know if the hair on your nape prickles and chill bumps race across your skin."

Frode frowned back at her, but when she glanced away, his hand went up to rub the back of his neck as if the hairs were already standing on end.

"So, what do you call out before you charge at the enemy?" Libby asked, trying to climb up on a stack of crates to sit. Her foot slipped. Frode stood and wordlessly picked her up around the waist and seated her carefully on the top before regaining his own seat.

Nial cleared his throat. "We yell our war cry, slå hjertet."

In unison, Trix and Libby repeated it.

"What does it mean?" Libby asked.

The men looked at Erik who was the one most knowledgeable about English translations. "Strike the heart."

"Strike the heart!" Trix yelled, pretending to thrust a sword into an imaginary foe. She smiled broadly at Erik and nodded. "I like it. That would be buail an cridhe in Gaelic."

Sten and Frode repeated the Gaelic words, while Nial's mouth moved in silent repetition.

Frode looked at Nial and then Erik and spoke in Bokmål. "We should come up with some biblical words to herald us. It sounds effective."

"Are there wolves in the Bible?" Sten asked.

"English, please," Libby said, rebuke in her tone.

"We are discussing biblical words to herald us as you suggest," Sten said.

"We could use Norse mythology instead with Sköll and Hati or Geri and Freki," Frode said.

"Those are names of wolves?" Trix asked.

Hannah nodded. "Yes, from Norse mythology." Her gaze met Erik's. "But if my brothers are speaking their ominous biblical passage and you're yelling your stories about wolves it might seem...comical."

Frode crossed his arms. "Not if we say ours first."

"But," Libby said, "you don't have anything to say."

Erik watched the storm clouds gather on his men's faces.

"We will," Frode mumbled in Bokmål.

Erik leaned against the rail and looked out at the calm water. They weren't moving fast with the weak breeze, but he wasn't anxious to reach Denmark anyway. The water reflected the muted sun as it began its descent to the horizon edge. "So, is that part of your plan, Hannah? To have us frighten your brothers long enough that we can talk to them?"

Her voice came from behind him, calm and poetic as a sunset on still water. "My brothers do not become frightened. The only thing that makes them pause is surrender."

"Surrender?" Nial asked, anger lacing the word.

"The Sinclair Horsemen do not slaughter those who drop their weapons," Hannah said. Erik could tell without turning that she looked toward him, speaking to him.

"Wolf Warriors don't, either," Sten said and one of them let out a gusty exhale.

"If you both lay down your weapons, there will be no slaughter," Hannah said.

"Faen i helvete," Frode said.

"Dritt!" Sten said at the same time.

"Those were all curse words," Libby said, and Erik could imagine her wagging a finger at his large, tattooed friends.

Erik turned, crossing his arms to tuck his hands in his armpits, and leaned back against the rail. The breeze ruffled Hannah's silky, blond hair. Her cheeks were rose-hued either from their exertions below or the wind above. Big blue eyes set in an angel's face stared at him, waiting. He was the leader of this mission, leader of the Wolf Warriors of Norway. What he said would be what his waiting army would do, unless his three friends, his three generals, chose to abandon their oaths to follow him. Erik could feel their stares.

"What exactly would that look like?" Erik asked.

Hannah inhaled as if she'd been holding her breath. "We land north of where you said for my brothers to land, and your army waits nearby."

Erik gave one slow nod. His army of two thousand would be camped near the coast southwest of Kronborg Castle where Sophie watched and waited, sending provisions out to them. With Erik's withdrawal from the Swedish border, the king's advisors had panicked and sent their army into Norway. Sophie must have had to answer for that, but Peter Kaas was definitely on her side of the conflict between the dowager-queen and the regents for her son, King Christian.

Hannah continued, holding his stare. "Then we proceed to the meeting point. Your armies will no doubt outnumber ours, since we must sail across. The Wolf Warrior leaders ride forward and...wave a flag of pure white."

"Dritt," Sten said again.

"My brothers will be surprised enough not to attack outright," Hannah said, her words growing faster to combat his men's agitation. "I'll come forward with you and explain that we must save Iselin from Sophie and Peter Kaas." She glanced at Frode and then back to Erik. "I will tell them what's going on, and Gideon will help explain to Sophie that we do not plan to take over Scotland. Once everyone talks, Iselin will be released, and the girls and I…" Hannah swallowed. "We will go home to Girnigoe."

"Our armies will turn against us if we surrender," Nial said calmly. "They will not stand for it, especially when we so obviously outnumber those coming to our shores."

Hannah didn't look at Nial but kept Erik's gaze. "I believe they have respect for Erik Halverson," she said, "and his men who have led them safely while keeping Sweden from encroaching into Norway. I think they would follow the Wolf Warriors to Hell if need be."

"That's what surrender would be," Sten said, his voice hard as frozen granite. "Hell."

Erik rubbed his jaw. "Wolf Warriors do not surrender." He looked directly at Hannah, hoping his words alone would crack through. "I do not surrender."

Hannah's brows furrowed. On her cherubic face, it made her look like a young girl dismayed with finding her doll dropped in a puddle. She continued as if he hadn't spoken. "Cain will pause when he sees the white flag," she said. "Everything he does is calculating. And Gideon."

"They would see our flag as the trickery it is," Nial said, shaking his head. "Your brother of war would know the odds are against them with our thousands. He cannot be fooled."

"How about we kill that one?" Frode said. "Joshua? He'd probably piss on our white flag and plan to splatter it red with our blood."

Hannah's furrow smoothed, and she seemed to almost smile. "Killing Joshua would be nearly impossible, but he would find favor with your description, Frode." She crossed her arms but pointed one finger at him. "Actually, you two would probably like each other if you were on the same side of this disaster."

Disaster. That's what this was. How could Erik surrender to a small group of Highlanders on Denmark-Norway land? It was preposterous and inconceivable. He drew in a deep breath. "We will get Iselin back as soon as we land, leaving Hannah in exchange at the Danish court." He crossed his arms. "Then my army will withdraw far enough back that the Sinclairs can land and march to Kronborg Castle to retrieve their sister."

"Kaas won't allow our withdrawal," Nial said.

"Our scouts will see Swedes trying to cross during the night north of Kronborg, and we respond by marching that way." Erik waved a dismissive hand as if the excuse would be easily accepted. "With the Danish armies being sent to Norway since we were called to Denmark, the Wolf Warriors would certainly defend the Swedish border in southern Norway. Without our army close at hand, Chancellor Kaas and Sophie will settle for peace over war, especially at sword point. And Hannah can stop her brothers from acting against them."

His gaze slid to his men. "No one need surrender."

Frode dropped his head in his hands, obviously relieved. Sten nodded, and Nial released a gusty breath. Hannah looked at Erik. Did she think his plan would work? She gave no indication.

One of the sailors spoke to Nial, and Nial turned to them. "There is stew below. We should take nourishment."

Libby thumped her heels absently on the crate where she sat, and her arms went out to Frode, who helped her down. Trix slid into Hannah's arms as if feeling the chill of possible war.

Hannah hugged the little girl back, her lips tight as she met Erik's gaze. "With the delay on Shetland, let us hope we still reach Denmark before my brothers."

Erik couldn't read her expression. Where there had been such raw passion below, up here in the light of war, with talks of slaughter and surrender, her face was pale, her brows drawn, and her lips pressed tight. He would do anything to see her bright and laughing again like when they walked in the meadow at the foot of the clootie-well hill.

Anything except surrender.

CHAPTER SEVENTEEN

"It's not just the wind that plays tricks in the fog.
Sound itself is morphed into strange beasts when
your eyes are removed from the sailing equation.

In fog, sound bounces off the water particles in the
air and the stillness amplifies those sounds so that
the rumble of a boat motor five miles away may
sound like five feet to the sight-starved
ears of a wayward watch stander."
LIFE OF SAILING.COM

I shouldn't seek him out.

Hannah stared at the small, dark window across
from the bed she was sharing with the two girls. *He's
the enemy.* She sighed, knowing her argument lacked
conviction. Erik was trying to save his sister. Sophie of
Denmark and Peter Kaas were the enemy, making
Erik and his Wolf Warriors act against the Sinclairs.

They could have killed Bàs or tried to. They could
have terrorized Trix and Libby, punishing them for
sneaking onboard. They could have left the Pedersens
to deal with Patrick Stewart on their own. But Erik
and his men had done none of those horrid things. *He
stole me away.*

The creaking of the ship kept her from falling back
to sleep. It must be close to dawn. She and Erik had
met again in the hull last night, coming together with
silent passion. They'd found release in each other's

arms even if solutions still eluded them.

Footsteps thudded softly overhead, and she turned onto her back to stare up at the shadowed ceiling. Was that Erik? She wanted to talk to him about his plan. If it worked, she wouldn't see him again after he left her at the Danish court. Didn't he want to know if he had a child? How could she get word to him?

Daingead. Her emotions seemed to fly up and down like a sparrow in a storm, battling to rise only to be thrown low with worry and regret. Could she even be with child after three tuppings? Her hand slid over her slightly rounded stomach. *I pray I am.* Even if Erik was no longer in her life. Although, then there'd be no hiding that she and Erik had come together, and her brothers would…act poorly about it.

One problem at a time. Hannah slowly and silently rolled out of the bed, dragging a smaller blanket with her. She paused as Trix mumbled, turning. "Boo, come back here." Her words came from barely moving lips.

Libby's arm shot out, whacking Trix. "Shhh," she murmured.

Hannah wrapped the blanket around her arms, waiting in the dark, feeling the gentle sway of the ship under her until both girls breathed evenly again. Stepping out of the room, Hannah paused in the heavy dampness hanging in the air. Fog. It had crept in the closer they got to land, and the wind's lower strength had allowed it to squat around them. She didn't mind the fog, not when it delayed them from arriving at the Danish court.

The lightening of the black sky to gray on one side indicated the east where the helmsman had pointed the prow of the ship. She walked in soft slippers, nodding to one of the watchmen who was running his fingers up a sail line, inspecting it.

"'Tis almost morning," he said in broken English. The fog seemed to warp his words, making them seem louder. "The captain is that way." He tipped his head toward the bow.

"Thank you," she whispered, feeling heat in her cheeks. Did the whole crew know that they had been together? That she would want to seek him out? Hannah considered turning back to her room, but privacy was precious here, and her time was running out.

She walked forward, stepping over ropes and around barrels of freshwater and a covered pallet of wool from Girnigoe that they'd traded their silver for before stealing her away. Water droplets from the dense mist dripped from every line. A figure stood in the fog, looking out as if he might spread his arms like Moses and part it. He turned when she neared.

Her heart sped as she followed the lines of his cheekbones and strong jaw. It was time to memorize every part of him in case they were parted forever. Thoughtful eyes watched her approach. His hair was down, brushing just above his broad shoulders.

"Did you sleep?"

"Yes, but I woke early. Perhaps I can sense land nearby." She looked out at the layers of fog. The entire world seemed swollen with it, pushing against their ship and wetting their faces. Wisps of it slid past them in the pre-dawn gray, but it was thick and showed no sign of clearing.

He leaned against the rail, looking at her, which made Hannah tug her hair over one shoulder. She must look tousled from sleep. "We will arrive at Denmark soon?"

"Aye,"

"And then…you will fulfill your mission to give me to Sophie."

She heard him inhale. "I have never questioned my orders before," he said, his words soft. "My men are perplexed by my actions over this whole misadventure."

She stepped closer, thankful that the fog could give them a bit of privacy. "They aren't the only ones perplexed." She swallowed. "You stole me from my home. You might try to kill the four men I love the most in the world or, at least, force them to bend to foreign rule. I should hate you."

"You should," he said. His hand rose, and he caught a loose strand of her hair between his thumb and finger, rubbing it as if testing the softness of it. The dampness made the curls twist even more. "You should very much hate me, Hannah Sinclair."

She stared up into his eyes, the dawn revealing more detail in the gray world. "But I don't. And that…is perplexing."

His brows furrowed. "This would all be easier if you did."

"This? You mean leaving me?" she asked, her chin rising. He'd yet to say anything about his own feelings, but he continued to stroke the strand of hair. His strong fingers were gentle and so talented at teasing pleasure within her. Watching them move over her hair teased the smoldering fire heating her body.

"Aye," he said and dropped his hand. "Our time together ends soon."

"We could still come up with a solution," she whispered, ire at his easy acceptance making her words tight. But she stepped forward as if he drew her despite her will. She gazed at the base of his throat above the edge of his tunic. She remembered kissing that warm hollow, feeling his wild pulse beneath her lips, licking the salt from his skin as they moved together under the stars on Shetland.

Erik's arms came up around her, pulling her close. "If I wasn't an enemy to your family before, I surely am now. Once they retrieve you, if they survive, they will never let you out of their sight, especially not to attend me in any way."

Hannah rested her cheek on his chest, breathing in the scent of him. His was a warm, musky scent of fresh air and leather. "You have a point, one I wish could be ignored. Why couldn't you have just been a bloody silver trader from Norway? Instead, you had to be a deadly Wolf Warrior bent on the destruction of my clan."

She felt rather than heard his low chuckle. The creaking of the ship and the lapping of the water obscured the sound. "Do I look like a simple trader?" His arms tightened around her, his muscles evident.

She tipped her face up to his, which she could see even better now as the sky continued to lighten above them. "Maybe not a simple trader, but my brothers trade things, too, and they are built strong."

"From training for war. 'Tis why your youngest brother was so suspicious of us."

"We all were," she murmured. "But I didn't care. My brothers scared everyone away, and those they permitted near me did not make my heart race."

She felt his hand slide down her back. "Do I make your heart race?" he whispered near her ear, which did exactly that.

"Yes. With both passion and fury."

The wind blew around them, making the sail fill with a snap, only to fall again with the wind's ebb. Several men came above deck, and Erik dropped his arms from around Hannah. Privacy was as fragile as the thick fog still cloaking them. They turned to lean over the rail, side by side. The dark water looked like cold death below them, lapping. She raised her eyes to the gray mist where one could imagine shapes of sea monsters and hulking ghost ships. It was as if they were stuck outside of time, buoyed only by the ship beneath them.

Behind her, she heard Trix and Libby giggle. "Tell us about your kittens again," Trix said.

"They fit into the palm of my hand," Frode said, his deep voice barely reaching them at the rail.

The rising sun tried to cleave through the fog in shades of orange and red. Layers of wispiness moved with the growing breeze as if the world yawned with its waking. With the increase in wind, they'd make landfall today, and she wouldn't have another chance to talk with him.

"Erik," she said, her face turned to the sea so her words couldn't carry to those behind them. "How will I get word to you once we part? Do you want to know if I'm carrying your child?"

From the fog came a voice. "Child? Carrying a child!"

As if the new day's light lifted a veil, before them a ship was revealed. The ghost ship of her imagination solidified a mere fifty yards away. This was no legend-ary vessel that rammed unsuspecting ships, taking the souls of all onboard, but a Sinclair ship.

"I'm going to foking kill ye," yelled a deep, bur-bling voice, hacking through the mist standing in its way.

"Bàs?" Hannah yelled back as Erik pulled her away from the rail, shoving her behind him.

"Let her go!" yelled a woman's voice.

"Ella?" Hannah dodged Erik's arm, her eyes opening wide at the sight of the hulking figure of a Sinclair ship growing sharper through the clearing air. What had they heard?

Staring back across the narrow stretch of sea, Hannah made out Ella and Shana, holding arrows nocked and pointed directly at Erik's chest while Kára held a cocked sgian dubh.

"No!" Hannah yelled, jumping before Erik. "Don't shoot!"

Behind them, thumping boots pounded across the deck while Nial called all below to arms.

Frode halted beside them at the rail. "The Sinclairs!"

"Don't shoot," Hannah called again, but her sisters didn't lower their weapons. Bàs stared across, and even though he didn't wear his skull mask, the prom-ise of death sat in the lines of his face. Hannah had to admit that, at the moment, Erik was right in that her brother would never surrender to Denmark or Norway's Wolf Warriors.

"Ye are going to die, Erik Halverson, after I cut your jack off," Bàs said. Bloody hell, he sounded like Joshua. That wasn't good.

"Trix! Libby!" Cait's frantic voice screeched from

higher in the misty air, and Hannah looked up the main mast where the girls' adopted mother stood, rope in hand.

Trix and Libby ran to the rail, waving. "We're here!" Libby called.

"We've had such an adventure!" Trix's words tumbled over hers.

Cait balanced on the outside of the topcastle, her legs, in trousers, wrapping easily around the rope. She slid down to the deck. Several men murmured behind Hannah at Cait's unique skill for climbing ropes and sashes.

"I'm coming over," Cait said.

"Nay," Bàs said.

"Don't try to stop me, brother," Cait retorted, climbing up on the rail with a thick rope that was used to swing across to other ships. "I'm coming, girls!"

Bàs threw his hands up in the air like he was severely annoyed. He looked across to Hannah. "Catch her."

The two ships had drifted closer, but the distance looked great. "Erik," Hannah said.

"I'll catch her."

Cait leaped out over the water, easily wrapped in the rope while Ella and Kára pushed her three times before she reached across far enough for Erik to catch the knotted end dangling under her. Hannah tried to help Cait off, but Sten grabbed her, setting her down on the deck.

"Girls!" Cait yelled, running toward them to fall on her knees, arms open wide to catch them. "Oh, my heavens." Cait's words were filled with a mix of anger, tears, and desperate relief. Her arms squeezed the two girls into her chest. "I thought I'd lost you forever."

Hannah's heart clenched for the woman, imagining the searing pain of worry stabbing through after her daughters had disappeared.

"We're sorry," Libby said, tears in her own voice.

"We climbed upon the Wolf Warriors' ship to save Hannah and Loinneil," Trix said, remorseful at first but then her tone lightened. "And Libby threw up all over Frode. Then a storm blew us to Shetland where we met Eydis and fought Patrick Stewart."

Libby's face came up. "I threw rocks at his men from the ship, and now he's tied up below. Chief Cain should like that."

"I threw rocks too," Trix added with a little frown.

"Wolf Warriors?" Bàs asked, all of them silent and desperate for any information.

"Erik Halverson and his men are Wolf Warriors of Norway," Hannah said. "Elite warriors ordered by the Denmark-Norway government."

Cait didn't seem to be listening to Hannah. She stared up at Frode and Sten with brutal fury on her face. "You stole two little girls from their home. They could have died."

The two Norse warriors crossed their arms. "We stole one big girl from her home," Frode said.

"Those two followed," Sten said.

"Hannah, stand aside," Ella called across, holding the arrow still nocked, the string of her bow pulled back to her ear.

"Not if you're going to shoot anyone on this deck." Hannah's voice carried easily over the water.

"Those bastards stole ye!" Bàs yelled, his usual apathetic voice abandoned for pure rage.

"There are reasons," Hannah yelled back. She shook her head. "Why are you all here? Where are Cain, Joshua, and Gideon?"

"Right behind us," Bàs said. "But we"—he glanced at his wife, Shana—"couldn't wait. A thousand cavalry will be here any day." It was a boast for certain. Even with the three vessels that they'd used to sail to Orkney, they wouldn't have room for a thousand men, let alone horses.

Neither Ella nor Shana lowered their arrows, although they trained them away from Hannah and on Frode and Nial. Kára seemed to target Sten. But Cait and the girls were mixed up with them, shielding them whether they knew it or not.

"They abducted you from your home," Ella said, calmly, her thirst for blood nearly as strong as Bàs's.

"Cain abducted you," Hannah said. "Aren't you glad you didn't shoot him?"

Ella hesitated and then the pull of her bowstring relaxed as she frowned back at Hannah.

"Ye said ye could be with child, Hannah," Bàs said. "Explain."

Heat raced into Hannah's cheeks. "You were spying on me through the fog? Didn't announce yourself, just listened?" She glared at her brother.

Bàs threw his arms out, indicating the fog. "We couldn't be sure who was in this foking mist, and then when I heard your voice…" He trailed off, his hands going to his head. He clawed through his hair as if worry had driven him to the brink of insanity.

"I'm certain Cait would agree that Gideon would judge Erik Halverson to die for rape," Kára said. Her gaze slid across the men, and her warrior-woman face condemned them all, thinking the worst. "All of you."

"There's been no rape here!" Hannah yelled quickly. "Lower your bloody weapons and listen." Her heart thumped hard, sending an ache to her head. She waved her hands as if washing away anything they might be thinking.

"Did you marry him, Hannah?" Bàs asked. "Marry him and run away to be with him?"

"No, but—"

"Then he dies," Bàs proclaimed, pulling his sword once again and pointing the tip of it over Hannah's head where she knew Erik stared back defiantly.

"I will meet you anywhere you wish, Sinclair," Erik said, the promise of death in his own voice.

This was going nowhere. Hannah stomped her foot and frowned, her arms outstretched and pushing downward. "Everyone put down your weapons and stop threatening one another. Discussion is what is needed, not violence."

"But violence will feel so much better," Kára said, sounding exactly like the man she married.

Shana went to Bàs and slowly uncurled his fingers around the hilt of his sword until it clattered to the deck. She whispered something to him, her hand sliding over her stomach absently.

"Bàs, how could you have brought Shana out here in the ocean when she's with child?" Hannah asked, wildly flapping her hand at his wife.

Bàs's fists rose into the air, his lips curled as he spun around, took two big steps, and turned back to stride to the rail. "Like I had any choice!" he yelled, his normally stoic personality gone, replaced by waves of irate emotion and frustration. "There are bairns onboard too!"

"I insisted," Shana said.

"*We* insisted," Ella said.

Shana gave up trying to catch Bàs's arm as he paced. She went to the rail. "And I'm perfectly fine. I'm a midwife, so I would know."

Bàs grabbed his sword off the deck. "They said it was their fault and they were sailing with or without me." His gaze lifted again to Erik. "But my brothers will have landed at Girnigoe within two days after me and will have turned right back out to sea to follow. Once we are all together, nothing here will stop us from seeking revenge on you and your men."

"Wolf Warriors," Trix called. "The fiercest fighting men of Norway."

"Then the Sinclair Horsemen seek revenge on the Wolf Warriors." Bàs said the name of Erik's army wryly as if the title lacked any weight.

"Wolves eat horses," Libby pointed out, nodding as she lifted onto her toes to lean over the water.

"Hush," Cait said, tugging both girls back from the rail. They yanked their hands away and ran to stand before Frode and Sten, their thin arms spread in protective stances. Kára lowered her sgian dubh, and Ella finally lowered her bow to her side. Only Bàs still held his sword as if ready to strike. If he had wings, blood would have already chummed the seas beneath them.

Cait turned to Hannah. "Clearly, things have… happened, and this abduction isn't exactly what we thought when we sailed from Girnigoe to rescue you and the girls." She took a full breath and released it, looking to Libby and Trix. "But everyone is sound." Cait turned to the rail so her voice could be heard easily. She took on the calm cadence that Gideon used when presenting evidence of a crime. "A discussion of the facts and motivations is needed to sort this out. Weapons and threats will only muddy the explanation."

"Meet me upon the shore, Sinclair," Erik said, obviously speaking to Bàs, "so we can...talk."

Hannah turned, scowling up at Erik's hard face. "I should be the one to explain...whatever this"—she indicated the two of them—"is."

Erik glanced at his men and then back at Hannah. "I let you within arm's reach of your brother, and he'll throw you on his ship, and I'll be chasing you all the way back to Scotia." He shook his head. "I must be the one to explain unless you want to shout it to him from far away."

She exhaled in a huff. "Don't provoke him then."

"Why not? He's provoking me."

"And he's an arse," Frode said.

Trix *tsk*ed. "Say it in Norse. Miss Cait doesn't like cursing."

Libby looked at her. "She doesn't care when adults curse."

"Well, everybody's cross at everybody and curses don't help." Trix nodded.

"And Bàs is not an arse," Hannah said, scowling at Frode. "He's worried, like you all are worried about Iselin."

"Who is Iselin?" Ella asked.

"Erik's sister has been forcibly taken by Dowager-Queen Sophie and her chancellor in order to force Erik and his men to infiltrate the Sinclair Clan and steal me away."

"Why?" Cait asked.

"'Tis a complicated miscommunication, I fear," Hannah said, "And I tire of yelling across." She indicated the water separating their ships. The fog was moving off with the increasing wind. 'Twas a wonder they didn't crash into each other.

"Then come back over," Ella said. "The girls, Cait, and you."

"Did you say you have that bastard, Patrick Stewart, on your ship?" Kára asked, her face tight with a mix of bloodthirsty glee and distaste.

Erik stood beside Hannah. "Aye," Erik said. "He's a gift for the dowager-queen to give to her daughter, Queen Anne of Scotland. Since King James has declared his family traitors."

"I don't think King James will mind if he arrives with a few holes in him," Kára said, obviously wanting to have a go at the bastard. Joshua and she'd had a poor experience with the man when Patrick, his brother, and his father tried to annihilate Kára's people on Orkney Isle.

"For now, send the women and girls over," Bàs ordered.

"I will send them all, except Hannah," Erik said.

Frode murmured something in their language that sounded angry and relieved at the same time, and Hannah saw Erik cast his friend a glare.

"Send them *all*."

"Or what? You will fire upon the ship that holds children and women?" Erik called back.

"Better yet, I'm coming over there, ye wolfy bastard," Bàs said, sheathing his sword and striding toward one of the ropes. Shana ran after him, tugging his arm and then grabbing his head in her two hands. Hannah couldn't hear what she said to him.

"Enough of this," Erik said, annoyance thick in his words. "There is a deep-water dock due east, north of Copenhagen." He glanced up the main mast to where the lookout stood in the topcastle, squinting east. The wiry man called Birch nodded to Erik, and Erik turned back to look across at the Sinclair ship. "Now that the fog is clearing, 'tis within sight. We will disembark there."

"And discuss how ye will be handing Hannah and the rest over immediately," Bàs said, his voice calmer. Hannah had never seen her youngest brother so openly angry before.

"You best control yourself, Horseman," Nial called over to him. "We have a few more countrymen waiting there than you do on your ship."

Hannah turned to Erik, and he cast his hard gaze down at her. Her breath caught at the ferocious warrior staring at her. His mouth was grim, and his deep blue eyes narrowed. Tight anger made all the angles of his handsome face seem deeper somehow, fiercer. It made her heart pound, which was foolish. She knew he would never hurt her, at least physically.

"Erik," she whispered. "He's worried like you would be if he had Iselin."

"That doesn't soften my stance. I must and will get my sister back." He looked like he'd say more but instead held her stare.

No, he didn't say the rest with words, but his inflection held all the information Hannah needed. He'd get Iselin back even if he must use Hannah to do it.

CHAPTER EIGHTEEN

"Úlfheðnar (pronounced "oolv-HETH-nahr"),
Norse warriors who wore wolf skin, went armor-less
into battle and were as crazed as wolves and as
strong as bears or bulls. They bit their shields and
slew men, while they themselves were harmed by
neither fire nor iron. This is called "going berserk."
YNGLINGA SAGA, SNORRI STURLUSON,
THIRTEENTH CENTURY

"Tell the men to stand down," Erik told Nial as the
man waited to disembark at Helsingør, Denmark
where several deep-water slips allowed the ships to
unload and load goods. "There's at most thirty men on
the Sinclair ship." And there were two hundred Wolf
Warriors waiting at the docks with another two thousand Norwegian warriors over the ridge to the
southwest past Kronborg Castle.

"And three lethal women on top of the one who
swung across," Nial said. He didn't look worried,
though. What was thirty men and four lethal women,
even with the Horseman of Death, when the Wolf
Warriors had faced down hordes of Swedes barreling
down on them during border raids?

"I'll let the other women and girls disembark as
soon as 'tis safe. They're not prisoners, only Hannah,"
Erik said, watching the Scottish sailors scurry about
their ship, lowering the sails to slow their movement
toward the dock. Erik's gaze slid to Hannah, who

stood on his upper deck, watching her kinsmen skill-fully aim the mid-sized warship toward the slip. The wind tugged at her golden hair, and the blue Norwegian costume made her look like a lovely, simple maid instead of a pawn in this dangerous political game.

His fingers curled along the rail. Nothing about her was simple, especially not this anxious knot tugging inside him when he thought of her being married off to Peter Kaas. *I won't let it happen.*

Nial slapped his hand down on Erik's shoulder and leaned in toward his ear. "Don't give her up to anyone until we have your sister back."

Erik turned his face to his friend, noting the question in the arch of his brows. "I know the plan," he said, feeling his teeth clench.

Nial's gaze was like a sharp blade, unbending. "The plan didn't have you bedding the woman. She's less valuable now that she's not a virgin." Nial quirked his head to the side. "Which you knew."

Erik stared back at him. "Do you believe all women are chattel, their worth tied to their maidenhood?"

A ruddiness came to Nial's cheeks, and he dropped his hand. "Chattel, nay. But Hannah Sinclair is a mission first, a mission to save your own sister. She's a woman second."

Erik looked out over his disciplined warriors, each wearing a tunic with a wolf head embroidered on it. "We are friends from childhood, Nial Kristiansen," he said, keeping his grip on the rail so he wouldn't punch him. "But don't forget I am your commander."

Nial didn't move for a moment. "Aye, I know. Just

watching your back, Erik." He turned, marching across the wide planks to the dock where several senior warriors waited to hear the news and plan for the approaching foreign ship.

The women who'd come, Hannah's sisters by marriage, had not played the warriors back on Scotia, although he'd seen evidence of their skill. But even the pregnant one had taken to the sea to follow Hannah, and at least three babes had been brought because they were still nursing. Erik could only imagine the height of Bàs's protests. The man hadn't stood a chance against all four women working together to make the voyage happen as quickly as possible. They'd probably departed as soon as the storm blew itself out, making their crossing in five days instead of the nine it took *Seieren* to cross due to their time on Shetland. Those days of worry had fueled the Sinclair women's anger and determination to rescue Hannah.

Right now, Nial was telling his generals they were not to kill the Highlanders and Horseman who came off the Scottish ship. Killing women, especially women who Queen Anne sponsored, one being pregnant and two carrying babes, ran counter to the plan Sophie and Peter Kaas had laid out to help her daughter as Queen of Scotland. And Erik would never allow the slaughter of women and children. Even if his ancestors had been cruel in raids, Erik had trained his Wolf Warriors to honor life, not blatantly destroy it.

Bàs Sinclair, the Horseman of Death, stared across at his sister. As long as he didn't attack, Erik was reluctant to kill the great warrior for seeking to rescue Hannah. He couldn't fault Bàs Sinclair for doing what he, himself, was doing.

Hannah escorted the girls and Cait Sinclair toward him and the plank to disembark. Cait walked behind Trix and Libby, her arms around their shoulders as if she worried they might disappear again. Before they even reached him, Hannah was shaking her head. "He's already put on his skull mask, and they've led his horse, Dòchas, up from below."

"He also has his ax out," Trix said. She imitated Hannah by shaking her head, which made her two braids swing. One braid hit Libby, making the girl huff and lean away.

Cait stopped before Erik and looked between Hannah and him, her lips pinched. Was the woman so perceptive that she'd noticed the strained glances between them? She exhaled as if making up her mind. "Bàs will likely take you on as soon as he disembarks." Cait glanced behind him at the assembled army of his elite warriors. "I've never seen him so agitated and irrational before. Once he's made up his mind, he swings immediately."

Like Erik had been when he'd found Iselin missing, and he'd torn apart their homestead cottage with impotent fury. "I understand," Erik said, meeting Cait's gaze. "I have a sister in jeopardy as well. 'Tis not an easy feeling, this helplessness."

"Exactly," Cait said. "None of the brothers do well under that feeling. Their father went mad under its weight."

He looked between them both. "How do you suggest I proceed?"

Cait's lips dropped open a bit, her brow rising as she glanced at Hannah. "The walking Norse corpse is asking for suggestions?" She turned back to Erik. "That's what Kára named you." She gave a little smile and tipped her head at Hannah. "Hannah will have to advise you on Bàs, though. She practically raised him and knows him best, maybe even better than his wife."

Cait's gaze snapped past Erik to the plank. "Be careful!" She dodged around him. They turned to see Sten and Frode pick up Trix and Libby, carrying them across the narrow bridge to the dock. Hannah didn't try to follow.

"Suggestions?" Erik asked her.

"Let me go talk to him."

"A suggestion other than me releasing you."

Hannah frowned. "I'm sure your hundreds of men could get me back from him."

"Aye, but you could be hurt, and he would be killed, which I believe we are trying to prevent."

Hannah reached into her pocket, pulling out a scrap of plaid. It looked like she'd ripped it from the ruined costume she'd been wearing when he took her from Scotia. She knotted it and handed it to Erik. The brush of her fingers against his made him want to clutch them. They lingered, but then she pulled away. "Give him that. Throw it at him once you get a few feet away."

"I'll hand it to him," Erik said. "He's not some diseased beast who will leap on my throat with gnashing teeth." Like the legends of the first úlfheðnar who fought like wolves in battle.

"Bàs is excellent with a sword and ax, and he gives no warning before executing whom he feels is guilty. Every head he lops off has a surprised look on it. Just throw the scrap at him and point out that 'tis knotted."

"What does the knot mean?" Erik asked, squeezing it between his thumb and forefinger.

"Not to act. 'Tis a system we have worked out with colors and knots. And if he's thinking rationally, he'd know I'd never tell you what it means." Even though she just did.

Erik led Hannah off the ship. One of his men brought over Erik's sleekly muscled, black horse, Loki, named after the troublesome god from the old legends. Loki had been wild at first, but they'd trained together, saving each other on the border with Sweden more than once.

"Have you gotten into mischief while I've been away?" he asked.

Loki tossed his head, and Erik slid his hand along the planes of his angular face, scratching the jawline in his favorite spot. Loki's nostrils flared as if taking in the scent of his travels. Did he smell Hannah on him?

"Stand back, milady," Nial said, taking a more formal tone with Hannah now that they were on Danish land.

Erik threw his leg up in a practiced move and mounted his warhorse. Feeling a weighty gaze, he turned in the saddle to see Bàs staring at him as his green horse was led off their ship. He'd lifted his skull mask to rest on top of his head like some macabre helmet. Hard emotions sat in the narrowed eyes, emotions that summed to a promise of death. Like staring down the brutish Swedish commander before battle, Erik let Bàs's look release him from any guilt about having to kill the man. *Faen.* Except that he was Hannah's beloved brother, the one she raised like her own child.

Erik broke the stare and turned toward his men. He raised his fist in the air. "Wolf Warriors," he boomed in Bokmål.

The two hundred gathered warriors shot their own fists in the air, bellowing. "Slå hjertet!" their war cry. Then, in unison, they thumped their chest once, the thud loud like the dull beat of a giant's heart.

The atmosphere was thick with waiting, and the gazes of his men before him turned toward the dock. Bàs Sinclair, the Horseman of Death, clopped across the pier on his pale green horse. The horse tipped its nose down, its mane ruffling in the breeze, and lifted its feet high in a beautiful display of restrained power. One could almost imagine the great beast unfurling a set of wings to attack from above.

Bàs halted before Erik's gathered army, and his voice boomed out from the skull mask that he'd lowered over the top portion of his face. "When the Lamb opened the fourth seal, I heard the voice of the fourth living creature say, 'Come!' I looked, and there before me was a pale horse! Its rider was named Death."

Not a man answered him. They stood, unmoving.

And then the Sinclair warrior repeated the bible verse in Latin, the words as strong. Several men in the group leaned to others to hear the translation of either English or Latin, but it was clear that the tone and presentation had caught their full attention, possibly attacking their courage.

"See." Hannah tapped his leg, and he looked down to her upturned face. "You need a poem or something about wolves. Something as ominous as Revelations."

"There's nothing as ominous as Revelations," he

murmured. "And we have a war cry."

She looked out at Bàs who remained mounted while the sisters came to stand beside him. Had she realized that her hand remained on his calf? "Quite right, but we should look for something…a bit longer."

She tipped her face back to him, and he studied her calm, angel face. *We?* Was she on the side of the Wolf Warriors then? Never. Like a mother with her child, there was no doubt that Hannah Sinclair would die to protect Bàs and probably all her brothers.

"I still think I should go up to him first," Hannah said.

"Stay with Nial," he said from atop his horse.

"I'm not the one he wants to slay," she muttered, dropping her hand from his leg.

"I will take care," he said. The Swedish Hussars, riding down icy slopes like avenging angels, had been known to send soldiers to their graves by making their hearts explode with fright. One Horseman was not a problem. Although one or two of his youngest men looked scared enough to piss themselves as Bàs swung his ax in an arch over the heads of his wife and sisters, making it whistle against the breeze. The women stood still, staring out, holding their own weapons, trusting Bàs not to mistakenly slay them. Their trust was their strength.

Bàs turned his horse toward Erik and spoke low in the same ominous tone he'd used reciting from the bible. "I challenge ye, Erik Halverson, to a contest to the death for the crimes ye've committed against my sister."

Hannah rushed toward Erik, standing beside his

horse. "Don't you dare accept that," she said with force, poking his leg. Hannah didn't wait for his reply and turned toward Bàs and her sisters, her voice raised. "There is to be no challenge before discussions." She hit Erik's leg again. "Give me the scrap." No matter his instructions, she'd decided to jump into the middle of this. A glance back at Nial showed the man was confronted by Libby and Trix, both of them with hands on their hips as if they dared him to move past their little frames to get to Hannah.

Hannah punched his calf hard. "Give it to me," she said in an angry whisper.

Erik handed it down to her. "You don't trust me to show it."

"I don't trust Bàs to see it with vengeance coloring his gaze."

Hannah waved the scrap. "I've knotted it, Bàs. We must have discussions before any bloodshed. I demand it and, since the crime of abduction was done to me, Gideon would surely rule that I am entitled to it by the law."

"A trial," Cait called out from where she stood with her daughters. "'Tis a discussion really."

Frode stepped even with Erik on Loki. "We have no time for a trial," Frode said. He was so close to Iselin again. She was held in Kronborg Castle to the south, over the hill, less than an hour's march away. Frode would carry Hannah there himself if he thought Erik would allow it.

Hannah glared at Frode. "Discussion first."

"A scout would have been sent to Kronborg as soon as our ship was spotted," Nial said, having made his way around the girls.

"Well, then," Hannah said, "let's talk right now." Hannah turned back to Bàs, her voice raised high. "Erik's sister is being held by Dowager-Queen Sophie and will be released only if I am traded for her. If you try to interfere, the Wolf Warriors are to kill the Sinclair Horsemen."

"They will fail." His voice was hard, uncaring. Right now, Bàs was not at all the compassionate man she'd raised but a warrior who'd been tortured with regret over this past week, regret that had hardened his heart to anything but vengeance.

Hannah took a full breath, her chest rising with the effort of yelling across to him. "You and Erik are both fighting for a sister most beloved, and your sister, me, has decided to help him. So, stand down, brother, Horseman of Death." Her beautiful face was hard in challenge, like a sculpted masterpiece in marble. "Restrain your ax and help us devise a plan to solve this debacle together. In the name of God and in the name of peace between Denmark-Norway and Scotland."

Her words reverberated along the dock, spanning out over the gathered men. Strong and without fear, Hannah Sinclair was a fierce beauty, like a Valkyrie from the old legends. If he hadn't seen it before, Erik truly saw now how she was the sister of the Four Sinclair Horsemen. Foolish pride filled him. Foolish because she wasn't his, would never be his.

"Stand d—" Trix's words were stopped behind him, probably by her mother.

Hannah raised the knotted sash high in the air and waited. Everyone waited, not a word even whispered among the two hundred men assembled ahead of the rest of Erik's army.

Bàs was too far away for Erik to hear any mutterings from him. Erik leaned forward enough to make Loki take a step before he started speaking. "I seek an audience to judge the suspected treason by the Sinclair Horsemen against the Scottish King James and Queen Anne." Hannah stepped up even with him again.

"As ordered by Dowager-Queen Sophie of Denmark and her chancellor Peter Kaas," Erik said, his voice booming. He repeated it in the native language of most of his soldiers, Bokmål. There could be no evidence he might lean against Danish royalty, otherwise he and his close commanders would be exiled or executed. Even though they'd been trained to be a deadly defensive unit, King Christian's advisors didn't fully trust the Wolf Warriors because of that power. Much like the king and queen of Scotland being wary about their powerful Sinclair Horsemen.

Lady Ella met the shadowed eyes recessed inside Bàs's half skull mask and commanded such dignity that it was as if they stood on equal ground. She said something to Bàs, quiet words that must have been powerful, because the Horseman of Death lowered his ax, attaching it to a special holder built into his saddle.

Erik heard a gust of relief issue from Hannah's lips. She touched Erik's leg. "Is there a building nearby where we can talk, before we march to Kronborg?"

There were several old buildings that lined the cobbled road off the docks. Erik motioned to Nial to follow them toward a two-story meetinghouse raised up on thick pillars so that steps must be climbed to a long porch before the doors. Vertical planks of warm brown oak made up the walls and cut shale fit overlapping to create the pointed roof. Dampness from the fog clung to the steps and wooden rail, making everything slick. The scent of the sea, which was eerily calm, and the remaining mist gripped the scene in silent dread.

Erik dismounted Loki, handing his reins to one of his generals who stood grim-faced. He turned to the Sinclairs. "Lady Ella Sinclair and Horseman Bàs Sinclair, come for discussion. Without weapons."

"No weapons for ye, either," Bàs called back.

Erik pulled his sword from the sheath strapped to his back and laid it on the porch. Bàs dismounted and walked forward, leaving his sword and ax behind. Erik pulled his short sword from his side and laid it next to the other. Bàs pulled a dagger from each boot, dropping them at the foot of the steps up to the porch. Ella did the same and so did Nial. Erik knew Hannah had a blade on her, which he wouldn't ask her to surrender.

"All weapons," Erik said, looking down from the porch.

"Ye too," Bàs answered.

Nial lowered his daggers and Ella handed her bow and arrows to Cait Sinclair. Bàs and Erik each produced three more blades hidden upon their bodies. They stared at each other. Was the horseman remembering how they'd dropped their weapons during the harvest festival at Girnigoe? Did the memory flaunt how Erik had infiltrated and tricked the Sinclairs?

Erik held his arms out to the sides. "I have only my fists and cleverness now."

Bàs made the same gesture and strode to the steps, taking them quickly and entering the room. Erik's arm slid without thought around Hannah's shoulders, escorting her to the stairs, Nial leading them up.

Nial entered the room first, going toward the covered windows to open the indoor shutters, letting in light and releasing the musty air inside. The room wasn't often used, a place to facilitate trading at the docks before the newer post was built with glass windows and proper locks. Erik and Hannah stopped just inside the doorway.

Bàs's gaze centered on Hannah immediately. Erik dropped his arm, and Hannah strode to Bàs, right into his arms. Her brother was a head taller than her even though she was tall for a woman. He closed his eyes as he hugged her, his mouth dropping to her head to kiss it. "I thought I lost ye," Bàs said, emotion thick in his voice.

Ella hurried inside and hugged her from behind. "We are so sorry, the ladies and me, to encourage you." She shook her head. "We came at once." She released her, but Bàs continued to hold Hannah as if he would never let go.

"I am hearty and well," Hannah said, pulling back so she could look into Bàs's eyes. "Truly. No foulness has occurred."

Bàs's face hardened as his gaze lifted to fall on Erik. "No foulness? Ye were forced onto a ship after several Sinclairs were knocked unconscious and tied up. No foulness?" The volume of his voice rose, and Erik could imagine the hate and promise of vengeance swirling around like black smoke in the rafters of the pointed ceiling. Bàs lowered his voice and looked down at Hannah. "Ye said ye might be with child."

Hannah tried to step back, but Bàs wouldn't let her go, holding her upper arms. "'Twas my will to… I seduced him."

"Release her," Erik said, feeling his hands tighten into fists. The man was her brother, but he held her to him like he'd reclaimed some treasured possession.

Bàs raised his daggerlike gaze to Erik although he spoke to his sister. "Ye were a virgin, Hannah, innocent and protected all yer life. What do ye know of seduction? Nay, the fault is his."

"There is no fault," Hannah said, her voice firm, and she brought the heel of her boot down on Bàs's toes. "Let go of me." She reached up and gripped his earlobe, twisting it.

He grunted and dropped his arms. Only then did she release his ear and tugged on the bottom edge of her bodice as if righting it. She frowned at Bàs. "Do you want me to tell you detail by detail how I convinced Erik to touch me, to pleasure me?"

Bàs's eyes opened wider as he dropped his gaze to his sister. "Nay!" The word shot out like a defensive blast.

Hannah reached for his arm. "Then you will have to believe me when I say that I encouraged him fully."

Bàs shook his head. "Ye were a maid."

"A maid of nearly thirty years old, brother. I am no cloistered nun, yet I've been treated as such." She shook her head. "But that is not what we're here to discuss." She looked back at Erik, and he could see the stain on her cheeks. "We must get Erik's sister free of Kronborg Castle and the Dowager-Queen

Sophie. Iselin Halverson was taken a month ago from her homestead in Norway."

"Two months now," Nial said, standing next to Erik, his arms crossed.

Erik watched Hannah's steps, which brought her to the middle between him and her brother. She held her arms out from her body as if trying to hold back two massive forces.

Erik spoke while staring across, meeting Hannah's beautifully expressive eyes. "To prevent my sister being forced to marry within the Danish court, I was tasked to bring the Four Horsemen of Scotia to heel."

"Under Denmark's heel?" Ella asked.

"Aye," Nial answered. "Iselin's freedom traded for a way to control the Horsemen. We were tasked to discover if the sister was loved."

"Which was easy to ascertain," Erik finished. "Hannah Sinclair is much beloved."

"And she was unguarded," Bàs said.

Ella flushed. "A woman must be able to live, too," she said softly.

"Your village was unguarded," Erik said. "No roaming patrols."

"We have no nearby enemies," Ella said. "There is peace in our land."

Nial gestured toward her. "Something that worries Queen Anne. The Sinclairs have so many allies, they could mount a civil war against the king and queen."

Ella looked at Bàs and then Hannah. "Queen Anne worries about a civil war?"

Hannah sighed. "Anne must have said something to her mother or King Christian about King James being uneasy about the Sinclair Horsemen. That our strength, if turned against the royal Stewarts, could take the throne. Sophie has always been a loving mother to Anne. I could see her interfering to ensure her safety."

She gestured to Bàs. "So, you see, brother, 'tis a misunderstanding we need to rectify."

"Or I take ye home and go to Edinburgh to emphasize our allegiance," Bàs said.

Nial stood, his legs braced and arms crossed. "'Tis not that easy. There are twenty-two hundred trained warriors out there under Sophie's orders to bring the Sinclair Horsemen to heel. Two hundred are the elite Wolf Warriors. If you try to take Hannah, we will kill you and any Sinclairs who land here."

"We must talk to Sophie," Ella said in the thick silence.

"Sophie has been alerted of the arrival of Bàs Sinclair," Erik said, "and the wives of the Horsemen. You are all in jeopardy now."

Hannah clutched her hands before her. "I will go to Kronborg—"

"Nay!" Bàs said.

"I must," Hannah said. "They will release Iselin, and then"—she looked at Erik—"you will get me out."

"We will be hanged as traitors," Nial said in Bokmål.

Erik felt the fissure inside his chest, like a giant tear between his friends and heritage and this clever, honest woman with beguiling blue eyes. If it were only him that he risked, the plan was obvious. But it wasn't just him. Sten, Frode, and Nial would be considered accomplices in whatever treason he committed. They were a team, friends since childhood, fighting their way together up the ranks of the Danish-Norwegian military until they were considered the elite Wolf Warriors who kept their country safe from constantly encroaching Sweden.

Erik cleared his throat. "After Iselin is out, I will help Lady Ella, Bàs Sinclair, and your team get inside Kronborg to get Hannah out safely. But my men"—he glanced at Nial—"must be free from any treasonous act." He looked back at Hannah, willing her to understand. "I will act alone to help."

Hannah stared at him for a long moment. Did she truly understand? Could she put herself in his place? Responsible for the lives of his friends?

"It may not come to that," Ella said, "if Sophie listens to reason. If she believes us when I explain that her daughter is friends to us, a patron of our school and orphanage."

"'Tis our hope," Nial said with false confidence.

Erik looked at Ella. "The dowager-queen was most adamant the Horsemen will start a civil war in Scotia. Mere words and assurances will not be enough."

Ella sighed. "We will try diplomacy first."

Hannah frowned. "I hate the idea of me being used to ensure Sinclair obedience." She turned back to Bàs. "If we can't get me free, then—"

"All of Denmark will die," Bàs finished. His words were so fierce they seemed like an oath. "If not by my ax alone, then by the thousands of allies we have."

Erik caught Nial's frown. His friend's eyes had widened slightly, but it was enough to show his worry. And Nial was seldom worried.

Rap. Rap. Rap. "Peter Kaas is riding this way." Sten's voice came through the door. "He does *not* have Iselin with him."

"He's the chancellor of Denmark," Nial said. "The one supporting Sophie in this plan despite the regency advisors not wishing to provoke war."

"He must be quite powerful." Ella took Hannah's arm to leave.

Erik stopped them and took Hannah's arm himself, drawing her away from her sister. "I must be in control of her."

Bàs snorted. "Ye don't know Hannah well if ye think ye'll ever be in control of her." He trudged out of the door before Ella.

"This should be interesting," Nial whispered behind Erik as he escorted Hannah outside.

Her arm felt stiff linked with Erik's. A distance had grown between them inside the dilapidated structure, and there was no time to speak with her alone. What would he say? *I'm sorry for dragging you into this.* He'd had no other choice. *I won't give up until you're free.* For the sake of his sister's life, his friends' lives? Perhaps silence was best.

As Bàs descended the stairs, his thirty warriors encircled him as if making him as large as possible. The Sinclair women stood in a row before the warriors, apparently having decided to hide Bàs in case he was a target. The man didn't look happy about it, but one of his warriors, Kerrick, if Erik remembered correctly, spoke in Bàs's ear. Bàs kept his skull mask off and remained with them while Ella took a step forward.

Nial spoke in Bokmål close to Erik's ear. "We do

need to come up with a saying, some legend. Even alone, on that green horse, speaking biblical words like God himself, the men looked uneasy. And that was just one brother."

"One might see why King James mentioned being nervous to his queen," Erik answered.

Hannah spoke without looking at either of them. "If you two are talking about your plans, 'twould be the decent thing to do so in English." She stood tall and dignified, but her grip on his arm had increased, almost like she didn't want to let go. Was that fear?

He laid his palm over her cold hand, leaning in. "This will be solved, do not despair."

Her face turned to him. It was tight with questions and yes, a hint of fear in her large eyes. She blinked, swallowing, and gave him the slightest nod. "When words and actions align…" She wet her lips as if her mouth had gone dry. "Then I will trust you."

Her words impaled him, quivering like an arrow freshly shot into a target, a target in his chest that beat with deep thuds.

CHAPTER NINETEEN

"Kronborg Castle has existed at Helsingør (Elsinore) since 1420. It's been burned to the ground and rebuilt since, but always maintained its vital position at the head of the Øresund Sound. Ships passing into the Baltic Sea paid tolls at Kronborg Castle and Helsingør was once one of the most important towns in Europe."

Visit Denmark.com

Hannah sat as straight as she could on the borrowed horse's back as she rode beside Erik. His black horse was majestic and strong like his master. She glanced to her other side where the Danish chancellor rode a stout dun-colored horse that was native to their land.

The man was short in stature and wore a false smile, framed by a waxed mustache. When he looked at her, that grin slipped between her ribs like a serpent, making her stomach churn. *Do not despair*. She held on to Erik's words as if they were the thickest armor.

Hooves thudded as they crossed the drawbridge into the walled inner bailey of Kronborg Castle. The wind tugged at her loose hair, causing strands to tickle her ear as she listened to the clopping of the horses' hooves and the slight jingle of their tack. Frode, Nial, and Sten rode their own horses. Ella and Cait also rode horses borrowed from Erik's men. They didn't want to worry about freeing Loinneil or Dòchas if they were captured.

Prickles of unease danced along Hannah's back, and she tried to relax into the rolling gait of her horse. If things went wrong, the Danish court could imprison two wives along with the sister of the Horsemen. Was Queen Anne's mother so cruel and manipulative to do such a thing?

Do not despair. Erik couldn't openly go against his sovereign's orders, but he would help her. Hannah believed that in her heart. She glanced at him riding with such strength next to her. Everything about him commanded attention and respect from his straight, easy seat on his shiny black horse to his steadfast stare ahead as if riding to battle.

From right behind Erik, Frode made a noise, murmuring something like a relieved prayer in their Norwegian language. Standing before the doors of the massive, encircling fortress were two women, one older and most royal and another younger with simpler clothing. Sophie and Iselin.

Their group halted in the bailey before the ladies and four armed guards. Hannah could almost feel Frode's desperation to reach the golden-haired young woman with smooth features. The roundish, balding Peter Kaas dismounted first and bowed low to Dowager-Queen Sophie. Straightening, he spoke, his overly long mustache bobbing on both ends like a wooly caterpillar trying to hold onto his upper lip. "As you directed, Erik Halverson and his Wolf Warriors have brought the sister of the Sinclair Horsemen, Lady Hannah Sinclair."

Hannah bowed her head. "Your Majesty."

"In exchange for my sister, Iselin Halverson," Erik

said, the force of his words making Hannah jump. "As agreed upon." The anger lacing his tone was obvious, but the dowager-queen of Denmark-Norway didn't seem to notice. Or perhaps she didn't care.

She stepped forward with a smile. "And who are these other ladies?"

Ella spoke from the back of her horse. "Your daughter, Queen Anne, is our patroness and friend. I am Lady Ella Sutherland Sinclair of Girnigoe Castle in Caithness, Scotland, and this is Lady Cait Sinclair of Varrich Castle."

Sophie's brows rose. "Wives of Chief Cain Sinclair and his brother, Gideon Sinclair?" The woman had done some investigation, so she knew the vulnerability they'd offered with this meeting.

"Yes, Your Majesty," Ella said, inclining her head.

"What brings you to our shores?"

"My abduction, and to discuss the conduct and loyalties of my maligned brothers," Hannah said.

Watching all the players in this stiff exchange carefully, Hannah caught the slightest smile touch Iselin's pale lips. The woman was young, twenty from what Erik had said. She had a natural smoothness to her features and piercing eyes like her brother. Her golden-brown hair was pulled back in a loose braid that fell down her back. She wore a blue Kraga cape draped around her shoulders.

Sophie's welcoming smile tightened, her eyes narrowing. "We shall all go inside then." She signaled to attendants who ran over to each horse.

"Not until Iselin is delivered to my man, Your Majesty," Erik said. From his tone, one would think he spoke to an enemy, not the mother of his king.

Perhaps, Sophie had done more damage to her country than she anticipated by infuriating one of Denmark-Norway's greatest commanders.

Sophie tipped her head as if considering this damage but then smiled. "Of course. Lady Hannah Sinclair can walk here to stand with me while Iselin Halverson can walk to your man. An even exchange, although I invite all the ladies inside."

"Thank you, Your Majesty," Ella said. "We can *visit* to discuss this problem, but then we will return to our ship to await our husbands who follow with their warriors."

Sophie smiled without moving her head. The woman didn't even blink. It was almost as if they stared at an expertly composed portrait of Denmark's monarch. "We will welcome them too, of course."

Welcome or attempt to kill? A dark intent seemed to hide behind her words.

Frode dismounted quickly as the guard beside Iselin led her forward, and Erik dismounted, walking slower to stand next to Hannah's horse. A shiver ran through Hannah at the hard, blank look on his face as he reached up to clasp around her waist, lifting her down. He leveled his gaze over her head instead of into her face. Was he playing a part? The worry wriggled inside her.

Hannah waited, but there was no squeeze to her hand or reassuring glance. Erik was a stiff and brutal warrior as he walked Hannah the distance to the middle while Peter Kaas and four palace guards walked with Iselin. Hannah met the young woman's gaze as they stopped before each other briefly, and Erik's hold on her arm dropped away. The absence of his touch turned her cold.

As Iselin passed, her large blue eyes blinked with the shine of tears. Had she been mistreated?

"Move," Cait said to one of the guards who'd stepped up beside Hannah. She elbowed the man over so she could take Hannah's arm while Ella took the other. The three women walked sedately toward Dowager-Queen Sophie. But all three of them paused at the sound of the thunderous hooves of another horse, practically flying into the bailey. They turned as one to see one of Erik's warriors pull his horse up short.

"The Horsemen," he said, his eyes big. "They have come."

Hannah's face turned to Erik, and she drew in breath when he actually met her gaze. But then it stopped hard in her chest, aching at what she saw in his determined blue eyes.

Remorse.

• • •

Two ships had collapsed their sails, and Bàs could see his brothers standing at the port side of one, their gazes searching the dock as they neared.

"Kára!" Joshua yelled, apparently having seen her standing on the porch of the meetinghouse where Patrick Stewart now languished inside. Joshua climbed upon the railing as if he were going to dive into the sea to reach her.

Kára ran down the steps, her arms out as if to hold back a flood. "Stop, you arse," she called, a smile on her lips as she raced to the dock. Neither of them seemed to care that two hundred Norwegian warriors watched from the field beyond. "Bloody hell, just wait and stay dry."

Cain and Gideon stood, their gazes searching for their wives. Joshua was so loud in his cursing about the ship moving too slowly that the other two brothers just watched, their hard gazes finally landing on Bàs when they couldn't locate their wives.

Bàs looked toward the distant hill that hid Kronborg Castle. When he turned back to his brothers, both Gideon and Cain stared in that direction with grim faces.

"They aren't happy," Shana said next to Bàs.

"Everything about this…debacle is dangerous and infuriating."

She placed her arm through his. "And yet you dove right into it because you love your sister." She squeezed his arm, and he looked down into her brilliant greenish eyes that held so much love. "A man who loves his family with a huge heart would do nothing different, and I am blessed to be loved by such a man."

He sighed softly. "I am heartsick that ye and our wee one are in jeopardy."

She shook his arm back and forth. "We are helping solve this mess, a mess we allowed." She huffed. "And I'm tired of seeing you sail away without me."

He kissed her forehead. "Just do what ye must to keep yourself and our bairn safe. Even if that means sailing away without me. Keenan has orders to get ye on that ship." He motioned to the larger of two where Sinclairs held poles out to stop the ship from ramming into the dock.

Bàs couldn't hear her whispered response with Joshua's roar as he swung across the space between the ship and the dock on a rope. He thudded to the boards in a crouch and leaped up to grab Kára. He hugged her so close it was as if he tried to shove her inside between his ribs. Bàs didn't understand much about what went on in his second brother's head, but he did understand his need to protect his wife.

Shana and Bàs walked to the dock, catching the last of Kára's words. "…to Dowager-Queen Sophie at Kronborg Castle beyond that hill."

"And the bairns?" Joshua asked.

"Safe and hearty onboard our ship."

Joshua halted for a second, his eyes shutting as he released a big breath.

Crack! The wide gangplank hit the dock. Gideon and Cain strode down the plank without even checking that it was situated correctly. The Sinclairs dropped a second plank next to the first and led their horses down after them.

"Ye let Ella go with them?" Cain's voice throbbed through Bàs's ears.

"And Cait?" Gideon asked, his voice slightly less thunderous, but not by much. "They'll imprison them along with Hannah."

Bàs released Shana's arm and glanced at Keenan. The loyal man pulled her slightly back to get her and her belly out of the line of fire. "They would not be dissuaded," Bàs said. "Your wives are as stubborn as my own who would not be left behind at Girnigoe, either."

"That's right," Kára said, her tone fortified into belligerence as if delivering a preemptive attack. "We were not and are not going to let Hannah be taken away without helping to get her back. Especially as we encouraged her to errr…well, we are partly responsible for Hannah trusting those Norwegian bastards."

Bàs gave a small nod. "Aunt Merida alerted me that the ladies were planning to drug me and take the ship on their own if I didn't relent and let them accompany me. And I was not prepared to tie your wives up and leave them behind. Not to mention having to pay off any ship owners within a hundred miles of coastline to stop them from following me," Bàs said. "I didn't have time for that."

Cain's glare slid past Bàs to the men waiting in straight lines behind the meetinghouse. The Norwegian warriors looked strong and disciplined, waiting for their commanders to return from Kronborg. "I see," Cain said in Gaelic, "that the Danish court has sent out their welcoming army to meet us."

"They are Erik Halverson's army," Bàs said. "Two hundred armed men here called Wolf Warriors and another two thousand hird, as they're called, behind that ridge. I had Keenan ride out there to check that Halverson's man, Nial Kristiansen, wasn't exaggerating."

"So, they aren't loyal to King Christian?" Gideon asked, his brilliant legal mind already working.

"Nay. I think they are Wolf Warriors first, Norwegians second, and lastly soldiers for Denmark-Norway."

"And King Christian wants Hannah?" Cain asked.

Bàs exhaled. "Nay. 'Tis his mother." He quickly explained the convoluted story that Hannah had told him about Sophie's fear for her daughter, King James's wife.

"King James gifted us five ships," Cain said, shaking his head, "for bringing Robert Stewart and his soldiers from Orkney."

"'Tis a misunderstanding from what Hannah says."

"And she thinks she can go in there and explain things?" Joshua yelled, still clutching Kára to him. She pinched him hard on the arm. "Ow," he said, releasing her.

She frowned at him. "Cait feels that we need to try diplomacy first," Kára said. "Especially since…" She indicated the army behind them. "'Twould be twenty-two hundred to…" She glanced around them at the three ships. "One hundred and fifty."

"One seventy-three," Joshua corrected.

"And two stowaways," Shana said, pointing to Trix and Libby who waved from the deck of the meeting-house.

Gideon made a noise and ran across the distance to the girls, throwing himself up the steps. He grabbed them both to his chest in a giant hug. They clung to him, too, and Bàs felt a tightness in his gut. Would a child, his child, ever hug him like that, as if he were a lifeline to this world? His need to protect Shana and the life inside her warred with his duty to help his brothers and sister. It felt like being tied to two horses made to run in different directions. He scrubbed his hands down his face.

"And we have Patrick Stewart tied to a chair in that building," Kára said with a grim smile at Joshua.

"Patrick Stewart!" Joshua growled. "That foking bastard."

Gideon walked over, one girl's small hand in each of his.

"We can use him," Cain said.

"Alive," Gideon said, looking at Joshua. "King James wants him along with his father."

Bàs stretched his shoulders, looking south toward Kronborg. "We first need to free Hannah."

"Without sacrificing Iselin Halverson," Shana said. "She's innocent in all this."

"She is the sister of our enemy," Cain said, his voice grim. "Hannah is our priority."

"Just like Iselin is Erik's priority," Kára said.

"Although…" Shana started, "I think Hannah and Erik have become…close. I think he's torn, too."

The tamped-down anger inside Bàs sputtered out like the warning sign of a waking volcano. He cursed low, drawing Joshua's and Cain's gazes.

"Close?" Joshua asked. "How close?" His face took on a hard, red look that heralded the entire volcanic mountain exploding apart to destroy the world.

Kára patted his arm, and, for the first time, Bàs was truly glad she'd come on this mission. No one else could calm his brother. "Hannah is a woman of almost thirty years, Joshua. And 'twas consensual."

"Consensual!" Gideon and Cain yelled at the same time.

"He tupped her?" Cain's voice was fierce even though he kept the volume down.

"That foking, rutting pig," Joshua said. "I'm going to cut his jack off first—"

"And shove it somewhere gruesome and probably unreachable," Gideon broke in, pulling his adopted daughters tightly to his legs, his hands pressed to their outer ears. "Which we don't need to describe." Both lasses stared at Joshua with wide and wary eyes.

"Riders!" Keenan called from atop his borrowed horse.

"I'll watch them," Shana said, striding over to take Trix's and Libby's hands.

The brothers each turned to their horses, mounting them smoothly. Bàs placed the skull mask over his head and nodded to Keenan. "Ye will lead the men," Bàs said.

"Aye," Keenan said and turned his horse to the groups already congregating as trained into four small groups. They didn't have their horses, but they wore tunics dyed in black, pale green, red, and the rest bleached white. He saw the men who accompanied them on the first ship quickly yanking off their tunics to replace them with green ones.

Bàs glanced down when he felt a touch on his leg. He pushed his skull mask back to rest on the top of his head and bent down to kiss Shana's soft lips, his hand sliding along the soft, smooth skin of her cheek. He pulled back, staring into her green eyes, so full of spirit and strength.

"'Twas not a farewell kiss, Bàs Sinclair," Shana said sternly.

"Of course not." He gave her a small grin and dropped the skull mask back in place.

Shana, Trix, and Libby hurried to climb the steps of the meetinghouse. He slid a hand down Dòchas's dyed coat and pulled the beast around to take his place next to Gideon seated on his black horse. The worn bone of the mask pressed into the usual spots on his face. As the riders galloped closer, he could make them out. "'Tis Erik, Frode, Sten, Nial, and the woman must be Iselin, Erik's sister."

"Ella and Cait must still be with Hannah at Kronborg," Cain said.

"As prisoners?" Gideon added.

Bàs ground his teeth at the anger in Gideon's voice, but he kept quiet. They knew he had no choice but to let them go. Ella had ignored all his pleas for her to stay behind, as did Cait, who demanded to be the negotiator. And they wouldn't let him ride with them, saying that he must remain there to keep Erik's army at bay.

Erik and his men and sister slowed as they neared, stopping twenty feet away.

"I am Erik Halverson, commander of this legion of Wolf Warriors." As if cued by his words, the army of two hundred before them raised their fists in the air and then thumped their chests once over their hearts in a single beat.

"They're trained," Joshua mumbled in Gaelic. "Good. I hate having to slaughter lads and incompetent arses given—"

"Hold yer tongue," Gideon whispered.

"I am Cain Sinclair, Chief of the Sinclairs of Caithness, Scotland. And ye have stolen our sister, Hannah Sinclair, Lady of Girnigoe Castle. Ye will bring her, Ella Sutherland Sinclair, and Cait Sinclair to us now, and we will leave ye unbloodied. Although, ye will still be our enemy for coming to our land and waging war against us without provocation."

"King Christian of Denmark-Norway had nothing to do with this mission," Erik said. "Nor his regents. Your war is with Sophie, the dowager-queen, and her chancellor, Peter Kaas."

"And with ye, ye foking bastard," Joshua said. "Hannah—"

"Hold yer bloody, foking tongue," Gideon said, his words fierce but his tone quiet in comparison.

Joshua was saying what Bàs was thinking. Hannah had been the most important woman in Bàs's world until he met Shana, and even still, Hannah was the mother who'd stepped in when his birth mother had died. The person who soothed his pains, in his head and on his body while he grew into a man. She'd cared for him through illness and did her best to make Bàs who he was today, never shaming him for a caring heart when others might think that made him weak. Always whispering that Bàs was good when everyone shrunk from him as soon as he began to grow into his name. The only thing that tempered Bàs, which Joshua hadn't yet seen, was the look that passed between Erik and Hannah more than once before the Wolf Warrior had hardened in front of his men. Even Bàs could tell there was more between them than mere lust.

"And, since ye work for the dowager-queen and her chancellor," Cain said, "our war is with ye and yer Wolf Warriors."

Joshua produced a wolf's howl under his breath.

"I'm going to beat ye," Gideon said to Joshua, just under his own.

"Should I fetch Kára to keep him in line?" Bàs asked.

Joshua snorted, and no one answered Bàs.

Cain moved Seraph forward, and each of the brothers followed one after the other equidistant apart to stop next to each other six feet from Erik and his three men. Iselin rode on the back of Frode's horse, her arms wrapped around his waist, her eyes watchful over his shoulder.

"Your sister, Hannah Sinclair," Erik said, his voice loud, "is a protected captive of Dowager-Queen Sophie of Denmark until such time as she sees fit to release her."

"And Cait and Ella?" Gideon asked.

"Visitors while Hannah gets settled."

"Hannah will never get settled," Cain said. "Because we are taking her home." Slowly, he withdrew his sword, the steel sliding at an angle that scraped the inside of the scabbard, making a noise that released warrior's lightning within Bàs's blood.

Well hell. It would be a battle then.

Dear God, keep Shana, the bairn, and Hannah safe.

CHAPTER TWENTY

"Queen Sophie used her energy, money and knowledge of administration to become a successful estate owner and ran a prosperous lending enterprise. When her own son was in trouble financially, she was able to lend money to the Danish King, and Christian IV became one of her biggest debtors." When the Dowager-Queen died in 1631, she was the wealthiest woman in Europe at the time.
HISTORY OF ROYAL WOMEN.COM

"Your Majesty, we are friends of your daughter's." Ella sat straight in the chair provided, her arms moving to emphasize her words. "She's our patroness for our school and orphanage. We have visited and exchanged Hogmanay gifts."

"I sent her a beautiful ebony mare," Cait added, "which she rides daily."

"Queen Anne and I have spent time walking through the wildflowers around Girnigoe," Hannah said. "My brothers"—she shook her head—"our clan, plan no overthrow of Queen Anne's reign. We are content with residing in Caithness away from court and venturing forth only when our king calls us to do so."

"Like when our men captured the traitor, Robert Stewart, the Earl of Orkney, for King James," Cait said. "He is your enemy, Your Majesty, threatening the strength of King James's reign, not the Sinclairs."

"And what of these alliances your brothers have formed with other clans?" Sophie asked and ticked them off on her long fingers. "Clans Mackay, Sutherland, Gunn, Oliphant, Campbells. Their armies number in the tens of thousands."

"They are loyal first to King James and your daughter," Hannah said. She wasn't certain of this, but she surely wasn't going to question it now. Gideon worked to foster personal relationships with these clans where King James did not. But no discussions of taking over the throne had occurred since their father had died three years ago. At least none Hannah had heard.

Ella folded her hands in her lap, meeting the dowager-queen's gaze calmly. "Any alliances are made so that King James can call up added troops to battle against threats to Scotland. A united country of strong warriors is needed to ensure the safety of your daughter. Turning the Sinclair Clan against her by this…" She indicated Hannah. "This will not be received well and will reflect *against* your daughter, not *for* her."

Sophie's eyes narrowed. "You are saying my interference will hurt my daughter, not save her from civil war?"

"Yes," Hannah said. This woman's meddling could bloody Scotland as well as turn her Wolf Warriors against the Danish crown.

The three women stared at Sophie across from them on her throne. Hannah tapped the arm of her own chair with a fingernail. "Right now, out on the field beyond your walls, a battle may be commencing. It will spark a civil war on Scottish soil when word

returns there that King James's most powerful warriors have been ambushed and slaughtered by his
wife's mother, leaving Scotland weakened and ready
for a successful invasion of our shores."

Sophie frowned, her already thin lips nearly disappearing. "Or your brothers can safely return home,"
she looked to Cait and Ella, "with their wives, knowing that their sister is treated well here in Denmark."

"As a prisoner."

"As a *wife*," Sophie countered. She nodded to
Peter Kaas. "To a wealthy and kind member of our
government and gentry."

The man nodded to Hannah, and her stomach
slithered as if filled with serpents. The thought of
sharing a bed with the man, letting him touch her as
Erik had, was unthinkable without a bout of nausea.
Hannah's face snapped back to Sophie. "You were
going to force Iselin to wed him first." Did Erik know
trading her for his sister meant condemning her to
marriage to the chancellor?

"Yes," Sophie said. "My Wolf Warrior general
knew that Peter would marry Iselin or you." She
tipped her head back and forth. "Erik Halverson's
love for his only remaining family ensured he would
succeed in his mission."

Hannah's breath caught with the dowager-queen's
words. For a moment, she couldn't swallow, her mouth
dry. Erik knew she was to wed Peter? She felt her
cheeks fill with heat and looked at Peter. Had he been
disappointed that Iselin was traded? She would have
been more biddable than Hannah. "Don't you wish to
have some say in your bride?"

He smiled. "Either woman will be kept well and

bring me joy." He talked of Iselin and her as if they were mares.

Hannah snorted. "I will not bring you joy." She looked at Sophie. "I'm not a maiden and might be with child." The words were out, but Hannah felt no embarrassment over using this weapon. And it could be true. She'd been with Erik more than once, and he hadn't withdrawn before releasing. "I would bring an illegitimate child to the union."

"Peter is not cruel, are you?" Sophie asked, nonplussed.

"No, Your Majesty." He smiled at Hannah.

"You will take responsibility for any child," Sophie continued.

He inclined his head dutifully. "And we will have children of our own." The mild temper jolted Hannah more than any glare. They acted as if Hannah was already married to the round, middle-aged chancellor with the fuzzy caterpillar perched upon his upper lip. That it was all inevitable and they merely waited for her to come around to it. Was there a reverend hiding behind the drapes ready to pounce out and proceed with the nuptials?

"In Scotland," Ella said, her words terse, "we do not force women to wed where they do not want."

"No?" Sophie said, ignoring a serving maid who entered with some form of liquid refreshment that she sat on the sideboard. "I could name numerous marriage alliances where the bride was unwilling." She tipped her head to Ella. "In fact, I hear that your courtship with Cain Sinclair was not desired. That he actually locked you up in a tower until you agreed to wed." She played with a loose gold ring on one finger.

"And yet you wed him to keep peace. That is what Hannah Sinclair will do."

Sophie looked at Hannah. "Peter could lock you up in a tower if that would make acquiescing more agreeable."

Erik had told Hannah not to despair, but what did that mean? Did he know that Peter was mild and kind, someone who wouldn't hurt her despite her distaste? Was that why she shouldn't despair? Hannah released her hot, angry breath. "Nothing will make me agreeable to wedding anyone here or remaining in Denmark. Nothing."

"Not even the lives of your brothers?" Sophie countered. She stared hard at Hannah, her rosy cheeks flanked by the high ruff collar. "One word from me, and a man will ride out there to the field to order my Wolf Warriors to kill the Sinclair horsemen and those sailing with them. I believe the count is twenty-two hundred Danes to about one hundred fifty Scots. They will—"

"The Wolf Warriors are Norwegian, not Danish," Hannah interrupted.

Sophie's lips thinned, and she continued. "My warriors will slaughter the men and bring the women to me." She nodded to Ella and Cait as if they discussed their admittance to a royal fete instead of murder.

"But if you wed Peter, Lady Hannah," she continued, "your whole family will be allowed to leave peacefully."

"You think by forcing me to stay here you can control my brothers?"

Sophie smiled as if delighted, the edge of white teeth exposed. "I do indeed."

Hannah showed her own teeth with her grimace as if she'd stepped in horse dung.

Sophie's smile faded a bit, her face softening. "You think me an uhyre, Lady Hannah, a monster, but once you have a child of your own…well, you will understand how a mother can be a monster to protect her daughter who fears for her kingdom, husband, and her own life."

"Queen Anne said that?" Ella asked. "That she fears us?"

"Your brothers and their power." Sophie lifted a letter from a small stack beside her. "That your clan will lead Scotia to civil war."

"May I see it?" Cait asked.

Sophie handed it to Peter who set it into Cait's hands. "'Tis written in Danish," Cait said.

"Of course," Sophie said. "'Tis her natural language with her mother."

"So, we have no way of knowing if you speak the truth," Hannah said.

Peter clasped his hands before his belly as if he was prone to resting them there. "I have already hired a tutor for you, Lady Hannah. You will be able to read our language soon."

Hannah stood suddenly, fury at her helplessness leaping up inside her. She stared at Peter. "You will be dead by my hand before I can read the greeting."

His calm smile dissolved like ink from a letter dropped in a puddle. "But I could make you happy."

"No," she said, shaking her head. "I will not be happy with you, nor being here. I will perish, and you will have no reassurances then or control of my brothers." Hannah turned her gaze to Sophie. "Once I am dead, they will gather those tens of thousands of warriors to war against Denmark no matter what Queen Anne says. You and your chancellor will bring war to your shores and turn King James's loyal warriors against him and his queen."

Before anyone could move, Hannah snatched her sgian dubh from her pocket and, stepping forward, hurled it through the air. It turned once and landed with a *thwack*, point first, into a portrait of some royal ancestor behind Peter. The blade vibrated. Peter's face paled, and his hands pressed hard against his chest over his heart. Several guards ran to stand in front of Sophie, shields held ready.

Let them see Hannah's true mettle as the sister of the Four Horsemen. Rarely did she let her temper rage, but she tossed Gideon's cautious behavior aside and embraced Joshua's wild fury.

Hannah stepped to the side so she could peek at an angle around the barrier of guards. She bared her teeth again. "We Highlanders will never acquiesce agreeably. Perhaps Queen Anne hasn't been in Scotland long enough to write about that in one of her letters."

Dowager-Queen Sophie stood, pushing aside the guard who tried to block her in case Hannah had a second blade. She still had three tucked around her body that Ella and Kára had given her as they'd mounted at the docks.

"And you, Lady Hannah, do not understand the loyalty of my Wolf Warriors, who will block any threat to my realm, slicing through any foreign power as soon as it lands on our shores. I will have you locked up if you remain a danger here, but here you will stay."

"You will have to kill me to make me stay."
Hannah leaned slightly forward and would have
charged up to Sophie if her guard wasn't between
them. How dare this woman, who had little backing
from Denmark's government, move her and her
brothers around on her political chessboard, ready to
sacrifice all of them to keep her daughter protected
from imagined threats.

Hannah's temper pushed her tongue onward despite feeling Ella's or Cait's restraining hand on her
shoulder. "How loyal do you think your most powerful Wolf Warrior will be when he finds out you are
responsible for the death of his unborn child?"

For the first time in the confrontation, Dowager-
Queen Sophie's confident mask slipped, leaving her
with wide, disbelieving eyes.

"Yes," Hannah said. "I may carry Erik Halverson's
babe." Her face held firm triumph even as her insides
quaked with warning. She'd revealed a secret that
might mark Erik as a traitor to his country.

• • •

Erik watched the four huge Scottish warriors with
steely readiness. Mounted and full of biblical refer-
ence, they stood equidistant apart along the docks.

This was not what he wanted. He'd managed to
keep his weakened loyalty hidden as he retrieved
Iselin, trading Hannah away as if she were merely a
pawn in Sophie's game. He'd told Hannah not to despair, but that disease of hopelessness threatened him
now. In the face of capture, Hannah had been

composed and courageous, her large blue eyes open to the foreign world of Kronborg as he released her to Peter Kaas.

You know Sophie will make her wed Peter in my place. Iselin's words, when she came to his side, had shot straight into Erik's chest like lethal arrow tips. Aye, he'd known it, but he hadn't told Hannah. Partly because it would make the situation harder and partly because he had no intention of letting the wedding happen.

Now, seated on their horses before the Sinclair Horsemen, the silence was thick as Sten, Frode, and Nial waited by his side. Cain Sinclair wore a gold crown on the white horse, Joshua Sinclair nearly foamed at the mouth in gnashing anger on red, Gideon Sinclair held a lethal stare from his seat on the black horse, and Bàs stared out through the empty holes of the skull from the back of his green horse.

"We will battle the four Wolf Warrior leaders," Cain called across. "For our wives and sister."

"We will not fall," Erik said, "but if we do, my army will slaughter you."

Frode raised his voice. "Only Trix and Libby will survive to take word back to your people about what has occurred."

"And the mothers and babes," Sten added quietly.

The Sinclairs had ushered the girls and the two remaining wives onto one of the Sinclair ships docked behind the Horsemen. Erik saw them, sad faced, at the rail, watching this prelude to battle. *Fy faen.* Hannah didn't want them to battle. Despite it being his profession, the overwhelming numbers that would see the Sinclairs easily killed left only a sourness on Erik's tongue.

Cain yanked a bow out from behind him and began to talk, his voice booming in the hushed tension moments before the break of battle. In precaution, the front row of Erik's warriors lifted their shields, peering over them at the spectacle.

"I watched as the Lamb opened the first of the seven seals. Then I heard one of the four living creatures say in a voice like thunder, 'Come!' I looked, and there before me was a white horse! Its rider held a bow, and he was given a crown, and he rode out as a conqueror bent on conquest."

"Hannah and the girls are right. We need words like that," Sten said.

"Hold your tongue," Nial said.

Joshua held his sword high, his chest muscles swelling, since he'd taken off his tunic to show off the etched pigment on his skin. "When the Lamb opened the second seal, I heard the second living creature say, 'Come!' Then another horse came out, a fiery red one. Its rider was given power to take peace from the earth and to make people kill each other. To him was given a large sword."

"Foking hell," Frode whispered in Bokmål.

Faen. The Horsemen were using the words to strike fear as surely as their swords could strike. Hannah was right, the resounding lines from the bible sent prickles up his nape. Erik had to do something to break the spell. The fear would dissolve from his warriors as soon as they remembered the numbers behind them, and Hannah's brothers would die. He must stop it.

When Gideon began his recitation of Revelations,

Erik spoke the words at the same time, his voice as powerful as the Horseman's. "When the Lamb opened the third seal, I heard the third living creature say, 'Come!' I looked, and there before me was a black horse! Its rider was holding a pair of scales in his hand." Erik was seated on a black horse as large as Gideon's and raised his hand as if a scale sat there.

Gideon stared coldly at him and didn't finish the words about not damaging the oil and the wine. Maybe he left that part out normally. They weren't threatening.

"When the Lamb opened the fourth seal," Bàs started, and Erik chimed in, his voice full of power. "I heard the voice of the fourth living creature say, 'Come!' I looked, and there before me was a pale horse! Its rider was named—"

Bàs said "Death."

But Erik yelled, "Bàs Sinclair, a courageous warrior from Scotia, not Heaven."

The counter name pulled faces toward Erik, faces of his men and the Horsemen.

"Says Erik Halverson," Joshua said, "who will lose his jack first and then his life today."

Gideon said something to his brother, his face tight with irritation.

Erik leaned the slightest forward in his saddle, and his black horse took a step. With an underhand toss, Erik threw the scrap he'd been holding with his reins at Cain. Cain caught the ripped plaid from the air, holding it by the end. It was the knotted strip that Hannah had flashed before Bàs earlier.

"Your sister wanted you to have that," Erik said.

"She's a wise woman, your sister. A woman I will not abandon."

His words were like a small ripple through his men, starting with Nial, who turned to look at him. "We are riding against the Danish crown?" Nial asked, his voice lowered.

Erik didn't answer as he held Cain's steely gaze. Let Hannah's eldest brother see the truth in it.

"Ships!" yelled a voice in Bokmål.

Erik tore his gaze away from Cain to look at the harbor behind them. The hulking shapes of three galleons sailed toward the mouth of the Kattegat Strait. A yellow cross on a blue field. The vibrant Swedish flags flapped from the main masts over the sails.

"I knew they'd come," a wiry, young Sinclair warrior that Erik remembered as Osk said. "A thousand Swedes who are happy for an excuse to bloody Denmark and take Kronborg Castle." These last words he yelled in Norm, an ancient language of the isles north of Scotia that was close to Nynorsk, a Norwegian dialect spoken along the coast.

Erik doubted the three ships held a thousand warriors; two hundred maximum, unless more were following, or ferries were being readied to carry ground troops across the channel.

Cain didn't look behind him but kept his gaze on Erik. "The Sinclairs have allies outside of Scotland, Wolf Warrior."

"We slaughter Swedes on a daily basis, Highlander," Frode called out. "'Tis nothing new to us."

Enough of this posturing. Erik inhaled deeply. "Hannah wished for us to have a discussion before we act. I would honor her with that action."

"We've already discussed the situation," Bàs said.

Erik kept his gaze on Cain. "A discussion with *all* the Horsemen."

Joshua shifted in his seat, his bay-colored horse standing still. "Because we now have like numbers ye—"

Gideon cut him off with curt words in Gaelic. Perhaps it was Erik's imagination, but Joshua, the great Horseman of War, looked to have chill bumps on his bare skin even though his words and eyes were full of fire. He couldn't imagine the man being frightened. Was he cold?

Bàs said something in Gaelic, and Gideon nodded once. Cain kept his gaze on Erik. "We will speak. Your four and my four."

"In the meetinghouse," Erik said, tipping his head to the structure.

"Osk," Gideon called, and the wiry man turned his head. "Greet the Swedes. Tell them to remain on their ships."

"Think they will listen?" Nial asked.

Sten snorted. "Once you bring the Swedes here, there is no stopping them."

"Kára," Joshua said and the woman, who stood in trousers with the girls on the deck, met his gaze. "Help Osk hold them off." He looked back at Erik and Sten. "She has a convincing nature."

Erik dismounted and spoke to his five other generals who had kept his men in line while he was away. "Send a runner to our forces over the ridge. Bring half of them here. If that devil Captain Larsen orders an attack, I want them picked off as they land their ships. Leave the other half south of Kronborg to keep the sound free of more Swedish troops trying to cross over there."

The five men nodded and turned away. "Aksel," he called to a slim warrior in his top ranks. The man ran up to him. "Ride to Kronborg and let them know Sweden is bringing their troops to shore in support of the Horsemen." The man nodded and ran for his horse.

Things were out of hand. No longer was this a mother worried about her daughter in a foreign country; this was war on Danish soil. If Sophie wasn't the loving mother of young King Christian, she might be tried for treason herself.

Erik led his three men up the steps of the meetinghouse. They walked inside to see Patrick Stewart pacing along the back wall.

"I demand to be released!" he yelled.

"I release you then," Erik said with a wave of his hand.

Patrick stopped, a look of astonishment on his face. After a pause, he strode across the floor to the door and halted with a small jump as Joshua filled the doorway. The Horseman's frown relaxed into a wicked grin as he came face-to-face with Lord Robert's son.

"Greetings, Patrick Stewart," Joshua said with serpent-like maliciousness. The Highlander didn't even need to use his gruesome threats to make the dandy, who'd terrorized his people on both Shetland and Orkney, look like he might piss himself.

Patrick jumped back. "Father said ye were alive," he said, but his face paled as if he watched a ghost before him.

"I am come back from the grave to see ye gutted," Joshua said.

Patrick retreated to the back of the room, his eyes wild. "I have money, Sinclair, money ye can use to buy back your sister from these people." He indicated Erik with an outstretched hand.

"Dowager-Queen Sophie is the richest woman in Christendom," Erik said. "Your money means nothing to her." Even after paying his army from her own coffers, she still had enough to keep the Danish government running smoothly for her son, King Christian. Another reason she might be forgiven for bringing war to her people.

Joshua stalked into the room, one step at a time toward Patrick until he grabbed him by the tunic. "Ye're not so brave without your brute now, are ye?" Joshua said in his face. "Who decays with a stinking seal in my grave."

"Leave him alive," Gideon said as he walked through the doorway. "King James wants to put him on trial with his father."

Joshua continued to glare in Patrick's eyes, his fist under the man's chin as he nearly lifted him from the floor. "Let him go, Joshua," Cain said as he followed inside with Bàs and Erik's three men. Joshua released him with a shove against his chest and pivoted as if he needed to put some distance between them before he lost control and skewered him.

"Go sit over there." Gideon pointed to a corner for Patrick, and the man hurried to sit on the floor as if he were a school lad sent to the corner.

Erik's three men stood in a line beside him. No one had removed their weapons, but hands remained empty, at least for now. Cain and his brothers lined up opposite him in their own order with Cain across from Erik.

"Hannah wished for us to discuss before we act," Erik said. "So, hear me out." With a nod from Cain, Erik explained as succinctly as possible how Iselin was taken while he was fighting the Swedes on the border. How she would be forced to wed the chancellor if the Sinclair Horsemen weren't made controllable. "Taking Hannah was our mission ordered by Dowager-Queen Sophie and her chancellor, Peter Kaas. Once I confirmed she was important to her brothers." Erik's gaze slid across to Bàs. "Luckily, one of you came back earlier from Orkney, and I could verify the love between sister and brother that your wives expressed. Hannah Sinclair is beloved by all."

Bàs's frown intensified. "And we will kill to get her back."

Erik nodded, thinking of Iselin. "I would, too."

Joshua shrugged. "But ye didn't, did ye? Instead of marching into Kronborg to take your sister back, ye sailed to Scotland to take our *innocent* sister." He stressed the word with a sneer.

"We could have waited until you returned from Orkney and killed the Four Horsemen," Sten said, his arms crossed. "But 'twas forbidden."

"You could have *tried*," Bàs said with quiet authority, "but ye would have died doing so."

Gideon squinted slightly. "If she worries about us taking over Scotland from her daughter, why were you forbidden to kill us in Scotland?"

Erik studied the Horseman of Justice, the brother

with the most cunning from Peter's report. "She doesn't wish to take you from protecting Scotland and her daughter. She wants to be able to control you."

"My brothers barely control me," Joshua murmured on an exhale, but his look said otherwise. Worry sat heavy in his brow. "Fok," he snapped. It seemed that even the most volatile brother could be controlled to protect his sister.

Gideon held up his hand to quiet Joshua but looked at Erik. "I know King James. He's proud and will not be happy if your dowager-queen is in charge of his best warriors. He would question our loyalty out of his lack of confidence and his worry, but he depends upon our strength to keep Scotland strong against invaders." Gideon shook his head. "Nay, James will not like Sophie's interference on behalf of his wife."

Before Erik could respond, Cain's quiet words caught him like a bird in a net. "Hannah will kill herself rather than weaken her clan."

Erik felt his blood surge but breathed evenly. "Sophie plans to lock her up until she's convinced Hannah won't harm herself." Erik swallowed hard. "And…if by chance she is with child, Hannah would not endanger it."

Was this the reason Sophie wanted Hannah wed? If she remained pregnant, she'd want to protect her child. The thought of Peter forcing himself on her made Erik's jaw clench. Suddenly, the sociable man, rumored to be kind, turned sinister in Erik's mind. Aye, he'd have to die if he forced Hannah into bed.

Tension swelled with the silence in the room as

Erik's blood heated. His hands fisted, and he yearned to roar.

"Maybe this is why ye stole my sister's innocence," Bàs said, his words soft, belying the promise of death Erik saw in his eyes. "Because ye knew she wouldn't harm herself if she thought an innocent life might be growing in her?"

Joshua's bellow covered any denial Erik might give.

"Ye foking bastard," Joshua yelled, charging forward, his fists pulled back.

CHAPTER TWENTY-ONE

Holmgang – A Scandinavian Duel

"Once the holmgang had been agreed, it had to occur in the following three to seven days. If the man who sought the duel failed to appear at the arranged time, he would be banished and outlawed. Similarly, if either of the two men failed to appear, the other man's cause would be seen as just, and the matter thus settled.

A man that did not appear at the duel would be formally proclaimed to 'have no honor,' and was thus socially ostracized and outlawed. An outlawed man was outside of the bounds of law, and any man could kill him without suffering repercussions."

ANCIENT-ORIGINS.NET

Erik sidestepped Joshua's attack, but Joshua turned, his leg sweeping against Erik's calves, bringing him crashing down with such force, it was a wonder the old floorboards didn't cave in. Joshua leaped upon Erik. *Crack!* A fist like a granite boulder hit Erik's jaw. Despite the lightning strike of pain through his head, Erik unleashed his strength, and flipped Joshua over onto his back.

Crack! Pain again erupted in Erik's knuckles as he delivered a similar blow to Joshua's jaw, followed by one to his nose. Fy faen, his hand would remain bruised and bloodied, but 'twas a familiar feel.

Blood poured from Joshua's nose as he rolled, leaping to his feet. The wrathful Horseman of War didn't even wipe at the gushing blood, and barreled forward again, grabbing Erik around the waist to hoist him in the air. Erik balled his fists and struck against the soft indents on the sides of Joshua's head. The man grunted, dropping him.

Erik turned to see Nial pinning Cain's arms with a squeeze, lifting him in his bearlike grip. Sten battled with fists against Bàs, and Frode had taken on Gideon. No one pulled steel. As soon as one did, blood would flow freely.

Crash! Nial threw Cain against the wall of the building, but the man barreled back into him like a charging bull, lifting Nial clear from the floor, despite his weight, and threw him. *Crash!* The small table splintered under Nial's body.

Sten and Frode were holding their own against Bàs and Gideon, trading punch after punch and dodging strikes by their opponents. They seemed equally matched. Joshua dropped his fists and roared, giving Erik warning of his next charge. The two grabbed each other's shoulders as if trying to throw the other to the ground, but the vast strength in each made it impossible. One would have to give way. Erik dropped to the floor, using his arms to throw Joshua over his head to the floor behind him.

The door of the room swung open, banging the wall. "Enough!" Ella yelled, Cait standing beside her.

"Ella," Cain said, turning away from Nial to run to her, grabbing her up in a hug. Gideon did the same, trying to carry Cait back out the door. Shana's face appeared around the corner before mumbling something about getting bandages and disappearing.

"I love you too," Cait said. "Put me down."

"There's no time for brawling," Ella said, struggling to loosen her husband's hold on her. "Sophie is going to make Hannah wed Peter Kaas. We must do something."

"By God!" Kára exclaimed as she ran inside and up to Joshua. She grabbed a rag from his belt and pinched his nose. She put a finger under his chin to tilt his head back. "Let me guess. You started it."

"He took Hannah's maidenhead," Joshua yelled, his blood-stained hands moving in the air, but his words sounded comical with his nose pinched, although there was nothing comical about what had happened between Erik and Hannah.

Erik walked up to Joshua, who tried to push his wife behind him as if Erik might still try to fight. Erik stopped and stared Joshua hard in the eyes. "I would beat any man who did the same to Iselin if I thought what you thought. But there were no calculated intentions when your sister honored me. There was nothing except two adults desiring each other. I swear it."

Joshua breathed hard but didn't attack.

"We must plan now," Ella said. "Sophie already has a reverend at Kronborg."

"Now we have Sweden in our harbor," Nial said. He looked pointedly at Cain. "And don't believe for a moment that they will listen to you. They didn't come here because they want to help you. They are here only to try to take our country."

"Of course," Gideon said, as if they'd made the decision to use Denmark's enemy anyway.

Shana dodged Cait to come inside, right up to Bàs, balancing jars and strips of clean rags.

"My army will battle the Swedes while you"— Erik pointed to the Sinclair brothers—"break into Kronborg to extract Hannah."

That way Sophie wouldn't blame him for Hannah's escape, not with Swedish ships anchored so close to shore. He would be too busy protecting Denmark to worry about what the Sinclairs were up to. Only Sophie's elite group of fifty soldiers remained at Kronborg to protect her.

"We can't be seen helping you rescue her," Nial said. "Or we will be labeled traitors." He passed a hard glance at Erik.

Ella looked over to Erik while dabbing at the cuts on Cain's knuckles. "You need to know…" She inhaled. "Hannah let Sophie know that she might be with your child."

Could she know so soon? Erik's chest opened with something that might be hope.

"Sophie was quiet," Cait said, attending to Gideon. "But her twitches and tense face said she was not pleased at all by the information."

"I knew it," Nial murmured. "Hannah would turn against us."

Erik spun toward him, speaking in Bokmål. "Hannah is using every weapon she possesses not to wed Kaas. To her it must seem we have abandoned her now that we have Iselin."

He spoke to Ella and Cait in English. "I have not abandoned her and will do what must be done to free her."

He looked at Cain. "You will need to take at least

fifty warriors to help with the liberation," Erik said. *Dritt*. He tasted blood from his cut lip. Its tang made his warrior blood run faster. Torn between his duty to Denmark-Norway and his sister and what had been growing between him and Hannah, Erik had welcomed the pain of the fight, but it hadn't distracted him for long.

Erik nodded toward the door where Patrick Stewart was stepping out into the gray day.

"Go ahead," Kára said to Joshua, dropping her hand from his nose. In three long strides, he grabbed Patrick's shoulder.

"Don't kill him," Gideon reminded him, turning his face back to Cait, who applied some balm Shana had brought for his swelling lip.

Cait *tsk*ed as she dabbed. "'Tis a good thing no weapons were drawn."

Gideon met Erik's gaze. "Aye."

"Else there would be more blood," Erik said. As it was, the table and chair had been smashed and there were pools and drops of blood flung across the floorboards.

Iselin ran in, going to Frode first with her own jar of ointment and bandages draped over her arm. "I can't believe you all were fighting when their sister is locked up in that dungeon castle," Iselin scolded, turning her frown on Erik.

"I'm sure my husband started it," Kára said.

"Of course I did," Joshua said, carrying Patrick Stewart over his shoulder to plop him back down in the corner. "The bastard laid with my sister, out of wedlock."

"I don't know your sister well," Iselin said, cutting

Joshua a cold glance, "but I doubt she would like you yelling that about everywhere."

Kára smiled. "I like her." Kára tugged Joshua to follow her. "Let's get you a tunic that isn't covered with blood." She rubbed his arms. "You have chill bumps."

"No, I don't," Joshua answered quickly. "'Tis warrior's power leaching from my skin."

"No doubt," Kára said, leading him toward the door.

Joshua looked down at his bloodied chest. "I rather like the blood, especially if others think 'tis from someone else." He stopped at the threshold to frown back at Erik. "But we aren't finished, Dane."

"Norwegian," Erik corrected. Erik would never think of himself as Danish, even if he fought their battles. They might be one country in the political arena, but they were different cultures.

Gideon finished binding Patrick Stewart's wrists and ankles, leaving him in the corner of the room. Gideon and Bàs filed out, along with Sten and Nial, who would find bandages and ointment from their men.

Cain remained, standing opposite Erik. He crossed his arms as he met Erik's gaze with intensity. "My brothers and I will rescue Hannah, and ye will stay away from her. We will leave these shores immediately tonight. If we do so without your interference, I will ensure the Swedish ships return to their side of the strait without attacking Kronborg and your men."

"And what if I interfere?" Erik asked, his face stony.

"Then we will fight again, but this time with steel.

Hannah will suffer by seeing you struck down, and we will be delayed in getting her safely home."

"You have decided she will leave here?" Erik asked. "Without asking her." His gut tightened. Not at the worry over battling with blades. He could battle and maim without killing Hannah's brothers. No, the tightness came from somewhere else, and it seemed to move up into the muscles of his chest, as if it bored into him, creating a hole.

"'Tis always been the plan to rescue her and return to Scotland. Gideon will ride Patrick Stewart down to Edinburgh to stand trial and meet with King James about the letters his wife has been apparently sending to her mother."

"That plan was before… She could be with child. My child."

A cold, dark fury radiated from Cain's features, his clenched fists, his entire bearing. "I will send a missive to Dowager-Queen Sophie if my sister delivers a child from your dalliance."

Dalliance? Perhaps the meaning was different across countries, but what had occurred between Erik and Hannah was not trivial. She had tricked him, trying to make herself less valuable to Sophie, but what they'd shared…it was considerably more than a dalliance.

"Hannah should be asked about this," Erik said.

As if breaking free from some tether, Cain closed the gap between them, fisting Erik's tunic. Even with his strength, Cain couldn't move Erik. They stared hard into each other's eyes. "Hannah needs her kin and to go home."

"Hannah needs to decide on her own what she

requires to be happy," Erik said, his voice as hard as Cain's. "You haven't given her the freedom to figure that out, at Girnigoe or here."

"She is free on Scottish soil, and her happiness can be decided on after she is safe," Cain said. "Without the likes of ye, an experienced seducer, swaying her." Cain shoved at Erik as he released his hold and jabbed a finger in his chest. "Stay the fok away from my sister." Without waiting for any type of reply, Cain pivoted and stalked out of the room.

Erik had forgotten about Iselin being there and the bound Stewart in the corner. When he felt a gentle squeeze of his hand, his gaze snapped to his sister. Her eyes widened at the hard look on his face, but she didn't retreat.

"What are you going to do?" she asked in Bokmål.

Fy faen. That was a question without a clear answer, and Erik hated not having a step-by-step plan in a mission. But this was no longer a mission. He'd completed that, rescuing his sister. But, somehow, that mission had transformed into something bigger, more complicated. And, damn, he hated complicated.

He was going to lose Hannah before anything more could grow between them. Erik grabbed the back of his head at the tightness running from his shoulders up his neck, making Iselin drop her hand. The tension within him was growing to the point he might explode. "I need to kill some Swedes."

Iselin huffed. "Spilling blood is not going to fix anything."

"It could," he said, rubbing his jaw that was tender and bruised from the earlier fight. He didn't mind the pain. It was familiar and on the outside of his body. It might distract him from the breath-stealing ache inside his chest.

Iselin shook her head. "Killing Swedes or even Sinclairs won't fix what you're feeling."

He snorted softly. "And what am I feeling?"

"Pain."

He rubbed a hand over the torn skin on his knuckles. "I know pain. 'Tis familiar."

"Not that type of pain," she said, pulling his hand to her so she could rub some ointment on the cuts. "This is a new, deeper pain," she said in Bokmål and touched his chest. "In here."

"A warrior doesn't suffer pain of the heart." He frowned, wishing for something to numb the tightness there.

She pinched her lips, giving him a look that balanced between scolding and pity. "I saw your face when you brought her to trade," Iselin said. "I know pain in the crease of your brow, pain when you watched her walk to Sophie." Iselin tilted her head. "You care for the Scottish woman. She is more than a mere dalliance."

Was he so easily read? Apparently, yes, at least by Iselin. "Aye, she is more." He let his hands drop to his sides, the closest he'd ever allow himself to get to defeat.

"And now she's being forced to wed Peter in my place."

"Her brothers will break in tonight and save her."

"And take her away on the tide."

"If I try to see her before she goes, I'll have to spill blood, blood of her kin."

Iselin had seen the hardness in Cain, the threat. Cain wouldn't allow Erik near Hannah, but would Hannah insist on seeing him? Would her brothers lie to her that he'd left?

"Fy faen," he muttered, looking toward the open door. "And now I have Swedes to fight. If I leave that fight to rescue Hannah, I'm a traitor to the crown. Sophie will order me dead, and the Sinclairs will try to kill me for being a threat to Hannah."

"First, Sophie might already consider you a traitor for lying with Hannah." Iselin stared up into his face, her head tilted, studying him. "If you don't find a way to speak with her, you will lose her forever."

"Faen i helvete!" he yelled with such force, Patrick Stewart jumped a bit in the corner.

"If ye let me go," Patrick said, "I will see ye well rewarded."

"If he lets you go, Patrick Stewart," Iselin said without looking at him, "Joshua Sinclair will make certain you're dead by daybreak."

Erik couldn't take the confines of the room any longer, nor the pitying looks from his sister. He clenched the pommel of his secured sword and traipsed to the door, throwing himself through it.

Below at the docks, Gideon issued orders to the Sinclair generals of the men who'd sailed over with them. The three ships, flying Sweden's flags, still sat in the strait, waiting. Their ground troops were probably lining up on Sweden's coastline, a mere two and a half miles across the strait. Even sending his fastest skiff over to Norway, the rest of Erik's massive army wouldn't have time to mobilize their force before the Swedes attacked here.

A thousand of Erik's men were marching closer to the docks while the other thousand waited over the eastern ridge for the Swedish infantry. Erik's group of two-hundred elite warriors waited behind the meetinghouse, watching the Sinclairs ready their ships to leave.

Shana and Ella spoke with some of the men about supplies for the journey home. He watched Cait and Kára on the deck of one ship, holding their babes. Even while nursing one, the other strapped to her back, Kára Sinclair looked like a battle maiden ready to take up her sword.

The afternoon sped by quickly as the Sinclairs readied and Erik and his men prepared for attack if the ships in the harbor came closer. The sun sank below the western landscape, growing shadows into giants across the docks.

Erik watched the Four Horsemen mount their different colored horses. A fifth man brought Loinneil out and mounted. *I should be going with them.* His pulse pounded with readiness even though they would leave him behind.

A group of approximately fifty Sinclairs jogged off toward Kronborg's western side, carrying torches and two small gunpowder kegs. At least the Sinclairs had taken his advice about taking more men in case Sophie's guards were alerted.

Erik marched down the steps and strode across to his horse, Loki. Sensing his friend's fury, Loki nodded his head, his nostrils open to pull in large draughts of air, readying himself for battle.

Nial ran up to him. "Where are you going?" The cutting worry in his friend's tone infuriated Erik even more. His men would never understand him risking his head for a woman. Maybe Frode, but definitely not Nial.

Erik looked down at the warrior, his lips curled back almost like a beast. "To see if the Swedes are advancing across the strait." Without waiting to see Nial's look of relief, Erik leaned forward, and Loki leaped forward into the growing darkness. The Wolf Warriors parted quickly to create a path for their mighty leader. As Erik galloped toward the ridge beyond Kronborg, he drew his sword.

The cold air hit his hot face, and he yelled into the night. 'Twas not a word but a guttural growl of pent-up anger and something more, something hotter and debilitating. He slashed his sword against an invisible foe, the blade whistling as it caught the wind. Loki surged ahead, all muscle and power under Erik as he raced off as if in battle, avoiding the moving Sinclairs by heading west first.

Cold enveloped him despite the heat in his muscles. The cold was vacant of the brightness of mischievous laughter, the softness of a courageous touch, the taste of honest passion. He roared again, ripping his sword through the air as he rose up tall in the saddle, clenching Loki with his thighs to remain seated.

The horse, despite seeing no one about, surged onward as if racing to battle. Because he felt and heard the battle in his friend and master. Erik flew through the night passing Kronborg Castle, passing by an imprisoned Hannah, fully realizing this action meant he would lose her forever.

CHAPTER TWENTY-TWO

"Cattle die,
kindred die,
every man is mortal:
but I know one thing
that never dies,
the glory of the great dead."
HÁVAMÁL – VIKING POEM TRANSCRIBED IN THE
THIRTEENTH CENTURY CODEX REGIUS

Hannah worked quietly in the luxurious room she'd been given. She used the three-inch blade that Sophie's guards hadn't found in her stays to slice the fabric of her petticoats and tied the petticoat and smock around each leg to resemble trousers. She used the blue ribbons in the armoire to secure them well and squatted to make sure they wouldn't pop open.

"Not as sleek as Cait's," she murmured, speaking about the slim leg coverings Cait had given each of them for Hogmanay. "But they'll do." She tucked the blade back in her stays and went to the window, pushing open both sides of the paned glass. Her heart lurched at the dizzying height. "Bloody hell." They'd put her in a chamber on the third floor, probably to deter her from escaping exactly the way she'd planned, out the window.

Do not despair. Hannah had been holding onto Erik's words through the whole afternoon and evening. But she didn't know what they meant. Were they a promise he'd come get her? She'd heard Peter talking with regimented soldiers, their words soft but frantic, but she didn't understand the Danish language. Were they concerned about the additional Sinclair forces?

Do not despair. They were good words even if they meant little coming from a man who had traded her away. "Daingead," Hannah muttered. Trading her for Iselin had been part of the plan. Of course, Erik didn't want to do it, but it had to happen. The fact that he'd known she would be forced to wed Peter Kaas, however, heated her blood.

Hannah looked down the side of the tower and felt her heart lurch at the height. "A wee bit of heart-pounding fear can't stop a Sinclair Horsewoman," she whispered. She just had to be clever about it. She couldn't fall to her death. That would catapult her brothers and clan into a war, and if she were with child… "No," she whispered. "I must be clever."

Hannah was glad she hadn't brought Loinneil. She needed to worry only about getting herself out of this fortress. She searched the night, her eyes wandering over the dark landscape. Erik would come, wouldn't he?

Hannah turned back to the room with its ornate bed, thick rugs, armoire full of petticoats and bodices, and a chest full of silk stockings, smocks, and aprons in the traditional Danish and Norwegian style. *A bloody wedding trousseau.*

Long strips of silk hung around the bed. She'd tie them together and lower herself down like Cait did at the end of her performances. Hannah had learned alongside her brothers how to create knots that didn't slip. Even as she told herself this, her heart thumped wildly inside, and her hands felt tingly. "God's teeth," she whispered, irritated at her body's reaction to the thought of hanging outside the window.

Blast!

Hannah jumped at the explosion and looked outside the window. Fire flew up into the darkness to the east of the castle. Running steps thudded past her locked door. Was the explosion a distraction? She scanned the dark wall and saw a shadow dropping down it on the inside. Erik? She squinted, trying to see if the scaler wore trousers or a plaid wrap, but it was too dark. They didn't even know where she was in the castle. If she waved her arms, would Sophie's guards see her, sending men to intercept Erik? Between rescuing her and her telling Sophie that they'd lain together, Erik could be hanged for treason.

"Daingead." She ran for the bed, yanking the drapes. Silk was strong, wasn't it? But was it strong enough to hold her dropping down a three-story castle wall? "Clove hitch to tie it to the bedpost," she murmured, taking the end. "Bloody hell." The bed was so far away from the window. She'd have to use her sheets as well.

"Square knots for the lengths," she said, pulling the ends through her grasp. Six knots tied, she threw the end out the window. Now she could see four men crouching in the shadows inside the wall. Hannah raised her hands to her mouth, took a deep breath, and made the sharp call of a hawk. A face turned up to her, and the light from a torch hitched inside the wall showed bare legs. Disappointment tugged at Hannah's middle, but she kept her fingers moving along the silk drapes.

With a final tug on the knots, Hannah pushed her way up onto the window ledge, patting her petticoats around her legs. Her palms were sweaty, and her heart hammered. She took even breaths despite the instinct to gulp air. "Slow and steady," she whispered and reached one leg down, wrapping it in the fabric like Cait had shown them. *Use your legs as much as your arms*, she'd instructed.

Another flash of fire was followed by a boom on the other side of the castle. Cait's gaze snapped over there. Groups of castle guards ran toward the explosion and away from Hannah's tower.

"Lord, save me," she whispered and clenched the fabric wrapped around her legs, letting it slide through as she lowered down hand over hand. Her muscles grew hot as she used not only her arms but her legs to slow her descent.

"That's it, Hannah," came a voice below her. "Just a bit farther."

A bit farther? She was still halfway up the side of the tower.

Bàs's hands grabbed her around the waist. "Untie the sash right before ye." He wobbled slightly, making her gasp. She tried to look down, which shifted her in Bàs's grasp. "Don't look down," he said quickly. "Cain is balancing me. Cut the sash if ye must."

Hannah withdrew the blade from her bodice and sawed three times to cut through the fabric with the razor-sharp blade. The sash dropped to the ground below.

"Now, Cain," Bàs said. "Hold on to me, Hannah."

Hannah's trembling arms held tightly to her

youngest brother as they lowered. She glanced over his shoulder to see Cain's hands wrapped around Bàs's calves, holding his feet planted on his shoulders as Gideon and Joshua held their arms out as if waiting for her to fall. Gideon reached her from Bàs's hold, and Bàs jumped down off Cain.

"I didn't know I was frightened of heights," she whispered. "But I could have made it all the way down."

Gideon grabbed up the fabric. "We didn't want the sash to dangle to the ground. It would be seen before daylight for certain then, and we need time to sail."

"Sail? Away tonight?" she asked, her gaze going beyond her brothers. Was Erik out there waiting for her?

"He did not come," Bàs said.

A hollowness spread inside her, and she swallowed hard. "'Twas not part of the plan."

"We need to go now," Cain said, reaching to lift her, but she turned to hurry forward into the shadows.

With her tied petticoats rustling with each step, it was difficult to stay quiet. Gideon surged forward to lead the way to a hidden door in the wall. The ten-foot-thick wall was a storage area, filled with casks of wine and ale and provisions if needed for a siege. Gideon hid the balled-up fabric in a barrel. In silence, the five of them moved across the way to where a door stood ajar. Two men were tied and gagged, lying on their sides near it.

In a moment, Hannah and her brothers jogged out on the dark meadow. A man stood by a group of horses, and Hannah's foolish heart leaped. But 'twas only Keenan. The familiar warrior lifted Hannah onto

Loinneil and climbed on behind her. He gave her the
reins, and she put her heels to Loinneil's flank. They
surged forward, her brothers surrounding her: Bàs
behind, Cain in front, Gideon to her left, and Joshua
to her right. They'd come for her without hesitation,
each one of them having so much to lose, each one
having found happiness and love elsewhere. And, yet,
they still came, ready to sacrifice for their sister. They
had come when Erik had not. Tears stung her eyes,
welling out hot to dry on her cheeks in the cool night
wind as they rode fast toward the ridge.

As they reached the top of the climb, Hannah held
her breath. She wasn't sure what she'd expected, but it
wasn't this.

Nothing. The space between the ridge and the
dock was dark and empty, the muted moonlight showing a peaceful night. Three ships sat like hulking
monsters, dark and silent, in the bay. The three
Sinclair ships and Erik's ship sat silently at the dock.
But where were Erik's Wolf Warriors? *He's left?*

As they drew closer, Hannah could finally make
out Sinclair warriors moving smoothly in the shadows
to load the ships. *We are leaving tonight.* The thought
nearly choked her as her gaze moved between the
plaid clothed men, looking for a giant wearing
breeches and a white tunic. The only people in
breeches were her sisters by marriage, organizing supplies, gesturing quietly.

Kára led Patrick Stewart by a lead tied to his
bound wrists, walking him toward the larger of the
two Sinclair ships. His eyes were downcast, and
Hannah saw he was gagged.

She stopped Loinneil, and Keenan dismounted

quickly. Hannah followed, annoyed when she felt his hands grab her waist. "I can do it," she said, her tone rigid, but he still held her until her feet were planted on the ground.

Turning away, she went straight to Cain. "Are we leaving now?"

"Aye. The tides are high, and we can sail out of the reach before Sophie's guards even realize you're gone." He walked off, issuing orders to load the horses.

Hannah followed and grabbed Cain's arm. "What of Erik and his warriors?"

"They are over the ridge to the south past Kronborg where his larger army is stationed."

"Is he just letting us sail away?" *Is he just letting me sail away?* She and Erik hadn't talked about the plan after she was rescued, but this couldn't be it. It couldn't.

Cain wouldn't meet her gaze but motioned to Bàs to come over. "Hannah wants to know about Erik." Her eldest brother didn't handle weeping well and treated her like a snake that might shoot venomous tears at him.

As soon as Bàs stepped closer, Cain jogged over to Seraph, whose tack was being disassembled for comfort on the voyage.

"Erik? He's…gone?" Hannah asked Bàs, less worried about keeping the hurt from her voice with her younger brother. Of all the brothers, Bàs knew pain of the heart intimately. He'd lived with it for decades until he met Shana.

Bàs's hands rested on Hannah's shoulders as he stooped to look straight into her eyes. "He stole ye away from your family, your home, and your country."

"But he—"

"He stole your innocence, Hannah."

"No, he didn't," she said, her voice rising, but then she lowered it. "I told you I wanted him. I've said that already."

Bàs exhaled long, pulling Hannah out of the path of some Sinclair warriors carrying bundles of turnips and other harvested vegetables onboard.

Hannah stood rigid, her hands fisted at her sides. "We must be given a choice. Cain can't take that away from us."

Bàs looked into her eyes, and she blinked against the sting of unshed tears. His hands stroked her arms. "Explain," she said, realizing his body language said there was more to this story.

"Cain told Erik to leave, and he did. Erik chose to accept his duty as a warrior and commander. He went against what might have been in his heart in order to protect his men and his country. A warrior's greatest honor is to die a good death protecting his people." Bàs squeezed her hand even though she barely noticed with the numbness spreading through her body. "Erik Halverson withdrew to protect his men, to lead them another day against his country's enemies. It shows he's an excellent leader." Bàs lifted his thumb pad to wipe a tear that slid down her cheek. "But a poor husband."

Hannah reached up and clenched his fingers, bringing his hand down from her face. "'Twas a test then? By Cain? To see his feelings for me."

Bàs looked back. He wouldn't insult her with pity, because she'd never done so to him as he grew up ridiculed and shunned. "He chose his army." Bàs's voice held approval, not censure. "He chose his duty to protect his dowager-queen and his country, Denmark."

The numbness advanced through Hannah, removing her strength to hold back her tears. "His country is Norway," she whispered as hot tears streaked down her cheeks.

Bàs pulled her into his chest, holding her there. Behind her, she heard Gideon, Ella, and even Joshua come up to see if she was all right, but Bàs brushed them away, letting her mourn without having to explain.

All those years as Bàs grew from frightened, sorrowful boy to strong man, she'd held him, giving comfort he couldn't get anywhere else. And despite the need to scurry around readying the ships, he chose to hold her there instead, keeping everyone at bay so she could grieve. So even though she should pull away, saying she was well, she leaned in to him and accepted his comfort as pain washed through her like poisoned wine.

"Libby! Trix!" The frantic edge to Cait's voice drew Hannah's gaze from Bàs's drenched tunic.

Hannah wiped at her cheeks and sniffed, taking the rag Bàs offered her.

Cait's face had a wild look as she ran to Gideon. "They're gone. From the ship."

Kára was on the deck where Patrick Stewart sat bound and helplessly waiting to sail. "I've even checked down in the bilge hull," Kára said, shaking her head.

"Bloody hell." Gideon turned to scan the darkness

where men hurried quietly, finishing their preparations to leave before daylight revealed a dangling sash
from Hannah's window. "Where have those two trou-
blemakers gone?"

Hannah turned to look at the dark ridge to the
south. She had a pretty good idea.

• • •

Erik paced before a large fire built in the center of the
encampment. His men were ready for the Swedes
when they landed. The darkness hid their numbers
across the strait. It was two miles across the narrowest
section of the strait, so they'd arrive by ship or ferries,
and Erik's Wolf Warriors would pick them off. He'd
left a small contingent of men to observe the Sinclairs
leaving. If the Swedish ships pulled into port, they
would start shooting, sending one man racing back to
gather five hundred warriors.

"I wouldn't go near him," Sten said to one of the
generals. "Go ask Nial."

Frode and Sten stood nearby but far enough away
to dodge Erik's fist or kick, which he'd initially delivered when dismounting Loki. Erik had lost control of
his temper that he thought he'd reined in on the
meadow when they started praising him for not incit-
ing Sophie. For abandoning Hannah to her brothers.
Nial had stayed away, and Iselin had pulled Frode
away, motioning to Sten. Which was fine with Erik. He
wanted nothing to do with any of them anymore. *Fy
faen!* He was letting her foking sail away. *I'm going
after her.*

The words, echoing in his head, made him stop

before the fire. The dancing flames flashed before his eyes, but he saw only Hannah's form as she danced before the Beltane Fire, so free and joyful. She'd had bitter loss in her life, ignored and avoided by men for fear of raising her brothers' wrath. And, yet, her smile was full of happiness as if she didn't worry that fate would deliver a blow to wipe it away. *Hannah.* Her presence created a wild, fresh air that helped Erik breathe. To lose her forever would be like losing his very breath.

He turned as a murmur rose behind him. "Pis," Sten said and jogged toward the back of the encampment.

"Dritt," Frode murmured and ran after him.

"Hannah?" Iselin asked, looking to Erik.

Erik's chest opened on a big inhale, and he blinked to rid his eyes of the spots from staring at the bright flames. He rushed through his men, but the weight of disappointment slowed his steps as his sight cleared.

"Trix? Libby?" Sten's confused voice floated back to Erik.

"What are you doing here?" Frode asked. "And what are you dragging?"

Trix dropped a bundle of folded fabric at Sten's feet. "You must hurry," she said.

"Before they sail," Libby said and trudged toward Erik. She stopped, letting go of her load with a huff. "These are so heavy," she said, shaking her slender arms.

"But they're perfectly waterproof," Trix said, smiling up at Sten and Frode. "Good Highland wool that's been fulled."

"What's this?" Nial asked, coming up to the pile, and the group of men closest to them gathered, several of them bringing torches to light the area.

Trix smiled broadly, rubbing her arms as if the muscles were cramping. She looked straight at Erik. "They are wraps to replace your trousers."

"Why would I do that?" he asked, his voice still rough.

"So you can sneak back to the ships," Libby said, her hands propped on her hips. "So you can kiss Hannah before she leaves."

Trix looked at Sten and Frode. "We brought enough for four of ye," she said. "So ye can protect Captain Erik."

"Without the wool wraps," Libby said, "you wouldn't be able to get close, but in the dark you'll look like Highlanders."

Erik's gaze moved between the two girls and their piles. Had they tricked four poor Sinclair warriors out of their clothes, leaving them naked? He wouldn't put it past them.

Trix propped her hands on her hips. Her familiar, toothy smile changed to something like a vicious frown to match Libby's. "Are you really going to let her sail away without a word of farewell?"

"Faen," Libby swore. "Surrender enough of your bloody pride to put the Highland wrap on and ride your arse over that blasted hill." She pointed.

As if not to be outdone with curse words, Trix jumped in. "Fy faen. If you're bloody afraid they'll discover you and shoot you," Trix said, "wave a white cloth like a flag of surrender."

There was no humor left in Erik or he would have smiled over the ferocity in which the young girls had learned to swear. But his mind had latched onto something else Trix had said. "Surrender?" Erik murmured.

Nial cleared his throat and spoke as if instructing the girls, but Erik considered that he also meant to remind Erik. "Wolf Warriors, especially the leader of the Wolf Warriors, never surrender."

"We don't even have a white flag," Sten said.

"No army of courage would," Frode said.

Nial stared frowning at the girls as light from the torches his men held splashed over their young serious faces. "King Christian would have no faith in us," Nial said, "if we laid down our weapons before another army. He and his regents and probably Dowager-Queen Sophie would see us as traitors, loyal to another government."

"Loyal to another government," Erik murmured. He glanced at the ridge blocking the ports north. His heart thumped as if he were about to charge into battle.

Frode crouched before Libby. "Aren't you afraid they will leave without you, vennen?"

Libby looked at Trix who looked back. They shook their heads slowly in unison. "Cait won't let them leave without finding us," Trix said. Her confidence made several of the men around them chuckle, and Sten snorted.

"Gideon either," Libby said.

"They're probably correct," Sten said in Bokmål.

"We will take you back to your clan," Erik said, motioning to the pile of plaids. "Dressed as Highlanders." He looked at Nial without blinking. "And carrying a white flag."

CHAPTER TWENTY-THREE

"Soldiers have been using white flags to signify
capitulation for thousands of years. The ancient
Roman chronicler Livy described a Carthaginian
ship being decorated with 'white wool and branches
of olive' as a symbol of parley during the Second
Punic War, and Tacitus later wrote of white flags
being displayed as part of the surrender of Vitellian
forces at 69 A.D.'s Second Battle of Cremona. Most
historians believe blank banners first caught on
because they were easy to distinguish in the heat of
battle. Since white cloth was common in the ancient
world, it may have also been a case of troops
improvising with the materials they had on hand."

HISTORY.COM

Hannah moved slowly along the narrow walkway
around the meetinghouse and peered into the black
night. No noise came from Kronborg, which sat over
the rise to her left, south on the most western point
jutting out into the strait. Had their trick of cutting
the sash way up high hidden her escape until morning?

Erik's encampment was also south, but on the
other side of Sophie's castle, directly across the narrowest portion of the strait to Sweden. All Hannah
could see from her lofty lookout was darkness and
shadows of low bushes and a few branching trees.
"Where are you?" she whispered, straining to see two

little girls through the dark. The moon cast a faint glow when the clouds passed it.

They'd given up calling the girls' names. Gideon and Cait had taken horses to ride up to the ridge, staying west of Kronborg Castle, their dark colors blending in with the night. Joshua grumbled about Wolf Warriors abducting the girls, but Hannah couldn't believe that.

Her fingers curled around the top of the wooden rail of the meetinghouse, rubbed smooth by thousands of hands over the lifetime of the old building. Her throat felt tight, her chest stuffed with a mix of hurt and longing. The cool night breeze made her shiver.

Cain ordered Erik to leave, but Erik hadn't fought to stay, to see her again. Her heart ached. She breathed in the night air. By letting her leave, Erik was saving his country from civil war between his men and Sophie's men. He was saving his men and himself from accusations of treason. He was preventing a war with her brothers and possibly a civil war in Scotland.

Erik was letting her go for good reasons, but she still hurt, hurt so fiercely that she felt weak. *I must not be selfish.* The thought brought back years of tamping down her anger about being ignored at Girnigoe. The world wasn't about her. She mattered only to her immediate family, and that should be enough.

Hannah peered at some movement in the darkness. A white patch rose over the ridge. She squinted at the flag, searching for an emblem, a coat of arms, but it was blank. "A blank white flag?" she whispered. Was someone surrendering? Who would be surrendering? And to whom?

"Someone comes," she called down to Bàs, who was organizing a search for the girls below her perch. "They're flying a white flag."

Bàs pivoted toward the ridge as the waving flag came closer. "Hold your fire," he called out to the dozen or so men who had firearms and bows. Joshua and Cain strode from the docks to stand with Bàs below Hannah.

The distant sound of tabor drums beating out steps came from multiple spots along the ridge as movement over it increased until the entire ridge seemed full of marching men. 'Twas a sea of men, stepping with the beat in uniformity so disciplined it sent a shiver through Hannah, and she wrapped her arms around herself. 'Twas an army marching behind a white flag.

At the front of the advance trotted two horses with riders on their backs. Gideon led one with Trix and Libby sitting bareback, one in front of the other. Cait rode beside them. "Thank God," Hannah murmured. Her gaze moved to the rider holding the flag, and her breath caught.

"Erik?" Hannah turned and ran, her skirts still tied around her legs, down the steps to the ground. She stopped short next to her brothers as the strange army marched out of the darkness. As Erik drew closer, Hannah realized his knees showed while he sat his horse. He was wearing a plaid wrap in the style of the Highlands.

"What is he doing?" Joshua asked, his voice full of suspicion. He held his sword. Bàs held his ax and Cain had his longbow ready to fire.

Erik's torch rose in the air, which made other torches rise, reaching far back into the darkness, and the drums quieted as he halted his horse. His army of thousands stopped behind him in lines, but from what Hannah could see, none of them held a weapon ready, only a few torches. Several men came forward to flank Erik and two of his friends, all three of them in Highland dress.

Gideon walked up, leading his horse. "The lasses were leading the Wolf Warrior army out of their valley when we came upon them." He shrugged. "No one will tell me what's going on."

"Not even my beautiful informants," Cait said, nodding to Libby and Trix. Libby sniffed, her chin tilted up, but she didn't respond further.

Hannah helped the girls down from Gideon's black horse. "Where have you been?"

Trix pointed at the army and the ridge but didn't utter a word.

Cain cupped his hands around his mouth. "What do ye want?" he yelled out.

Erik handed the loose flag, which seemed to be a rent sheet, to Frode and dismounted.

"Where did they get Highland plaids?" Hannah asked Gideon.

He shrugged. "Again, no one is saying anything."

"I bet if I slice someone's arm off, they'd say something," Joshua said.

Kára had stopped next to him and softly punched his upper arm. "I could have used this bloodthirsty Joshua when we first met on Orkney," she said.

"He likes to talk bloodthirsty," Gideon said.

Joshua opened his mouth, probably with a

gruesome example of his bloodthirstiness, when Erik began to walk forward, once again holding the white flag above his head, his chest exposed.

"No one fire," Hannah called out, lest the Sinclair warriors forget. She ran forward, dodging Cain's arm that shot out to catch her.

"Hannah!" Cain called, and she heard someone pounding the ground behind her, but her focus was on Erik. He stood like a rugged Highland warrior, his hair loose to brush his wide shoulders. Arms held straight up to spread the field of white above his head, his large biceps strained against the white tunic. The flag's bottom edge blew in the breeze, grazing the top of his head. His gaze fell on Hannah.

She stopped short right before him. "Erik?"

Bàs stopped next to her, his arm going out as if to block her, but she shoved his arm away. Cain, Joshua, and Gideon halted beside Bàs in their usual line, and their wives hurried to stand between them. It was a solid front of strength.

Erik looked directly at her, the torchlight flickering across his handsome, hard face. "I've come to surrender."

Hannah's intake of breath froze inside, and prickles crawled along her jawline. *Surrender?* Erik never surrendered. Nial had boasted of it. The words had never passed his lips before.

Erik's gaze moved to Cain and down the line of her brothers. "Now 'tis your turn, Horsemen."

• • •

Erik stood with his arms stretched overhead holding the bleached tunic that had been roughly cut into a rectangle. Frode and Sten stood on either side of him, wearing the wrappings of the Highlanders that the girls had brought. Nial had stayed behind, cursing, and asking for a flask of strong aquavit.

In this position, his chest unprotected, he was the most vulnerable he'd ever been in his life. It was foking uncomfortable. "I have come to surrender," he repeated. "To the Sinclairs of Scotia."

Hannah's eyes were wide. They looked damp, though, glassy and a bit puffy, as if she'd been crying. It added to his discomfort. Hell, he wanted to pull her to him.

Cain stepped forward, and Erik had to look at him instead of Hannah. "Surrender?" Cain said, his face full of disbelief. "Your two thousand warriors are surrendering, on your land—"

"Twenty-two hundred," Frode corrected.

Cain glanced at him and continued. "To my one hundred fifty warriors."

"One hundred seventy-three, plus five vicious women," Joshua said next to him.

"Aye," Erik said, focusing on the burn in his shoulders from holding up the tunic instead of the sacrifice he was making. But he met Cain's gaze without flinching. "I wear the plaid of the Highlanders and surrender to them."

"Why?" Gideon asked.

Erik's gaze moved to Hannah. "I've learned that a commander must sometimes pull back in order to move forward."

Hannah's hand went to press against her mouth. She'd recognized her advice on his tongue.

He continued to look at her. "I have a plan." He

swallowed. "It has to do with a wager between the sun and the wind."

Hannah made a slight choking sound, and Cain looked at her and then back to Erik. "Sun and wind?"

Erik lowered his arms slowly, his gaze connecting with the Horseman of Conquest, the chief of the mighty Sinclairs. "I have a plan to keep Sophie from going after Clan Sinclair again."

"We would hear it," Gideon said quickly, as if he was very aware that the Sinclairs sailing away wouldn't be the end of her meddling.

"You surrender to move forward," Nial said, coming up from behind. The man hadn't changed into the Highlander plaid, but he was there. He glanced at Erik and then at Cain. "The Sinclairs of Scotia march on Kronborg to surrender."

"Bloody hell that," Joshua said.

Cain held a hand out to quiet his brother. "I would hear more of this."

"It needs to happen before dawn when Hannah's absence is discovered," Bàs said.

Erik nodded but looked at Hannah. "After I've had a word with Hannah. Alone."

"Nay," Cain said.

Hannah overrode his dictate by grabbing Erik's hand to lead him away. The touch sent power through him, like when a battle swings his way. Iselin would call it hope.

He pushed the white flag into Nial's chest for him to hold. The man looked like it burned to touch.

Hannah led Erik past both silent groups of men, Wolf Warriors and his other warriors. Did they question his strategy like Nial? That Nial even arrived was a testament to his loyalty and lifelong friendship. If this plan didn't work, Erik would never win back his loyalty.

Hannah led Erik up the steps of the meeting room, grabbing a lantern from Ella as they passed. Cait held Trix's and Libby's hands like manacles, but the girls nodded to Erik with large grins. Trix even pinched her lips together in an exaggerated kiss. Someone needed to talk to these girls about what kissing could lead to before they reached an age when undisciplined boys lost their foolish minds around them.

They walked into the room, and Hannah set the lantern down, closing the door. She turned toward him, but there was no rushing into his arms.

"What is your ultimate goal, Erik?" she said, her arms crossed as if to ward him off.

He stayed back in the shadows. The windows were closed, holding in the heat of the day. It would make him sweat, but he didn't move. "I want the Sinclair Clan safe from Sophie's games." That was true. "I want you safe."

"In Scotland? You release me to go home with my brothers?"

What did she want him to say? His brow pinched. "I want you safe," he repeated.

Her arm went out. "None of us are safe in this world. I was at home, protected by the feared Sinclair Horsemen and all their allies, and yet I was abducted. And you weren't my first abductor, either."

He came forward, desperate for her to understand. His hands alighted on her shoulders, sliding gently down her arms to capture her hands. They were cold and clenched into small fists. "Read my actions," he said. "Like you reminded me, actions are truth. I have brought my armies in surrender and lay my sword at your feet. My ancestors are spitting down at me from Heaven or Valhalla."

He pulled her forward little by little, waiting for her to understand, waiting for her to yield and rejoice in the sacrifice he was making. She didn't pull back, so he lowered his face to hers and kissed her.

After a moment that felt too long, Hannah's rigid body melted into him as her lips opened to the kiss. He heard her sigh, and he brushed her hair back from her face. The kiss was unhurried despite the waiting crowds below, and for a moment Erik lost himself in the sweetness of it. His heart pounded hard as she wrapped her arms around him, holding him to her. Despite showing his weakness by surrendering, hopefully *because* he'd shown his weakness, her touch made him feel stronger.

Rap. Rap. Rap. "Hannah," Cain said outside the door. "We need to plan before dawn strikes."

She stepped back, her hand rising to rest on Erik's cheek. "When actions and words align, that is when trust grows." She gave the smallest shake of her head. "I want to trust you, Erik."

"You can."

"You knew Sophie would marry me to Peter Kaas once you traded me for Iselin."

"It didn't matter what I knew," Erik said, guilt spreading through his chest. "I wasn't going to let it happen."

"But you knew that was the plan, and you kept the information back."

He went to deny it, but she placed her finger over

his lips. "You had to make sure I would cooperate to rescue Iselin. I understand, and you didn't lie. You said nothing with your words, and your body, your touch…" She stopped, her face sad. "As we grew closer, and then in the field under the stars, your touch said you loved me, but the words didn't follow. Trust requires both."

The door behind them opened. "We can't wait any longer," Cain said, coming into the room with his eyes closed.

Her brothers came in one after the other with their eyes closed. Hannah snorted. "Since when do warriors enter a room without seeing their enemy?"

"When they don't want their minds scarred by what they see," said Joshua, opening one eye. "She's fully dressed," he announced, and her brothers opened their eyes. "Ye can come in," Joshua called, and Erik's three friends also walked in.

"Dawn will break in a few hours," Gideon said. "We need to have an action plan figured out and implemented by then."

Hannah left Erik's side, and he felt the absence like a cold wind. *Your touch said you loved me*. Did it? Did he love her? His body tensed, becoming an iron fort instead of a man. He shouldn't love her, because Hannah could die of disease like his vast family. She could be lost on the sea or be tricked by a band of warriors from another country or clan. And then… then he would hurt until he died. Nay. He would never love, never open himself to such vulnerability.

He swallowed the lie down like the bitter draught it was.

CHAPTER TWENTY-FOUR

"All warfare is based on deception...The whole
secret lies in confusing the enemy, so that
he cannot fathom our real intent."
THE ART OF WAR, SUN TZU

"I don't like this," Joshua Sinclair said once again.

"The plan has merit," Gideon countered. "The sun
made the man take off his jacket."

Joshua snorted. "I never liked that story. If I was
wind, I'd have stripped the man bare." He rubbed his
side where his sword usually rested. "And I'd rather
march up to Kronborg Castle totally bare than without my sword. Completely naked."

Erik ignored the grumbling Highlander while they
walked southwest to meet Sophie when she woke at
Kronborg. Since her soldiers hadn't marched on them
or sent scouts during the night, Hannah's absence
must not be known.

Despite the bickering between Hannah's two
brothers, his thoughts and gaze kept sliding to
Hannah, who walked with her sisters several yards
away. She looked straight ahead.

"Being naked would also mean ye're not wearing
yer sword," Gideon said to Joshua.

"Nay," Joshua said, flapping the plaid wrapped
around his hips. "The loss of yer tunic and wrap make
ye naked, yer body exposed for all to see."

"Doesn't one *wear* a sword?" Gideon said. "Like

one *wears* his clothes?"

"One can also carry a sword," Frode suggested.

Joshua threw out a hand toward him, his eyes wide. "Aye, very good. I would rather go naked and carry my sword."

Erik had watched Hannah's expressions as soon as there was light enough to see them. She displayed few. A mild smile at something Kára said. An annoyed grimace as an insect landed on her. Other than that, she kept her face a neutral mask. For a woman who expressed much in the movement of her lips and brows and the largeness of her blue eyes, this lack of expression made her look numb. They hadn't gotten but an hour of sleep, if that, so she might be half asleep on this march. The Horsemen and Hannah had left their horses at the dock as if they had been confiscated by Erik's army. Erik's elite men rode behind them on horses, fully armed.

They walked in silence for a while as the sun rose. "Bloody hell, I'd rather lose my hand than my sword," Joshua said as if he couldn't keep quiet.

"How would ye even *hold* it without your hand?" Gideon asked.

"With my *other* hand," Joshua said slowly as if Gideon were a child who needed special instruction.

"If those Swedes attack," Nial said, "this whole plan could fail. Sophie might be very happy to employ the Sinclair warriors to keep Kronborg safe."

"The Swedes won't attack," Cain said as they strode through the calf-high grass.

"They don't need a provocation," Nial said. "If they attack from land and their ships dock, we must return immediately to keep them from pushing into Denmark."

Erik watched a glance go between Cain and Gideon before Cain once again looked forward. "There are no Swedes," he said. "The three ships in the strait are Sinclairs and Sutherlands."

"And a few MacKays," Cait added from beside Hannah.

"What?" Nial asked, tripping on a small hummock in his path.

"They're flying Swedish flags," Cain said. "And I have no knowledge of any Swedish infantry gathering on the opposite coast."

Frode snorted, shaking his head. "I have Iselin being guarded by Aksel and Kyle. They are ready to throw her on Erik's ship and set sail if the Swedes attack."

"With the sun rising, yer men will see no armies gathered on the Swedish shore," Cain said. "Unless by happenstance."

Sten's hands cupped the back of his head, his elbows jutting out. "Fy faen," he muttered. He sounded angry, but Erik knew he was relieved. A horde of Swedes would complicate this venture, and with little sleep they'd be at a severe disadvantage.

Nial's mouth remained open, and he suddenly choked as if one of the grass beetles had jumped down his throat. "No Swedes?" he croaked between coughs.

Joshua grinned. "'Twas my idea. Find the enemy's enemy and either entice them to join ye or pretend they did."

"But the lad who spoke Norm?" Sten asked. "Osk."

"He acts as well as Kára," Joshua said, nodding

toward his wife who walked on the other side of Hannah.

Kára called over, "There was no time to contact distant relatives in Sweden, and my brother is excellent at subterfuge."

"Our ships will wait there," Gideon said.

"Wait for what?" Nial asked.

"If we fail to appear back at the docks within the day, they will land and attack," Gideon said darkly. Regardless of his comment about Erik's plan having merit, the Horseman didn't sound confident.

"You are still outnumbered," Nial said, but Erik overrode his words.

"You'll be back before night falls." Erik looked at Joshua. "You just have to be convincing."

Joshua chuckled darkly. "I played the part of a faltering warrior with black bulbous plague hanging by my ballocks, so I can play this part with ease."

"Would you rather give up your cod or ballocks than your sword?" Sten asked.

Gideon rolled his eyes. "Ye encourage him?" he asked Sten.

Sten shrugged. "'Twould be a boring march without him."

"Not boring," Gideon said, "peaceful."

"Nay," Joshua said, shaking his head vigorously and shivering dramatically. "My jack and ballocks are sacred." He cupped the spot on his wrap covering his giblets. He looked over to his wife. "Kára would mourn the loss forever."

Kára laughed and moved over to Joshua, throwing her arm around his waist. "Perhaps you should not talk for a while."

"But I was—"

"Oh look." Kára pointed outward, interrupting him. "A castle with a horde of Danes inside. Let's talk about that."

Joshua moved his head back and forth. "I suppose that's not boring." He glanced at Gideon. "Although we've discussed it all night."

Gideon sighed. "We must be prepared to look somewhat resigned to our new fate. Placate Sophie into taking off her jacket, metaphorically."

"Naked, I tell ye. I'd rather strip naked," Joshua muttered.

Kára patted his chest. "Think of how cold that would be. Now hush."

Activity at the gatehouse showed that Sophie's men could see them marching their way across the field. Soldiers with muskets lined the wall.

"Hold the flag up," Erik said.

With a look of pure disgust, Cain lifted the white rectangle above his head as he marched forward like Erik had done at the start of the night. Ella came over to stand beside him with a grim look of support as if she, too, woke from nightmares of surrendering her clan.

Joshua spit on the ground, making Erik wonder if they'd suddenly start vomiting over the act of giving in to an enemy. Kára looped her arm through Joshua's as they walked. "'Tis not comfortable surrendering one's people, is it?"

He frowned while still looking forward. "I didn't ask ye to surrender your people, just leave Orkney." After a moment he looked down at her. "But aye, 'tis bloody uncomfortable."

Her handsome face softened with a light so bright, Erik knew it was love. And suddenly Erik envied Joshua Sinclair.

Erik made his way over to Hannah. Kára had slid closer to Joshua so it was easy to find room. Hannah didn't look at him.

"Riders are coming out," Nial announced. 'Twas the signal and reminder for them all to play their parts. "Erik."

His time was limited, and if things went poorly, he might not get another chance to show his true self.

Erik grasped Hannah's hand where it swung by her side. "Hannah Sinclair," he said, his voice calm despite the surge of emotions flooding him. She turned her face toward him, and he caught the shine of unshed tears in her eyes. "Hannah Sinclair," he repeated. "Marry me."

"What?" Gideon said down the line. "Don't answer him, Hannah."

"Erik," Nial called. "You need to be over here in front."

Erik squeezed her hand as she stared at him, blinking. "Do not despair," he whispered and released her to stride back to march next to Cain, who still held up the white flag. His wife, Ella, had taken one side, helping him with the obvious burden.

"Father is yelling up at us from Hell," Bàs murmured, the first words Erik had heard from him since the start of this march.

Joshua snorted. "Aye."

Erik strode quicker to advance before the Sinclairs. "Dowager-Queen Sophie," he called but knew she would not be out among her warriors before Kronborg. "Chancellor Kaas."

The easily recognized man pushed forward on his mount. "What do you bring to the doorstep of your sovereign?"

He could have pointed out that King Christian was his sovereign, but his anger at Sophie's demands of power wouldn't fit into this farce. Erik opened his arm out to the side where Cain and Ella held the white flag. "Your Wolf Warriors bring Clan Sinclair in surrender to her majesty."

Behind him, he heard Joshua gag and Gideon tell him to hush.

· · ·

Hannah stood still, her numb feet planted in the grass, while her heart beat like a raven taking flight, so hard it was likely to burst forth and fly from her chest.

Marry me. Marry me.

Erik Halverson had asked her to wed. Why would he do that? Her mind raced, searching for a strategy that would make sense.

When stars sparked in her vision, she drew even breaths and counted to release them. Cait appeared next to her, her arm through hers. On her other side, Shana did the same. "She's too pale," Shana whispered.

"Just breathe, Hannah," Cait whispered on her other side.

Daingead. I'm too pale. How could she marry Erik? He was a Wolf Warrior in Norway. She was a protected sister in Scotland. A protected, old maid of a sister in a castle full of brothers in love and sisters bearing children. And after this she'd never be allowed to be alone again, not when she was Clan Sinclair's weakness. The story of this adventure would be passed from clan to clan throughout Scotland, to every Sinclair ally and enemy.

"Yes," Hannah called out, the word bursting from between her lips. "My answer is yes."

She didn't look over at Erik, but he would have heard.

"Bloody hell," Gideon swore.

"Lady Hannah," Peter Kaas said, confusion obvious in his voice. "Good morn. How are you not in your chamber?"

"We must discuss this surrender," Erik said.

Kaas looked back and forth between Hannah and Erik and then cleared his voice. "Leader of the Wolf Warriors, in the name of Dowager-Queen Sophie, we accept this surrender."

Joshua made another gagging noise under his breath. "If this is a trick, I'm tearing Halverson's arms and jack off his body. I don't even need my sword."

If Gideon wasn't playing his part of subjugation, Hannah was certain he'd have punched Joshua by now. Hannah doubted her brothers were bickering out of some duty to her, but their familiar animosity gave her comfort.

"Bring the four leaders, their wives, and Hannah Sinclair inside. Our soldiers and yours can keep those Sinclairs outside the walls until we bring them in. How many are there?"

"One hundred seventy-three," Erik said. "Their weapons have been confiscated." He gestured toward Cain who came forward. Joshua, Gideon, and Bàs came in line with him. Kaas's soldiers came forward, one for each wife and Hannah. The man who took Hannah's arm was burly and smelled unwashed. His gaze slid over her with appreciation. Even though it was quick, and he looked forward again, Hannah's stomach turned, making her want to gag like Joshua.

They walked over the drawbridge to the arched main gate. Hannah's boots clipped, the smell of the sea washing the stink of the guard from her nose when the wind blew. The stone arch had the pointed portcullis tucked up underneath as if threatening to fall upon them. She trembled slightly, remembering the horrors of her first abduction when she was still a foolish lass back in Scotland. Since then, she'd changed, coming out of her corner more and more. And now Sophie wanted to shove her back into that corner as a married hostage. Anger strengthened Hannah, banishing the tremors and straightening her spine.

They walked across the pebbled, open-air square and entered the queen's receiving chamber. Despite the early hour, Sophie sat on her throne, a frown on her bow-like lips. "How frightening for your maid, Lady Hannah, to enter your chambers this morn to find you having flown from your window."

Hannah swallowed her terse response and bent her head to stare at the woven rug beneath her feet.

"Surrender?" Sophie asked. "The Four Sinclair Horsemen of Scotia have surrendered? How is this?"

Erik stepped forward and bowed to her. "We have outnumbered them, and they surrendered." He made it sound quite easy. Anyone who truly knew the Sinclair Horsemen wouldn't believe it.

"They may return to Scotia," Sophie said. "Only Lady Hannah will stay to marry Lord Kaas."

Never welled up inside Hannah, but she pinched her lips tightly together.

"They will not," Erik said.

"What?" Sophie asked.

Cain's voice boomed out. "Clan Sinclair of Girnigoe joins the Danish country as citizens."

"As does Clan MacKay of Varrich," Gideon said, stepping forward next to Cain. They both bowed low and then straightened.

Sophie said nothing for a moment and then looked at Peter. She said something in Danish. When Peter gave her a small shake of his head, Sophie turned back to Cain. "What is the meaning of this?"

"Your Majesty," Gideon said. He was used to speaking with King James and his voice held the right amount of deference without sounding weak. "We will not leave our sister, Lady Hannah, so we have decided to bring our mighty clans here to Denmark."

"Bring your clans?" Sophie said. "'Tis not possible."

"We have three thousand people preparing to move countries," Cain said. "Word has been sent on two of the three vessels that sat in Kattegat Strait."

"The Swedish ships?"

"They were Sinclair ships in disguise, Your Majesty," Erik said. "The third has been sent to King James of Scotland."

"King James?" The name fell from her slack lips. She rubbed them back and forth for a moment. "You sent word to King James? What word?"

Gideon spoke clearly, keeping her gaze. "That his

Four Horsemen are no longer his. They have been taken by the dowager-queen of Denmark-Norway. He must be made aware, since our…abduction opens up his country to French and English invasion."

"And Swedish," Cait added.

Sophie's hand went to her chest, and she stood. "My daughter sits with King James."

"Aye, Your Majesty," Gideon said. "She will need to take care without us there to protect Scotland's shores. Word of our surrender and move to Denmark will reach other countries within a fortnight."

"I do not desire you here." Sophie's words snapped from her pursed lips.

"Ye have taken our sister," Cain said. "If we take her back from Denmark, ye will send Erik Halverson and his Wolf Warriors after us again. 'Twill be easier to remain here so ye can ensure we won't do anything in Scotland."

Sophie stared at him for a long moment. "Lady Hannah is already betrothed to a Danish citizen."

'Twas a lie, since Hannah hadn't verbally agreed nor had she signed a betrothal contract.

"She agreed to wed before witnesses this morning. I believe even your chancellor heard her," Gideon said.

Sophie's face snapped to Peter. Peter frowned. "I…I do not recall—"

"Who will she wed?" Sophie asked, her voice rising with a shrill cadence.

Hannah's heart pounded as Erik turned to her. His face was hard, but his eyes shone with conviction. He held out his hand, and without thought, Hannah walked across the floor toward him. She set her hand, fingers open this time, in his warm palm. They looked at each other, and for one moment it felt like they were alone. "Yes," she said again. "I will marry you."

"No!" Sophie yelled.

Erik turned his face to his dowager-queen. "Your Majesty, Lady Hannah will remain here in Denmark-Norway with me, just like you'd intended."

Hannah's stomach tightened. They hadn't had time to talk about where she'd live, where they'd live.

"This is not what I intended!" Sophie yelled, moving a hand in the air toward Hannah's brothers and their wives. "All the Sinclairs leaving Scotia, leaving Queen Anne without protection."

She plopped down on her throne as if it must hold her up. Her eyes were wide. "No," she said. "Lady Hannah must marry someone at my court, and her brothers must return to Scotia to protect Anne."

"The ships have already sailed, Your Majesty," Gideon said. "King James and your daughter, Queen Anne, must prepare for invasion. 'Tis not right to leave them without notice."

"'Tis not right to leave them at all," Sophie said, her gaze narrowing at Erik. "How could you let this surrender happen?"

"I have no answer," he said with practiced confusion in his tone. "Your enemy has surrendered to your Wolf Warriors."

She waved her hands in the air. "This is not what I wanted."

Gideon cleared his throat. "We will need to build a town on the moor between Kronborg and the docks. Three thousand souls need food and lodging and ways to keep themselves from having to beg at the gates of

Kronborg. The effort will impact your treasury."

Sophie made a small, strangled noise. "They are not welcome here."

"They will follow where their chiefs go, Your Majesty," Gideon said. "They are quite loyal."

She pointed a damning finger at him. "Loyal to the Four Horsemen and not their God-anointed King and Queen."

"With our surrender," Cain said, "our people are loyal to ye and yer son, King Christian. We've let King James know we will be swearing fidelity to King Christian due to your actions to lure us from Scotland."

The words were all out. Sophie would be held responsible for opening the shores of Scotland to foreign invaders. King James and her daughter, Anne, would know she'd worked to doom their kingdom and rule—exactly opposite what Sophie had intended.

"And I will remain in Denmark with Lady Hannah," Erik said. "The Wolf Warriors will no longer protect your Norwegian border with Sweden." Erik pulled Hannah to him. "I would make our betrothal official before our sovereign. Hannah Sinclair, will you wed me?"

"No," Sophie yelled.

"Yes," Hannah said, her voice loud. "I will wed you, Erik Halverson." And he leaned in, his lips touching hers.

· · ·

"She can ask King Christian to break your betrothal," Gideon said to Erik as they walked out from Kronborg under the raised portcullis.

Erik held Hannah's arm wrapped in his. Her "yes" had boomed out through the queen's receiving chamber for all to hear, but she remained stiff, her smile absent.

"We are already married in the eyes of God," Erik said, speaking of their intimacy. "Hannah might even be pregnant." He glanced at her, but she didn't respond. "And the rest of our ploy has already swayed Dowager-Queen Sophie."

Gideon chuckled. "I don't believe I've ever been yelled at to get out of a country before. Her Majesty even offered us transport home if we no longer had the ships to see it done."

"Cain should probably follow up with a second letter to King James," Erik said, still watching Hannah from the corner of his eye.

"He never sent the first one. The ships have sailed out around the peninsula and will return."

The thudding of hooves made Erik turn to see Joshua and Kára galloping back toward the docks. The infamous Horseman of War smiled as they passed their group walking.

Gideon swore. "He must have commandeered one of your warrior's horses."

"Walking back 'tis my man's penalty for letting him take it," Erik said.

"We will prepare to leave on the next tide," Gideon said and strode off, finally leaving him and Hannah as alone as they could be surrounded by over two hundred warriors.

They walked for several strides together in silence. What was she concerned over? Missing her clan, no doubt. "Hannah—"

"I will not hold you to it." The words burst from Hannah's lips as if they'd been waiting there all along. "The betrothal. 'Twas a clever way to help sway Sophie." She glanced at him and then back to the field ahead. "But I will not stay here. My home is in northern Scotland. You need to know that." She shook her head. "I will go back with them on the tide."

"We would not live in Denmark or anywhere near the court," Erik said, his words measured even though they wanted to rush out of him. "Norway is beautiful. I would show you my home."

She looked at him. "Your home of ghosts? Live where your whole family perished, where every corner and hearth remind you of what once was that is no more? Reminding you how fragile life is even for a Wolf Warrior? That is where you would take me?"

Hannah pulled her arm from his. "I cannot do that, Erik. I cannot live in the shadows again. So, your words before about marriage…" She turned her face to him. Tears welled in her blue eyes, one breaking over the dam to trail down her cheek. "Your words were wonderful, and your actions…" She held her hand out toward the meetinghouse in the distance where he'd surrendered during the night. "Surrendering was the perfect trick to get my brothers to listen to your plan." She swallowed, her watery gaze making her eyes seem even larger and bluer. "But they aren't enough."

"I surrendered, Hannah, to keep you from sailing away." Didn't she understand? "I've never surrendered to anyone, ever."

Her fingers gripped his forearm. "Real surrender to a person is being truly vulnerable. No two thousand men behind you." She shook her head and squeezed his arm before slowly loosening her hold until her hand fell away, and she looked forward again. "'Tis too much, I know, for you to really surrender. 'Tis not in your nature, Erik." They were closing in on the meetinghouse by the docks. Sinclairs jogged past them as they ran to continue readying the ships to leave.

Hannah stopped, turning her face to him. Her tears had stopped, but sorrow was etched in every line of her face. "I…I love you, Erik Halverson. See it in my eyes and know it in your heart. This is no trick, only truth." She stepped in to him.

Erik's chest turned to marble but thin like eggshell, hard and fragile at the same time. Hannah loved him. Hannah was leaving him. When she slid her hands behind his neck, he let her pull his face down to hers.

Her lips touched his. He tasted the salt of her tears as she kissed him. It was over too quickly, and she turned, hurrying away. And…he let her go.

CHAPTER TWENTY-FIVE

"Many of the 'Scots' located in Scotland today have a
history connecting them to the Gaelic or Irish, while
others have connections to Scandinavian and German
roots. The diverse genetic history of the Scottish
people is a result of the country's colorful history, and
the interactions they had with different cultures.

The Vikings in Scotland had perhaps one of the most
significant influences on the development of the
country. The initial visit [eighth century] wasn't a
peaceful one. The Vikings arrived on the coasts with
the intent of attacking and overthrowing the region,
as well as looting precious objects. Most experts
believe the Viking raiders who landed in Scotland
came mainly from Norway..."

SCANDIFICATION.COM

Hannah wanted to remain forever under the blankets
heaped over her. It was warm and dark there and she
could cry without anyone seeing her broken heart.
The narrow berth she'd claimed onboard the larger of
the Sinclair ships was tucked away, and she could let
the waves rock her like she was back in her childhood
cradle at Girnigoe.

She couldn't remember her mother, really, but it
was the idea of her singing to her, brushing her hair
from her forehead, that comforted Hannah. She
would stay there until she arrived back on Scotland's

shores to go hide away in her corner once more.

Why had she allowed herself to fall in love with a warrior who lived on the other side of the sea? And now when Ella said that she'd make certain Cain ordered his brothers not to be so protective of her, Hannah no longer cared to find a husband. There was only one she wanted, and she'd left him behind, standing on the dock as their ships pulled away.

He'd stood like stone, watching her, Frode, Sten, Nial, and Iselin on either side. Frode and Sten had returned farewells with Libby and Trix who waved with both arms. Nial had clapped Erik on the back before turning away to give orders to the Wolf Warriors for their return to Norway over a course of days with many ships, from what Gideon said.

Hannah had remained on the deck, all feeling in her body diminishing as Erik's form grew smaller as the gentle breeze unfurled the sails. He never left, and neither did she. Standing there, watching as each grew too far away to see. And then she'd gone below, taking to her cot.

"Has she even eaten?" whispered Ella as she came into the small room.

"Broth, some bread," Shana answered. "Not enough. But she doesn't have a fever."

"Thank God," Ella murmured, coming closer. "Hannah? Are you awake, sweet? We are about to dock at Girnigoe."

Hannah took a full breath. *Home*. She slowly pushed upward from her nest of blankets that she'd rarely left over the last five days of crossing. "I am awake," she said.

Shana placed her lips against Hannah's forehead,

feeling for fever. "Cool." She smiled as if that meant Hannah would be fine, but Hannah wasn't sure she'd be fine ever again.

Ella and Shana helped her stand. Ella gently slapped Hannah's petticoats down, since she had not bothered to remove them. "Let's get you in a warm bath up at Girnigoe," Ella said. "'Tis been an exhausting adventure."

Hannah ignored the concerned looks from her family as the two helped her up on deck. She barely noticed when Bàs scooped her into his arms and rode her on an available horse back to the castle, wrapped in a blanket. He carried her inside, and Aunt Merida flew to her.

"Is she ill?"

"Nay," Bàs said.

"Injured?"

"Nay."

"What's wrong then?" she asked, following behind him up the stairs. He reached the landing and walked to her bedchamber, pushing the door open with his boot.

Bàs set her on the edge of her bed. "Hannah's heart has been sorely bruised." Hannah glanced up at him, and her brother met her gaze. "But she will recover, because she's the strongest woman I know."

"Bruised heart," Aunt Merida murmured, touching her palm to Hannah's forehead. "Whisky will help. Whisky and tarts." She rushed off.

Hannah searched her brother's eyes. There was no pity there, only comfortable confidence. "Thank you," she whispered.

He kissed her forehead and departed.

• • •

Ella, Shana, and Aunt Merida prodded Hannah through a warm bath, a real meal, and into bed that night. Hannah's dreams were full of misty landscapes and a need to find herself through a maze that would lead her to the crying bairn within. She woke agitated and needing bright sunlight. Shana and Aunt Merida came upstairs with a tray of tempting tarts, poached eggs, and warm bread with fresh butter.

Rap. Rap. "Good morn," came two small voices from the doorway. Trix and Libby slid through. "We came to make sure our favorite aunt was doing well," Libby said.

Trix came to perch on the bed next to Hannah while Libby stood. They both handed her freshly plucked wildflowers.

"Thank you," Hannah said, giving them a smile. The action felt difficult, her lips heavy.

Trix pointed at the tray. "The tarts are delicious."

"Don't thieve her tarts," Libby admonished.

"I'm not."

Libby's frown turned into a bright smile. "And I came to fix your hair."

Trix looked from the tarts to Hannah's face. "And I came to bring sunshine." She lifted her arms and smiled brightly.

Hannah handed her flowers to Shana to find water for them. "My two brave rescuers." Hannah smiled and felt the warmth of their happiness. "Thank you for your courage and cleverness." They had been the ones to give Erik the idea to surrender in the first place.

Libby and Trix both beamed. "We are quite brave together," Trix said. "And clever."

Libby led Hannah to a chair to braid her hair.

Aunt Merida snorted. "We can burn these in a cleansing ceremony," she said, pinching the traditional Norwegian costume between her fingers.

"No," Hannah said quickly, her hand rising. "I... Just please have them cleaned." Maybe one day she would burn them, but right now she didn't have the anger or the strength to do it.

Aunt Merida glanced at Shana, who nodded as if she'd taken charge of Hannah's physical and emotional care. Shana was a midwife. Were they all waiting, like Hannah, to see if her monthly courses would come? Her bleeding was expected soon. In truth, Hannah didn't know what to pray for. A bairn was what her heart wished for continuously, but a bairn with Erik's stormy blue eyes and strong features would remind her of all she'd lost. Ivy's sage advice from before this whole adventure made complete sense.

Had she chosen correctly? Should she have stayed? If she had, even if she'd married Erik, Sophie would have used threats against Hannah to control her brothers. As long as the dowager-queen was within reach of her, her brothers would be under her influence. And she could order Erik to undertake reckless missions until he was killed. No. She could not stay in Denmark-Norway.

"I wish to walk," Hannah said, glancing at the sunlit window. "'Twill do me good."

"I will go with you," Shana said.

"Us too," Trix said with excitement. "Where will we walk?"

Hannah rose from the chair to finish dressing in a thin woolen petticoat and bodice dyed in a shade of rose. "Thank you, but I would like to walk alone."

"I'm not sure your brothers would like that," Shana said.

Hannah released her breath. "I'm merely walking up to the clootie well. I have need for healing." She took her long cloak and picked up her bow. "I'll go armed." She gave Aunt Merida and Shana a weak smile. "I just need to sit and listen to the burbling water." *And weep without everyone noticing and pitying me.*

"We will follow you up after an hour," Shana said, "to make sure you're safe."

Hannah would give her family a week of following her around before she started to demand her freedom. After all, she'd become only too aware that her circumstances affected her whole clan and maybe the whole of Scotland. *Bloody hell.* She was both honored and horrified.

When they descended, all her brothers were absent. "They were called to the docks," Ella said, smiling to see Hannah up and fresh. While Shana explained where Hannah was going, Hannah slipped out a side door into Girnigoe's bailey and strode rapidly through the open gates. She kept her hood up as she traipsed the familiar lane through the village, not wanting to be stopped by well-meaning folks welcoming her home. Luckily, her brothers were down the other side, probably inspecting their ships and helping to clean them after the journey.

On the outskirts of town, Hannah lowered her hood and let the sunrays shine on her upturned face.

She paused, breathing in the sweetness of late summer in the Highlands. Wrapping her arms around herself, she felt her sorrow squeeze her, and she gasped at the power of it. Tears threatened, and she hurried forward, seeking the coolness of the path up to the clootie well.

At the base, she paused, her gaze on two footprints in the dried mud: one large and one medium. She stepped into the medium one. It was hers and the other must be Erik's from when they'd walked together. The tale of the sun and wind. Their banter and lies by omission. Tears slid down her face as she left the footprints behind. Hannah lifted her skirts and traipsed quickly as if demons chased her.

One foot in front of the other, she climbed the root-filled path. Watching for tripping hazards helped her focus on something other than loss and sorrow. At the top, the burbling sound of the freshwater spring mixed with the breeze whispering through the leaves. The clootie rags, offerings for healing, fluttered with the bright green leaves. The small fertility dolls sat in a row along the edge of the spring where the Beltane brides had left them. Hannah crouched to pick up her little woven doll, wondering if she should let it float away.

She sat holding it there for so long she suddenly worried that Shana, Aunt Merida, and the little lasses would show up any minute, ending Hannah's solitude. She stood, still holding the doll, and turned when she heard a *crack* below on the trail like someone breaking through a troublesome root. The heavy thud of boots hitting earth followed. *Not one of the ladies or girls.*

Hannah set the doll down and grabbed her bow, pulling and nocking an arrow in one swift motion. She pulled back the bowstring and waited.

"Hannah? Hannah, are you up there?" called a deep voice with a northern accent.

Everything in Hannah froze, her breath, her half-way open lips, every muscle turned to stone. Only her heart continued, jumping into a hard, swift cadence.

"Erik," she murmured.

His anxious face came above the incline. A slight sheen of sweat marked his brow, and his chest rose and fell with vigor as if he'd been running.

"Erik?" she said louder, and his gaze fell directly on her where she stood by the tree where he'd sat.

He slowed to a walk and lifted his hands in the air. "Will you shoot me?"

Hannah realized she was still holding her bow-string back and ready to release, and she let it drop by her side, releasing the string tension. "You are here? In Scotland?" She shook her head slightly as her watery gaze took in his handsome features and a beard that looked to have grown without thought for the last week.

"Aye," he said, taking slow steps toward her. "I came for you." But then he shook his head. "Not to take you, but I came to…" He lowered to his knee as if he were swearing his fidelity to his king. "I came to surrender to you, Hannah Sinclair." From his position he shook his head. "When you sailed away…" He clasped his jawline, sliding his hand down to rub his chin. "Part of me, the best part of me, sailed away with you, growing smaller and smaller until it disappeared."

Hannah blinked as the tears in her eyes broke free again. "Are you really here?" she whispered, her bow slipping from her fingers to the ground. Or was she losing her mind like her father had when her mother died? Seeing Alice Sinclair everywhere as he grieved her loss.

Erik stood and walked closer, stopping before her. He gently slid the quiver of arrows off her shoulder, setting it on the ground while never leaving her gaze. "Aye, I'm here," he said. The warm honey quality of his familiar voice mixed with her own desperation, and a sob broke from her lips. She clasped her hands before her mouth.

"I sailed a day behind your fleet," he said and lowered onto one knee again. "To surrender my heart to you, Hannah Sinclair." She realized he was holding out a silver ring. "Will you wed me properly before the kirk? I have come to Scotia to make my home with you."

Hannah's knees gave way, and she sunk to the ground before Erik. "You...you've come here for me?"

"To stay," he said.

"The Wolf Warriors—"

"Will be led by Nial," he finished. "Denmark-Norway no longer holds my loyalty." He met her gaze fully, and she felt mesmerized by his clear blue eyes. "You hold my loyalty," he said. "And my heart, Hannah. I...I love you."

Hannah threw her arms around his neck, burrowing her face against his shoulder. "Erik, oh Erik," she said and pushed back so he could see the absolute truth in her eyes. "I love you too." Her palm rested against his bristled cheek. "I love you. I surrender my heart willingly."

He released his breath, his eyes closing for a moment. A smile spread across his mouth as they stared at each other, and he pulled her to him as they sat on the mossy ground. Warm lips met hers in a kiss that melted away the painful anguish in which Hannah had been locked. Released from her shackles, she gave in to her hopes and dreams. With every beat of her heart, she knew that this was right. This was truth, and this was love.

• • •

Erik clasped Hannah's hand as they walked down the path leading out of the forest. Just like he expected, all four of her brothers, with their wives, and Hannah's aunt waited at the base of the hill. Joshua frowned with arms crossed, openly judging him poorly. Gideon and Cain held neutral faces while they assessed him and his motives, and Bàs, Hannah's closest brother, grinned. Erik guessed that they would become close friends.

The ladies laughed with Hannah as she wiped her eyes of happy tears. The joy radiating from her made Erik smile, too. Coming up to them across the moor were Frode and Iselin, holding hands, while Trix and Libby each took one of Sten's hands, swinging them. Erik's chest still tightened with gratitude that his sister had asked to accompany him to his new home.

There's nothing left for either of us here except ghosts and bad memories, she'd said. *Frode has agreed.* And Sten wouldn't be left behind. Only Nial wished to stay, taking the reins of their elite warriors to lead them back up to the border of Sweden in Norway.

Hannah hugged his sister. "We can have a double wedding."

A bright, full smile grew on Iselin when Frode translated. Iselin nodded and spoke in broken English. "I...like"—she pointed at Hannah—"your plan."

Hannah squeezed Iselin's hand before looping her arm back through Erik's.

"We will make it a festival with the wedding at the beginning," Ella said, excitement blossoming on her face, and she rose up to kiss Cain. He didn't let her pull away, and she laughed as he kissed her again.

Gideon pulled Cait into his arms, too. "Perhaps you can perform," he said. "I've been meaning to build ye a sturdy structure to anchor your sashes from."

"Yes," Cait said with a huge smile and a hug for her husband.

Libby and Trix were hopping through the grasses collecting late summer wildflowers to hand to all the ladies. "And we will throw wheat and flowers during the ceremony," Libby said.

Kára pulled Joshua's arm, opening his hand to weave their fingers together. She smiled at Iselin and Hannah. "We will carve wedding spoons for the couples to use at the wedding feast."

"We didn't use wedding spoons," Joshua said, his brow raised.

"'Tis a Norwegian tradition that the couple uses carved wooden spoons joined together by a chain as they eat. I think Iselin will appreciate something from her home."

Frode translated and Iselin nodded, smiling at Kára.

Erik drew Hannah against him, his arm hugging her close. "And we will plant fir trees beside our cottages." He kissed her forehead as she looked up at him.

"Fir trees?" she asked.

"In Norway, the newly married husband and wife plant them on either side of the door to bring them many healthy children."

"Maybe that explains why Kára is having so many bairns," Cain said. "Isn't that house ye built her in the trees surrounded by firs?"

"I knew I distrusted trees for a reason," Kára said.

Joshua picked her up, swinging her around. "Nay, 'tis my hearty seed that brings so many bairns and the fact I can't keep this lusty woman from wanting me all the time."

She laughed, kissing him firmly. When Joshua tried to tug her toward the hill and some privacy, she tsked. "This *lusty* woman must return to our bairns who need feeding." She gave a little shriek as he scooped her up in his arms and trudged toward Girnigoe.

Ella laughed and smiled at Cain. "I believe the water at Hempriggs Loch is still warm, and I'm in the mood for…a swim." They walked off together.

Bàs met Erik's eyes, the animosity having turned to something much lighter but just as powerful. "I like him, Hannah." He pulled her into a hug for a moment. "And I'm so happy to see ye happy." He stepped back, glancing at Erik. "Aye, I think he'll make an excellent brother." He extended his arm. Erik grabbed up his forearm in a solid clasp.

"Tapadh leat," Erik said, trying out the bit of Gaelic he'd learned.

Bàs's brow rose, and he nodded in approval. "Ye are most welcome."

"Beò's come," Shana said, nodding to the tree line. "I think he was on the clootie hill watching out for Hannah."

They turned to see the majestic wolf before he trotted off. Bàs nodded. "He protects his people."

"Back to the castle," Aunt Merida said, swooping her arms about as if shooing the two little girls who ran ahead. "And we can start planning the weddings." She tipped her head to the side and smiled at Hannah. "Perhaps we will make it three. Kenneth Sutherland has asked me to be his bride."

Before anyone could say anything, the elderly woman hurried forward with the little girls, looking spry indeed.

Hannah laughed and looked up into Erik's face. He turned, immediately losing himself in the joy making her pale blue eyes sparkle. "It seems love has found us all."

Bàs cleared his throat softly and looked up at the blue sky. "Mother is smiling," he said.

Hannah pulled Erik's face toward hers. Their kiss was pure love, giving and taking in equal measure until they were completely one. Only love could do that, love filled with trust and honed with commitment and joy. Forever.

EPILOGUE

"James," Queen Anne said as she walked toward her husband at his desk in his privy chamber. "I've received the strangest letter from my mother. First of all, 'tis written in English, but 'tis her handwriting."

"Oh," James said, cocking a brow. "Does she fret again about not having control of your brother, King Christian?"

"She always will," Anne said, rereading the scrawl across the parchment. "But this is about the Sinclairs."

James stood, walking over to her. He took the letter from her fingers, earning him a frown from his young wife that he didn't notice. Anne pointed to one paragraph. "Did you send the Sinclair Horsemen over to Denmark?" she asked.

"No, I did not," he murmured as he read.

"It says she doesn't want them there. That they must remain here to protect us and our future children. That they are exceedingly loyal to the house of Stewart."

"You know I've wondered about their loyalties," James said, glancing at his wife. "The Sinclairs are too powerful."

"In the letter, Mama says their power is good to protect us and the shores of Scotland." Anne shook her head. "Perhaps she's received some intelligence that proves their loyalty." She patted James's arm. "And my mother is quite thorough and tenacious, believe me. If she says they are loyal, we have no fear of them trying to take the throne of Scotland."

"Excellent," James said. "I believe this calls for a celebration."

Anne laughed. "You always want to celebrate."

"Life is best when we celebrate, my dear," James said and kissed Anne's hand.

She giggled at her husband's rare show of affection. Perhaps her mama would have a grandchild to fret over soon.

• • •

Hannah walked behind Trix and Libby, who were dressed in white and throwing flowers and barley along the path. Hannah stepped in the cadence set by pipes playing a slow procession toward the dock at Loch Hempriggs. The dock had been expanded to allow Pastor John to stand with three men on one side, two in buff-colored breeches and one in the Sutherland plaid.

Hannah held a small bouquet of flowers with fir boughs in it. Would Erik understand the significance? Just in case he didn't, she'd nestled the fertility doll that she'd left at the clootie well among the boughs. She smiled mischievously as giddy excitement flooded her.

Hannah's deep blue skirt trailed slightly behind her. She'd spent the last week embroidering the hem with silver vines and the interlocking valknut, the Norwegian symbol of unity. She wore a circlet of silver that her own mother had worn at her wedding, but Hannah had added wildflowers twined within it. Her golden waves were left partway down with small plaits looping upward to catch in the crown. She walked confidently through the throng of silent people, a full smile on her lips. Her gaze remained on Erik, who stood closest to Pastor John. He was her anchor, her other half. Today they would be officially joined as one.

Behind Hannah walked Iselin, wearing a traditional Norwegian gown of blue and red, the white apron crisp, and a large silver headpiece that jangled when she walked. Aunt Merida followed in a wedding costume in rose-hued tones accented with blue plaid. Each bride was distinct and ferociously in love with the man waiting for her at the end of the aisle jutting out into the loch.

Hannah stopped before Erik in the middle of the rectangular dock. She smiled up at him, and he grinned. He was getting better at smiling. She glanced at the fir twigs in her bouquet and back up at him. He followed her gaze, and his grin fell away as he stared at the hidden little doll.

Erik met her gaze with eyes opened wide in question. She nodded, her teeth setting on her bottom lip. She was pregnant. They hadn't yet planted the fir trees beside the cottage Erik had been painting and furnishing for them in town, but their offspring were already starting.

He reached for her, and the bouquet crushed between them as he caught her up in a kiss. The giddiness in her chest filled her with such joy that tears leaked from her closed eyes.

Around them, people laughed, and Pastor John cleared his throat, whispering, "Usually we wait until the vows are said for the kiss."

In Hannah's mind, they were already wed, their vows honed into the most unbreakable bond through the pain they'd endured. But she let him pull away.

"Let the pastor put God's blessing on ye first," Joshua said from the side of the lake where he stood with Kára next to Cain, Gideon, and Bàs with their wives. Cait crouched low, beckoning Trix and Libby off the crowded dock to stand with her and Gideon. Everyone looked on with huge grins, her brothers all happy to watch their sister find her own joy.

She turned back to meet her handsome husband's gaze as Pastor John began to speak about the seriousness of marriage. But Hannah only wanted to laugh and rejoice. She and Erik were one through action and word.

Love had prevailed.

ACKNOWLEDGMENTS

Thank you, readers, for coming along with me on the Sons of Sinclair adventures and falling in love with the mighty Sinclair family! I wanted to make certain everyone in the series found their happily-ever-after, even Aunt Merida. Maybe someday Trix and Libby will grow up and have their own adventures!

A special thank you goes out to AJ Siemon for guiding me through the intricate dialects of historical Norway and Denmark. Any mistakes are completely my own. And thank you to my amazing, warrior-woman friend, Kathy Siemon, for tracking down her brilliant son on an archaeology dig to answer my questions.

A huge thank you goes out to my fabulous agent, Kevan Lyon, for helping me convince my publisher that Hannah needed her own story. Thank you also to my talented editor, Alethea Spiridon, who loved this book the first time she read it! Yay! And thank you to the Entangled production team who put together such a beautiful package.

And of course my heartfelt gratitude still goes out to my own Highland hero, Braden, who reminds me all the time that I can do just about anything. You are the love of my life and my happily-ever-after.

Also...

At the end of each of my books, I ask that you, my awesome readers, please remind yourselves of the whispered symptoms of ovarian cancer. I am now a nine-year survivor, one of the lucky ones. Please don't rely on luck. If you experience any of these symptoms consistently for three weeks or more, go see your GYN.

- Bloating
- Eating less and feeling full faster
- Abdominal pain
- Trouble with your bladder

Other symptoms may include: indigestion, back pain, pain with intercourse, constipation, fatigue, and menstrual irregularities.

GET TO KNOW THE
BROTHERS OF WOLF ISLE!

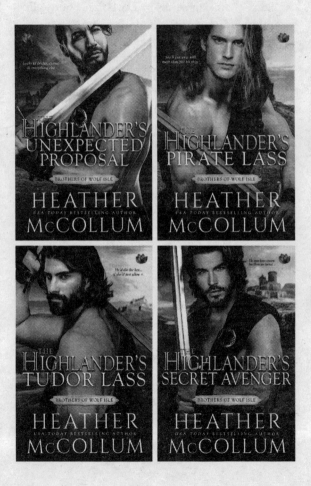

Highland Surrender is the last book in the very popular Sons of Sinclair series by *USA Today* bestselling author Heather McCollum. However, the story includes elements that might not be suitable for all readers. A woman being bound, mentions of attempted assault bordering on rape, kidnapping, beheading, threat of forced marriage, along with harassment and possible endangerment to an older child are in the novel. Readers who may be sensitive to these elements, please take note.

AMARA
an imprint of Entangled Publishing LLC